INSIDE
Part 3

by Kyra Anderson

THE
AMIVERSE
www.the-amiverse.com

Website: www.kyra-anderson.com

Published by K.J. Amidon

ISBN: 978-0-9832280-8-0

1st Edition © 2014
2nd Edition © 2024

Cover Art by K.J. Amidon

Printed in the United States

Table of Contents

Dedicated to:

My friends and family who inspire me everyday

R&D&Z, who put up with brainstorming sessions until the wee hours of the morning. You guys are awesome!

Beckers, for listening to me talk about this book incessantly!

Cheryl, you are my rock in turbulent times. You helped me through this darkness.

Author's Note

Hello, Reader!

Here it is! The final part of Inside! The conclusion to this disturbing venture will have you spiraling into the darkest parts of the Commission of the People and testing the limits of humanity.

As I stated in the first two parts, this story is not for the faint of heart or easily-offended. The story elements of this novel are meant to provoke intense and often unpleasant emotions. This is not a warning to try and sound edgy—this is to cover my bases in case some readers do not heed all the other warnings before purchasing this book.

Like all authors I ask that you suspend your knowledge of reality and step into the world created in these pages. Please remember that this is a work of fiction! Any similarities to people, places, or situations are not intentional. None of these events are meant to push political agendas, nor should anything in this book be taken as politically accurate. The politics, laws, and scenarios in Inside are 100% fiction.

Due to the very dark nature of this particular part of the book, I feel the need to stress the gravity of the warnings above. This is about to become much darker than the previous two parts, but the entire book has been leading up to a very specific juncture. This book was meant to mirror the horrors—to the extreme—of the world of Inside. For that reason, the ending of this book may seem unsatisfying, and frightening, but that is my goal as we round out Lily's horrifying journey.

If you have struggled with the severity portrayed in the previous two parts of the novel, then I urge you to back away from this ending and read the Alternate Part Three, which is far more palatable.

Also as I stated before, there will be no detailed recap of the first two parts. If you have picked up this book first, please note that the first chapter in the book is Chapter Sixty-Five. It is imperative that you read Part One and Part Two before proceeding in order to have an understanding of the characters and plot.

Let us venture once again into the dark, twisted world of the Commission of the People and the rebellion attempting to reform the government.

When you last saw Lily Sandover, the rebellion had launched and was gaining support not only from others in the Commission of the People, but also from the American people. After successfully leading a mass-breakout and several raids, Lily has successfully put Dana Christenson in a difficult position.

But Dana, determined to end their game, uses Lily's own family to bring her into the Commission's grasp. Her own mother called her in as a traitor to the country, running her out of her home and causing her parents to declare her dead in their eyes.

Chapter Sixty-Five

I confessed to Mykail where I had been. He held me as I cried, both of us disappearing into the privacy of the empty medical room. I was certain I would have been unable to handle the pain without Mykail holding me.

When I returned to the bunker, I found myself fascinated with the way life was run in the fort.

In the two months that everyone had been living in Fort Daniels, they had created an incredible system. Everyone had their chores and they rotated depending on the day. Several people had already gone through the tasks of cleaning the weapons to be sure they were ready if and when we needed them. Inventory was meticulously kept and the bunker was always exceptionally clean to keep everyone healthy in such close quarters. Cleanliness was a big priority.

Food rations were obsessively preserved, but I could see around lunch time the following day that we were already beginning to run dangerously low on the food that had been discovered in the fort. I figured that it was the highest priority to discuss with Tori and Griffin as soon as possible how we were to keep everyone in the bunker fed.

But I was pulled away in the early afternoon before I had a chance to speak to either of them.

Josh showed up at the bunker and was greeted with hugs and cheers as he made his way to me.

"Lily," he greeted, relieved. "I'm very happy you got away from the Sweeps team."

"Me, too," I chuckled brokenly.

"I bet you're happy to be here," he said, nodding to Mykail at my side. I squeezed our laced together fingers.

"I am."

"I hate to pull you away, but Clark wants to meet with you," Josh said. "I'll take you to him."

"He's not coming here?"

"Not yet. He'll explain."

"Are you taking her away?" Tori teased, stepping up to Josh and putting her arm around his shoulders.

"Just for a few hours," he said. "I will have her back before dark."

"Sounds like you're taking her on a date," Mykail chuckled. Josh blinked and looked around, surprised.

"It does?"

I could not help but laugh at the startled expression on Josh's face. "I-I didn't mean that," he laughed nervously.

"It's okay," Tori laughed, hugging him tighter and rubbing his shoulder. "Have her back before dark."

Josh took me to the downtown area via one of the fort entrances, where his car was parked. I got into the passenger's seat as Josh started the car.

"Thank you, Josh."

"For what?"

"For watching out for me," I elaborated. "For…believing enough in what we're doing to risk everything." I stopped quickly, looking around the car, remembering that there could be bugs in the vehicle.

"Don't worry," Josh assured with a smile. "Hyunwoo and me took them out this morning."

I relaxed.

"And I should thank you," he continued, driving along the river-walk in the north end of downtown Central and stopping at the park next to the river, pulling to the curb. "Without you, we could not do this."

My smile broadened and I reached over, giving him an awkward hug over the center console.

"I also like that you give so many hugs," I said, backing away. "Mark doesn't hug."

"No, he doesn't," Josh laughed knowingly. "Hyunwoo and me will be at the camp where we usually talk. When you're done, you can come meet us."

"Okay," I agreed, climbing out of the car and crossing the street to walk along the river. I came across Clark sitting on the dry riverbank.

"Hey," I called, running up to him. Clark turned and smiled, standing.

"Hey," he repeated. "How are you?"

"Not bad," I said truthfully. "How about you?"

"Not bad," he said, nodding down the path. "Walk with me?"

We strolled along the river in silence. I watched the water rush over the rocks, trying not to think of my narrow escape from the Sweeps team in the freezing water of the tributary near my former home.

Clark brought it up anyway.

"How did you manage to escape?" he whispered, his gaze pointedly locked on the path in front of him.

"I ran like hell," I said. "They didn't come for you?" I tried to ask as casually as I could. He shook his head.

"I'm not as popular as you," he tried to tease.

"I don't think it has anything to do with popularity," I grumbled, though I was smiling. "What are you going to do?"

"I think I'm going to have a fight with my parents," Clark mused. "But...it's hard to do that when they're never around."

"I've noticed that about your family," I said. "Busy parents."

"Parents who don't care," Clark corrected. "All I hear around the house is follow what Dana is doing, do what Dana says, don't aggravate the situation. They don't even see me." He rolled his eyes. "I'd say the situation is pretty well aggravated..."

"Understatement," I snorted. I shoved my hands deep in my pockets, trying to keep them warm in the chilly March air. "So, you're going to have a fight with them and run away? Why not just run away?"

"...I'm worried about Mark," he admitted. "I'm trying to make it so that he doesn't get in trouble for not catching me, or not going after me. He's driving me around today, and if I just randomly disappear out of nowhere, then people are going to ask how Mark was unable to find me. I think it's better to have a fight with my parents and sneak out," he put air-quotes around the two words, "in the middle of the night."

"Yeah, we definitely need to keep Mark on the inside as long as we can," I agreed with a strong nod. "If Mark gets found out, I think the entire Eight Group gets exposed and then we don't have any inside information."

"True," Clark agreed. "How's living at the fort?"

"Pretty cool, actually," I said. "How's school?"

"Boring," he laughed. "I was going to try my best in school, but that's gone all to hell in the last month. I just don't care anymore."

"I know how that feels."

"Besides, this is much more important than school," he continued. "Speaking of which, your posse surrounded me yesterday wondering where you were."

"What did you tell them?"

"I told them that I didn't know."

We sat on a bench near the eastern parking lot, finally reaching the end of the park. I asked why Mark was at the campground where we normally had our strategy meetings if he was driving Clark around.

"He left the car here, but he wanted to take a walk, or something." Clark shrugged.

"You're not worried?"

"About Mark? No, not really," he said. "I'm pretty sure he's able to take care of himself. He was beaten down by Dana and still is helping us. I think he's smart enough to know how to cover his tracks by now."

"When did you get him as a gift?"

"About three or four years ago," Clark explained. "Right after his voice got..."

"But you were in the Commission before that," I noted.

Clark nodded, letting out a long sigh.

"Yeah, we had another gift, but a neighbor found out," he said. "She was a young experiment who exhaled a poisonous gas when her adrenaline spiked, so she always had a mask on."

"Seems like a dangerous experiment to just give away..." I muttered.

"Dana is obsessed with keeping my family safe. He gave us gifts that were supposed to protect us against anyone who might try to capture my mother or kill her because of her close connections with Dana. After Leila was seen by our neighbor, Dana had to pay a lot of hush money and had doctors draw up fake notes about her medical condition in order to cover the Commission's ass. In the end, he decided to save everyone the trouble and took her away, giving my mom Mark instead."

"Hiroki told me about when Mark had his voice taken..." I said slowly, looking distantly over the parking lot. "It was horrific."

"Why did he do it? Was it because they were talking to one another in their own language and planning against Dana?" Clark asked. "Because that's always what I was told."

"Not entirely," I said. I spelt out the terrible story in the same detail it was told to me. Clark blinked in surprise and rested his elbows on his knees, pressing his mouth to his hands.

"Fuck..." he breathed. "So he's almost killed Dana before..."

"Yeah. It's no wonder he had so much of this already planned."

"No kidding. That's really ballsy, plotting all of this behind Dana's back, gathering information and stealing things from the Commission, even after being caught once."

"But he can't stay hidden forever," I whispered. "Just like us, he's going to get found out. What are we going to do then?"

"Hopefully this revolution will be stronger and we won't need to get inside information from him."

"Hopefully," I murmured. "Speaking of which, I didn't think the start of a civil war would be so calm..." I tried to chuckle. Clark looked around us.

"I know, right? There are little demonstrations taking place, mostly about the innocents who were killed, and it's splitting the army against itself even more. But otherwise, it's pretty calm."

"We're going to have to start planning our next move."

"Very soon," Clark agreed with a nod. "I'm hoping I'll find a good opportunity to pick a fight with my parents and join everyone else in the fort." I could not help but giggle at the statement. Clark chuckled, too.

I shivered, looking around the park again.

"Should we head out?"

"Sure." Clark glanced around but hesitated in standing when his eyes settled on the parking lot. I followed his gaze and my blood ran cold. There was a black van sitting between the parked cars, idling, tinted windows hiding the people within.

"Shit, Commission van," I whispered.

"Wait for them to get out of the van..." he hissed. "When they're out, run like hell."

"Can we outrun them?"

"We're about to find out..."

The van door slid open and four men leapt out, rushing toward us.

"This way!" I yelled, darting back along the path we had walked, following the river. The men yelled at us to stop, proving to me that they were pursuing on foot. I crossed the street and started running up the sidewalk, further from downtown, feeling my lungs burn from the labored inhalation of cold air. I did not bother to look back at Clark, knowing he was close behind, hearing his frantic panting.

When we reached the last intersection before the open road leading out of town, I ran across the street just as the light turned green and traffic started moving. People honked at us angrily, but I hoped they would continue to drive after us, delaying the Commission employees.

I sprinted along another road, parallel to the river, darting across the street yet again, Clark close behind, the angry cursing of the men following loud, but at a distance.

Cutting through an alley of outlying buildings, Clark and I leapt into the tree line, moving in a diagonal direction to meet the dirt road that would tell us where we were in the park and where the campground was.

"Is it really...a good idea to run...*to* Josh and Mark?" Clark yelled behind me.

"Do you have another idea?!"

We pushed our tired muscles and burning lungs harder, particularly when I heard the roar of an engine gaining ground behind us.

"Is that them?!"

"I don't know!"

I darted into the trees and off the road again, knowing that the van could not follow in the crowded foliage, even though it slowed our escape, as well.

I continued forward, keeping my eye out for the campsite that had become so familiar.

"There!" Clark gasped, pointing as he saw a black car and two men in suits.

Clark and I were completely out of breath by the time we stumbled into the campground where Josh and Mark were standing. They both straightened when they saw us.

"What happened?" Josh asked.

"Commission van…" Clark panted, leaning on his knees, trying to catch his breath as I crouched completely down, light-headed and weak. "After us…"

Mark's head turned in each direction as he stepped forward, grabbing my arm and pulling me upright. As he was pulling me to wherever he was going, we heard the sound of tires rolling on the dirt and all of us saw the van skid to a stop in the campground. A few of the men jumped out of the car before the vehicle came to a complete stop.

"Grab them!"

I was surprised when I felt Mark turn me around and grab both of my arms, pulling them behind my back almost painfully. But as I began to catch my breath I remembered that Mark was a master at keeping up appearances.

I had no idea how we were going to escape.

"Great." Two men who had been kneeling on the ground and pointing their guns at us stood. "It's a good thing that little fucker's gift is one of us," one of them chuckled darkly, putting his gun in its holster.

"Fucking moron, he ain't one of us," the other snapped.

"Who would have thought that the Markus kid would be part of that bitch's group." The third man shook his head, disappointed.

I counted seven people around the van. I glanced at Clark and saw Josh holding him as Mark was restraining me. My heart was beating angrily against my ribs, not just from running to escape, but in fear that we were going to be turned over to Dana and that would be the end of our plan. After evading the Sweeps team the previous day, it seemed like a really stupid way to be caught.

"Get some restraints," the driver ordered, putting his gun back in the holster and moving to the other side of the car. "You two, clean out the back. We're gonna have to throw the boy in the trunk."

"Craig, I'm gonna smoke," one of the men said, turning out of sight behind the car as the driver groaned.

"Fuck, Zac, are you serious? *Now?*"

"Fuck you," Zac snapped irritably. "I haven't had one all day. I'm going crazy."

"Just fucking quit," another man groaned. There were three people on our side of the car. One was standing to the side of the open sliding van door, taking the ropes that the other two were handing him from the compartment under the floor.

One man glanced at us and then turned to the driver.

"Hey, what the hell were the chinks doing out here anyway?"

"Who gives a shit? They got the little fuckers."

Mark moved my arms for me, simulating struggle. I started fighting against him, though his strength kept me from moving much.

"Come on, I know the chinks are strong, but the kids are getting feisty," the one holding the ropes snapped.

"We gotta get the tracers, chill the fuck out," another growled. "They're not going anywhere."

As I was being pushed by Mark toward the car, I struggled more and my steps became stumbled and awkward.

On one stumble, Mark's hand dropped lower on my arm and wrapped around my wrist. He guided my hand to his waist, inside his jacket, where the gun sat on his left hip. I stilled for a moment before, while still pretending to struggle, I pulled the strap on the holster and unclipped the gun, taking hold of the handle and pulling the heavy, cold weapon out.

When it was free of the holster, Mark's foot pushed mine, causing me to stumble and allowing him to grab the gun.

"Alright, got it. Bring them—"

Before the man turned around completely, Mark's arm was over my shoulder and he shot the man in the temple, the silencer effectively minimizing the noise.

"What the fuck?!" the other two gasped, watching their friend fall. One didn't even complete the sentence before Mark shot him in the head also, and then turned the gun on the third one, killing him instantly.

My mind turned white.

It was the first time I had seen someone killed. When we had broken people out of the Commission, I had seen the dead bodies of the security guards, and I saw the dead woman at the parade two weeks previous, but watching these men fall limply to the ground as the life left them was something else entirely.

The driver reached for his gun, but Josh had had time to release Clark and get his own gun, shooting the driver in the head on the second shot.

Mark pulled me behind him to shield me as the remaining three Commission men screamed orders at one another, but they never tried to round the corner of the car. Through the tinted window across from the open van door, I saw two of them press their backs to the car, readying their guns as the third ducked out of sight.

Mark pulled me, motioning with his gun to the van.

"Come on, get in," Josh told us sharply, pushing Clark and me before climbing in after us.

I crouched between the two seats in the middle of the car, my heart knocking against my ribs. I tried not to stare at the dead man slumped half-way in the van. Josh locked the already-closed side door, crouching by it, his gun ready as Mark grabbed the collar of the dead man and pulled him out. He took the door handle with the bottom of his jacket around his hand, nodding once to me and shutting the van, sealing us in the bulletproof vehicle.

"What about Mark?" I gasped, whirling to Josh. Josh glanced at Mark's silhouette as he pressed his back to the window and carefully stepped toward the back of the van.

"He's fine," Josh assured with a tight nod. "He's the best, remember?"

"Are you fucking insane?!" Clark snapped. "They can trace the bullets of the Commission guns!"

"Not a Commission gun!" Josh retorted, moving the gun in his hand for emphasis.

I watched Mark as he reached the back of the car, ignoring how Clark angrily asked to see the gun to be sure it was not from the Commission. One of the Commission men was moving along the back of the car, his gun extended. They were stalking closer to one another. My heart was in my throat, choking me. I could not hear the argument between Josh and Clark as I watched the two figures draw closer and closer.

The Commission man hesitated before inching just barely forward so that his gun was just past the edge of the car.

His hand fell out of place as Mark reached forward and pulled the gun away faster than I could blink. Before he had time to notice his weapon was gone, Mark rounded the corner and grabbed the man's arm, twisting his body and elbowing his bicep. I heard the cry of pain and then saw the two shadows move, circling. Mark's hands were around the man's jaw and, with a quick movement, the man's head jerked in a way I had never seen a human head move before and he fell out of Mark's grasp.

Before I had time to let out my sigh of relief and realize that Clark and Josh were still arguing about how they were going to cover up our crime, the side window of the car shattered inward, causing all of us to jump and me to let out a scream.

The man laughed, pushing the lock open as he dropped the device that had shattered the window and reached for the handle.

The hand on the side of his head kept him from succeeding in opening the door. Mark violently bashed the man's head into the side of the half-broken window. Even though the glass was polarized, the force caused shards to embed in the man's temple and chin as he let out a cry of pain.

Mark turned away briefly, lifting his gun and shooting at the final man, who I assumed was hit in the arm because he let out a loud yelp of pain then began shouting profanities into the air.

Mark dropped his gun and pulled the man out of the window, punching him a few times so hard that his head rolled back into the broken car window before Mark bashed his forehead against the bottom of the window frame, finally snapping his neck.

As the man fell to the ground dead, Mark ducked to retrieve his gun, running to the final man, who was still screaming angrily in pain. Josh peeked out of the broken window and opened the side door, ignoring the dead man below. I also tried to pretend he wasn't there as I stepped out of the car on shaking legs, watching Mark as he ran after the man limping away with a bloody hole in his leg.

Mark tackled him and rolled him over, smacking him across the face with the gun repeatedly. The man's screaming made me feel sick. Mark dropped the gun, resorting to his fists as he pummeled the man until he stopped screaming.

When all seven were dead, Mark was very still, sitting on top of the man he had just beaten to death while the three of us studied his tense back.

I became aware of a quiet buzz that sounded like static. It caused all of us to whirl in the direction of the dead driver, who was laying on the ground by the front tire.

Mark stood and grabbed his gun, jogging to us when Josh whistled to him. Josh dropped to a crouch beside the dead man. With one hand keeping his gun ready, he used the other to pat the front of the man's suit, stopping near his lapel. He reached into the man's jacket and grabbed a small, clear communication device, watching as the wire unwound from the back of Craig's ear and pulled loose.

Josh turned to us, his eyes wide with fear that the slaughter had been heard and we were going to have other Commission employees on us soon.

We all leaned close to the earpiece.

"...nmit, what the fuck, Craig? What happened? What was that screaming? Report!" a male voice snapped urgently.

We looked at each other, not sure what to do.

Josh nudged Clark, looking at the earpiece expectantly.

"What?" he mouthed. Josh nudged him harder and Clark cleared his throat, dropping his voice.

"Craig! Fucking answer!"

"Alright!" Clark snapped, trying to keep his voice from shaking. "Can you fuckin' hear me now?"

"Finally, what the fuck, Craig? What was that screaming?"

"Just Zac fuckin' around," Clark tried to sound annoyed. I was thrilled to hear the man's response because it proved that he could not hear us very well.

"Zac's fuckin' a cow?"

"Fuck! No!" Clark snapped, though Josh and Mark pursed their lips against their laughter. "Scarin' off some teens. They're drinking up here."

"What the fuck, Craig? We got other shit to worry about. Get the fuck out of the camp and go to your section, now."

"Yeah, yeah..." Clark groaned. Mark grabbed the device from Josh, tossing it to the ground and crushing it under his heel.

"Quick," Josh said. "Clark, pull up the section map."

"What?"

"In the front!" Josh snapped, pointing. Clark was about to reach for the driver's door handle when Mark grabbed his wrist and shook his head, reaching into his pocket. He pulled a black glove over his hand and opened the door for Clark.

Clark climbed into the front seat, looking at the screen on the front of the dash.

"Lily, ropes," Josh ordered, motioning to the other side of the car. I nodded without question, climbing through the van and opening the other door, covering my hand with the sleeve of my sweater. I looked at the ground to the dead men, their heads only slightly bleeding from their wounds now that their hearts had stopped. Their eyes were open, staring under the car or up at the sky in glassy fear. My gaze was locked on their chalky, dead faces, terrified and sick.

"Got it!" Clark called, breaking me out of my stupor.

I saw Clark move away from the driver's seat, being careful not to touch anything and turning to help me. I slipped my sweater off my shoulders, wrapping it around my hands before extracting the rope from the dead men's hands, trying not to look at them or think too much about what I was doing.

By the time Clark got over his shock at the men and took his sweatshirt off to help, I had gotten the ropes back in the car.

"Hey!" Josh called, standing at the other side of the van with one of the dead men. "Help." Josh pulled at the limp man's arms and tried to pass him off to Clark, but both of us froze, staring at the dead man stupidly before Josh lowered his arms again, rolling his eyes. "*Now*!"

Clark took a deep breath and reached forward, taking the man's wrists with his arms still wrapped in the sweatshirt, pulling the corpse into the van. I tried to keep myself from passing out as the dead body was brought closer to me.

"Back! Back!" Josh snapped, motioning for Clark to move the body as Mark stepped awkwardly into the car, carrying the dead man's feet. Clark followed Mark's nods to sit him in one of the back seats where Mark, wearing gloves, buckled the corpse in. My stomach was somersaulting at the morbidity of the situation.

Mark stepped out of the van as Josh began ordering us.

"Get them in the car," he snapped, motioning to the dead men on our side of the van.

"What?"

"No time! We need to go!" Josh yelled, pointing harshly again.

"But—"

"Do it!"

"Shut the fuck up!" Clark snapped. "Fucking hell! What are we going to do with them?!"

"Explain later!"

"No!" Clark protested.

Josh began yelling very strongly in his native language, which took us aback, having never seen Josh so angry. Mark, who had been trying to move another man, whirled around with appalled eyes before walking to Josh and smacking him sharply across the back of the head. Josh's head snapped forward as he caught himself on his hands on the floor of the car.

With a whine, he rubbed the area on the back of his skull and turned to Mark, who stared at him expectantly before grabbing his elbow and bringing him to the man he was trying to move.

Clark turned back to me. I knew my face was pale and my eyes were showing my mortification. I was not sure how Mark and Josh planned to cover up what had happened. Even though they seemed to know what they were doing, I could not stop my anxiety from creeping higher and higher with each passing minute.

Steeling myself for my task, I grabbed Clark's arm and pulled him to the other side of the van, wrapping my sweater around my hands and lifting another man into the van, though I was not sure where to put him. I moved him to lay between the two seats and as I was about to step out, Mark and Josh brought the man who had been shot in the leg before beaten to death, setting him on top of the dead man we had carried in. I assumed we were just piling the bodies in the car now, rather than strapping them in like the first.

I decided not to question why the one corpse got a seatbelt and the others didn't.

Clark and I pulled another body we were charged with into the van, trying to lay him on the other two, but he fell limply to one side, wedging between the seat and the other two bodies. I cringed and quickly got out of the way as another body came in from the other side.

Clark and I had one more body that we tried to curl to fit in the space behind the front passenger's seat. When we finally got him to fit, both of us closed the door and moved around the back of the van, picking up the boxes and tools and replacing them in the back, taking special care not to touch anything with our bare hands.

Once that was complete, Josh and Mark loaded the driver into the van and closed the door, sending some of the broken polarized glass from the window scattering to the ground.

Josh turned to Mark, who nodded once and went to the driver's seat, climbing in and starting the van.

Josh ushered us out of the way and Mark peeled away, driving down the dirt road out of sight.

"What now?" Clark asked, pale and shaking.

"We find other Eight Group members," Josh said, motioning to his car.

"Could...could I have a second?" I breathed, feeling my stomach turn sickly as I replayed the memories of the men falling dead to the ground and then the horrific scenes afterward as we loaded the dead men in the van.

Josh did not look willing to wait, but when I crouched to the ground, putting my head between my knees to quell the nausea, he remained quiet, waiting for me to collect myself. Clark darted away and threw up behind a tree.

Chapter Sixty-Six

Despite the number of times I had heard about the structure of the Eight Group, it still startled me how organized they were.

Josh drove Clark and me to another part of town, near the main branches of the banks, where another black van was parked on the curb. I could not stop the shiver of apprehension at seeing another black van, unsure if we were about to flee from another team.

"Come on," Josh said as he turned the car off and got out, walking quickly to the other van and knocking twice on the door before opening it without waiting for an answer.

There were a lot of familiar faces in the van. Ichiro and Rin were the first ones I noticed. Minsoo was in the front seat and Yi Ling was driving, finally back from her Sweep run in the Western Region.

"Lily, get in!" Rin said with an exasperated laugh as Ichiro turned on the scrambler he was carrying. "You're a wanted criminal. You can't just stand in the middle of downtown."

Both Clark and I clambered into the van, still feeling sick from what had happened earlier in the day.

Rin closed the door and turned to Josh.

"What happened?"

"Another team found them," Josh explained.

"Woobin...you didn't..." Ichiro looked at him with wide eyes, allowing his sentence to trail off.

"Hyunwoo started it," Josh defended quietly, looking at the floor of the van. Rin blinked at Josh incredulously.

"Are you insane?!"

"Where are the maps?" Josh asked. Minsoo pulled the tablet off the dash, passing it to Josh.

"Josh, this is very bad," Yi Ling whispered. "Where is Mark?"

"Driving to their section," he said, flipping through the various frames on the tablet as I watched, my brain numb and my stomach turning. Ichiro put a hand on my shoulder, which made me jump.

"Are you okay?" he asked worriedly.

"Yeah," I answered before I had time to think. I could tell that no one was convinced, but I forced a smile, figuring I would need to get used to such horrors with the way our revolution was progressing.

Josh stared at one of the maps and then glanced at his wrist watch before rubbing his temple worriedly.

"What?"

"Huan-yue is going to be in the area," he mused. "But she is alone..."

Minsoo asked something over the seat and Josh lifted the tablet, pointing to the map somewhere.

"What does Mark plan on doing?" Rin asked. Josh looked up from the tablet, turning it around.

"He's taking the car here...and he's going to stage it to look like an attack."

"Is that their section?" Yi Ling asked.

"Later today," Josh said. "I'm worried about someone seeing him."

"You better go help, then. Why did you stop here?" Rin asked.

"If there was anyone in the area, there would be a problem," Josh whispered, motioning to me and Clark. He handed the tablet back to Minsoo. "Tell everyone," he ordered.

Ichiro and Rin nodded before they turned to Clark and me, worry clear in their expressions.

"I'll take you to the fort," Josh whispered, motioning for both of us to follow as he opened the door.

"What about Mark?" Clark asked.

"I'll pick him up after I have you two safe."

* *** *

That night at the fort, I was anxiously waiting to learn if Mark and Josh had gotten away with the murders. I told everyone what had happened and though everyone was worried, many of the experiments, particularly Tori and Griffin, were telling me not to be concerned, assuring me that Mark was the best of the best and he could take care of himself.

Everyone started moving into one of the hallways on the far side of the strategy room. Sitting with Mykail in the main bunker, I turned to him, confused.

"What's going on?"

"It must be almost seven," he said. "Time for the news."

"You guys watch the news down here? How do you manage that?" I asked, standing when he offered his hand to me.

"Some people who are a lot smarter than me set it up," Mykail chuckled. "We have some highly-educated people here. You would be surprised."

"Why didn't anyone watch yesterday?"

"They did," Mykail corrected, taking my hand and leading me in the same direction the others were walking. "You and I were in the medical room."

I did not particularly care about what was going on on the news. I was still having difficulty processing the events from earlier in the day, which was why I was sticking so close to Mykail, holding his hand, grounding myself in reality. He knew what happened, but he didn't press me to talk about why it was bothering me so much. I could not help but notice the difference in the way my friends at school used to comfort me, constantly asking if I wanted to talk about it, trying to get inside my head, telling me that everything was going to be alright even though they had no real grasp on the situation.

The people that had been in the Commission did not provide comfort the same way. It was silent, supportive, and completely devoid of pressure.

The room of old computers and monitors was crowded with people watching the three screens as the program before the news wrapped up. Tori and Griffin were leaning against the back wall with us. Tori sighed and leaned against Griffin's arm, watching tiredly.

"Tori," I called. She turned quickly. "Are you alright?"

"Yeah. Just a little tired."

"She's been awake for the last week and a half," Griffin said. "Her batteries are about to die." Griffin turned to her. "Will you sleep tonight?" he asked, lifting his eyebrow.

"Will you stop snoring?" she teased.

"I do not snore."

"Yes, you do," more than a dozen voices, including my own, contradicted. He looked around, shocked, pretending to be indignant.

"Get earplugs," he snapped playfully.

It still impressed me how well everyone got along. The two bunk rooms were very crowded and with the trauma levels of the experiments and those who had been captured by the Commission, everyone had some form of sleep disturbance. I shared a bed with Mykail, which proved to be extremely difficult due to his large wings. He slept on the top bunk and allowed his wings to drape down each side heavily, but that also meant that the heavy wings were over me, practically suffocating me with their weight.

After some rearranging, we finally found a way to somewhat-comfortably share the bed.

However, the close quarters, I was sure, were taking their toll. There were some tensions that Griffin and Tori had told me about when I saw some people snap at one another, but they told me that it was just a response to the worry of the rebellion, the less-than-desirable food, lack of sleep, and close quarters.

I was worried that if it got out of hand, we would implode as a revolution. I needed to talk to the main strategy group soon to discuss the food shortage, the high tensions, and what we needed in order to quickly, but smartly, speed up the process of getting everyone out of the fort.

But, at that moment, there was too much going on in my mind to even try to think of our next big move, or use the teasing as a way to bring up ways of solving our problems.

"How much have I missed lately?" I asked, nodding to the screens.

"When was the last time you watched the news?"

"…a week ago?" I answered, unsure.

"The CEO and four corporate managers of the Carolina Media Group have been arrested," Griffin said.

"Arrested? For what?"

"Treason," he said. "There is a big public outcry about it. They had to move them out of the prison and bring them to Central because people were rioting outside and causing trouble."

"They're in Central now?" I asked.

"Welcome to your seven o'clock news, I'm Debbie Peats," the female anchor said.

"And I'm Joseph Walsh," the man next to her said. "Our first story of the night comes from deep space. The Altereye team just contacted Central…"

"The people were angry about the Carolina managers getting arrested?" I continued, turning to Griffin and Tori when I realized that the first story had nothing to do with us. "What are they asking the government to do?"

"Nothing…" Tori said with a smile.

"What do you mean?"

"They're asking *us* to do something," Mykail clarified. He wrapped an arm around my shoulders. "You've done a good job."

"*We* did a good job," I laughed.

"Group hug!" Tori declared with a beaming smile, pulling Griffin away from the wall and dragging him to us, throwing her arm around my shoulders. I laughed while Griffin groaned and Mykail, slyly, was able to escape the hug.

"Tori…" Griffin said, pretending to be annoyed.

"Don't be so grumpy," she teased, though she did release us.

"What have they been asking us to do?" I pressed.

"Mostly they've been asking us to break them out," Griffin said. My eyebrows went high.

"And the thoughts on this are…"

Griffin sighed and turned to Tori, who looked at him for a moment before turning to me.

"We need to prove how dedicated we are to this," she said. "If we answered and broke these people out of the camp, they would see that we stand with those who support us, and we could gain a very strong following."

"I agree." Mykail said. "It would be best to find a way to break them out and show everyone that we mean what we say."

"Do we know where they are?" I asked.

"The location is secret. But don't worry," Tori winked, "we got men on the inside."

"Our second story of tonight," Debbie said, the camera focusing on her once again. "The outcry at the imprisonment of Carolina Media Group CEO Jerry Parker has spread through the country. There have been seventeen reported demonstrations across the regions of people holding signs outside city halls, demanding that he be freed. There have been reports that the number of people at such demonstrations have doubled since Mr. Parker was moved to an undisclosed location, raising fears that he will soon face punishment from the Commission of the People for his public support in the recent rebellion against Central and the Commission of the People."

The image changed to footage of men and women holding signs, saying "Support Central Angels" and "Free the Rebels!" They were chanting various phrases, garbled from the number of voices.

"This is one group outside the city hall of New Boston," Debbie's voice said over the montage. "Despite their demands to release CEO Parker, they claimed that they were unwilling to ask Central directly for his acquittal."

A woman came on the screen, being interviewed as she held her sign proudly in front of her.

"It's obvious that Central and the Commission of the People are trying to get rid of anyone who supports the rebellion. The Commission is trying to keep their power. It needs to be dismantled completely."

A burly man was next to be interviewed.

"We have to step in fast, before the Commission makes him into some kind of secret weapon," he declared. "We hope the Central Angels can do something."

When the camera went back to the studio, Joseph spoke next.

"As we've stated before, this is just one of seventeen reported demonstrations taking place across the nation. Beyond these protests, reports of vandalism and graffiti continue to pour in, all showing sentiments in agreement with the movement now known as the Central Angels."

"I like that name…" I mused. Mykail squeezed my hand.

"The Commission of the People has yet to respond to the accusations against the transfer of CEO Parker, and their silence has led to some devastating crimes," Debbie added. "Earlier today in south Central, a van was discovered near an abandoned motel with seven bodies around the scene. The dead men were identified as employees of the Commission of the People, and once Central Intelligence and the Commission of the People were called to the site, news crews were banned from the scene. Our informant was able to take pictures of the crime beforehand, though we are unable to share most of the photos due to the graphic nature. There is one photo we are able to share. Here you can see the side of the van that was found spray painted with wings."

I could not help but bark a laugh, shaking my head in disbelief as I looked over the picture.

"See? Mark knows what to do," Griffin told me with a smile.

"Central Spokesperson Leana Grey had this to say about the crime," Debbie concluded, nodding as the shot cut to an informal press conference on the front steps of the Chamber of Regions building. Leana Grey was an older woman with a hard face, wearing a suit and looking extremely aggravated.

"This rebellion has taken things too far," she said sharply. "Attacking Commission employees in such a violent fashion shows disregard for human life. This was done just because of their employment. These traitors are criminals and terrorists and must be held accountable for this heinous crime."

Cutting back to the studio, Debbie closed the story.

"We will bring you more updates as this story progresses. If you have any information about the crime, please call your local law enforcement," she concluded.

"In entertainment news, RM Entertainment announced…"

"Won't it be a little too much if we make ourselves out to be murderers?" I asked, turning to Griffin and Tori.

"It was a Commission van," Griffin said. "For now, I think we're safe. But it would be best to be very careful from here on. I'm pretty sure that was just a one-time thing. We probably could not get away with it again."

After another ten minutes of watching news that had little to do with our revolution, I went to help Tori with dinner preparations. Mykail stayed with the others, continuing to watch the news.

"So…do I need to ask you if you're going to be okay?" Tori asked as she pulled out pouches of the rations that everyone had been living on. I hated the rations, but the hunger in my stomach always pushed me to eat them anyway.

I took the ration packs, sorting them by type into our serving bins.

"I'm fine…"

"Are you just saying that?"

"Yes."

Tori chuckled and grabbed another handful of rations, kneeling next to me as we both sorted our stacks. I remained quiet before sighing and stopping in my work.

"Mark wouldn't have killed them if I hadn't…" I finally muttered, unable to finish the thought.

"Don't be so sure about that," Tori said. "Mark has a vengeful streak in him. Anyone who has ever done him wrong has paid for it dearly. And hurting you is something he would deem worthy of revenge."

"…is Mark dangerous?"

"Extremely," she said, turning to me. "But so are you. Look at what you've accomplished and you have never pulled the trigger on anyone. People are dangerous. It doesn't matter who they are."

I picked up the next ration, resuming my sorting.

"I just wonder if it was avoidable, that's all…"

"Probably not," Tori sighed. "We're at war now. These things will happen."

I looked back to the diminishing crates in the supply room.

"We're running out of food really fast…" I noted, trying to make the comment sound off-handed. Tori sighed dejectedly.

"Some of us have been trying to find a way to get more rations. Several of the experiments only need one meal per day, but the humans are getting hungry, and when they get hungry, tensions rise."

"I thought we had a lot of food, though."

"We did," Tori agreed. "Some of it had to be disposed of because it was no longer edible. Griff found the schematics of the fort. They kept supplies enough to last six months for sixty people. We have twice as many." Tori stood, pulling the two bins full of rations off the ground as easily as if they were empty. "We will need to figure something out quickly," she said. "But we can worry about that another day."

Members of the rebellion trickled into the main bunker for rations. Tori handed me a serving, reminding me that I was also human and couldn't survive on one meal a day. I thanked her and took my dinner, walking to Mykail and sitting with him to talk about nothing in particular.

Everyone dispersed to different activities. A large group was playing cards in one corner, cheering when someone lost and another person could jump into the group, the low radio music drowned out by the excited players. Tori disappeared, as did Griffin, and I was left with Mykail, who was dozing off, staring at the various groups of people as they lounged around the main bunker.

As some were heading into the bunk rooms in an attempt to get some sleep, I remained wide awake. Mykail had gone to sleep on his side, his head resting on my leg as I played with his hair. The fine strands were tangled, so I slowly worked my fingers through his hair, trying not to wake him.

I looked at his wings, which were still pristine and white, though some sections were dirty from being on the ground. I noticed some darker spots barely hidden by the feathers that covered the scarred area where his skin met the wings.

I moved the feathers gently out of the way and was shocked to see sores along the base of his wings. I was about to wake him and ask when I remembered Dana coming to our house to give Mykail his shots.

I was mortified that Mykail had not said anything earlier.

I debated whether or not to bring up the topic with the sleeping experiment. I tried to tell myself that I was overthinking things and that there might have been some light irritation from the dirty conditions of the fort.

I nervously recalled what Dana had said about caring for the experiments, wondering how many more experiments were hiding their pain.

There was a clunk and then a resonating boom that caused everyone to look at the warped spiral staircase leading into the fort from the power plant above. Everyone in the main bunker silenced. Only a few people knew where the staircase led, so everyone was particularly anxious about that entrance.

When I saw the thin man coming quickly down the stairs, holding a bag at his side, I relaxed.

Josh smiled, seeing me first as he descended the final flight of steel stairs. He was greeted with smiles and waves all around him. Everyone loved seeing Josh.

The noise woke Mykail and he sat up, blinking tiredly.

"Where is Peter?" Josh asked, looking for the med-school dropout.

"I'll get him," Gracie offered, jumping away from the card games and running into the first bunk room.

"Where have you been?" Mykail asked the Eight Group member. "We were getting worried."

"Things got busy," he said with a shrug. Josh held the black bag forward. "Rin finally got some."

"She did?" Mykail breathed, a relieved smile spreading across his face.

"Some what?" I asked.

"The shots to help with my wings," Mykail answered, trying to sound nonchalant. I was about to tell him I had seen the sores, but I decided against it. He was trying to keep his pain concealed, and I felt that bringing it up would make him feel worse about his condition.

"Josh?" Peter grumbled, blinking the sleep from his eyes as he joined us. "What's going on?"

"This is for you," Josh said, extending the bag. Peter's eyes went wide and he grinned, taking the bag.

"Thank you. I was getting worried about Alex and Mykail."

"I told you I was fine," Mykail said with a chuckle, standing.

"Well, you are now," Peter agreed. "Come on, let's go to the medical room."

"I'll be back in a little bit," Mykail told me, squeezing my hand again as Peter asked a few others to gather the experiments that needed medical attention.

"Josh, Josh," a teenage boy named Luke, who was the best technician we had in the bunker, called, running to the experiment. "Did you get any more pictures of what happened this afternoon? The news is saying it was a hate crime."

Josh pulled out his phone, turning to his photos and showing one to Luke.

"Oh, you are *awesome*!" Luke beamed, taking the phone. "This is perfect!"

The teen ran off with Josh's phone and I laughed. Josh sat down next to me.

"What picture did he see?" I asked as casually as I could.

"The section maps. Marked targets for Sweeps, notes about what to do with the people captured..."

"Wow...And he's going to go spread those online?"

"I hope so," Josh said. "And then delete them off my phone," he added with a chuckle. He looked at me for a moment before nudging me. "Are you okay?"

I turned away, nodding slowly.

"I'm okay…" I murmured. "It was…it was just a lot to process…"
Josh reached around my shoulders, pulling me close.

"I'm sorry if we scared you."

"I'm alright," I said. "Where's Mark?"

Josh laughed and shook his head, rolling his eyes.

"He's at the Commission, making sure that everyone thinks
someone else did it," he explained. "Ruining evidence…"

"You two are pretty good at covering your tracks," I said with a
teasing eyebrow. "Like you've done this before or something."

"Three times." Josh held up three fingers.

"*Three*?"

"There was another time where Mark killed two people and we
had to hide them," Josh elaborated. "They were about to rape Eun and
he stepped in."

"You two are always saving his sisters…" I tried to tease. Josh also
smiled. "Do you regret what you did for Mark's older sister? Since it
led to you being captured?"

Josh groaned, his head rolling around on his neck as he withdrew
his arm, running a hand through his hair in frustration.

"How can you ask me that?" he whined. "Such a difficult
question…"

"I mean, I heard that the life you had before was…really bad," I
said as carefully as I could. Josh puffed out his cheeks, trying to think
of a way to answer.

"Our families were very strict," he said. "We were always
watching for people who were going to hurt us, but we didn't know
who they were…and as kids we were always wondering how our life
would be outside…but…we were happy."

"Hiroki said your father…tried to kill you," I mumbled. Josh bit
his lip, stalling as he thought about how to answer.

"Things…were different," he tried to explain. "He stopped doing
that when I was…fourteen?" He furrowed his eyebrows, thinking.

"That doesn't really change anything," I said. "What about your
mother? What was she like?"

"My mom?" Josh hesitated, surprised by my interest. "She was
very sick. She died when I was seventeen. I don't really remember
her…she was always sleeping or lying in bed. My father said I made
her sick."

"No offense, but your father sounds horrible," I said simply. Josh
laughed and looked at the ground.

"He was alright..." he murmured, though it was obvious he did not believe that himself.

"Mark's parents were nicer to you though, right?" I started. Josh opened his mouth to speak and then let out a little laugh.

"Lily...not all parents are loving," he said. My heart fell.

"What were Mark's parents like?"

"His mother was very nice, but...quiet," he told me, looking into the space of the bunker to avoid eye contact. "His father was..." He trailed off for several moments. "He was a...hard person...But he let me sleep in the house with them, so I thought he was nice."

"You don't have any brothers or sisters?"

"No." He shook his head. "Our parents were trying to stop having children, but some families still had them." His gaze remained distant, thinking about the life he led before being captured by the Commission. I watched his face, wondering what kind of memories he had of his childhood. I could only imagine what it was like to be raised in such seclusion and fear.

"Did you ever think about leaving the country?"

Josh laughed.

"A lot. But it was not possible with so many people...We look different." He folded one leg to his chest and hooked his fingers over his knee.

"Did you ever think about what kind of life you would have liked to have? You know, if you could?" I pressed. He was thoughtful for a very long time, and after an intense silence, I continued. "What do you like to do? What did you do for fun when you were younger?"

His face broke into a big smile and he finally turned to face me fully, light playing in his eyes.

"Dance."

I blinked at him and then laughed, confused.

"*Dance?*"

"I love to dance."

"What kind of dance?"

"Any kind." I stared at him, not sure what to say in response. "You don't like to dance?"

"Well...no, I guess, I don't know. I can't dance." Josh looked skeptical and shook his head, not believing me. "No, really, I can't," I chuckled.

"Then why do you go to the club?" he asked.

"That's different," I defended. "In the club, you're just in a group, jumping up and down and moving with everyone else. It's not really *dancing*."

891

"Is there music? Are you moving because of the music? Then you're dancing," Josh said simply.

"So, really, you like music," I deduced.

"I like music and I like dancing," Josh agreed.

"I remember when you did the dance while you sang after the parade," I giggled. "You were good."

"You think so?" he asked. "I should be on TV, then."

"Yes," I agreed, playing along. He clapped his hands together, standing. He turned and reached out to me. I stared at his hand for a moment before I took it slowly, not sure what he wanted me to do.

"We are going to dance."

"We *are*?" I gaped. He took both my hands and pulled me closer, though I backed away. "Josh, come on. I can't dance."

"Please," he whined, looking at me hopefully. I groaned and caved in. I let him pull me closer, one hand settling on my waist and the other taking mine. I looked at him skeptically, listening to the song that was playing on the radio.

"We're going to dance to *this*?"

"Why not? You can always dance, there's no music you can't dance to."

I laughed, letting him lead as we moved awkwardly around the bunker. Some turned to watch, which made me embarrassed and, therefore, clumsy.

"*Relax*," he teased.

"People are staring…"

"So?"

"You don't think this is weird?"

"No." He shook his head, spinning me under his arm. Stunned at the fluidity of his moves, my gaze turned suspicious.

"Where did you learn to partner dance?" I asked, coming back to him and putting my hand on his shoulder.

"Mana and I would dance sometimes," Josh said, turning me again.

"Mana? Mark's sister?" I asked. He nodded, crossing my arms and holding me for another part of the dance before spinning me outward again. "Was she your girlfriend?"

"No," he said. "Like my older sister, too."

"You would just randomly dance with her? Where did you get the music?"

"Sometimes we got radio," Josh explained, continuing to dance even though the radio had moved to another song with a completely different beat. He picked up the pace and I struggled to keep up. "But the community would sing and dance, too."

"Why?"

"Entertainment." Josh spun me a few times. "Yoshiro, Hyunwoo's father, told me I had been dancing since I was really small."

"I must say that I am impressed," I said, starting to relax and have fun as we moved around the improvised dance floor. "I did not know you could dance like this."

"I would dip you, but I don't know if I could," he said with a small smile. After a few moments of me staring, unsure what he meant, I laughed, deciding to tease him.

"Are you calling me fat?"

"Fat?" he repeated, horrified. He looked me over and then shook his head quickly. I laughed harder.

"When a woman says that, you don't look her over!" I gawked playfully. He stopped, backed away, and stared at me, confused and concerned that he had offended me.

"What does that mean?" he asked hesitantly. "Look her over?"

"I asked if I was fat, and then you," I looked him over in an exaggerated manner and then laughed, "looked at me as if you were trying to decide if I was fat or not."

"No, no, you're not fat," Josh said quickly.

"Josh, you better be careful," one of the men laughed from the fringes of the card game group. "Never call a woman fat."

"I wouldn't!" Josh protested, frantic, though he was laughing in his confusion. "When did I call you fat?" he asked, turning back to me.

"You said you couldn't dip me."

"No, it's because you're taller than me! I might lose my balance and fall on top of you!"

"Better not do that, either," a woman leered. "Might give people the wrong impression!"

"What?" Josh looked around at those in the bunker, a confused but amused expression on his face. I giggled and walked closer, hugging Josh and patting him on the back.

"It's okay," I said.

"I don't understand," he chuckled, hugging me back.

"We're just teasing you," I assured, breaking the hug and taking his hand. "Really, it's okay. Come on," I grabbed his other hand, pulling it to my waist, "dance with me again."

Chapter Sixty-Seven

I sat with the same people I always did during lunch, but there was an unusual addition to the group. Josh had spent the last two nights with us. When we asked how he was able to stay away from the Commission, he told us that he was supposed to go on a small reconnaissance mission just south of the city with a few others of the Eight Group and they had taken his tracers with them while he stayed behind to keep an eye on us, at Mark's request.

I had been in the fort for a week and we were still waiting for the fuss to calm down. The people were getting angrier as Central tried to keep the chaos to a minimum. There had been three attempts to storm the Commission building, but the small groups had been rapidly apprehended by the military forces that had surrounded all buildings in the Leadership District since the Rhodes Parade Massacre.

I was growing worried about our food supply, but was waiting for Mark before discussing any plans to replenish. Mark had been busy with whatever he was doing up on the surface, not even visiting after Clark had come to live in the fort the night after our encounter with the Commission team. If anything, Mark was even busier since Clark's arrival. Several members of the Eight Group regularly checked in and gave us gossip on Dana's dealings. However, the leader of the Eight Group had only checked in once, though he had not come into the fort. Josh, who had come to stay in the fort on Monday, suddenly started up the stairs toward the passage into the abandoned Makay Power Plant. When I asked where he was going, he told me that Mark was there.

Eager to see the experiment that I had not seen since he killed the Commission team, I had quickly followed.

Mark was obviously exhausted. I had assumed he was tired before, but I had never seen the signs on his face. In the dark shadows of the power plant, I could see the deep crevices in his features caused by lack of sleep.

Before Josh could say anything to Mark, I had run forward and thrown my arms around the leader of the Eight Group, hugging him even though I knew he disliked it, feeling as though we were reuniting after several months.

He hugged me back, but only stayed long enough to show something to Josh on his phone.

That was when Josh had started his stay with us.

It was Wednesday and I knew that, very soon, the core strategy group would have to gather and discuss what we were going to do about the dwindling supplies and the public's demands for our action.

But we were talking about nothing of the sort as we ate our tasteless rations.

"I'm really impressed with you two," Cody said, pointing at me and Mykail when our previous conversation about the crowded bunk rooms had exhausted itself. I blinked, confused.

"What do you mean?"

"You two have successfully kept your hands to yourselves," he teased. I laughed and looked at the ground, embarrassed, but surprised myself. I had not even thought about how long it had been since Mykail and I last had sex.

"Yeah, guys, you know, we don't mind if you want to slip away into one of the store rooms," Paula, a former teacher, teased. "I mean, it's not like you're the only ones sneaking off..." She looked at Griffin, who blinked in surprise before pointing to his chest.

"*Me?*"

"You and Tori have a tendency to disappear together," Paula pointed out. I turned quickly to the two of them as they both laughed heartily.

"Don't you play for the other team, Tori?" Meg asked.

"I do," she laughed. She turned to Griffin and hugged one of his arms. "Although, I am rather fond of these. He gives the best hugs," she teased, leaning against Griffin and smiling broadly. "Like a big ol' teddy bear!"

"C'mon, Griff," Cody leered. "Aren't you at least a little interested in Tori? She is gorgeous."

"She's like my little sister!" Griffin growled playfully, flicking a crumb of the ration at the younger experiment.

"Josh," Tori said, turning to the member of the Eight Group sitting between Mark's younger sister and me, "would you say you know Mark better than anyone?"

"Uh...yes?" he answered slowly. "Why?"

"It's just...you know, you two seem...*close*," she said, trying to sidestep the question I had asked myself before. While I had not seen a lot of interactions between Mark and Josh, there were moments where it was obvious how well the two of them knew one another and how deeply they cared. I had occasionally wondered if their relationship was beyond friendship.

"We are," Josh confirmed, looking around, seeing that we were all uncomfortable trying to ask the question.

"Do you love him?" Paula asked, trying to be a little more direct.

"Yes, I love him."

We all turned to one another, wondering if he had just confessed to a romantic relationship with the leader of the Eight Group.

"So, you have..." Cody tried to press, trailing off, motioning nonsensically.

"What?"

"I don't know if he understands," I mumbled.

"Understands what?" Josh asked, scanning the faces in the circle.

"Have you two slept together?" Clark tried, still being careful about how he phrased the question.

"Yes, we sleep together all the time," Josh said, still confused about why we were so interested in the information.

"Okay, you know what, don't worry about it," Tori laughed, shaking her head and waving the question away. I could tell that she was just as awkward as the rest of us about the topic, though the uncomfortable feeling had nothing to do with the question—we felt more uncomfortable gossiping behind Mark's back in such an immature manner.

"No, wait, what are you talking about?"

"Have you two kissed?" Mykail chimed in.

"Uh, yes, we have kissed..." he said. I blinked at him, surprised.

"What?" he said, shrugging. Mark's little sister asked a question to Josh, who turned and answered, though it was obvious that he did not entirely know what was going on in the conversation either.

"Okay, let's just say no," Griffin chuckled, shaking his head. "I doubt it..."

"No, I want to know what you're talking about," Josh laughed.

"Just ask *him*," Paula said, pointing at the opening door to the medical room. Mark had stepped into the fort.

The entire circle lit up from the sight of the leader of the Eight Group and cries erupted, first from us, and then the entire bunker, greeting the experiment as he entered. He waved awkwardly at everyone before his attention was brought to the two figures moving toward him. As she always did when Mark showed up, Eun hugged her older brother, keeping close to him. Josh also approached Mark, speaking quickly to him, clearly relaying our earlier conversation.

Everyone in the lunch group shared an embarrassed, yet extremely curious, glance with one another.

Mark's eyes went wide and then he rolled his eyes, exasperated. He lifted one of his hands and crossed his fingers, looking at the experiment in front of him expectantly. Josh gasped and smacked Mark's hand, starting to snap at him before he rounded on us.

"*No!*" he practically screeched. Without meaning to, we laughed at his mortified reaction. "With *him*?! No!"

Mark just sighed and shook his head, joining the circle, Eun and Josh in tow.

"Mark, we've missed you," Tori greeted. "You look really tired..." she noted sympathetically. Mark just smiled as he sat, his back close to the wall.

"Everything okay?" Griffin asked. He nodded, though his eyes betrayed the depth of his exhaustion. Some of us were sliding our eyes sideways to one another, nodding minutely when we understood the general concern for Mark's health. "Nothing bad?"

He shook his head.

"Did you just come to say hi?" Clark laughed gently. Mark nodded slowly, smiling.

"Well, you know what we were just talking about," Tori teased.

"How can you *think* that?" Josh whined.

"You two are very close," Paula defended. "We just assumed..."

Josh looked at Mark before making a face and shuddering.

"*No,*" he snapped.

"Do a lot of people have relationships here?" I asked.

"Not so much," Griffin answered. "A few reunited couples and families, but as far as I know, no one has been forging relationships."

"Seriously, you two, if you want to have some time alone, that's totally fine," Tori laughed, pointing between Mykail and me.

"Oh..." I was not sure what else to say, embarrassed. I looked away from Tori, trying to stop the blush from rising to my cheeks. As I was trying to look anywhere else, I spotted Mark's eyes sliding shut as he sat with his arms folded over his chest. As his head dipped, his eyes fluttered open and he straightened. I pursed my lips against smiling and turned to the rest of the group, pretending not to notice, though many shared my knowing smile.

"Actually," Mykail started, "I think we would like to have some time to ourselves tomorrow...for her birthday."

My eyes went wide, having forgotten that my birthday was around the corner. I always used to laugh at those people who said that they had forgotten their birthday, but with how busy we had been with the revolution and then me moving into the fort permanently, I had lost track of the date.

"Tomorrow is your birthday?" almost everyone in the group gasped. I opened my mouth a few times, trying to say something. I just laughed and shrugged.

"I guess so," I chuckled. "I forgot."

"Oh my God, we should do something for your birthday!" Tori declared.

"Like what?" Griffin teased. "We can't just go to the store and buy her something." His smile grew wider when he turned to Mark and saw the experiment leaning forward, his head hanging as he dozed.

"It's okay, really," I said. "I don't need anything."

"Well, we should figure *something* out," Tori insisted. "Mykail, you can have her for as long as you want, but you have to share her with us for at least a couple hours tomorrow. Deal?"

"Deal," Mykail laughed, flicking his gaze to Mark. His head had dropped, sitting at an angle I knew would be painful, his arms crossed as he slept. Everyone was looking at him with a smile, though I was certain our hearts were breaking for the exhausted leader of the Eight Group.

"Mark," Tori called gently.

His head shot up and startled all of us as he scanned the circle, blinking as he tried to wake up.

"Mark," Tori repeated with a gentle smile, "please, go find a bed in the bunk room and sleep."

Mark shook his head, pinching the bridge of his nose and closing his eyes tight, fighting his fatigue.

"Seriously, Mark, when was the last time you slept?" Cody asked, concerned. Mark did not make any move to answer. He remained in his position for a few moments before Eun put her hands on his arm, speaking quietly.

After a few moments, Mark heaved himself to his feet and walked across the bunker, waving and smiling at everyone who called a greeting to him on the way.

"He's completely drained…" Griffin murmured.

"No kidding," Tori said. "I guess that's a good sign, though."

"Why?"

"Because it means that Dana still trusts him enough to charge him with doing tasks," she explained, turning briefly to look at the closed bunk room door. "You know…he probably came here because it is the only place where he can let his guard down and sleep for a little bit, now."

"Let's give him a couple hours," Mykail agreed with a nod. "Tell everyone to leave him alone. We can wake him up later."

"He will set an alarm," Josh said with a shake of his head.

"Why?"

"He has to pick my mother up," Clark whispered, looking guilty. "With the raids on the building, Dana has told him to keep watch on her at all times and keep her safe."

"...how long do you think he can keep this up?" I murmured.

"As long as he needs to," Tori answered.

* *** *

Even though I had been angry at my family for everything that had happened the previous weeks, there was a sadness that pervaded my thoughts from not being with them on my birthday. I was annoyed by the lingering attachment. Even after everything, I still wanted to be with them and wanted everything to be as it had been before Central.

I decided that, starting that day, I would no longer let my emotions get in the way. I had more important things to worry about. Pining for the past was going to get me nowhere.

It was nice to wake up to Mykail kissing my cheek.

"Happy birthday," he whispered when I opened my eyes. I smiled, stretching.

"Thank you," I mumbled, pecking a quick kiss on his lips.

As soon as I got out of the bunk room, I was greeted with cheers and people crowding to hug me. Even though I knew that Tori had wanted to do something to celebrate my birthday, I was still surprised. It felt like everyone in the fort was there to wish me happy birthday at the same time. A few of the teenagers we had saved gave me hugs, thanking me for everything I had done and telling me that if I wanted anything to let them know. Even some of the Commish Kids who had run away from home were wishing me well.

The bunker sang happy birthday, which nearly made me cry, though I tried to keep my happy tears at bay. Eun wrapped her arms around the arm not holding Mykail's hand, hugging me through the entire song.

After what felt like an eternity of well-wishes, Mykail and I finally got to the other side of the bunker and he led me down the hall of mechanical rooms. I followed him silently, not sure where we were going, but not too concerned. There was a fluttering in my stomach as I realized that this was going to be our alone time, and I was highly anticipating it.

He opened one of the doors and pulled me into the boiler room. It was warmer than anywhere else in the fort, and I felt more comfortable and relaxed almost immediately.

Mykail walked behind me and pulled my jacket off my shoulders. I could feel him smiling as I looked around the room with wide eyes.

"What is this?" I gasped.

"It's not much..." he murmured, folding my jacket over one of the boxes near the door. I looked at the two mattresses covered with sheets and given pillows, surrounded by candles.

"Candles?" I asked, turning to him with a grin.

"Well I was going to find roses too and make this as stereotypically romantic as possible." He took my hand and pulled me close, wrapping his arms around me as I settled against his shoulder, closing my eyes and feeling the warmth coming from his skin.

"You've outdone yourself."

"I wanted to do something special for you..." he whispered, holding me gently, yet securely. "Admittedly, I feel a little responsible for everything."

"Why?"

"Well...I kinda helped you get into this whole thing," he started. "I was the one who kept telling you that it was a good idea to go after Dana and find a way to take the Commission down, but now you've been kicked out of your home, you're a wanted criminal—"

"And I've never felt better in my whole life," I interrupted, my gaze locking with his. "I have been going to school and listening to what everyone told me to do my whole life. I saw nothing I wanted in my future. And then you came along and showed me that I could help to change the things I didn't like. I have you to thank for that..."

He drew in a worried breath. "You're really happy with this?"

"I have a purpose now," I said with a nod. "I never had one before."

He pressed his lips to mine.

When we had gone to the boiler room, I thought we would be hungrily pawing at each other, too frantic and desperate to take things slow after our long stint of abstinence. But Mykail took control of the situation and set the pace.

He draped over me just as he had before, his wings supporting his weight so he could use both hands to touch me, lighting my body on fire and creating a dull, but exquisite, ache. We moved and danced with one another as though we had never been apart intimately. I was becoming impatient with the slow pace, though I tried to force myself to endure it.

When we were connected as one, there was a small twinge of pain as my body tried to readjust to the intrusion it had forgotten. The pain heightened my pleasure and sent a delicious shockwave through my body. I moved against him to bring him deeper, wanting to speed up. But he kept a painfully slow rhythm.

In a way, it was nice to have the slow build that led to my entire body bowing in pleasure, but I longed for us to move faster, more desperately. The slow pace made me nervous.

After we had rested, I initiated our second union. It was faster, more intense and it made me more comfortable than the slow lovemaking we had enjoyed earlier. There was no need for the sensual removal of clothes, both of us comfortably nude in the heat of the boiler room. There was no slow build into passion. I leapt on him, pushing him into a sitting position and climbing on his lap.

He held me and allowed me to take control, not opposed to picking up the pace either, though he was tired from restraining himself through our first romp.

I came down from the second high, holding onto him and shivering as the last ebbing waves of my orgasm left my body. He kissed my collarbone, gasping for breath.

"I've missed you," he whispered.

I leaned my head on his, kissing his temple, trying to slow my breathing.

"I've missed you, too," I said, swallowing hard. He smiled gently and his hands tightened around me. The action spoke volumes and an intense love poured out of me from every pore. I wrapped my arms around his shoulders and laid my head against his neck, seeing the still-visible sores on his wings. I looked at the spots of dark red, feeling the love in me change to pain at the danger I had put on his health.

Not only was Mykail someone I cared deeply about, he was also the symbol of our revolution, the element of unity that expressed our movements against the Commission, and that meant that he was the biggest target. I remembered with a sick feeling the Rhodes Annual Parade when the shots had been fired at him and how terrified I was that he was going to be shot out of the air.

Knowing that our revolution had turned into war made me feel as though I was the one putting him in danger. He worried he had been the one to endanger me, but I felt more responsible for his life since I had put him in danger not only because of the revolution, but also because of his body fighting the appendages Dana had attached.

All I could do was hold him until we both were asleep on the makeshift bed, kept warm by the boiler as it heaved and roared behind us.

I was awakened by hands on me, running over my chest and torso, familiar lips against mine. Still hazy from sleep and the heat of the room, Mykail and I worked each other into bliss once again.

I had no concept of time, or even where we were. We were simply enjoying one another to the fullest extent in the warmth.

We eventually redressed, cleaned up the area—though we did not remove anything from the room—and went back to the bunker.

It was another incredible shock when I saw what was waiting in the bunker. Everyone cheered for me as they had that morning, including a lot of very familiar faces that had not been present earlier. Josh hugged me, spinning me around as I laughed.

Again, everyone sang happy birthday, but that time, Josh pulled me into a ridiculous dance that had me grinning ear to ear as I laughed, spinning in a circle with him.

"And, we have a surprise for everyone!" Tori called when the song and applause died down. "There was a reason that we sent everyone to different rooms for different tasks. The Eight Group wants to show their appreciation for Lily on her birthday and for Clark as well, even though his birthday was a few months ago." Minsoo, Rin, and Ichiro ran to the door for the strategy room as we all turned. "So they have set something up for all of us to enjoy."

The three experiments slid the large door out of the way and my eyes went wide when I saw what was on the tables. There was food—food that was not rations—obviously from caterers with the way it was perfectly set up. People cheered and shouted in loud celebration.

I turned to Josh in shock, who was grinning devilishly.

"How the hell did you manage—"

"Don't worry about it." He waved the question away. "This is your present from us. Oh, and this." Josh reached into his pocket as Tori yelled at everyone to get a plate. Josh pulled out something wrapped in newspaper. I blinked at the parcel, surprised that he had a gift. Hesitantly, I unfolded the paper, discovering a small, gold-colored object with a hole in the middle, two brown strings tied to it to make a bracelet.

I picked it up to get a better look at the engravings on the thin gold surface.

"It's been my good luck charm," Josh explained. "It was my mother's. I was able to get it back a few years ago." He looked down at it. "It's a coin from our country."

My eyes were brimming with tears.

"This is very generous..." I said, failing at keeping my tears back. "But you should keep it."

"No, I want you to have it," Josh said. "Without you, this would not be happening. I want to thank you for that."

"Thank you, Josh," I whispered, hugging him tightly. We hugged for a short time before Rin grabbed Josh, pulling him away and telling me she would bring him right back.

I watched them disappear into the strategy room and then laughed, looking at the bracelet.

There was a tap on my shoulder and I turned to face Mark. My smile widened as he took the empty newspaper and folded it, putting it in his pocket. He then took the bracelet, tying it around my wrist.

"Thank you, Mark," I murmured. I looked at the excited frenzy as people enjoyed the food. "How did you pull this off?" I asked, looking at him suspiciously. He just smiled and put his finger to his lips, telling me it was a secret. Looking down at the bracelet on my wrist again, I took a deep breath.

"Did you bring me anything?" I said with a teasing smile. He looked at the ground for a brief moment before walking forward, wrapping his arms around me in a secure hug and holding me close.

I wrapped my arms around him as well.

"Is this my present?" I whispered. I felt him nod and my smile widened. There was nothing like the safety I felt at hugging Mark, as though his arms protected me from the negative feelings that pervaded my thoughts, shielding me from the blood of the growing revolution. It was one of the best gifts I had ever received.

Mark did not break the hug. I did when I was ready to let him go.

"You give great hugs," I told him. He laughed silently, looking at the ground, embarrassed. "You should give them more often."

He gave me a second hug.

Chapter Sixty-Eight

"We're finally all here," I said, looking at the people sitting at the table in the strategy room. For the first time in what felt like years, everyone in the main strategy group was in the fort at the same time.

"We have a lot of things we need to figure out," Clark said.

"I think the first thing we need to approach is whether or not we're going to do anything about the people in the camp that publicly supported us and were imprisoned for their trouble," Tori started.

"I think it would be foolish to not do anything," Griffin said. "We've already been out of public light too long. People are getting nervous about our disappearance."

"I agree," Josh seconded.

"Then, what do we want to do about it?" I asked.

"I've been thinking we need to get our supporters out of the camp, but do it quietly, at night, and let people find out about it after we are safe. Like what we did before," Clark suggested.

"To plan a silent raid like that again we would need a lot of information on the camp," Griffin said, shaking his head. "Right now, we don't even know where CEO Parker and the others are, or if they're even in the same place."

Mark reached into his inner coat pocket and pulled out several folded pieces of paper, sliding them across the table. All of us watched the papers move, confused and curious. Griffin slowly unfolded them, glancing at Mark briefly before looking over the information on the first page.

"What is it?" Tori asked.

"Holy shit…" he whispered. He looked at Mark, his hand falling heavily to the table as he shook his head in disbelief. "No wonder you've been so busy!"

"What is it?" I repeated Tori's question.

"The Carolina Media employees are in three different locations right now, but Dana plans to bring them into the Commission for interrogation. For that, he plans to move them to one location for one night before taking them in." Griffin lifted the papers. "This is the camp name, location, and the schedule for the transfers."

Everyone turned to Mark with wide eyes. He met eyes with each of us, confused why we were staring.

"*Damn,*" Clark chuckled brokenly.

"But there might be some actual criminals in the camp," Mykail interjected. "We don't want to break any of them out. How are we going to know who to get?"

Mark tapped the table to get everyone's attention and then pointed at the papers again. Griffin flipped through the sheets, stopping on the third page. He stared at the information for a moment before looking up with an affectionate, but surprised, smile.

"You are the most badass person I have ever met," he told Mark.

"He has the cell numbers?" I guessed.

Griffin nodded, looking back at papers.

"He has everything we..." He stopped as he turned to the fourth page, trailing off.

"What?" Clark questioned.

"This is one of the higher security camps," Griffin mused. "I never worked detail on one, but one of my friends did. He would always tease me that I got full meals while he had rations." Griffin turned the paper around and showed us a map of the camp compound, pointing at one structure. "The supply house...if we could lift some rations from the camp we could ease the strain on our own supplies."

"Food is not the only thing we need to worry about," Mykail added. "Bullets will become hard to come by later on."

"That's true," Griffin agreed.

"We did inventory on all the weapons, and we have enough weapons to outfit everyone," Tori noted. "But bullets will go quickly if we are called upon to fight. We need to be sure we have enough to last us through this war."

"There's no way to predict that," Clark lamented. "We haven't fought once, yet."

"The people can't easily access guns and weapons," I said. "Against the military, they are practically defenseless. They can't offer us any support in that respect."

"Mark, you bought your gun off the black market?" Griffin asked. Josh spoke for the silent experiment.

"We've bought several guns and several cases of bullets."

"You have?" Tori blinked. "Where are they?"

"I don't know," Josh admitted, making a face as he looked at Mark suspiciously. "He never told me."

Mark smiled and put his finger to his lips, motioning a few things very quickly.

"...okay," Griffin said. "I guess that's a good idea."

"What?" I asked.

"He wants to keep them secret until we absolutely need them," Tori translated. "It makes sense. If we count what he has as accessible, we're more likely to be careless about the bullets we already have."

"How much time do we have?" Clark asked, nodding to the papers. "If Dana is only keeping them there for one night, then that is the only night we have to strike."

"We have four days," Griffin answered.

"But..." Mykail looked at Josh and Mark, "isn't it dangerous to attack on that night? It will expose the fact that we have inside information on what Dana is doing, and that could expose you as well."

The table fell silent, all eyes on Mark. The leader of the Eight Group looked down, his eyes pensive. We waited. He finally reached into his outside coat pocket, pulling out the small notebook and pen he used for short messages when he was around us. He scribbled something and turned it for us to read.

"*He's going to find out eventually. I can't keep this up much longer.*"

"Why? Does he suspect something?" Clark asked quickly. I felt my own heart race as I thought about Mark being discovered by Dana at the wrong place and wrong time, which would cause us to lose one of our strongest allies along with our information on Dana's dealings inside the Commission of the People.

Mark shook his head, writing another message.

"*I don't want him to suspect anything before I leave.*"

"What happens to the rest of the Eight Group if you get found out?" Griffin asked, glancing at Josh.

"We'll be killed," Josh answered. "Dana said that after our first rebellion."

Mark nervously looked at his lap as Mykail leaned over to me.

"He went up against Dana before?" he whispered.

I cleared my throat and tapped the side of my jaw in response. Mykail quickly turned back to Mark, his eyes surprised.

"How did I not know this?"

"It was almost four years ago," Griffin said. "Many of the experiments who remember it don't want to talk about it."

"I'm surprised Dana didn't kill you then," Mykail said.

"Mykail," I scolded quietly. I knew about the torture Mark had endured and figured that there were times when Mark wished Dana had killed him. Everyone else who knew of the incident also seemed uncomfortable discussing it. I glanced at Mark and saw him looking at me with an unreadable expression. I schooled myself, trying not to show that I knew about his terrible ordeal.

Eventually, his dark eyes moved away from me.

"Sorry, Mark, I didn't mean to be insensitive," Mykail apologized.

"Does the Eight Group have a way to get out of the Commission if everything goes south?" Griffin asked.

Josh nodded, tapping the band around his wrist that he had shown me briefly before. It was similar to the band that Mark and Josh had had when they were younger and someone would spot a Commission car around their hidden community. It would tell them to run and hide by vibrating quietly. It was the way the Eight Group told each other about nearby danger.

"So, for the camp," Tori started, pulling us back on track as she grabbed the papers, "what do you think is the best approach?"

"I think that, as soon as possible—tonight even, if we can—we should have a group go to the camp and see what kind of guards they have. We'll need to have some people who know what they're doing and can find gaps in their security," I said, looking between Mark and Griffin as the two of them looked at one another.

"I will be willing to lead some people there," Griffin offered. "We can let Mark rest a little. If you want, Mark, you can come with us, but I'll be in charge of this. You have enough on your plate."

Mark bowed his head in agreement.

"Can we start that tonight?" I asked.

"I'll get some people together. Mark?" he asked. "Can you do this tonight?"

Mark nodded, looking at Josh who shook his head.

"I'll stay and watch the fort."

"Can I join?" I asked.

Mark shook his head strongly, which stopped whatever Griffin was going to say.

"Why not?" Griffin inquired.

Mark quickly jotted another message.

"*Too dangerous.*"

"Lily will be fine," Tori defended as I stared at Mark. It was nice that he was protective of me, but I wanted to be a part of our attacks against Dana. "The others know that she's a big part of this revolution. If she's not involved, they are going to wonder why."

"*The public does not know who she is, and we should keep it that way. She needs to remain safe so the rest of the revolution can continue to believe in her if things start getting bad.*"

I sighed and turned to Griffin.

"Fine, I won't be part of the scouting, but I want to be part of breaking people out," I told him. I turned quickly to Mark. "I don't have to break anyone out, but I want to at least help in getting supplies."

Mark made no effort to hide his displeasure at the idea of me being part of the raid at all, but I wanted to be sure that I had an active role. Mark slowly tapped the end of his pen against the pad of paper, studying me with his piercing gaze. He sighed, setting the pen down gently and closing his eyes, nodding once to show he had conceded.

* *** *

It was a very full and busy four days of preparation. Because Mark still had to keep up appearances, he was unable to assist in the daytime preparations. Tori and I worked together on getting the teams in order. Griffin worked with the men and women who had handled a gun before and kept them in the shooting range for target practice while, at night, going out on reconnaissance missions and coming back to the fort with updates about the number of guards and their positions, which occasionally caused us to shift our plans.

One of the prisoners was transferred on the second day of our preparation, and Griffin gave us the information about the increased security he saw on reconnaissance. With his information we were able to better predict how many guards would be present at the time of our infiltration.

Getting transportation was another problem. We could easily get people out of the camp and into one of the secret passages to the fort. The supplies were an entirely different matter. We had no car that we could use without being linked to the Eight Group.

When Mark joined us the day before our raid, we asked him if there was anything he could think of that would help us get the supplies from the camp to the fort.

He led Tori and me out of the exit near the water tanks and took us on a short hike into the still-snowy area around the reservoir. In one location, he pulled a large tarp from some wooden slats that covered a ramp where an old van was barely hidden underground. After digging up the key near the back tires, he got in the car and drove the vehicle out of its hiding spot.

When he got out of the car, Tori and I could only stare at him.

"Is there anything you're *not* prepared for?" Tori gaped.

Mark just smiled.

He parked the van in a motel parking lot about twelve kilometers from the campsite so we could access it the following night and get to the camp quickly. He insisted Josh would drive because he knew which back roads to use to keep us from getting caught.

Even though I was fully behind the idea of breaking out more people, I was not nearly as comfortable with the plan as I was with the Commission breakout. I had known more about the Commission before our infiltration and had understood the plan completely. I had never seen the camp compound. While I knew my job of getting into the supply tent and starting the train of people loading the supplies into the car, I was worried that everyone else might somehow fail because I did not know what they were supposed to be doing.

It made me very nervous not to understand the entire plan.

I barely slept the night before we went into action.

The final twelve hours before we left were a nightmare. I was a ball of nerves. Even though I had confidence that everything would go well, there was no calming the anxiety inside me. All weapons were checked and rechecked and the plan was reviewed again and again. The first group of infiltrators, the ones who would be breaking into the prisoners' cells, left in the late afternoon to watch the transfer of CEO Parker and see if we needed to increase our numbers with the backup group we had prepared.

Mykail stayed, watching over the fort and the remaining members of the rebellion.

Tori and I slipped away from the group that was heading toward the downtown exit from the fort and went to the motel where Josh was to meet us. We would drive to a certain spot before turning off the engine and pushing the car to its final position so as not to alert the guards to our presence.

It wasn't until I got in the back seat of the empty van with Josh that I started feeling thrilled, excited, and alive—the same feeling that had invaded my body when we were about to break out prisoners from the Commission.

None of us spoke on the drive, watching the streetlights pass in silence, feeling the tension and exhilaration of what we were about to do.

I ran through every aspect of the raid in my head. When we broke into the Commission of the People, I did not think we would perform something similar again. But war had passed beyond the idea of forming lines and having armies shoot at one another. Now, war was secretive, taking place in the dark of night and being sure that the little acts were performed with the most publicity manageable. It felt less like a war of humans and more like a war of symbolism.

After driving on a dirt road for five minutes, Josh turned off the headlights and the engine, putting the car into neutral. Tori got out of the front passenger's seat and went to the back of the car. Josh kept one hand on the steering wheel while the other one pushed on the outer frame of the car. I also climbed out of the car, keeping the van door open as I pushed on the frame.

Josh tapped twice on the car, loud enough for us to hear, telling us to push.

I had never pushed a car before, but I was sure that a car, particularly a large van despite being empty, was meant to be heavier. There was no strain. Once the car leveled at the top of the hill, the van slipped from my grasp and I watched as it moved along the road easily, the two experiments with enhanced strength pushing as though the vehicle was made of paper. I walked near the car, one hand keeping the side door open, the other resting on the gun strapped to my leg. I kept a close eye to my right, looking through the trees for the lights that belonged to the camp.

It was worse than deportation camps, which were notorious in their own right. That camp was called a "deliberation camp," as Griffin had put it. It was where the higher level criminals were brought while their fate was decided, whether it was deportation, death or, the worst, the Commission of the People.

Most worrisome was the knowledge that there was a mafia boss and a few of his colleagues at that particular camp. No one wanted them broken out and, subsequently, under our care. No one was sure we could trust people in organized crime.

I caught sight of lights in the distance and whistled to Josh and Tori. Two taps answered.

The road stopped at several fallen trees and rocks used to keep people from accessing the road close to the camp. It had been the construction road when the camp was being built, but became a liability when operations started. The surrounding roads had been destroyed, leaving only one heavily-guarded way in and out of the compound.

Josh pulled the emergency brake and placed a block of wood between the frame of the car and the driver's door to allow for quick access and a quick getaway. Likewise, I was sure to place a longer plank of wood along the track of the side door.

When the van was ready, the three of us crept through the woods. My eyes were not nearly as good as the experiments' and seeing the bright lights around the compound nearby helped illuminate parts of the ground, but I was still clumsily tripping over roots and small bushes.

Tori ran to my side after my third stumble and guided me through the dark.

I noticed several people crouched in the dark as we drew closer. I approached the mixture of experiments and humans, looking over the brightly-lit compound. It was much bigger than I expected, making me nervous about getting the supplies to the van.

"There's the supply tent," Josh whispered, pointing. Even though my stomach tensed at seeing the large tent, I nodded in response. We had discussed identifying the supplies that were most crucial to us, but I was worried we would not be able to fit everything we had discussed into the van. I started running through the list of supplies in my head again, trying to decide what would take priority.

Griffin approached the group and crouched by Tori, motioning a few things in the experiment sign language that I still did not know. Tori nodded once and Griffin responded with a few gestures before kissing her on the cheek. He disappeared into the woods again.

"What was that?" I whispered.

"The convoy left twenty minutes ago," she said, putting her mouth close to my ear. "Parker is in his cell now, which means that we have five minutes before we can move. We're waiting for Mark's signal."

The wait was torturous. I could only watch the two cars patrolling the outer wall in their circular pattern, opposing one another, being sure that no one had time to sneak in. My heart was thrumming, pumping my blood hard through my body, both electrifying and terrifying me.

When the two cars disappeared out of sight on the other side of the camp, Josh placed a hand over the band on his wrist.

"Security's down," he told us.

That allowed me a little relief, as it meant our first group had climbed the wall and somehow safely made it into the prisoner's building to successfully deactivate the motion sensors and cameras of the camp.

Josh and Tori moved forward, leading our group down the slope of the hill as quietly as possible. I followed, trying to keep myself from smiling as we moved closer to the wall surrounding the compound.

Two people grouped close around Josh, me, and Tori. Ivo stood just behind Josh, ready to perform his task. Celina, another experiment of the Commission, stood next to me as we watched Tori jump, her hands locking on the top of the wall. She swung herself easily to crouch on the narrow space under the circular barbed wire on top of the wall. Throwing a quick glance around her, she grabbed the edge and pulled the barbed wire sharply, causing it to snap. She bent the sections she had broken to open a space.

Tori looked into the camp and then motioned Celina to join her. With the same altered strength, Celina leapt up and grabbed onto the top of the wall, swinging over and dropping to the other side.

Ivo linked his fingers together near my knees. Supporting myself on his shoulder, I stepped into his hands and was raised to grab Tori's hand as she remained perched on the wall. Carefully stepping on the narrow ledge, Tori grabbed my other hand and lowered me to Celina, who guided me the rest of the way down to stand inside the camp.

Celina and I darted to the surplus tent. When she heard nothing within or nearby, Celina ripped through the canvas and made an opening for us. I ducked inside and was immediately overwhelmed. With the influx in guards that had come in for the prisoner transfer, the supplies had also grown. But it was clear that they were also disorganized, shoved into the tent in haste however they could fit.

"Great..." I groaned, studying the haphazard boxes.

Celina came to my side. Aware that we did not have much time, I read the narrow writing near the corner of the crates closest to me, seeing crates of medical supplies. Knowing we had enough medical supplies already, I carefully picked my way through the crowded aisles until I stumbled across the crates of bullets.

"Here." I motioned Celina over. "Only four crates," I whispered. "We need more food."

She grabbed the first box, running it back to the hole in the tent, where she would throw the case to Tori, who would drop it to Ivo and the train would take the supplies to the van and load them.

While Celina moved the cases of ammunition, I scoured for boxes of rations. As I drew closer to the front of the tent, I spared a few seconds to look at the rest of the camp through the plastic window on the door.

Mark and the others were taking the prisoners out of the building, but in order to get the supporters of our revolution out, we had to distract the guards.

Mark had obviously done that already with the way the guards had moved to one section of the compound, leaving the grounds eerily deserted. I hoped that the first distraction would be enough to buy us time to get out before things got frantic following our second distraction.

Moving away from the discolored plastic, I stumbled upon the boxes of rations. I turned around to call to Celina, but she was walking another box of ammo out of the tent. I was worried we were moving too slowly.

I lifted one of the heavy boxes of rations and unstacked it, carrying it only a few meters before dropping it heavily and running to get another. After Celina had taken the fourth case to the back of the tent, she took the first ration box as I set the second one down.

We worked quickly. I knew I was lifting boxes that were far too heavy for me, but the adrenaline and excitement made me stronger and I was able to bring crates about as fast as Celina could take them. She would take the box and run to the back, stepping just outside to throw the case to Tori, glancing around each time before returning to grab another case.

On my eighth box, just as I was getting tired, I heard four loud gunshots followed by a bellow.

"Breach!! We've been breached!!!"

I stopped, my eyes going wide as yelling and gunfire filled the air.

No sooner had I started moving again, a deafening explosion rattled my eardrums, shaking the earth and causing me to drop the wooden case of rations, the wood splintering, sending packages of dried military food to the canvas floor, blocking my path.

Our second distraction had started. The grenades were meant to take out the wall for our false means of escape, causing confusion in the guards while the fugitives fled through the front gate, pried open by Griffin.

"Lily!" Celina snapped, grabbing the box I had left for her further up the aisle. "We have to go!"

I grabbed one more box, determined to bring it. Celina ran toward me as quickly as she could, stopping just on the other side of the broken case of rations.

"It's chaos out there! We have to go now!" she snapped over the deafening gunfire. A siren whined angrily into the surrounding woods.

"Take this!" I ordered, shoving the box into her hands.

"Are you crazy?!"

"Go!"

She carried the box to the hole in the tent. Turning once more, I grabbed another box, my ears ringing from the explosion and the continuous attack of the blaring siren.

I heard a crunch and explosion before a dull groan came to my ears. I was forced to the ground by a sharp snap over my head and shoulders. I fell, my body contorting around the case of rations I was carrying, causing intense pain to radiate through my back and chest. It was completely dark, and I was too stunned at first to realize that something had crashed into the top of the tent and made it collapse.

Trapped in the small opening created between the crates, I tried to find a way out. I turned my head toward the front door of the tent and saw an orange glow, increasing in brightness.

It hit me too quickly that the canvas tent was on fire.

Unable to think, I forced my injured body to crawl over the crates to my right, pushing the heavy canvas up, though I only barely managed to wiggle in the narrow give the canvas had.

Amazingly, I was not panicking, even as I thought about the explosive weapons in the supply tent and the fire growing over the canvas. I was calm, trying to find a way out, wishing I had a knife.

I crawled on my elbows over another crate, pulling myself toward the edge of the tent, wondering if there was a space at the bottom I could crawl through.

My hand slipped off the edge of the crate in front of me and I tumbled to the floor once again, rolling and feeling a sharp bite against my lower back. Spinning away, I spotted part of the canvas floor already ablaze, lighting my jacket on fire. Rolling immediately, I attempted to put the flames out, scrambling to my hands and knees when I was no longer on fire.

The flames were closing in around me.

A ripping sound somehow made its to my ears over the crackling of the fire. I saw a knife in the canvas to my right, slashing the part of the roof that was not yet engulfed in flame. Creating a hole, I saw two faces peek inside.

"There!" Celina gasped, pointing.

I ducked as the knife returned to the canvas and cut away the tent that was quickly being devoured by flame. Two hands grabbed my arms, pulling me sharply through the slashed canvas and falling backwards to the dirt ground.

Mark did not allow me any time to regain my bearings. He got up from under me and claimed my arm, pulling me upright and running. I forced my legs to work, running, too disoriented to look around.

Just in front of us, Celina stumbled and fell, a torrent of blood jutting from her leg as a bullet bit into her calf.

Mark let me go and ran to her, helping her up as I turned to see who had fired.

I saw one man silhouetted by the growing fire of the supplies tent, pointing his gun at Mark and Celina.

Without thinking, I grabbed the gun on my leg and clicked the safety off, pointing at his dark form, which was distorted by the heat of the fire behind him. I fired four shots, hoping I at least scared him to buy us some time.

Mark's other hand grabbed mine just as I watched the dark shadow of a man collapse.

Mark pulled me to the front gate while he held Celina around the waist, supporting her out of the camp.

The area past the mangled gates of the compound was dark and cold compared to the wild chaos of the fire inside the walls. Mark did not stop moving, pulling the both of us into the darker woods and through the underbrush. After a few moments, when I adjusted to the sudden chilly air, I pulled my hand from Mark's and returned the safety on my gun, replacing it in the holster as I focused my attention on Celina's injury.

Realizing we were going toward the van, I ran ahead. I found Tori and Josh, who were snapping at the final people to follow our practiced escape plans.

"Lily!" Tori gasped, running to me. "Are you—"

"Celina's been shot," I snapped. "Hurry!"

I led Tori to Mark and Celina. Tori took Celina's other arm and the two carried the wounded experiment to the van. Josh helped bring her into the van. I took the board away from the tracks, feeling a painful twinge somewhere in my body that I was too frantic to pinpoint.

I closed the door as Tori and Josh went to the front of the car, pushing it as quietly, but quickly, as they could manage back on the path we had come. I turned to Mark, who was rifling for something near the passenger's seat.

"Celina, are you okay?" I asked stupidly.

"I'll be alright," she said with a tight nod. I could just barely make out her silhouette until Mark found the flashlight and clicked it on. He shined the light on the bullet hole in Celina's calf. My stomach turned at the sight, but I forced myself to calm down and study it, my worry for Celina outweighing my squeamish nature. Mark put the flashlight in his mouth and used both hands to move the leg of her pants out of the way, cutting one of the strings off a nearby case and tying the fabric out of the way.

Josh jumped into the car and turned it on as Tori climbed into the passenger's seat.

"How bad is it?" Tori asked, turning to look at Celina. The other experiment shook her head strongly, grimacing.

"It's fine..."

"The sooner we get you back, the better," Tori declared. She turned to me. "Are you alright, Lily?"

"Yeah," I answered quickly.

Less than ten seconds later, I was reminded otherwise. A particularly large bump in the dirt road caused me to jolt and my back to hit the upholstery, which made me cringe in surprising pain. The scramble getting out of the compound had made me forget my pain, but it was clear the fire had left some damage. Now that it was brought back to my attention, the pain was acute and strong, amplified by the other aches of my body from where I had fallen.

I tried to hide my pain. Celina's bleeding bullet wound was more pressing.

Josh drove us to the freeway, turning away from the agreed direction of our escape.

"Where are you going?" Tori gasped.

"We're going another way," Josh answered. "It's not clean enough through the tunnels with an open wound."

He drove as close to the hilltop entrance in the cave as he could and stopped, helping Mark get Celina out of the van. I climbed out after her, being sure to remain facing Mark so he could not see my back. I did not know what the burn looked like, but I could tell that my burnt clothes were not covering the area, since the edges of my jacket and shirt continued to brush the edges of the wound. I turned to keep Josh and Tori from seeing as well, closing the van door, trying not to wince as I moved.

"We'll unload and return quickly," Tori called to me and Mark.

They drove off as Mark helped Celina up the hill and I followed close behind. By the time we were half-way up to the rocky slope, I was in agony. I was trying to hide my pain, not wanting to worry Mark any more than I already had that evening. My head was spinning and I felt nauseous as the pain radiated through my entire body from the burns. My pained limbs from my falls were not helping either, making it difficult to climb the hill at my normal pace.

With the slow climb with Celina's injury, neither experiment noticed my sluggish pace.

We finally made it to the entrance to the fort. I was unsure if I was going to throw up or pass out from pain, but I almost told Mark to stop moving. I bit my tongue, deciding it would be better to tell him I was hurt when we were safe.

Gritting my teeth, I closed the heavy door, locking it. I tried to convince myself that the tunnel vision I had was just because of the erratic flashlight along the walls of the tunnel and not due to pain.

It seemed like eternity before we found ourselves in the main bunker.

The bright lights overloaded my hypersensitive brain and I recoiled. Several who had been on the raid had already returned and were greeting the new people in the fort, celebrating another successful raid. I smiled when they called to me, but thankfully their attention was deterred by Celina. They cleared a path to the medical room, calling for Peter as Mark walked with her. I moved along the wall, trying to keep my back hidden as I moved toward the medical room as well.

"Lily! Lily!" Clark called, running to me, leading a man with him who was wearing a blue jumpsuit with a number on the left chest. "This is Jerry Parker, CEO of Carolina Media," he introduced. "This is Lily."

"Hello, Lily," Jerry said, extending his hand. I took it and immediately regretted it as he shook my hand and jarred my entire body. I hid my cringe behind a smile.

"It's nice to meet you."

"I want to thank you for everything," he said. "All of you. I mean, you have exposed the Commission and just when I was about to become a victim myself, you swoop in and save me." He smiled. "I am here to help however I can. I'll help you take down the Commission of the People."

"Thank you," I said. "We will need all the help we can get."

"Speaking of..." Clark said nervously. "Mr. Parker, why don't you find your colleagues? I want to meet them."

"Oh, sure," he said, walking into the crowd that was growing as more people were brought into the bunker. Clark turned to me.

"We might have a problem," he said, dropping his voice. I sighed and closed my eyes, the black starting to encroach on my vision. I was in no condition to be hearing about problems.

"Okay, just let me go check on Celina and then we can—"

"The mafia boss is here...and his colleagues," Clark whispered, interrupting me.

"*What?*"

"They say they know Mark. They want to help us and we can use their contacts to get supplies," Clark elaborated.

"They know Mark? *How?*"

"I don't know. That's why I said it might be a problem."

"Okay, well, I'll deal with it later. Let me go check—"

"There you are," a relieved voice said. I turned quickly and managed to see Mykail through my tunnel vision. "I was getting worried."

"Sorry..." I murmured. He moved to hug me and I backed away quickly. Both Clark and Mykail blinked at me.

"What is it?" Mykail asked.

917

"Nothing...I...I just need to go to the medical room, alright?" I babbled desperately.

"Okay," Mykail said, reaching his hand out to lead me. I hesitated, knowing that if I turned, both of them would see the wound. The pain finally got the best of me and I quickly moved in front of Mykail, determined to get to the medical room.

Judging by the gasp and the hurried pace at which Mykail followed, I knew the burn was bad.

"What the hell happened?" he asked.

"An accident," I breathed. "I'm alright, really. I just need a few minutes."

I opened the door to the medical room and stepped in. Peter was seated on a stool while Celina sat on one of the examination tables, watching him treat her leg. Mark was standing near the table, watching. All three of them turned when we entered the room.

"Lily is badly burned," Mykail said before I had a chance to speak.

"What?" Celina gasped.

"Let me see," Peter said, standing, careful to keep his hands from touching anything. Mark also approached, his eyes wide with concern. Mykail took my shoulders and turned me, showing my back to the others in the room.

"Oh, God," Peter said. "Okay, Mykail, help her get the clothing away from it. Lily just lay on your front. Mark, get some of the heavy painkillers and give her two. I'll be over there when I'm done with Celina. That should let the painkillers work into her system a little."

I did as I was told, moving closer to the table as Mykail pulled the jacket from my shoulders and then helped me extract myself from my shirt, though I bit back a cry of pain as my body protested all movement.

Mark held out two pills for me along with a bottle of water. Forcing the pills down, I felt the tears spill down my face. Mykail stroked his thumbs over my shoulders. Both Mark and Mykail guided me to the table, supporting me as I lowered myself, trying to find a way to lay down without being in pain.

I was finally on the table, cold and shivering, the tears coming down my face as Mykail kept my hand in his.

Mark continued to pace by me. I could not see his face, but I could tell by his movements that he was worried.

Peter finally came to me and injected me with something to numb my lower back, letting it take effect before he started cleaning the burns. I did not say anything about my fall over the crate, knowing that no bones were broken, and not concerned with the forming bruises. The burn was bleeding in a few places, but was not as severe as first believed, much to my intense relief. Peter did the best he could considering his limited training and dressed the burns. He told me they would have to be checked every day and cleaned to avoid infection.

I remained in the medical room long after Peter had finished my treatments. I did not want to deal with the problems in the bunker yet, waiting until I felt stronger.

Chapter Sixty-Nine

Already haunted by nightmares of a shadow falling to the ground after I shot him, I did not sleep as long as I wanted. When I woke, people were still celebrating in the bunker, reminiscent of when we broke everyone out of the Commission.

Mark and Mykail were still in the medical room. Mykail was holding my hand, though it was obvious the two had been locked in conversation when I woke. They fussed over me a little when they saw I was awake but did not pester me too much when they saw how unreceptive I was to their concern.

Mark brought me clothes that were loose enough not to aggravate my burn. I dressed and went into the bunker, exhausted but feeling slightly better.

Clark quickly stood from his conversation with Tori, Griffin, and four men I did not know when he saw me. I studied the strangers worriedly, wondering if they were the mafia members that we had agreed not to release during our original plan.

"Lily, are you okay?" Clark asked.

"I'm fine. Who are they?"

"The men I was telling you about."

I nervously approached them, Mykail and Mark beside me. The man next to Griffin jumped when he saw Mykail and laughed nervously as he deflated.

"Seriously, I don't know if I'll get used to seeing you," he said apologetically.

"It's okay, it takes most people some time," Mykail said. I sat stiffly with the group, Mykail following suit, though Mark remained standing behind me, scanning the group diligently.

"I heard you know Mark and that you want to help us." I got right to the point, feeling safer and braver with Mark standing guard.

"That's right," one of them said.

"How do you know him?"

"He used to be a Fixer," the man chuckled, looking at Mark. "The most expensive one, but he sure as hell got the job done. Had an incredible reputation"

"A Fixer?"

"A hitman," Griffin clarified quietly. My eyes were wide as I turned to look at Mark.

"How in hell did you manage *that*?"

Mark turned his gaze to his feet.

"Your boy there was the best Fixer, but I only met him face to face once. When we saw him being a part of this group, we knew it had to be something good," the man who had been startled by Mykail said.

"And what do you gain from this?" I asked. "No offense, but you're in organized crime, and we're not starting this revolution so that the Commission won't be a threat to crime anymore."

"I understand, little miss," the second man said. "I like that you get straight to the point. No playing around."

"We don't have that luxury here," I said. "After we get some inventory, we might ask you to use your connections to get us some weapons and ammo."

"You got it," the fourth man said.

"Yeah, we owe you," the first agreed. "You got us out before we were sent to the Commission."

I did not like having them involved, but we were certainly in need of more supplies, and there was no reason to turn away their connections.

The following day, inventory had been taken and we came away with even less than I thought. The food rations were minimal, particularly with the influx of people living in the fort. When the breach had been announced and the explosion happened, all cells had been opened for evacuation due to the fire and several of the other criminals had followed us to the fort. There were some I was wary of—it felt as though outsiders were intruding on our family.

However, when the mafia members stated they could get in contact with others who could get us weapons, I was not about to turn down the opportunity.

With minimal hesitation, the strategy group agreed to send them to one of their contacts, leading them out of one of the entrances, telling them that was the only way into the fort before we posted people along the route, armed, in case they brought more people with them when they returned.

Three days after they left the fort, they had not returned.

Our supplies were becoming incredibly strained. The main strategy group had to figure out how to combat our dwindling food. It was finally decided that we would send teams out in pairs to procure food, whether it was from dumpsters or if they had to lift food off of trucks being unloaded at supermarkets.

In order to feed the people of our revolution, I had to put aside my moral issues with theft.

On the fourth day of the mafia members' absence, Mark decided to track them down. I demanded to go with him, my burn close to being healed, though he strongly denied. We fought with one another for at least twenty minutes, with him angrily trying to find a way to tell me that I was not going with him no matter what argument I threw his way.

I finally gave up and stormed off. Mykail found me fifteen minutes later and tried to talk me down, telling me that Mark was just worried for my safety, particularly after the raid. I agreed, but I was still angry at the overprotective nature—it made me feel like he didn't trust me.

When Mark returned, he showed a picture to Griffin, but refused to let anyone else see it.

"What is it?" I asked, trying to ignore Mark like a petulant child throwing a tantrum.

"They're dead…" Griffin said.

"*Dead?*"

Mark pulled out his notebook and wrote four letters.

"*Dana.*"

Clearly Dana was not only connected with the international community, but also the underbellies of society.

The morning and evening news had been flooded with images of people celebrating our success at freeing the captives of the camp, calling it a triumph, though there were some among the population unhappy with the information that we had also freed dangerous criminals.

The social support was at an all-time high. People were posting messages online and on the streets, telling us that they wanted to join our cause, though they did not know where to find us.

I was unwilling to let more people know our location or plans. The people in the fort were there because they had to be, because it was not safe for them among the population. Letting people in at random would compromise our safety and would also strain our already-dwindling resources.

The following Monday, my burn was practically healed. Mark and I had more or less made up after our fight since Mark hugged me and that seemed to make everything better. But I still wanted to do my part. I wanted to go out and find a way to get more food at the very least. I was the only one besides Mykail and the others who would stand out too much who had not gone to procure food. I felt like I was slacking, and I did not want to appear as though I did not care about the revolutionaries. As a figurehead, I had to keep a certain image and keep the morale high.

Once again, Mark and I were butting heads in the strategy room about whether I could go outside or not.

After telling him that there was no way he was going to keep me in the bunker and that I would just leave when he went back to the Markus house, he finally conceded to let me go out as long as he was with me.

Deciding I wanted to go out more than fight with him, I agreed.

He drove me in his Commission car to the large, open park at the center of town, agreeing that I was going stir-crazy and just needed to see the sunlight. When he parked the car, I turned to him.

"Mark," I started, "can I just walk around the park for a bit?" I pleaded. "Please, I just need some fresh air. You can see the whole park from here. You can watch me."

Mark opened his mouth to protest, but hesitated, finally sighing and dropping his head as he turned off the car.

I could not explain my restlessness. Even with how much support the revolution had been getting, I was not satisfied with anything. I needed to get away from the fort, away from Tori and Griffin and Mykail, away from the bickering members who were trying to figure out how they were going to survive on one meal a day while fighting such a stressful war.

We were at a high point in our revolution yet, for some reason, I had a feeling that everything was about to crash down around us. Hearing about the dead mafia members made me think very carefully about Dana's connections. It had been forever since I had devoted such thought to the leader of the Commission of the People. I had almost forgotten he was a real person. I had been so focused on what was going on in the world of Fort Daniels that I had forgotten his incredible control of the surface world.

I wondered what he was planning. He had clearly been waiting for the four mafia members to seek out their connections, and he took the opportunity to kill them, though I had no way of knowing if they were connected to our revolution. Dana had said that our game would end when he said. I was beginning to think that he was getting bored with our game, that he was planning earnestly to end our revolution swiftly and decisively. I wracked my brain as I walked around the park, desperate to think of how he could quash all the support we were receiving from the public, worried that his next moves would spell disaster for everyone in Fort Daniels.

What frightened me most was that I was certain Dana was not only trying to defeat us, but was trying to tear us down so completely that he could rip us apart until there was nothing left.

I had to find a way to combat his influence.

"Well, well, well," a voice said behind me. I halted, my blood running cold as I registered the voice. "Imagine finding *you* here..."

I did not want to turn around. Keeping my face as straight as I could, I turned to the two men I had not seen in so long.

I stared at the two figures in suits before me, my heart forgetting how to beat. Dana smiled, his eyes covered by his dark sunglasses. Sean remained behind Dana, watching, his own expression also hidden by sunglasses.

We were in a crowded park, and it was to my advantage that I remain someplace public. Even Dana would not risk doing something drastic in front of so many people. No one outside the Commission even knew what Dana Christenson looked like. He would be exposing himself by trying to capture me in a crowded place and saying it was Commission business.

"You've caused quite a lot of trouble, Little Lily," Dana said. "You've really made a mess of things."

"At least you're no longer bored," I quipped, trying to pull together a plan of escape that did not involve exposing Mark or leading Dana to the fort. "You should be thanking me."

"Thank you for entertaining me, but really, we both know how this is going to end," Dana said. "You will eventually come to me on your hands and knees, so why fight it?"

"I won't come begging to you, Dana," I growled. "You and the Commission destroyed *everything*."

"Not as much as you have." Dana shook his head with a broken chuckle. "You're a traitor to your country. You've caused unrest and fear within the people, and you will answer for what you have done."

"What about what *you've* done?" I snapped, finally making the decision to run into the nearby trees and weave until I got someplace I could hide. I just needed to get Dana to move slightly one direction so I could run with a few steps of an advantage. It wouldn't buy me more than two seconds, but it was the best I could hope for. "What about the way you've destroyed America?"

"Destroyed?" Dana echoed. "I have done nothing other than improve America. I have kept the people happy and safe. Before you came to the Commission, I bet you used to hear about the way the country once was. And I'm sure you used to think that you were so fortunate to be born into a time when the unrest had been settled and the population was harmonious." I saw one eyebrow arch over his glasses. "Am I wrong?"

"Then why make the weapons?" I asked. "Don't you see what will happen when you finish Eina? He's stronger than you. He'll turn against you and kill you."

"That should please you, Little Lily," Dana said. "That's what you're trying to do, after all."

"But after he's done with you, what do you think he'll do? He'll be unleashed on the world and who knows what kind of destruction he'll be capable of."

"It sounds like you need me," Dana said. "I'm the one thing standing between you and Eina."

"So kill him," I said. "Stop the program now while you still can!"

"It's too late, Little Lily." Dana shook his head slowly. "He's finished."

I stilled, forgetting all plans of running for a few moments while I processed the short statement. After a few silent seconds, I shook my head and retreated a step, my eyes wide.

"You're bluffing…"

"Would I really do something like that?" Dana asked. "I don't need to bluff. He's finished. If you had come to the meeting two days ago, you would know that."

My brain turned to static.

Dana reached a hand out and his smile widened.

"Come, Little Lily," Dana commanded. "There's nowhere for you to run."

I shook my head and took another step backward.

"I wouldn't even try if I were you," Dana warned. "You're surrounded." I looked over my shoulder to see another man in a suit with dark glasses. Mark was slowly walking toward me. My heart picked up pace and several horrible scenarios ran through my mind, but I spotted the small movement of Mark's hand as he tapped his pointer finger once against his leg.

"*Calm down.*"

I turned back to Dana, worried but now confident. It would be the day Dana would learn that Mark was on our side and while that put our strongest ally in danger, I knew I could trust Mark to get me safely away from Dana.

"Mark, grab her," Dana ordered.

Mark stopped behind me before stepping to the side, pulling the gun with the silencer out from its holster and flashing it, hiding the gun from general view at my side.

Dana was still, his smile gone. Sean's jaw dropped slightly as he shook his head.

"I don't believe it…"

"Well," Dana chuckled, "I certainly wasn't expecting this." He looked over Mark as Sean unholstered his own gun, keeping it concealed by his jacket. "I should have known you would sympathize with this movement. After all, Mark, you were the only one who ever attacked me and was able to draw blood."

Dana sighed.

"I'm quite sad, though," he said, tilting his head contemplatively. "I'm sad that I have to kill you now. You always were one of my favorites. That's why I didn't kill you the first time. I wanted to give you a second chance while you were still useful. Oh well, you know what they say, fool me once, shame on you, fool me twice, it's time to die."

I jumped at the sound at my side, but was even more shocked when Dana's right leg folded underneath him and he fell to his knee, a bleeding hole in his thigh.

I did not have time to see if Dana was cringing in pain, or even his reaction past falling to his knee because Mark's hand had a vice grip on my arm in the next second. He yanked me away, tucking the gun into his jacket as we ran. I followed, confident that Sean would not shoot in the crowded park while we were weaving in and out of the confused and indignant people around us.

Mark pulled me into the parking lot. He jumped into his car and I clambered into the front seat, breathing hard.

Mark peeled out of the parking lot, his covered eyes glancing every now and then in the mirrors before he turned to me and tapped the plastic buckle of my seatbelt, reminding me to strap in.

I did so, my hands shaking.

I turned around and spotted the car following ours, rapidly gaining on us, black in color with tinted windows that did not allow me to see the driver.

"Mark," I whispered. He had taken off his glasses, his eyes glued to the rearview mirror. He glanced at the other two mirrors and took a deep breath to calm himself, studying the street as he turned away from the park.

My hands were gripping the seat, frightened and shaking as I glanced in the side view mirror. Mark made another turn, driving above the speed limit, watching the car behind us with hawk-like intensity.

Every turn we made took us closer to the industrial district. The car followed us turn for turn, keeping close to our bumper.

Mark sped up, his foot flooring the accelerator and his hand shifting gears, causing the engine to roar. Mark sped around a corner, our back tires skidding on the asphalt before finding traction and racing down a wide street lined with businesses and crowded with semi-trucks.

Mark was weaving in and out of traffic at terrifying speeds, his eyes sharp and his reflexes quick, not even phased as he slipped into the opposite flow of traffic to get around one truck while I panicked. There were horns blaring and tires screeching. I flinched at every sound, certain that there was going to be an impact on the car at any moment.

Mark followed the large sweeping curve of the street and drove north, away from the industrial area and to the freeway.

I could hardly breathe.

The road was crowded with trucks and transportation trailers preparing to enter the freeway. Mark tapped the brake when he had no room to move. My hands were locked on the door panel and the bottom of my seat, my eyes wild about the road as I threw random glances into the side mirror to check how close Dana and Sean were.

They were only one car behind us and were just switching lanes.

"Fuck..." I hissed.

Mark looked over the road, assessing the situation before his foot pushed in the gas pedal and the clutch, his hands fast on the wheel, turning us abruptly and cutting off Sean and Dana. Mark leapt across the lane, over the median, and into the opposite lane of traffic, where the light had just turned green and cars were starting forward, including the semi-truck blaring its horn at us.

Mark shifted into a lower gear and challenged the semi while I tried not to scream. Just before Mark collided, he turned, bouncing over the median again and flooring the car, darting across three lanes of traffic, forcing one car to swerve to avoid collision, creating a chain reaction as another semi-truck moved the opposite way, crashing into the stopped semi as we sped to the onramp, flying up the slope at an amazing speed.

My breath left me loudly and I slumped.

"Holy shit..."

Mark shifted the car, jumping into the far lane, flying through traffic.

"Mark, slow down. The police—"

I stopped, realizing that Dana had probably already called the police on us.

"We need to get to the fort, *now*."

Mark sighed and looked at me with an exasperated expression before turning his eyes back on the road. I mentally mapped where we were in the city—we were nowhere near access to Fort Daniels.

As we flew past another onramp, three police cars entered the freeway, having difficulty keeping up with our speed. The other cars were trying to move out of the way at the same time, which added to the confusion and worked in our favor.

"Shit!" I pointed at a familiar black car entering the freeway at the onramp in front of our car. Mark slammed on the brake, causing another skidding of tires behind us. Shifting to a lower gear, Mark turned across four lanes of traffic as another crunch was heard from a collision behind us, which kept the police cars at bay. Mark turned onto the off ramp just as the black car in front of us pulled to the shoulder and threw their car into reverse.

Mark sped to the next freeway, causing the engine to roar and my panic to increase.

The leader of the Eight Group darted back across the other lanes of traffic to another off-ramp. I knew exactly what entrance we were going to—the one in the cave with the dead-bolted, bulletproof door.

But as we started up the hill of the off-ramp, we were met with flashing blue and red lights stopped in a blockade.

Mark did not slow down.

He moved into the shoulder, aiming the nose of our car at the two opposing noses of the police cars. His right hand extended in front of me, holding me in my seat. I closed my eyes. I was launched violently forward and then thrown back with the force of the collision. Our engine roared and the crunching and groaning of distorted and strained metal faded as Mark pushed through the gap between the two cars and turned violently, the car bumping onto the curb and in the dirt, tires skidding, before Mark regained control and pulled us back onto the road.

My eyes were wide, looking at the dented front of the car and the crack in the windshield, as well as how fast Mark was speeding down the nearly-deserted road.

He turned onto a dirt path toward the hill where we could gain access to Fort Daniels and plowed through the gate, causing the windshield to crack as the mangled metal smashed into the glass. The windshield did not shatter, which made it nearly impossible to see.

Mark rolled down his window, looking out it as he drove along the dusty road, trying to keep control of the speeding car on the dirt.

He slammed on the brakes and the car slid as he reached over and unbuckled my seatbelt.

Needing no further instruction, I clambered out of the car and ran around the front, not knowing where I was going, but knowing I needed to head uphill. Mark's hand was on my back, pushing me in the right direction. I heard tires rapidly approaching, so I forced my shaking legs faster up the hill.

A gunshot sounded and I flinched, but Mark retaliated with a shot of his own and then pushed me again, shielding me. I saw the cave and quickly stumbled over the rocks, around the first corner to the bolted door. Mark remained at the corner, listening for the approaching group as I heaved the latch to the side, adrenaline giving me strength. When the bolt was undone, Mark helped me get the thick door open, pushing me into the dark corridor before slipping in just as I heard Sean's voice say we were "over there."

Mark slammed the lock shut as I caught my breath, my whole body shaking.

There was banging on the other side of the door as Mark kicked the second and third bolts down. He grabbed a large rock, somehow able to see it in the dark, and slammed it into the main lock, causing sparks to fly as the metal bent and twisted, pinching the lock permanently.

I pulled out my phone, my fingers shaking to activate my flashlight, but I finally got some light to the corridor. Mark put an arm around my shoulders, pointing his gun at the door as the banging continued. My breath was shuddering out of me violently as I listened to the commotion.

"Don't shoot it, you morons!" Sean's voice growled.

"Wait by the cars. This is Commission business," Dana ordered. "Little Lily...I know you can hear me."

Mark's grip tightened on my shoulder.

"I'm not sure what's behind this door, but I have a feeling that your secret hideout has been compromised...but it's not because of me," Dana continued. "Well, okay, I guess mostly because of me, but the truth is, I have had inside information almost the entire time. You did some of the work for him by leading me here. He won't have to sneak out to tell me where you are."

I blinked, staring at the door, an impending sense of doom lurking around me at what I dreaded was coming.

"Oh, Little Lily, you are so naïve. So is Mark. I'm surprised that that chink didn't figure it out already if he was able to hide his support of this movement for so long. You didn't think it was strange how easily you bonded with Mykail? How willing he was to risk everything to help you? I sent him to you with orders to report everything you did to me."

"You're lying..." I choked, knowing he likely could not hear me.

"I sent him to your family to stoke that fire in your belly. I knew you were angry. I knew he was just charming enough to seduce you and get you to this level. He talked you into going against me, didn't he? Told you that he hated me and he wanted nothing more than to kill me? I told him to say those things to you, Little Lily. And in exchange, I would consider removing those wings once I had you in my grasp. You had all the potential to pull this off, but you needed the final push...You needed to feel empowered, and angry, and he followed my orders exactly and riled you up just as I wanted him to."

My stomach was churning. Mark's hand on my shoulder was the only thing keeping me from collapsing.

"How do you think I knew so much about you without ever setting foot in your house? Why do you think Mykail would only talk to you and not the rest of your family? And you fell for his sob story, his charms, and his beauty because you wanted so badly to think that you had some sort of power over me. I told him exactly what to say and do. He played you, Little Lily, and he fed me every juicy detail."

I cringed against the words.

"Knowing that Mykail has become the figurehead of your revolution, I know he's in there—in your secret headquarters. Don't think I don't know that there are other ways to get in. Rest assured, now that I know where this one is, I can map other possibilities. I will find your hideout before Mykail has a spare moment to get to me and tell me where you are. He probably hasn't been alone in a very long time, has he?"

Mark guided me backward, Dana's last sentences fading as we moved away from the door and through the dark tunnel. I felt numb. Empty.

Somewhere in my brain, I had always suspected...

Mark kept my hand in his as we walked, keeping me grounded to the present. My brain was replaying every instance with Mykail that had probably been relayed to Dana, remembering how hesitant Mark was to have Mykail involved, my own apprehension when I learned that Mark did not trust him, the way Mykail had been so secretive about things that were bothering him...

It made sense.

Mark opened the door to the empty medical room, holstering his gun so he could keep his hand around mine.

But as soon as we walked into the main bunker, he released my hand and all hell broke loose.

I watched with numb disbelief as Mark darted forward, ignoring those in the bunker who turned to greet us, and slammed into Mykail with his entire body.

The two fell to the ground heavily as several began yelling at Mark to stop, though everyone knew better than to step in, in case Mark turned on them. Mykail was stunned and, for several long moments, could not gain his bearings enough to fight back. Mark flipped the angel onto his stomach and pulled both of his hands behind his back.

"Mark, what the hell are you doing?!" Griffin snapped.

Mark opened his mouth but no sound came out. I saw him struggling to find a way to communicate what he knew while he still had Mykail pinned.

"Mark, let him go," Tori ordered.

Before she completed her sentence, one of Mykail's wings violently connected with Mark's side and threw him to the ground. Mark rolled and got to his feet as Mykail scrambled to stand.

Clark was at my side, though I did not turn to him, focused on the confrontation.

"Lily, what the hell is going on?"

"What the hell is wrong with you?!" Mykail snapped, raising his fists to defend himself against the leader of the Eight Group. Mark threw a punch at Mykail's face, ducking under the wing that was thrown in front of Mykail to protect him.

The humans were backing away from the confrontation as several of the experiments surrounded them, trying to find an opening to interfere. I was frozen, watching, knowing I needed to speak for Mark, but I could not command my mouth to form the words, even as Clark asked me again what was wrong.

"Mark! Enough!" Griffin yelled, finally finding an opening in the fight and grabbing onto Mark's arms, pulling him back. Mark kicked at Griffin, who barely managed to avoid a very painful kick to the groin, though it did cause him to release one of Mark's arms. The smaller experiment turned around and grabbed Griffin's other arm, kneeing his forearm to release himself before running back at Mykail.

Tori ran to Griffin, worried, and then turned to watch the two experiments fight.

"Mark! Stop fighting him and tell us what's wrong!"

Mykail's wing swept angrily at the leader of the Eight Group and Mark fell to his side, using his position to kick Mykail's feet out from under him. Off balance from the weight of his wings, Mykail fell heavily and Mark jumped to his feet.

When Mykail turned, the barrel of a gun was pressed between his eyes.

"Stop!" I finally managed to bellow.

All movement ceased. I stumbled forward, eyes locked on the gun pressed to Mykail's forehead.

"Lily, what happened?" Griffin asked, massaging his arm.

"Get some chains and chain him up," I said, my voice shaking.

"What?"

"Get some chains and fucking chain Mykail up!"

"Lily, what are you—"

"Chain him up! He's been lying to us! He's been feeding Dana information the entire time!"

"Lily..." Mykail started, his eyes wide.

"Don't fucking talk to me right now," I growled. To emphasize my point, Mark pushed the gun harder against Mykail's skin, pushing his head back.

"Please, listen to me. I can explain."

"Shut up!"

Ichiro, Rin, and Keiko darted to get chains and returned shortly after, all of them moving to pull Mykail's arms behind his back. Mykail did not fight, his expression conflicted.

"Be sure you find a way to secure his wings, too," I warned.

"How do you know this, Lily?" Tori asked, stepping to my side, realizing from Mykail's expression that my claim was true.

"I've suspected it...but Dana just confirmed it for me." I sighed and rubbed my face before turning to Griffin and Tori. "Dana knows the passage to the medical room, so we need to get some dynamite and permanently seal it. We'll figure out what to do with him later."

"Lily, please, listen to me," Mykail said. "What Dana told you—"

"What? It was a lie?" I snarled. "I'm not taking any chances."

"Please, let me explain! Dana did send me in to give him information!" Mykail said desperately, cringing as his wings were forced to fold painfully against his back. "But...I swear to you, I started lying to him!"

"I don't believe you."

"I fell in love with you! I meant it when I said that! I started leading Dana on a false trail. If he really did know everything, don't you think I would have told him how you were planning to break everyone out of the Commission?"

"I didn't tell you the whole plan," I said darkly. "Now that I think about it...I didn't really trust you then, either."

"You told me enough. Dana is not an idiot. But everything went through as planned. When I saw that Mark had put together a plan that could actually work, I began to really believe in this revolution...I really began to believe in what you could do..."

"And yet you were about to doom this revolution?"

"I have not been telling Dana the truth!" he gasped, his eyes wide and desperate.

"Someone throw him in one of the store rooms," Griffin ordered. "We'll figure this out later."

Mark pushed the gun and Mykail's head finally fell to the side, slicing his forehead on the edge of the barrel before the others of the Eight Group hauled him to his feet and dragged him away.

"Lily, are you alright?"

"I'm fine."

In that moment, I was fine. Nothing was going through my head other than what I needed to do next.

"We need to deal with that passageway from the medical room."

Griffin and Tori looked at me worriedly. I rolled my eyes.

"I'm serious, I'm fine." I told them strongly. "Let's get some explosives and deal with that entrance. We don't have a lot of time."

Mark joined us, holstering his gun.

"Also, I hate to say it, but Dana knows about Mark, too."

Griffin and Tori looked at the leader of the Eight Group worriedly before turning to everyone surrounding us, agitated by our behavior and the realization that the symbol of our revolution had been feeding information to the man we were trying to defeat.

"We need someone to get one of the cases of dynamite," Tori began to give orders. "Just one case. Jodie, you and Kyle."

The two scurried off. Tori and Griffin began talking to another group about going up the tunnel of that exit and being sure that the police and Dana were no longer there. I turned to Mark.

"Will the others of the Eight Group be able to get out in time?"

Mark sighed and looked at the band on his wrist, which was already blinking red. I could tell from his expression that he did not entirely know if the others could get out fast enough. My thoughts immediately went to Josh.

Forcing myself to focus, I returned to the problem of the compromised tunnel.

Several sticks of dynamite were used near the door in the cave and a little further down the tunnel. Everyone waited in the main bunker, where the fuse stopped, going through the medical room and up the tunnel. Griffin lit the fuse and all of us hugged the far wall of the main bunker. My experience with dynamite was nonexistent, and seeing how nervous everyone else was, it was clear that no one else entirely knew what they were doing either.

It felt like agonizing hours before we heard the resounding concussion of the dynamite. For how far away the dynamite had been placed, the blast managed to shake the bunker.

Followed by the initial blast, there was a dull roar that progressively grew louder and caused some panic. The groan of strained metal and the rumbling became almost deafening. There was a loud boom and the sound of screeching metal and tumbling boulders could be heard in the medical room. Listening to the racket, I shared worried looks with the others, knowing what the sound meant.

I tried to get up from my crouching position, but Cody held me back, hearing some of the remaining groaning of what could only be a cave-in. Cody was sure to keep me still for several long minutes after silence fell over the bunker. Tori was the first to walk to the medical room. I followed, along with nearly everyone else.

Tori had to push the door open against the fallen rocks. I craned my neck around her, squinting through the settling dust in the nearly-destroyed room. The tables were mangled from the fallen boulders and the larger equipment was practically buried under rubble. There was the sound of trickling water that could be heard from the distorted door leading to the former tunnel. I stepped into the room with Tori and Griffin, covering my nose and mouth with my hand as I tried to move over the boulders.

I looked around the shelves of medicine, seeing most of them blocked by the rubble. Some were completely destroyed while some shelves only had a few toppled bottles, leaving others relatively unharmed.

"Lily, you should stay back," Griffin said. "We're going to see what happened."

Mark pulled me out of the room and we watched from the door as Tori and Griffin moved over the rocks, getting closer to the other door and finally managing to climb over the boulders and look into the tunnel.

Both of them disappeared for only a short time before cautiously picking their way back, Griffin helping Tori.

"What happened?" Clark asked.

"Looks like there was a reservoir of water above the tunnel," Griffin explained. "There's a lot of water coming through the rocks, we're going to have to build something to keep the water from flooding into the fort."

"A reservoir?" I repeated.

"From the melting snow," Griffin said. "Freeze-thaw would have eventually caused the tunnel to collapse and the fort to be flooded, but we helped speed the process." Griffin got to the door and shooed everyone into the main bunker.

"Alright, Cody, Vic, Ivo, David, and any other experiments, go to storeroom seven and get shovels, bring some for Tori and me, too." He turned to Peter and some of the others. "Once we have the water diverted and we know that the tunnel isn't going to collapse further, we're going to need to sort through everything that survived and make sure to clean up the room as much as possible. I'm putting you in charge of that."

"Yes, sir."

"Mark, keep guards around Mykail at all times," Tori whispered.

"Lily." Griffin turned to me. "Can you and Clark go through another one of the exits and make sure that there is no physical change in the mountain that would cause people to notice what happened?"

"Sure," I said.

Mark did not protest my leaving the fort.

* *** *

Thankfully, there was no visible evidence of the cave-in from outside, though it worried Clark that there was a large empty space above the cave-in that would soon collapse on top of us as well. I tried to remind him how far away the actual fort was from the entrance we had now blocked, but I also shared his concern.

I did not tell anyone that Dana would start looking for other entrances to Fort Daniels. Due to the threat, I felt pressure to get the revolution moving faster to eliminate Dana as a threat so that we could move out of the fort and find another base of operations while we took down the rest of the Commission of the People, including the new threat of the Machine of Neutralization.

When I got back to the main bunker, there were a few members of the Eight Group there, who assured us that everyone had gotten out and that they were on their way. They also told us that the cops were swarming the city discreetly, looking for anyone associated with the revolution.

I made a decision, telling those who were not working on the other projects to grab a gun and station themselves at the passages of the fort to be sure that the groups collecting food were not followed, even if that meant that we would have to kill whoever was following them.

They obeyed.

I called Tori and Griffin out of working on the tunnel and brought them into the strategy room, grabbing Mark and Clark as well.

"We have another problem," I told them. "Dana said that Eina's complete."

Everyone's eyes shot wide and Tori looked at the ground, her eyes conflicted. Griffin leaned against the table behind him and crossed his arms.

"Shit…"

"Maybe he was bluffing," Tori tried to explain lightly. Mark slowly shook his head, his gaze on his feet. I turned to him, having figured that the Eight Group would know about the finished Machine of Neutralization with their close proximity to Dana.

"Why didn't you let us know?" Griffin snapped at the leader of the Eight Group. Mark did not offer a response.

"We have to find a way to kill him," Tori said somberly.

"What do you know about Eina?" I asked. She sighed heavily and rubbed her face.

"Not much, really," she admitted. "The experiments all try to stay clear of him during our times in the Dome."

"They let him into the Dome with other experiments?" Clark gasped. Tori nodded.

"He's only killed one other experiment when he was in the Dome, but it was out of self-defense," Griffin explained. "And let me tell you…you think Mark knows how to snap a neck? Eina had so much force in attacking that experiment that he shattered each vertebrae."

"He is considered the ultimate weapon…" I breathed. "How do we kill him?"

"We don't know what he's truly capable of," Griffin whispered. "If he kills Dana and gets loose, there's no telling what he'll do."

"Is he coherent?" Clark asked. "I've never seen him when he's not sedated."

"He's coherent," Tori answered. "But all the things that Dana has done to him have destroyed him mentally. He talks to things that aren't there, carries on actual conversations with himself, keeps talking about dragons…trust me, you don't want him loose in the world."

"That's not the only problem," Griffin murmured, seeing Mark lift his hand, motioning that he wanted to say something. Griffin took over the task for the mute experiment. "Dana wants to mass produce Machines of Neutralization. Not only will we have to destroy Eina, but also his sister and any records of how he was created."

"But to do that, we have to get past Dana," I said. "And with Eina at his disposal, we don't know what we'd be facing."

Having the super-weapon at his disposal gave Dana the element of surprise once again. We were poking at a nuclear missile.

Deciding to think it over for the next few days, everyone returned to their tasks. Clark and Mark stayed close to me as I met with the groups who had been collecting food. I asked them how they had done and if they had seen any police or Commission cars when they were out before I explained what they had missed.

I had to keep busy.

Josh finally showed up about five hours after the cave-in. I was so happy to see him alive and well that I ran to him and threw my arms around him. He hugged me back tightly.

"Are you okay?" he asked.

"Yeah," I answered automatically. Mark motioned for Josh to follow him and the two disappeared to the storerooms. I looked at Eun, who was agitated knowing that her brother had been found out by Dana. I wondered if she had been forced to watch the previous torture with the others or not, and found myself giving her a hug around the shoulders regardless, just to reassure her.

I paced the bunker, waiting for the final seven groups to return from procuring food. Since it had been so long since I had sent the first set of guards to the entrances, I asked others to relieve them and stand at the posts for a few hours, which would allow the others to get some food and rest.

Clark and I sorted rations, picking through the fresh food as well, seeing what would spoil quicker and bringing it to the strategy room, which had also become the room where we handed out the food to keep everyone in a straight line and be sure that no one took more than their share. Giving out food at meal times—which was now only twice a day—had become a chore. I did not like that we were unable to trust anyone to keep their share, but we had to be sure to protect our limited resources.

When Clark offered me my ration, I shook my head, telling him I was not hungry.

It was the truth. I was nauseous, a feeling that had been hanging over me for the better part of seven hours.

I walked into the main bunker, taking some empty boxes to their proper spot in the back of the final storeroom, trying to ignore the collection of Eight Group members standing around one particular storeroom door, who were sure to fall silent when I walked by.

On my second trip with two more empty boxes, I came out to see Josh standing in the hallway, waiting for me.

"Can I talk to you?"

I looked at him and then at the others of the Eight Group before shaking my head and swallowing the painful lump in my throat.

937

"I don't think it's a good idea," I said quickly, ducking my head as I walked past. He caught my wrist and my stomach flipped over with a fear I did not understand.

"Please?" he asked. "It's important."

I hesitated. I knew what he wanted to talk about. I turned to Mark, who was standing with the others of the Eight Group. While it seemed like he knew what Josh wanted to talk about, he did not appear to have any intention of following and being part of the conversation.

"Fine," I conceded. "Where do you want to talk?"

Josh motioned to the ammunition room next to us. I opened the door and walked in, turning the lights on and trying to stop the fluttering of my stomach. Josh closed the door behind us as I turned to him. I cleared my throat, folding my arms over my chest and trying to school my expression.

"What's wrong?"

"Well...about Mykail," he started gently. I cut him off before he could continue.

"Josh, please. I really don't want to discuss him right now."

"No, I'm not asking that," he said. He looked at the ground, nervous. "See...what I want to tell you is that...it's okay to be upset," he said gently. "He hurt you...and you don't have to pretend you're not hurt."

The feelings were swelling in me like an angry tsunami, threatening to drag me under, into a dark place I was trying not to go.

"I just want to tell you...it's okay to cry. You don't have to put up a front for us."

"Yes, I do," I said, almost cutting him off again. "I am one of the leaders of this revolution. I can't have people thinking that I'm too emotional to handle the things that have to be done."

"But, right now, you are," he said, stepping closer. I backed away, keeping my arms crossed as a barrier against him, trying to discreetly get rid of the ball in my throat choking me. "You love him...and he hurt you."

"*Loved*," I corrected strongly. "I loved him. Not anymore."

Josh remained still and silent for a long moment before he looked at the ground again. I cleared my throat and turned away. I could feel the pain clawing at my abdomen, making me feel sick and dizzy.

Josh took a step forward. I retreated immediately.

"What are you doing?"

"I'm going to give you a hug," he told me simply. My eyes went wide, horrified, knowing that if he touched me I would break down.

"No, no," I said, pushing past him. He grabbed my arm and turned me around. "Don't, Josh," I snapped. "Don't do this to me, *please…*"

"You can't keep this inside, Lily."

"Yes, I can."

"No, you can't," he said. "If you don't want to let anyone else know how hurt you are, fine, but you are not going to hurt yourself like this. I won't let you. It will kill you."

He jerked me forward and wrapped his arms around my shoulders, locking me to him. I pushed away in horror, but his strength kept me close and I felt my barriers crack.

"You were not weak," he whispered against my ear. "*He* was the weak one. He gave in to Dana. You are not weak…" he repeated, holding me tight.

The tears were coming on too quickly for me to stop. I tried to control them, taking deep, rhythmic breaths, trying to combat the terrible emotions that were ripping through my body.

"Please, Josh, l-let me go…" I pleaded. "I can't…"

"You're safe here," he said, keeping his hold on me. "It's just me. It's okay."

That proved to be my undoing. Josh had given me permission to accept being upset and, before I could stop myself, my arms went around him and latched onto his jacket, holding him close.

I was not even sure what I was crying about as I buried my head against his shoulder, unable to stop my sobbing as I trembled, clutching to him. My thoughts were a muddled scene of white, like static, buzzing and moving around erratically, but not forming anything coherent. It was as though my lungs had been cut out of my chest, slowly, and my entire body was trying to find a way to gasp for breath around the pain.

Josh lowered us to sit on the ground where I held onto him tightly, crying, clawing at the fabric of his jacket as he continued to tell me it was okay.

Chapter Seventy

"We now bring you an update on the twelve-car accident on eastbound-60 yesterday," the female anchor said, switching stories. "According to the official report, law enforcement was working with the Commission of the People to apprehend members of the domestic terrorist group called the Central Angels. Two members of the terrorist group stole a Commission car and caused the accident while evading police pursuit. The fugitives abandoned the car and are still at large.

"Most supporters of the Central Angels are commending the actions of the two who stole the vehicle. However, Danielle Markus of the Commission of the People had this to say earlier today."

Clark's mother appeared at a press conference that had been recorded earlier.

"This group has, once again, put the lives of the people of America at risk. First, they cause a riot during a demonstration that killed nine people and costs tens of thousands of dollars in damage. Then, they break into a security compound and release known criminals, including members of organized crime families, and now they are stealing government property and creating accidents that have killed one and hospitalized several others. These terrorists are not a group that the American people should support. They are dangerous. Central is working with the Commission of the People to find them and bring them to justice before more lives are lost."

The anchor reappeared on screen.

"An official statement claims that fourteen members of the Central Angels terrorist group have been caught and are going to be questioned later in the week before they stand trial for disturbing the peace and treason."

"That explains the people we're missing..." Clark muttered.

"We just have to hope that the people caught won't be able to tell Dana where the bunker is," Griffin added.

"We tried to make sure that each person only knew one or two entrances," I said, rubbing my eyes as I tried to get rid of the headache that had settled in my skull the previous night. "We should keep rotating guards at the entrances for the rest of the week, just to be sure. We can give them the Eight Group bracelets so that they can tell us if we're in danger and we can find a way out."

"We need to ask the groups we are sending out to be more aggressive about getting food," Tori said. "Maybe we should have someone go around in the van rather than asking them to carry it themselves."

"We'd need to make sure the van rarely stops moving," Clark pointed out. "We can't risk having a vehicle tied to us."

"Or being pulled over for not having license plates," I added.

"We could probably take some from an impounded car," Griffin suggested. "Maybe only use the car once a week, get a few different plates and rotate them…"

"Maybe…" I whispered. "All I know is that our food supply is getting dangerously low."

"We could pay for some, potentially," Tori said. She turned to Mark. "You have money, don't you?"

He nodded.

"But we don't want to become dependent on buying food," I interjected. "That means we're going to go through money and food far quicker, and it is entirely possible that we're going to need more ammunition and weapons. What we lifted from the camp was minimal, at best."

"True," Griffin agreed.

"Do you think there's any way to get a message to the people who support us to give us aid?" Clark asked. "Maybe ask them to leave food somewhere to support the fighters of the revolution."

"Potentially…" Tori said.

"But that would make people realize that we're running out of supplies, and if we don't appear strong, it could make them nervous." I shook my head. "We're going up against the most powerful institution in the world and the government. If we don't look like we know what we're doing…we could lose a lot of support. People are going to stand behind who they think will win."

The group fell silent, staring at the ground or at the television as the news reported on the international response to our attacks against the Commission.

"We *need* outside help…" Tori whispered.

I sighed heavily and walked out of the communications room, trying to think past the fogginess in my head.

"Lily?" a voice asked. I turned and saw Jerry Parker had followed me.

"Mr. Parker," I greeted. "Is everything alright?"

"Forgive me for eavesdropping, but it sounds like you're worried about getting food…" he said. I hesitated. I did not want the others to know that we were running low on rations. Everyone already knew that we had to be careful with our supplies, and though they grumbled about getting one and a half meals a day, they knew that we were trying to preserve our supplies. They did not, however, know how dire the food situation had become.

"Yes..." I said, hesitant to admit the problem.

"I could talk to the company about sending out a message for donation of non-perishables," he suggested.

I smiled. "Thanks, but I don't want to make this a pretense for charity or anything. It would feel wrong."

"No, I mean...it's already known that my company was supporting this cause, and everyone who supports you knows that you broke me out. Rather than try and make it seem like we're running low on supplies, we could make it so that my company does it to support me and the other people you broke out of the camp."

I blinked, a little surprised at how appealing the idea sounded.

"Would...would you be willing to do that?" I gasped. "I mean, that could get your entire company in trouble."

"The country is in trouble," Mr. Parker said. "You made us see that. Having companies turn a blind eye to what is going on is one of the things that made the United States such a disaster. If the company gets into trouble, it's okay. It's a company. These are people we're trying to help. I want to do my part."

If I had not cried myself out of tears the previous night, I would have been crying again.

"I would really appreciate it if you could do that."

* *** *

The following morning, amid the late spring snow lightly falling over the city, Mark, Josh, Jerry, and I made our way to the middle of the city. Mark and Josh were dressed in casual clothes. The snow was a perfect excuse to wear hoods and scarves to cover our faces.

Slipping under the awning for the bus station, I nodded to Jerry, who went inside with the few coins we had given him for the payphone. Payphones were almost obsolete, but there were still a few places, mostly public transport hubs, that had them. I just hoped that Jerry would be able to finish the call before we were spotted and identified.

I stood with Mark and Josh under the awning, staying outside so we could have an excuse to be covered up.

"I really hope this works."

"Me, too," Josh agreed.

"Do you think the others are okay?" I asked, worried about sending five teams out to get food despite the recent captures. Josh hesitated.

"They'll be careful."

I looked through the windows at Jerry, hoping he was able to get some help from the public. The people demanded we break out the people who had been imprisoned, which put us at risk. It seemed only right that they support us and ease the strain the extra people had on our supplies.

"Mark," I started, "you got all your money from being…a Fixer?" I caught myself quickly. He nodded. "How much money do you have?"

He lifted two fingers and placed them against the palm of his other hand, tapping them three times.

"Two thousand?"

"Two million," Josh corrected.

I know my jaw hit my chest because I got the fibers of my scarf in my mouth. I coughed and spat out the scarf before rounding on Mark in shock.

"Two million dollars?" I whispered. He nodded. "How much did you get paid for each job?"

He tapped three fingers against his palm twice.

"Three hundred thousand," Josh translated.

I was unable to speak for several long moments, looking between the two members of the Eight Group, dumbfounded by the numbers.

"Did you…" I turned to Josh. "Were *you* a Fixer?"

"Only two times." Josh shrugged. "I got one hundred thousand each."

"Holy shit…" I gasped. "How did you two even get away with doing that? Didn't they notice how you looked?"

"Not until much later," Josh said. "We were very careful. It was extremely secretive. Only after working multiple times for the same family did Mark meet them. They didn't really care."

I decided I did not want to know. I did not want to think of Mark being a hired gun for the mafia, no matter how much money he had gotten from it. When I factored in the guns, ammunition, car, and whatever else he had bought, I realized he had likely made a lot more than two million dollars as a hitman. I turned to Mark with one final question about the sordid past.

"Did you do that just so you could get money to support this kind of a revolution?"

He nodded.

Jerry came out of the bus station and smiled as he wrapped his scarf around his face again.

"Well?"

"They're going to start with the employees first," he explained. "They will bring in non-perishables throughout next week. In the meantime, they will put up signs around the city telling people about the donation with little wings in the corner to be sure that the supporters know," he continued, dropping his voice. "In two weeks, we can gather those donations."

"Perfect," I said. "Thank you so much."

"My pleasure. But, we're going to need someone to keep contact with them as often as possible, to help put up the signs and keep an eye out for Commission cars."

I nodded. Most of the Commish Kids were also living in the fort now, having run away from their families around the same time that I had been chased away from mine. While I wanted them to be the ones to keep in contact with Carolina Media, I knew that their faces would be too recognizable, meaning the task had to be delegated to less-vetted members of our group.

"Wait, I need to make a call," I said, darting inside the bus station.

It was very warm in the building, but I forced myself to keep on my jacket and scarf. I did, however, lower my hood. I looked around nervously, seeing the young backpackers and older citizens waiting for their buses away from the chilly storm outside.

I stepped in the phone booth and closed the door behind me, fishing in my pocket for more coins. Putting in the quarter, I picked up the receiver and dialed the number I wanted.

I listened to the ringing for a few seconds, praying that there would be an answer.

"Hello?" a voice answered hesitantly.

"Hey," I said. "Remember how you said you would be there to help me? I need a favor."

It was a short conversation. I could not stay in the station long and she would not be able to stay on the phone much longer. We made arrangements to meet in the park to talk.

Of course, the day I chose to meet Becca in the park also happened to be the coldest day of the year.

It was later in the afternoon, so the sun was starting to set behind the hills and cast cold shadows around the park. While that worked well for hiding me and Mark from inquisitive eyes, it also dropped the temperature several degrees.

I was shivering, huddling into my scarf and jacket, trying to keep my teeth from chattering. Mark did not seem at all concerned with the cold as he sat with me, always casting a wary eye around the park. He had refused to let me out of his sight. I had no problem with him tagging along. After realizing he had been right not to trust Mykail, I wanted to be sure that he trusted Becca, though I knew that he was already apprehensive.

I saw a girl quickly shuffling through the light powder of snow to us, waving, though she did not call out to me.

"Hey," I greeted as she hugged me. I hugged her back, surprised at how happy I was to see her again. "How are you?"

"Bored without you around," Becca said. "Everyone kept asking where you were. But after all the other Commish Kids vanished, I think they got the idea."

"What are the rumors?"

"The two theories are that you all joined the revolution or the Commission locked you all up," Becca told me. She hugged me once again. "I'm so happy to see that you're okay."

"Yeah, I'm alright."

"Did you really do what the news said?"

"Um...now is really not a good time to discuss it," I laughed nervously. "You know Mark," I motioned to the silent man at my side.

"It's good to see you again," she said, extending her hand. He took it slowly and I watched the apprehension on his face. Taking careful note of it, I began to strategize how I wanted to ask for her help. Becca turned back to me. "So, you want me to help. What can I do?"

"Well, I don't need you to do a whole lot. And I'm going to make this quick so we can get out of the freezing cold," I laughed, my teeth chattering. "Basically, we're getting a little low on supplies. It's nothing serious, but we want to make sure it doesn't get worse."

"Okay."

"Carolina Media is holding a kind of can-drive for us of non-perishables, since we released their CEO. I was hoping that you could be my eyes and ears out here and try to get more people to donate food to us."

"Sure, sure," she said, shivering in the biting cold of the clear dusk sky. "You know you can ask me for help with anything. Do you want me to talk through the gossip channels of the school?"

"Sure," I said, hoping to get as many people to help as possible. "But don't get yourself in trouble. Say that it's just a collection of food and that's it. Don't make it a recruitment thing. Carolina Media will be putting up fliers with wings at the bottom. That should tell them where they can drop off the non-perishables."

"Okay."

I did not think she understood how serious I was. I felt that our fort was already severely compromised with the missing members of our revolution and Dana's knowledge of one of the entrances, plus whatever he had learned from Mykail previously. I did not want more people knowing where we were and compromising our limited security.

"Is that all?"

"For now, yes," I said. I hugged her again. "Thank you so much. It would be a big help."

"No problem," she said, hugging me back. "And if you need me to help you up here with anything, I don't have to know all the plans, but if you want me to look into something, you let me know and I will do my best."

"Really? You mean that?" I said, tears of happiness rising to my eyes. It was nice to know I still had Becca as a friend, particularly after everything that had been happening recently.

"Of course," Becca said strongly. "I told you, having the Commission gone is a lifesaver for me."

Mark turned to me, confused. Catching the movement out of the corner of her eye, Becca looked at him, dropping her voice to a whisper.

"I like other girls."

Mark straightened in surprise, and then looked away, uncomfortable. Becca and I both laughed at Mark's awkwardness.

"Does your phone still work?" she asked.

"No," I groaned. "I was planning on calling you from a payphone in two days to get an update on what you've got, and call you again another day depending on what you tell me."

"Okay," she agreed. "But be sure you call after four. And remember, I'll be at Archangel on Fridays, so you better be sure you call me at the right time." She nudged me playfully. "Remember? Remember when you weren't such a badass and you used to have a normal life?"

"To be honest…it's really hard to remember," I tried to tease. She laughed but, once again, I was sure that she did not understand I was telling the truth. My life before the fort seemed a distant memory. The mundane days of going to school and sitting in class were muddled into one, dream-like portion of my life. I could hardly remember the times before the war against Dana.

Becca left, running out of the cold as Mark and I hustled back to the fort. When we were in the drainage pipes and walking to the fort, nodding to the two people we had posted as guards, I turned to the leader of the Eight Group.

"Do you trust Becca?"

Mark was still, his hands remaining in his pockets as he walked with me. After a few steps of him staring pensively at the ground, he sighed and raised his hand to his face, rubbing the corner of his eye in a familiar, yet ominous, warning.

"Be careful."

* *** *

It was time I faced the problem I had been avoiding all week.

I paced for what felt like hours in the strategy room alone, trying to summon the courage to go through with the plan I had devised earlier. My stomach was tied in knots, my hands shaking as I wrung them together.

I had to face Mykail.

Before I could second-guess myself yet again, I walked out of the strategy room and made my way to the storage rooms, ignoring the curious eyes that followed from the main bunker.

I approached the familiar faces outside the storage room. They turned, surprised to see me walking with such purpose. Josh, who had been speaking with Rin, looked me over.

"Lily…"

"I want to see him," I said, surprising myself with the strength and steadiness of my voice.

The experiments looked at one another worriedly before Josh cleared his throat.

"…are you sure?"

"Yes."

"Do you want one of us in there, too?" Rin asked.

"No. This is something I need to do alone."

Hesitantly, Josh nodded to Ichiro, who opened the door. I took a deep breath and started forward.

"We'll be right out here if you need us," Rin said. I nodded, gathering any final bits of courage I could to walk into the room.

He was chained to some of the larger pipes, though I could see the strain it put on his wings, making it painful for him to sit against the pipes. He looked at me, his eyes tired and his face dirty, but not hurt. There were some light bruises on his right side and scrapes on his left from his wrestling with Mark. The scratch on his forehead had scabbed over and was almost healed.

"Mykail," I said to him in cold greeting. I saw a bottle of water near him and picked it up. Giving him water would allow me a few moments to adjust to being back in his presence. Seeing his eyes made the memories rush back. The memories of how I had been so captivated by those eyes, the times when I had seen love and happiness in them…the painful nostalgia threw me off-guard.

I unscrewed the top, pressing the lip of the bottle to his mouth. Carefully tipping it, I poured water into his mouth. After giving him a few gulps, I set the water down and backed away, composing myself for the confrontation.

"I figured it was only fair that I listen to what you have to say."

"Before anything, I want to say I'm sorry…" Mykail whispered, trying to shift, though the chains kept him tightly bound on his knees. "I never wanted to hurt you like this. I really wanted to tell you the original reason Dana put me in your house, but…"

"But?" I prompted.

"I was terrified," he admitted, looking at the ground. "I really do love you, Lily."

The words hit me like bricks, but I remained as calm as I could.

"You understand that it is hard for me to believe those words," I told him. He nodded slowly. "Tell me your side. Don't lie to me anymore."

"Dana wanted me to go to your house and to…coerce you, I guess, into acting out against him. He never told me why he wanted you, only that he wanted you in the Commission. He wanted to have you, whatever that meant."

"And what did he want you to do while you were with me?" I pressed. "Did he want you to make me fall in love with you? Did he want you to have sex with me?" Mykail hesitated before answering.

"Yes," he whispered. "He wanted me to seduce you…"

"Congratulations, you succeeded in your mission," I snarled.

"No, I didn't," Mykail said quickly, his eyes shooting wide. "Listen, I really pushed for us to get close at first. I wanted to push you to do something faster so that I could get out from under Dana's influence, but you were smarter than that," Mykail told me sincerely. "You did not fall for my tricks or his. Yes, we got close fast, but…as we did…I actually fell in love with you. And it wasn't just your fiery spirit or your commitment to take down Dana, it was all the little things. The way you laughed and smiled, the way you looked when you got angry at the little things at school…every moment with you made me feel more alive than I ever had before…and I realized that I could not do what Dana commanded me to do."

I swallowed hard, trying to keep my composure.

"How am I supposed to believe that?"

"I know I can't ask you to believe me," Mykail said. "I have no right to ask for something like that. But I want to tell you the truth. I owe you that." Mykail dropped his head again. "Honestly, when I heard that Mark, the leader of the Eight Group, had a plan, and that the plan could work...I decided that, rather than avoid telling Dana anything, I needed to tell him things to get him on the wrong track."

I looked at the ground.

"Lily, if there was any way for me to prove this to you, you know I would."

"I want to believe you, Mykail," I murmured. "I really do. I honestly felt that I loved you and knew you...but that shattered so quickly, I'm starting to think that maybe I didn't love you as deeply as I thought I did."

"What I did was unforgivable," he said. "I don't blame you for distrusting me."

"I distrusted you before I heard what Dana said," I whispered. He looked at me, confused. "There was a moment when I realized that I was the only one who trusted you completely...and because of that, I began to wonder why it was that none of the other experiments trusted you. But rather than stand beside you and say that they just didn't know you, or that they were being paranoid...I trusted them more than my knowledge of you."

Mykail looked down, ashamed. I swallowed hard.

"I won't forgive you for playing me, even if you did turn away from Dana at a certain point. The fact is, I will never know if what you're saying is true. I will try my best to think well of you...but I can't trust you...and I don't think I will ever forgive you."

"I understand," he murmured. "I want to thank you, Lily...for coming in here and telling me that. And thank you for at least listening to what I had to say." He sniffed, the tears making his voice waver. "You were always better than I deserved."

I stood, clearing my throat before walking over and kissing him on the cheek. I walked out of the room, feeling pained, but somehow lighter.

Chapter Seventy-One

There was an interesting story on the Saturday morning news that caught my attention as I was about to go out and find a payphone to call Becca. I walked into the communication room to get Mark, who insisted on being with me whenever I left. He was standing in the back of the room while Tori and Griffin were sitting at the computer with Clark, everyone's attention fixed on the news.

"…the culprits of the tagging have not been identified, due to their use of masks in the video, which quickly went viral," the male anchor explained. I watched the video change to a clip taken on a phone, jarring as the person taking the video ran to the group of young men and women excitedly spray-painting a brick wall, laughing, wearing Thomas Ankell masks.

"…This thirty-second long clip shows the taggers spray painting profanities at the entrance of the Third Tier building. Here are pictures this morning from police, depicting demeaning slogans, violent scenes, and the image that has become the symbol of the Central Angels—wings. School will open normally on Monday. Officials hope to have the graffiti cleaned off the school by then. Central has yet to make a statement about whether this is the work of vandals or if this is also connected to the terrorist group, the Central Angels."

I studied the pictures of the tagging. While some of the words were blurred out to censor the profanity, it was clear what the messages were saying.

Fuck Central!

This is War!!

There was a picture of a distorted angel violently stabbing a large C and the flag of America was painted as being on fire.

"What the hell is this?" I whispered.

Everyone had been so absorbed in what they were watching that they jumped and turned to me.

"Lily, you startled us," Tori laughed, a hand on her chest.

"What's this about tagging a school?" I repeated, appalled to think that some of our revolution had done something in such a demeaning and terrifying manner.

"It wasn't ours," Griffin said. "There's no way it could have been. Everyone was in last night."

Remembering accounting for everyone as they returned the previous night, I accepted that it was probably the work of some young teenagers who were trying to make a splash in the media. While I did not like the idea of our public supporters getting violent and defacing property, I had to let it go.

But there was something about the story that continued to bother me.

Mark went with me into the city and to the post office, another place with an outside pay phone.

I called Becca with Mark standing close by, keeping an eye out for possible eavesdroppers.

"Hello?"

"Hey, Becca."

"Hey," she greeted, a smile in her voice. "How are you?"

"Not bad, you?"

"Great, actually," she laughed. "Listen, rather than talk on the phone, can you come over around seven tonight? I have something for you."

"Uh..." I said, suspicious. I turned to Mark. "Hold on."

I pressed the receiver to my chest and whispered what she had asked. He looked thoughtful, torn about the idea.

"Can we meet somewhere else?" I asked.

"I wish, but I have to be home tonight. My mom is out with her...*person* and my dad is sick, so it's my job to take care of him."

I turned to Mark and shook my head. He furrowed his brow in thought, not liking the idea of going to her house without knowing what was waiting for us. After pursing his lips, he nodded slowly.

"Okay, your house should be fine," I agreed, though there was a tone of disbelief in my voice at Mark's agreement.

"Great," Becca said. "I really don't want to talk about this over the phone, just in case."

"Okay, thank you, Becca,"

"Sure, I'll meet you out front of my house around seven."

"Great, see you then."

I hung up the phone and turned to Mark.

"You really think this is a good idea?" I asked. He nodded for me to follow him and we returned to the fort. As soon as we got back, I followed Mark to the normal meeting spot for the Eight Group, which was in front of the storage room in which Mykail remained chained until we could decide what we were going to do with him.

Motioning a few quick things to the three guarding the room, Rin called a few names. The other fourteen members of the Eight Group gathered around their leader, bringing some attention from the others in the bunker, though no one approached or tried to eavesdrop.

"What's going on?" I asked.

"We're going to do surveillance," Rin answered.

"What's the address?" Josh asked.

Giving them Becca's address, I watched Mark point to a few of them, making a few gestures that they understood. The three that had been standing around Mykail's door left and Mark turned to another two, ordering them in the same silent fashion. After they left, Mark turned to Josh and nodded once. Josh left briefly, going into the communications room as Mark ordered another three to take up post outside Mykail's door.

I felt a little better, knowing that Mark was having some of the Eight Group accompany us to Becca's house to be sure that we were not walking into a trap.

Josh returned with a box and pulled out the clear earpieces that I had seen the security of the Commission wear, though a few were attached to a box with a clip on it, used as the main communication device.

I sat with them as they sorted through the earpieces. The two members that had disappeared from their positions at Mykail's door came to the strategy room and helped sort, trying to find the earpieces that were connected to the main communication devices. As they leaned over, I saw that each had four guns—two under their arms and two at their hips.

I was not going to Becca's house alone or unprepared.

Mark put on one of the earpieces as Josh joined us, the main communication line attached to his belt. The three of us walked into the mains and got as close to the neighborhood as we could.

Backtracking when we could not find a better way out, Mark lifted a grate in the residential street and looked around to be sure that no one was watching. Skillfully moving it out of the way, he pulled me up, pointing at me to go to the sidewalk corner, which I obeyed while he and Josh closed the hole.

No one in the Eight Group was wearing their sunglasses which, even though it was dark, made me worry about their safety. Having a large group of people dressed in black moving through the darkened neighborhood was suspicious enough.

Josh went one way while we took another turn, walking around the block to Becca's house.

"What about your glasses?" I murmured through my scarf, turning to Mark. He shook his head, pulling his hat down over his ears and brow. "Why not?"

He tapped his ear, where the communication device was seated, the speaker resting just behind the top of his ear, pressing into the skin. The precisely placed speaker would have to be moved for the glasses.

I was nervous as we approached Becca's house. Josh had told me not to worry, since no one on the Eight Group surveillance team had seen anything threatening around Becca's home. Becca was sitting on the curb outside, huddled in her jacket and scarf, waiting. When she saw us, she leapt to her feet.

"There you are," she said, hugging me as she normally did.

"Sorry to keep you waiting."

"You smell...interesting."

"That's what happens when you take the subway," I teased, pointing to my feet.

"Oh, I guess that's true," she laughed. "Mark." She nodded to him. He bowed his head in greeting.

"What did you have for us?"

"First, I have to tell you what happened yesterday at Archangel," she started excitedly. "We went to Archangel, and now that all the Commish Kids are gone, the balcony is used for the people who are kinda supporters of the revolution. I went up to tell them about what Carolina Media was doing, and you will never guess what they were doing..."

"What?"

"They were mapping out other high-security camps to raid," Becca said. "They said that if they protested enough, that the revolution would raid more camps because they needed to make a statement."

"I would rather not," I chuckled brokenly. "One was enough."

"I talked them out of protesting, but I did get these." She pulled out some folded pieces of paper and handed them to me. It was difficult to get the papers apart with my gloves on, so Mark took them, opening them and as I leaned over to look. I could not see as well in the dark what was written, but I did see some photos that had been printed out with writing below them.

"What's this?" I asked.

"They're pictures and locations of seven other camps around the city," she said through her scarf, her body shuddering in the cold. "It was all over the news that you guys set their supply tent on fire, which made a huge mess and everyone had to be transferred out of the camp," Becca explained. I cringed at the memory.

"Yeah...something like that..."

"It got me thinking about their supply tents. There has to be food in there, right? Food that lasts for a while." She looked at me excitedly.

"While we're gathering the food up here, you could raid the supply tents and steal food."

I turned to Mark. He shrugged with one shoulder and nodded, giving some thought to the idea.

"That could work really well," I agreed. "We'll have to do some more surveillance but we can definitely plan something. Thank you," I said.

"I told you I wanted to help," she said. "Let me help with this."

I turned to Mark again to see his reaction.

"You have to get past the guard," I teased. The leader of the Eight Group hesitated.

"I don't have to go where you are. I would actually prefer not to," she said. "I don't want to know. The less I know about the technicalities, the better," she laughed. "But, I do want to help in any way that I can. I wouldn't mind getting out of this house more often."

My heart fell.

"I'm sorry…" I murmured, hugging her again as Mark looked between the two of us, confused. Becca saw his expression and bluntly told him that her mother was having an affair and it was tearing the family apart. Once again, Mark got awkward. I laughed at how he was so nervous when he learned something personal about others. He wanted to help everyone who was in a bad situation, which was obvious by his concern and desire to understand why Becca was upset, but with how bluntly Becca had told him her two big secrets, he was immediately taken aback.

"I love how flustered you get," Becca chuckled.

"Tell you what," I started, "we're going to collect the food from Carolina Media on Monday, around ten at night," I explained. "Meet us there and we'll let you know if we need you to do anything."

"Sounds good," she agreed. "This is kind of exciting."

"Maybe right now, but it might get really nasty."

"That's okay," Becca said, her expression hardening in determination. "I can handle it."

* *** *

The information Becca had given us had been extremely helpful. That same night, eager for something to do, a group led by Griffin went to do reconnaissance on two of the camps while Tori took another group to watch a third. Josh led the Eight Group to another two camps, Mark joining them, while I was left with Clark and most of the humans in the fort, waiting for them to return, watching Peter and the others meticulously sort through the wreckage that was the medical room.

A lot had been destroyed from the mishap with the tunnel. While Peter said he did not yet know what had survived, he told me there was no need to find more medical supplies yet.

I decided to take at least one case of medical supplies from each camp if we did decide to raid anyway, just to be safe.

Early in the morning, I went into the main bunker to see if any of the teams had returned. Hearing Griffin's typical snoring from the side of the bunk room, I knew that at least his group had made it back safely.

Tori was in the strategy room with Mark and the rest of the Eight Group. They filled me in on the different camps and which they thought would be best to raid first. The larger camps were the better targets, since they would have a greater number of supplies. I told them that we should take at least two cases of bullets from each camp and one case of emergency medical supplies. They agreed and said that they would do reconnaissance on the final two camps that night.

I stayed with them in the strategy room, pulling out a map of the city and putting Xs where the camps were to see if we could hit more than one camp in a night. After what had happened to the first camp, it would be foolish to wait between raids and give them time to prepare and fortify other camps.

Griffin and Clark joined in the planning once they woke, easily helping us decide which camps to raid and how many people would be needed to accomplish the heists.

Refusing to sit out on the plan, Mark and I had another one-sided argument about whether I should be a part of the raids or not. I finally won, though I had to continuously tell Mark that what had happened last time was the result of an accident when the light tower fell on the tent. It was no fault on my part.

However, I was outnumbered on the decision regarding my role in the raid.

Monday, a small group went to collect the goods from Carolina Media around seven. I had felt bad about lying to Becca about the time to meet, but she was not someone I saw every day, and it was entirely possible that Dana or the Commission could meet with her and I would never know. Therefore, I told her to meet us three hours later to allow some time for us to get the food back to the fort.

Mark and Clark stayed with me outside Carolina Media, hanging around in the back alley and waiting for Becca as it got colder and the night descended.

Poor Mark had a moment of panic when Clark said he was going to get coffee for us at the coffee shop down the street. The snow had disappeared from the streets, but the clear sky of early April left a chill in the night air that bit to the bone. Mark was not sure if he should go with Clark or stay with me. Finally persuaded to stay with me when Clark told him that he would look strange at eight-thirty at night wearing sunglasses, Mark anxiously waited for Clark to return.

The coffee did wonders, warming me up and making me more alert. I also felt better realizing that we had just gathered food for the revolution and that we were about to go through with another plan that I was sure was going to be successful.

Becca showed up as promised around ten o'clock, peeking around the back of the Carolina Media building where we had been standing since loading the van with the food.

"Hey," she said, hugging me before hugging Clark as well. "I haven't seen you in forever. How have you been?"

"Not bad," Clark said shyly.

"Where is everyone else?"

"They just left," I lied.

"Oh, okay. Do you have anything you want me to do?"

"Yes." I said. "Will you be available Wednesday starting at seven?"

Thankfully, she was.

Mark teaching me how to drive the van had proven to be unsuccessful and stressful for both of us, so Josh had to take over instruction, taking me on a few practice runs on bumpy dirt roads near the van's hiding spot. I by no means felt comfortable driving the large van, but I put on a strong face, wanting to do my part.

I also wanted Becca to do well. This was, in a sense, her initiation. Mark did not trust Becca but he wanted to give her a chance, and our plans Wednesday were that chance.

She met me at the motel where we had left the van. She was anxiously scanning her surroundings as she approached me while I was standing by the van, waiting.

"Why are we here?" she asked. "It's really skeevy…"

"It's alright, we're not staying," I said. "These are for you," I said, handing her a batch of papers. "You're riding shotgun."

She got into the van and I moved around the front of the car, climbing into the driver's seat as she blinked at me incredulously.

"You're driving?"

"Yeah."

"But...you don't have a license..." she told me, as though I had forgotten that fact.

"We're only going to be on the main roads for a while," I said, turning the car on and buckling my seatbelt. "Josh taught me the basics."

"The basics," Becca repeated, her tone worried. "Great..."

I tried not to let her know how nervous I was. I was not worried about the raids, since I would not be in the action. My job with Becca was to pick up the supplies from three camps before dropping the crates off where those who had stayed behind, organized by Clark, would take the boxes into the fort. My anxiety rested solely in the fact that I had to drive.

I was tense the entire time, trying very hard not to go too fast or too slow while telling Becca to guide me based on the written instructions I had given her.

We made it onto the first dirt road with little trouble, stopping when we saw a person standing on the shoulder. We had a longer line of people to the road, which kept me from driving too close to the camp. I put the car in park and opened the doors to load the supplies. When we were ready for the crates, I turned to Becca.

"Okay, see the lines at the bottom of the map?" She glanced at the paper. "Those are for the supplies. Make sure we have one medical crate, four weapon crates, and seven ration crates. That's how much we're taking from each camp."

"Will all of that fit?" she asked skeptically. The seats had been taken out to fit as much as possible so that we could move quickly through each site.

"We tested it."

"Lily!" Jake called, telling me that the supplies were starting to come forward. I stood by the side door and waited for the first crate, which I could see being passed from one person to the next toward the van. Once the group finished this raid, they had to move to another location so they were moving quickly. We were hitting three small and two large camps that night with two groups of people, which meant everyone had to move rapidly and efficiently to hit all targets before the sun rose.

When Jake passed the crate to me, I turned it toward Becca so she could see the labeling. She squinted in the dark, crouching close.

"Ammo."

"Weapon," I said, climbing to the back of the van and putting the crate tightly against the back doors. I waited only fifteen seconds before I saw the next crate approach.

We had four weapons crates before long, and the food boxes followed shortly. Everyone moved smoothly, quietly, completely in sync and focused. We had to wait a little after the seventh food crate to get the medical supplies, since they had to be found in the tent before they were passed over the wall.

"Do I even want to know how you guys are getting these things over those walls around the camps?" Becca asked during the short waiting period, her eyebrows high.

"Let's just say you don't want to piss any of the experiments off," I said. "They're tossing them over."

"Of course they are," Becca chuckled brokenly. "They are weapons made by the Commission, of course they have super-strength."

When Becca confirmed that we had the medical supplies, I loaded the box and the line of people darted into the trees, moving to the next location. Some were going to take public transportation if they were inconspicuous, while the others went down the tunnels to move faster and out of sight.

I climbed into the driver's seat, backing down the path and into the parking lot, letting Becca swing the "No Trespassing" gate closed behind us.

Reading the directions from the next map, we made it onto a deserted section of the old state highway, which was surrounded by trees and extremely dark. I saw one woman, Emilie, setting the final crate on the stack she had made on the side of the road. Pulling over, I scrambled out and opened the side door. Becca did not need to be told what to do, using the lights of the car to read the sides of the crate and confirm that we had what we needed while Emilie disappeared into the woods to move to the next spot.

I did not feel the same kind of excitement from previous times raiding government establishments. Instead, there was a focused feeling of purpose.

I was feeling a little more comfortable driving as we went to the third location, though I was still driving slowly in care of the crates in the back.

The slope to get to the third location was bumpy from the abandoned asphalt that had cracked and sunken over the years. Even with how slow we drove, we had to wait for the crates from the third location. By the time the crates made their way to the car it was already eleven at night and we were running behind schedule. I was worried that we would not be able to hit all locations before the sky started to get light.

Stacking everything in tightly, we barely managed to close the doors of the vehicle.

Then, it was a mad dash to those waiting to unload the van and take everything to the fort. I did not drive as carefully, concerned with the time-crunch. Becca had to continuously remind me to slow down, worried about police pulling us over, since we were out past curfew.

I finally pulled up to the park where the group was waiting, Clark shivering in his jacket with many others. I threw the car into park and scrambled out.

"I was getting worried," Clark said.

"We're running a little behind, but nothing is wrong," I said, jogging to the back of the car. Everyone flooded forward and I started rapidly pulling out the crates, handing them to whatever hands were nearby. "Just stack these somewhere, we really need to get moving," I ordered.

We had the back of the van emptied in three minutes. Half of the people were helping me get crates out of the car while the other half were moving them out of sight of the road.

When the van was empty, Becca turned to Clark.

"Are you okay handling everything from here?"

"Yes," he affirmed. "We'll see you in a couple hours."

The next location was the furthest camp from town and the biggest one we were going to hit. That meant both teams were meeting at that particular site, though a few individuals were moving on to be sure that the other forts had not been alerted to the raids.

It took me and Becca forty-five minutes to get to the place in the road where we were supposed to stop.

"It's here," she said, looking at the map.

"Are you sure?"

"Yes, I'm sure," she said, looking up at the road and then back down to the map. "Stop, stop."

I slowed the car, looking around the dirt road, not seeing anything distinguishable on the shoulder. There was no one from our group, worrying me that we were in the wrong spot.

"Let me see the map." I glanced over the papers, turning the lights of the van off. "It looks like there should be a lot of some kind..."

Becca looked around and then pointed at the map.

"I was following the bends in the road, and we came here."

"But there's some kind of...space here," I said, pointing next to the X that marked where we were supposed to be. "I don't see one here."

"If we go any further up, we're going to get closer to the camp."

"Let's get out and see if we can find the lot."

"Why don't we wait to see if someone will find us?"

"We don't have a lot of time. I want to be in the right place so that we can get moving. If they're not here in a half hour, we have reason to worry and we'll need to book it out of here."

We got out of the van, but never wandered out of sight of it.

"Lily," Becca called further down the road after we had been searching for three minutes. "Over here."

I turned down the slope and walked to her. There was a dirt lot that could barely fit the van and a large ditch between that and the road.

"I think this is it," she said.

"I hope not," I grumbled, looking at the ditch. "I don't know if the van can make it through that."

"It should be fine."

"Let me see the map again."

After debating with each other for a few minutes in the cold, trying to keep quiet as we deliberated, I finally gave in and assumed Becca was right, going to the car and letting it roll down the hill before turning it to the lot. Becca guided me between the two massive trees that almost clipped the side mirrors as I grumbled irritably, knowing she could not hear me.

The van gave a jolt when it went into the ditch, and I pressed my foot on the accelerator, causing the engine to roar as it heaved over the other side of the ditch, barely clipping the back bumper on the road as the back tires descended heavily.

But I managed to clear the ditch, even though my hands were shaking with fear that the van had been stuck.

Becca climbed into the car and smiled.

"See?"

We sat in silence for a few minutes before Becca struck up conversation, both of us continuously scanning the surrounding trees for the others of the raid.

"So…Dana Christenson…you said he was crazy," Becca started quietly.

"Completely."

"And Leader Simon is too afraid of him to do anything?"

"Right."

"Then, why didn't you just…kill him when you were down in the Commission?" she asked.

"Apparently, it's not that simple," I murmured. "Mark tried it once and it cost him his voice. We needed to find a way to take him down from outside. Inside the Commission…it's like you've walked into another dimension. Everything is so…"

"So?" she prompted when I trailed off.

"This is going to sound stupid, but amoral, primitive, maybe even decadent. There is only one rule, and that's to obey Dana. Otherwise, everyone is having affairs, sleeping around, enjoying the torture and mutilation of people…"

"No one says anything?" she whispered, horrified.

"What *can* we say? Dana changes people. He even turned my mother against the family. She almost broke some of my bones before I got out of the house."

"*Why?*"

"I spoke out against Dana," I told her with a shrug, keeping my eyes away from hers. "Everyone is so loyal to him. They act like he's God."

Becca fell silent.

"Maybe, in a way…he is God," I mused, keeping my eyes in the trees. "He has the whole world in the palm of his hand."

There were ten seconds of silence before I saw a figure moving in the trees.

"Finally, they're here."

Becca followed me out of the car. Jake called to me quietly when he got closer.

"You didn't have to pull into the lot," he said.

"Told you!" I snapped at Becca, though I was smiling.

Even after Jake made it to his spot and the others had formed the line, there was still a long wait in the cold before we had crates to stack in the van. I used the time to ask Jake how everyone was doing.

"Fine," he said. "I'm starting to think the Eight Group are literal ninjas," he laughed. "They are moving so quickly from each location it's unreal."

"The Eight Group?" Becca whispered, nudging me for an answer.

"Mark's group of friends."

"Why are they called the Eight Group?"

"Kind of a long story," I evaded. I did not want to spend my time discussing the rankings in the wards of the experiments, or the other Asians who had become a part of the Eight Group. I did not want to reveal too much since they were so vital to our intelligence, even though they no longer had inside information on the Commission of the People.

There was a whistle deeper in the woods and we assumed our positions.

With twenty cases from that fort, it took longer to get all the crates into the van. When they were laid out in the back, I told Becca she had to ride in the back with them over the ditch to be sure that they remained stable. I turned to Jake before he left.

"Jake, how fast can you run?"

"Pretty fast, why?"

"Can you stay with a few others and make sure we make it through the ditch?"

Jake called a few others back and I climbed into the car, putting it in reverse as Jake came up next to me.

"Just go slow and get the back in the ditch, but try and give it enough power there to get up the other side."

Doing as he said, I told Becca to hold on and started the venture of getting back through the ditch. Thankfully, the weather was still cold and the ground was still frozen, meaning that the now-heavier van did not sink when it went into the ditch. However, I did have to have help pushing the van over the other side of the ditch. I scraped the nose, but continued to rev the engine and made it back on the road. I waved at the men and women who had helped, who darted away as Becca climbed out of the back and resumed her map reading.

"You know, domestic terrorism is way more fun than it should be," she teased. "It's exciting."

I had to agree.

We had no trouble finding the secluded parking lot for our next location. We went as far into the back as we could and passed the time rearranging crates to be sure that we had enough room for the goods of the final heist.

It was nearing three-thirty when the others made their way to the parking lot.

"Last place," I said. "Thankfully, this went a lot better than last time."

"What happened last time?" Becca asked.

"The tent collapsed and caught on fire while I was still in it," I recounted, watching the train of people for movement of the crates, though I could feel Becca's surprised gaze on me.

"Wow…and I thought Archangel was exciting. You really are a badass, now."

"Yeah," I laughed sarcastically. "Total badass…"

The passing of the crates went quickly, everyone feeling the energy that came with success. It was the first plan that had involved so many people of our revolution and everyone was pleased to have a part.

It gave them something to do besides sit around the bunker and wait for news.

Loading the final crate into the car worried me when there was absolutely no more room.

"I'll carry it on my lap, it's okay," Becca assured when I cursed at the sight.

After she buckled in, I placed the crate on her legs.

Once we got out of the parking lot and on the road, Becca squealed, pumping her fists into the air.

"This is incredible!"

I laughed, the same sense of accomplishment washing over me. I ended up speeding toward the park to unload the car without care. Nothing could touch us.

Thankfully, there were no police on the back roads.

Talking excitedly among themselves, the whole group moved to unload the van, going through the same process, racing against the approaching daybreak.

Becca and I remained where we were, watching the crates move from their spot in the clearing into the trees as people collected boxes one at a time. Clark sat with us, grinning from ear to ear.

"We did it," he said. "Thank you, Becca."

"I just hope it will be enough," she murmured.

"It's more than we had," I said, hugging her. "Seriously, thank you for your help. We couldn't have done it without you."

"You're going to make me cry," she teased, fanning her face. She put an arm around the both of us. "You have to tell me when you're doing more things like this," she hissed. "This was amazing. I have never felt so accomplished in my life!"

We agreed to keep her informed. I was sure that after that night's success she had won a little bit of Mark's trust and, therefore, would be able to participate more as our outside informer.

We only had to wait ten minutes before Mark appeared, Josh and Rin at his side.

Both Rin and Josh hugged everyone, thrilled at our success while Mark smiled, waiting for everyone to calm down before tapping his wrist, reminding us of the time.

"We'll take you home now, Becca," Rin said.

"I'm driving!" Josh declared, running to the driver's door and climbing in. Mark motioned for Rin to take the front seat and sat on the floor of the van with Becca and me. Becca was grinning broadly as the van returned to the road.

"I really want to thank you for letting me be a part of this," she said. "It feels amazing to do something good for people."

"Good for people, but bad for the government," I clarified with a chuckle.

"I told you when we first met, I didn't like the government anyway."

Rin and Josh thanked her for her help and Mark offered his hand for a handshake. She stared at it before looking at me, a question in her eyes.

"He doesn't like hugs," I said, throwing a teasing glare at Mark.

She shook his hand, respecting his space.

We dropped her off just as the sky was beginning to brighten. I apologized for making her so tired for school, but she assured me it was no concern and skipped happily into her house.

Josh drove out of the neighborhood as I turned to Mark.

"Is she trustworthy?" I asked seriously, wanting to know his honest opinion.

He hesitated before nodding slowly, relenting that, for the moment, he trusted her.

* *** *

Our revelry in the success of the raids did not last long.

We had stolen quite a few goods, but only some of the bullets were useful to us, and the medical supplies were almost exactly the same as we had been able to salvage from the medical room. Peter and his team had made it their goal to clean up the medical room, though they were moving relatively slow, being careful not to break anything that could still work.

The one triumph we did have was with food. While it was clear that we had gotten quite a number of rations, when we divided the food among everyone with two meals a day, we had enough for one month, even when the experiments only had one meal.

As a result, we decided to keep the policy of going out in small teams to find food and keep the strain on our resources limited.

It did not ease my worry. I was still concerned and on edge, wondering where else we could possibly get food, knowing that we could not pull the same trick again.

Friday morning, Tori called me into the communication room with a serious face. Worried that something had gone wrong, I quickly followed. She closed the door behind me, and pointed to the television screens, where Clark, Griffin, and Mark were focused.

"...the accident occurred around ten last night, when a man, clearly intoxicated, crashed into another car and then proceeded to get out of the vehicle and scream at the other driver. He proclaimed that he was a member of the Central Angels and that the other driver could not press charges because he would shoot the man," the anchor explained. The video changed to that of a man yelling violently, leaning over the mangled hood of the other car and waving a bottle around.

"This is footage taken by one of the many bystanders who saw the horrible scene with the Molotov cocktail play out."

My heart was in my throat. The man was yelling at the crowd, most of his slurred speech edited of profanities, though it was clear what he was saying.

"I'm a fucking revolutionary! We just attacked five other fucking camps! No one can touch me! Come on, you cock suckers!" He grabbed his shirt and clumsily pulled it over his head, spilling some of the bottle and cursing colorfully as he tried to gain his bearings, stumbling. He shoved his shirt into the neck of the bottle and waved it around.

"What do you think?! You think you can get me?! Just you try, motherfuckers! You go against the Central Angels and we'll fuck you up! You're all nothing but a bunch of pussies, kissing the asses of Central! We're the future!"

He pulled out a lighter, going to the driver's door of the other vehicle, waving the tail of the shirt around as the flames slowly ate at the fabric. The driver ran as the drunken man cackled loudly.

The crowd fled, though there was a sound of an explosion before the clip stopped and the anchor reappeared on the screen.

"The man was arrested and will face charges later today," he concluded. "We will keep you updated as more information is presented to us."

I was livid.

"What the fuck is going on?"

"I don't know what to make of this," Griffin admitted. "So far...they have not released information that we broke into the camps."

"Can you look up his name in the police computers?" I asked.

"I can look into the military computers," he told me. "There might be something there."

"Please do," I said. I turned, walking to the main bunker.

"Lily, where are you going?" Tori asked.

"I'm going to have a talk with everyone."

I walked into the bunker and raised my voice over the people finishing their breakfast.

"Excuse me, everyone," I called. The noise disappeared and everyone turned. "Can we get everyone in here? There is something I want to say before we start today."

It took three minutes to get everyone out of the various rooms and in the main bunker. Tori stood next to me, as did Mark, both of them wearing worried expressions.

When everyone was seated, I took a deep breath.

"I know that, right now, things seem like they're going well, but that does not mean that we can get careless," I told them. "We still need to be very, very careful. So, from now on, the groups going out for food are only allowed three-hour time blocks, and they are to be back by five. There will be no exceptions."

Confused and worried murmuring broke out and objections were raised about the ability to collect food in the daylight when they had had most success at night.

"I know it sounds extreme, but I will not have anyone making a scene right now. We managed to break into five camps, but that does not mean we have won. For now, this is the rule. Do I make myself clear?"

"Tori, Mark," one of the women said. "You can't be okay with this. We won't be able to do anything in three hours in the daylight."

"With the way things are lately, this is the most logical move we can make to keep everyone safe," Tori agreed. "We will find a way to manage."

I went to the communications room, leaving the stunned members of the revolution as they began murmuring among themselves.

"That is a bold move, Lily," Tori whispered. "They're going to start getting scared."

"I don't mind," I said, opening the door, causing Clark and Griffin to turn. "I'd rather they be scared than make a stupid mistake like what happened last night."

"There's no record of his name on the computer," Griffin said. "But we managed to get a still of his face. It's a little blurry, but I don't think he's one of ours." He pointed to the screen on the desk.

"He's not one of ours..." Tori agreed.

With his knowledge of what happened at the camps that meant only one thing. The drunken man was one of Dana's, sent out to make a scene.

Chapter Seventy-Two

I had to take several deep breaths before I walked into the room that I had been avoiding once again. That time, Josh and Mark came with me, which startled Mykail greatly.

"If we remove some of your chains, will you try to run?" I asked pointedly.

"No. I have nowhere to go."

After a few moments of staring to determine if he was telling the truth, I nodded to the other two experiments, who removed the chains around Mykail's ankles and loosened the ones around his wings to allow him more mobility. He let out a relieved sigh and winced as he stretched as much as he was able.

When we had loosened the restraints as much as agreed, I nodded once more to Josh and Mark, who left the room.

Mykail turned his gaze back to me when the door clicked shut. I sat on the floor, looking him over.

"Are you hungry?"

"No," he said. "I'm glad you came to see me, though."

"Please," I whispered, shaking my head. "This is already painful for me."

"Me, too," he agreed. "I know that I can never take back the pain I've put you through…but I still wish there was some way I could help you take down Dana. He's a dangerous enemy."

"I know," I said. "He's infiltrated us, and then he sent some of his men out to make us look like we're violent anarchists."

He bowed his head at the words and I sighed heavily.

"I'm sorry," I said. "I'm angry and worried. Not to mention you kinda deserve that."

"I know." He looked up at me curiously. "Why did you come in here?"

"If I managed to get Mark to give you a second chance, would you be willing to try and win back our trust?"

His eyes widened and his mouth opened and closed a few times before he spoke.

"Yes," he said strongly. "I know you don't trust me, but I swear to you that I will not betray the revolution."

"I trust a little too easily," I murmured. "It's Mark you will have to convince. I will see if I can find a way to give you a second chance."

"Thank you, Lily," he said, trying to sound as sincere as possible. I nodded, studying him to be sure he had no injuries. I did not want him treated roughly, and I had made that clear to the members of the Eight Group guarding the door that no one was allowed in to hurt Mykail.

Satisfied that he had no new wounds, I asked him a question before I could stop myself.

"Is there anything I can do to make this more comfortable for you?" As soon as the words left my mouth, I tried to catch myself. "I mean, is there anything I can get you? A pillow maybe?"

His shocked expression softened.

"No, thank you, Lily."

We sat in awkward silence. Finally unable to handle the strained, quiet air, I stood and brushed off my pant leg absentmindedly.

"I will talk to Mark."

"Thank you, Lily."

I walked out the door, where Mark and Josh were waiting. I turned to Yi Ling, who was standing guard outside the store room.

"Can you get him a pillow to sit on?" I requested. She left as I turned my attention to Josh and Mark.

"What did he say?" Josh asked.

"He said he would be willing to work with us and try to gain back our trust," I said, walking out of the hallway and into the strategy room where Griffin, Tori, and Clark were waiting.

"Well?" Tori pressed as I closed the door. Telling them what Mykail had said, they fell into pensive silence. We had decided that we needed to protest again, and show ourselves to dispel the negative air that had surrounded our cause, thanks to Dana's scheme. But we knew that if we appeared without Mykail, our demonstration would not have the same impact. He was our symbol, and we needed him now more than ever.

"We have no parades to crash this month," Clark muttered.

"Then we make one," I suggested. "We'll just show up on Main Street and protest. If we agree to let Mykail come with us, then we'll let him fly above us as he normally does. We'll make one march down the street and then scatter."

"We're going to have to call attention to the fact that the man with the molotov was not part of us," Griffin said. "We're going to have to find a way to show that he was a set up by the Commission."

"I just hope they'll believe us," Clark grumbled. "The online response to what happened has been clearly against us."

We discussed which day to protest, knowing it had to be soon due to our dwindling supplies and worried revolutionaries, as well as a growing lack of interest from the people.

The second food donation by the Carolina Media Group was much less than the first. The public had been wary of supporting the revolution after the incident with the drunk man that had sent three people to the hospital. The media company said that they were unable to risk giving us further support.

Sunday morning, I asked Mark to take me to the shooting range and let me practice. Even though I was still having nightmares about the shadow falling in the first camp, followed by dreams of Dana and I having our shooting contest, I wanted to handle a gun again, sure that if I mastered it, I would not be so frightened of having to use it.

Mark made sure it was just the two of us in the shooting range as I pulled my gun out of the holster. When we had gone to the first camp, Mark had given me one of the guns he had bought off the black market and said it was mine, but I had only used it twice. Once when I first got it to test it in the shooting range and the other time when I killed the man in the camp.

Knowing the rules of practice, I took the weapon out of the holster, removed the empty magazine, opened the chamber, and showed Mark that the gun was empty before setting the components on the table and backing away two steps.

Mark walked down the range and tied one of the water jugs to each rope at the end of the room.

When he came back to where I stood I had grabbed two sets of headphones and handed one to him.

I picked up the magazine and loaded it with the bullets on the table, then put it back in the gun, drawing in a deep breath and taking my stance, aiming at the first jug. I took a deep breath and gently squeezed the trigger as I exhaled.

A shot fired down the room and landed just below the first target. Aiming again and trying not to shake, I fired, hitting the target. I moved on to the next one, taking my stance, though Mark put his hand on my belly and pushed on my shoulders, reminding me to lean forward.

I missed the target twice before I hit it. When I went to the third target, Mark stood behind me and helped me line up the shot, which allowed me to hit the target the first time. I managed to hit the fourth one on my own.

I went through all six targets before unloading the gun and setting it on the table, lowering my headphones around my neck. Mark smiled and nodded once to tell me I had done a good job. He held up one finger, asking me if I wanted to try again and I nodded, reaching toward the gun again to load more bullets, assuring him that he did not need to replace the targets.

I was in the process of loading the final bullet when the door banged open and caused both of us to jump. Mark reached for his gun, but stopped when he saw Clark at the bottom of the stairs, his eyes wide.

"Clark?"

"You both need to come quick," he gasped. "Something's wrong with Tara."

Leaving the gun and bullets where they were, both Mark and I ran after Clark to the main bunker, where a large group had formed around the shivering fifteen-year-old experiment as she convulsed on the ground.

I pushed through the others to see Peter crouching next to her.

"What's wrong?" I asked, horrified as Tara let out a pained screech, her back arching off the ground.

"It's a result of the testing," he said. "Her brain is firing signals to her muscles to contract, but they're contracting too much."

"How do we help her?" I asked, going into a crouch, trying to ignore the prying eyes around us.

"I don't know," he admitted. "We don't have any muscle relaxants and our painkillers are not going to be strong enough to stop what's happening."

"Will it stop?" Clark asked.

I looked around the crowd and noticed something about the spectators. They were all humans. I caught glimpses of the other experiments, who were in the back, sharing knowing looks with one another.

"Griffin!" He turned to me. "You know what's going on. What do we do?"

"I don't know," he said. "This is what happens with the SID-3. All the experiments go through it."

"The what?" Peter asked, turning around, flinching at the sound of Tara's pained scream.

"The SID-3," Tori repeated, looking sadly over the situation. "It's sort of standard for the experiments of the Commission." I turned to Tara, seeing the veins bulging under her skin as her muscles trembled. "This is the negative side-effect and relapse. It tends to happen with the younger experiments."

"The injections I was giving her were to keep *this* from happening?" Peter asked. The experiments nodded. "Is she going to come out of this?"

"I don't know," Tori whispered.

"What are her chances?" Clark pressed. No one answered.

970

"We need to get her someplace else," I declared. "Is there any place in the medical room where we can move her?"

"No," Peter said dejectedly.

Tara screamed and her body convulsed violently, her head colliding with the wall, splitting the skin. She continued to twist and contort, her voice raw. The other experiments pushed through the group and picked her up, fighting with her convulsions, trying to take her toward the strategy room. Clark and I held the others back, telling them to stay out as we closed the doors, letting only Peter and a few other experiments inside.

"Is there anything we can do?" I asked the experiments as they tried to hold Tara to the table as she screamed in agony. "How long do these last?"

"It depends," Cody said. "I've seen a kid relapse into this and it killed him."

"Killed him?"

"The SID affects the heart, too," Griffin told me. "The heart is a muscle, and when it gets hit with this, it can cause the heart to explode."

"What the fuck?!"

"We don't have any more of the injections I used to give her," Peter choked.

"Just hold her down so we can keep her heart rate down," Tori said, desperately trying to get the convulsing teen to remain still. The other experiments pinned her down, trying to keep her from moving as she let out piercing screams that set my teeth on edge.

Clark and I remained near the door, watching in terror as Tara's body locked in painful spasms, her breathing labored and pained between screams.

Tara's body flailed against the people restraining her and, with a terrible screech, one of her arms broke under the tension of her muscles as she fought against the other experiments.

I felt sick.

"Come on, Lily," Clark said, taking my arm and leading me out, feeling just as ill. We both left, letting the experiments who had been through the same test deal with the horrific situation.

For an hour, the bunker waited in silence, barely able to hear the screams coming from the other room. Everyone was tense and nervous, not sure what to make of the screaming and worried for Tara's safety.

Zane, Cody's brother, sat next to me.

"Hey," he whispered.

"Hey."

"Are you alright?"

971

"I'm worried about Tara," I said. "Does that happen a lot?"

"No. Very few have reactions like that," he said, resting his chin on his knee as he looked distantly into the bunker. "It's like Tori said. Generally, the younger experiments have this kind of relapse several months after the test."

"Do you think she's going to be okay?"

He remained silent.

Finally, silence came over the bunker as the dull screaming from the strategy room stopped. For ten minutes, no one spoke. They remained as they were, throwing glances at one another, wondering if Tara had come out of the spasm, or if she had not survived.

When the door opened, everyone jumped, apprehensive and eager to know what happened.

Griffin stuck his head out of the door and looked at Victor, who was the nearest experiment. He whispered something to the man and Victor stood, walking into the bunk room. I watched Griffin as he searched the crowd for me. When our eyes met, I could feel the sinking in my stomach.

Slowly, he dropped his eyes to the ground and refused to meet my gaze again.

That was when I saw Victor come out of the bunk room carrying a single white sheet.

* *** *

The day that Tara's body was to be buried, I left the fort and went to my old school, Mark close behind. I felt completely out of place approaching the building during school hours, but I needed to get out of the bunker.

Tara's sudden death had shaken everyone, and there was a somber mood around the fort. Feeling responsible for the Eight Group being unable to steal the medicine that the experiments needed, I had a burning desire to get out of the fort, worried I was going to be judged, even blamed, for Tara's death.

I wanted to talk to someone outside of the situation.

When school let out, I hid around the side of the building, Mark close by, both of us hiding within our coats and scarves. I pretended to fiddle with my phone, acting like a normal teenager in case anyone happened to see me. Hiding behind his glasses, Mark was able to keep an eye out for Becca.

When he saw her, he nudged me.

Quickly moving toward her, I cleared my throat, trying to be discreet. She turned around.

"Oh my God," she gasped, surprised. "Hi." She turned to Jill and Taylor, who were looking me over, confused, not immediately recognizing me under all the layers. Becca turned to see their reactions before smiling at them.

"I totally forgot that I have a date already," she laughed. "I'll catch up with you later."

Jill and Taylor turned away, throwing concerned glances at me as I avoided their scrutiny. I guessed with how bloodshot my eyes were from the crying and the sleepless night before, I likely looked extremely suspicious.

"Did something happen?" Becca asked.

"Can we go talk somewhere?"

We ended up by the river, Mark close by, trying to pretend to be part of our conversation.

"One of ours died last night..." I finally muttered.

"What happened?"

"It's what happens when they don't have certain medicine," I said, my gaze distant on my feet. "Most of the experiments are sick in some way."

"Where do you get the medicine? Is there somewhere I can get it?"

"Only in the Commission," I said dejectedly. "But it does make me realize that we have to move fast and get the Commission taken down. We can't help the other experiments otherwise." I had come to the understanding that Tara was not the only one who had been in need of special attention. As Dana had told me before, all the experiments, except for the Eight Group, had something wrong and needed attention. Without the constant supply from the Eight Group, our revolution was in danger of losing our most valuable assets.

"Well...I don't know if it helps any, but I thought of another way for you to get food," Becca said, trying to smile. I looked at her, smiling before I could help myself, tears fresh in my eyes.

"You're really full of ideas that seem to help."

"Well, it just sort of came to me but I figured, why not hunt?"

"Hunt?"

"There are deer in the woods. If you need food, you can hunt them. Do it the way we lived thousands of years ago."

I laughed and shook my head, turning to Mark.

"How did we not think of that?" I asked. He smiled, shrugging one shoulder.

"My dad is a hunter, and he was talking about the next hunt he's going on, which made me think about it," Becca chuckled.

"You're dad's a hunter?"

"Yeah, well, he's friends with Kirk Sterling. You know, from Sterling Firearms?" Becca explained. "He got into hunting through him. Anyway, I don't know about how to help move the revolution along faster."

"Would you be willing to help in a protest?"

"Sure," Becca agreed without hesitation. "When are you thinking of doing something?"

"Thursday morning," I explained. "Everyone's making signs now, but we could always use numbers. There are some people who can't go out and protest, like him." I motioned to Mark, which caused Becca to nod in understanding.

"What about the school?" she asked. "Do you want me to send out some rumors that there will be a protest on Thursday?"

"Do you think anyone would come?" I groaned, rolling my eyes as I thought about the way people had been bashing us on the internet because of the stunt Dana pulled with his drunk man.

"Absolutely," Becca said. "A lot of people our age are still behind the revolution. We all know that you're not trying to become the new government. That was just some drunkard."

I heaved a sigh of relief.

"Thank God some people noticed that that had nothing to do with us," I said with a quiet laugh. "If you think you can get some help, it would be greatly appreciated."

"Of course. I told you, I will do what I can."

* *** *

The day was full of tension. It was not just about the fact that we were going to demonstrate again, even after the last appearance had ended with people dead, but we were unsure about how many people would show up, who would pay attention, or if we would be well-received.

And everyone was still upset over Tara's unexpected death.

Not to mention, everyone was also watching one of the members of our demonstration very closely.

Mykail had been set free of his chains, and I told him that if he tried to run, we would not hesitate to shoot him. He promised that he would not run, and reminded us that he believed in what we were doing and wanted us to succeed. I chose to give him the benefit of the doubt,

974

though I did not say anything when I saw the challenging glare Mark gave to Mykail.

It was a look that said: "Try anything and I will kill you immediately."

The group that was going to be walking down Main Street, backing up traffic to be sure that we got as much attention as we could, got out of the fort at different points, each of them knowing when to scatter and where to go. Most were also concealing guns, just in case we had to defend ourselves, though everyone was ordered not to shoot anyone center-mass.

The gun under my jacket felt heavy and I was constantly focused on it.

When we were gathered at the fountain at the top of Main Street, I saw at least forty people waiting, most being students from my school that I had passed in the hallways not registering their faces but aware of their presence. They were carrying signs and had already gained attention from some on their way to work. Already there were phones taking pictures and videos of us as we gathered.

Realizing how quickly we could get the police, or even the military, called on us, I knew we had to start.

From under the blanket Tori was walking next to, Mykail stepped out on my call and darted away, taking off into the sky with a powerful stroke of his wings, holding the banner he had tied to him, releasing it when he soared over our heads and between the buildings lining Main Street. There were gasps and cries as he started flying, circling to keep pace with us as our group, much larger than I anticipated, began our march.

"Stop the lies! Stop the lies!"

We chanted, holding signs and banners that declared the Commission had lied about making weapons and they lied to create a distraction and turn the people against us. We walked through the stopped cars at a red light, which prompted those within the vehicles to get out and take videos and photos as we passed them, causing more of a traffic jam. We tried to spread across the entire street, also taking up the sidewalks.

I was somewhere near the middle of the group at Mark's request, and watched as some spectators remained where they were, watching with fascination, others with indignation, and even a few with indifferent glances. Some started walking with us, repeating the chant, making our numbers swell.

We continued the long march down Main Street, aiming for Central City Square, where we would protest as long as we could before scattering.

We needed peaceful exposure.

It took thirty minutes for us to go down Main Street. Cars were honking, all for different reasons. The more people that joined, the more empowered I felt, thinking that we were swinging people back on our side. Mykail soared above us, his banner reading: "No More Secrets!"

We managed to get to Central City Square, something that exceeded my expectations.

There, we gathered in a large circle, turning to face city hall and continuing our various chants as news crews filmed our protest. We kept most of the experiments in the middle, also as a means of protection. Mykail circled above us, enthralling many as they got the longest look at him that they had ever been able to.

The spectators of the demonstration were shouting questions, asking us what we wanted in place of the Commission, telling us we were too young to understand, thanking us for standing up against the Commission of the People, and so many other muddled messages that I could not distinguish all of them.

I was starting to get nervous about how long it seemed to be taking law enforcement to appear.

I looked at Mykail and saw him circling higher, watching the streets for the police that would undoubtedly show up.

Things got ugly very fast.

It started when one older man came forward, yelling that the Commission was the best thing that ever happened to the country. He claimed we wanted to tear down the most stable society in the world to put in place something similar to the Washington System. While everyone in our group had been told to remain quiet and not engage anyone outside the demonstration, the students of my school were not under the same constraint, and a few yelled back at him, causing the chanting to weaken and more attention to be paid to the confrontation in the front.

A few who supported the Commission of the People began voicing their opinions alongside the older man. I could not entirely see what was going on from my position, but I could hear the increased yelling as the chanting died down.

Then, there was a great surge forward. People dropped their signs and tried to pull back the students who had rushed to attack those trying to take their signs away. I heard a whistle and saw Mykail pointing up

Second Street before flying away, gaining the attention of a lot of people.

"Now!" I bellowed.

Signs and banners were abandoned as we scattered. Tori and I started in our direction when we heard gunshots. It was impossible to tell where the noises had come from with the way the sound reverberated off the buildings, but the screaming started, and chaos ensued.

Rather than scatter as they should have, many of the revolutionaries pulled out their guns and tried to gather together to defend themselves, causing others behind them to be stuck and confused, rushed forward by others and pulled in disorienting directions, creating more confusion and danger for everyone involved.

The public was trying to find a path to get away from the gun-bearing revolutionaries and the police, who were also trying to maintain order, though some were turning their guns on the people scattering, not sure who was part of the Central Angels and who was an innocent bystander.

A few of the younger teens ran forward and tried to overtake some of the police cars.

I saw bodies drop to the pavement.

Tori grabbed my wrist and pulled, whistling loudly to remind everyone that it was time to retreat. We slipped into the alleys and ran along the shadowed areas, followed by a few others as we tried to get away safely.

It was much bloodier than the last demonstration, and while my stomach twisted at the thought of the dead, there was another part of me that scolded those who had stormed at the cars. It was supposed to be peaceful to avoid the violence that the people were going to associate with us.

Instead, they had managed to turn everything around and get us into trouble again.

I turned when we reached our designated entrance tunnel to see who was following us, relieved to see Becca trying to catch her breath.

"Thank God you're okay," I whispered.

"Lily, we need to go," Tori said, setting the iron cover aside and motioning for others who were living in the fort to climb down the iron rungs into the tunnels below the streets.

"Go," Becca assured. "Call me tomorrow and I will tell you what the news says."

"Thank you, Becca," I said, hugging her before joining everyone else in the dark tunnels.

According to what Becca had heard the following day, the news was reporting forty-seven injured, five in critical condition, and twelve dead.

The people lost while fighting for our cause had officially become statistics.

Chapter Seventy-Three

It was possibly the worst thing that could have happened.

Griffin was trying not to panic when he got me out of bed Tuesday morning, but I could see from the frantic look in his eyes that something was horribly wrong.

"Come quickly," he said.

I scrambled out of bed and walked past the Eight Group standing guard in front of the bunk room, being sure that Mykail—who was sleeping on the opposite end of the room from me—did not try to escape. There were a few people in the main bunker that watched us pass with tired eyes, but most were too sleepy, or thinking too much about the way things had occurred during our demonstration to pay much attention to my hurried pace.

Griffin brought me into the communication room where there was live footage on the news of buildings with plumes of smoke rising into the air. It was around downtown Central, and the commentary over the helicopter's blades was trying not to be frantic.

"What you are seeing now is the helicopter's view of the fires that have broken out as a result of the bombing. Our news crews are steering clear because of the military helicopters that are trying to catch the weapon still flying around the buildings of Central. If you are just tuning in now, this is the result of the winged man that is known as part of the Central Angels group, who was seen flying around downtown early this morning, during rush hour, yelling about avenging his comrades before he dropped several bombs onto the streets."

"Where is Mykail?" I gasped.

"He's *here*..." Tori told me with a dark look.

"Then how—" I stopped abruptly, my eyes going wide as my brain clicked into gear. "That *fucker*..." I growled, grinding my teeth together. I turned to Griffin. "Get Mykail in here."

He left as I moved next to Mark, who had his arms crossed, one hand on his face as he watched the news footage with hard eyes. My eyes were also glued to the screen. I watched the helicopter circle as the anchor continued to babble about what we were seeing, saying that they were waiting for their correspondent on the ground to get to the scene and report on what was happening.

The door opened again and we turned to Mykail, who looked confused and worried.

"What is it?"

"*That*," I snarled, pointing at the screen. "Dana let your brother loose on the city. Everyone thinks it's you."

Mykail's eyes shot wide and he stepped closer, listening to the anchor.

"Chris?" he breathed, scouring the screen for any sign of his older brother. I was so furious I was chewing the insides of my mouth to keep from throwing a tantrum. After the horrific events of the previous Thursday, where we were once again made out to be a violent rebellion hell-bent on bringing down the government, having someone who so closely resembled our symbol attacking the city would surely cause the people to turn against us.

"We just got word from our correspondent Nancy Trakin on the ground. Nancy, can you hear me?"

The camera cut to a young woman with blonde hair and green eyes standing in front of a row of police cars keeping people at a safe distance.

"Yes, I can, John."

"Can you tell us what's going on?"

"Right now, the streets leading into downtown Central have been blocked to allow medical crews and firefighters into the core of the city to tend to the injured and the fires."

"Is there any word yet on the number injured?"

"No, not yet. I have seen dozens of people with injuries being led away for treatment, away from what the police are calling the critical area. It was rush hour and there were a lot of cars that have significantly hindered the access and, with the creature still at large, it is impossible to tell if there will be more attacks today."

"Nancy, stay safe. We will come back to you in a moment. We're going to go back to our helicopter unit," John said, the picture cutting again to the shot of the tops of the buildings of Central. It was possible to see many military helicopters making their way around the city, trying to spot the experiment of the Commission of the People.

"This is really bad..." I murmured over the anchor's continuous babbling.

"It's a really bold move from Dana," Tori said. "He knows that swaying public opinion against us won't be easy, so he willingly put Chris out there." She rubbed her face. "We can try and deny it as much as possible, but it will be hard to prove that he came from the Commission of the People rather than from us."

"Because the Commission can just as easily say that they have stated before they had no knowledge of this technology and, therefore, could not have had another one just like Mykail," Griffin added. "*We would become the liars.*"

I watched as the military helicopters continued around the city, trying very hard to think of how we could smartly counter Dana's move.

"What you are seeing now is live footage, and if you look around the bottom of the shot, you can see the military choppers are quickly turning, which means they have spotted the man flying, and...Terry, can you zoom in to see what they are doing?"

The camera followed the choppers as they pursued a much smaller object flying toward the east side of the city.

"Oh my God, he is heading toward the Leadership District...There is no way to tell if he plans to attack any of the buildings. What you are seeing is the chase of the person, who is known as part of the Central Angels, flying toward the Leadership District, flying very quickly toward Central Hall with the military in pursuit."

Without realizing it, my heart was in my throat, horror gripping me as I watched the other winged experiment soar toward the beautifully constructed Central Hall and Chamber of Regions buildings. He stopped and as the news helicopter tried to follow the action. Before they could get too close, a blast emanated from the side of the Chamber of Regions building.

Everyone in the room gasped, mimicking the reaction of the people in the newsroom.

"Oh my God, he has just attacked the Chamber of Regions. This is a live broadcast. He appeared to throw something at the building and a large explosion just erupted from the Chamber of Regions."

"There is no way he could throw a bomb that powerful..." I breathed.

"You might be surprised..." Griffin said. "There are weapons that the military has with that kind of power. They're heavy as hell, but with him being an experiment, it's entirely possible."

My attention was brought back to the screen as the anchor began talking again.

"The military choppers have surrounded the creature and the gunner on the side has been trying to take aim at him. If you look closely, you can see people running away from the Chamber of Regions below and—oh, God..."

My eyes were wide as well as Chris launched to the helicopter and climbed into the aircraft, pulling the gunner out and throwing him to the ground.

"Oh my God," John gasped off camera. There were gasps all over the news studio as the footage was captured.

Chris climbed into the helicopter and violently pulled the pilot out of his seat, gaining control of the helicopter and tilting the aircraft to the side, tipping the pilot out.

"The creature has just hijacked one of the helicopters, this is something that he has done before if you remember the Rhodes Parade...and he seems to be grabbing something and, what did he just throw at the other heli—oh my God!"

The other helicopter, which had been aiming their gun at the cockpit of the hijacked aircraft, suddenly burst into flame.

"Oh my God...Oh my God..."

The fiery helicopter plummeted to the ground where the people were running from the Chamber of Regions building, which was slowly being engulfed in flame.

The mangled metal smashed into the front fountain of Central Hall's gardens just as Chris turned the other helicopter's nose to the ground. He jumped free three seconds before the second helicopter collided with Central Hall, causing an immense explosion of flame, smoke, and shattered glass.

There was nothing but panic in the studio for several minutes, even as the news helicopter moved the camera to follow the other angel as he flew rapidly away, disappearing after the catastrophe.

Everyone in the Fort Daniels communication room was silent, staring at the carnage in the Leadership District.

We were in a state of disbelief.

"Do we tell the others?" I whispered.

"They're going to hear about it at some point," Tori said. "We better tell them so they don't think we're keeping secrets."

Griffin sighed and stood straight.

"I'll tell them. Mykail, you better come with me," he said, motioning for the younger man to follow.

We did not let anyone else in to watch the news for a long time, eagerly watching for any new developments, but we eventually let them in, knowing that they were just as worried as we were about what the attack meant for the revolution.

Everyone packed into the room to hear the statement of the Commission of the People. I felt a sick ache in the pit of my stomach as the time drew closer for the government to say something about the attack. I was surprised that the Commission was the chosen representative for what the government wanted to say.

I felt even more nauseous when I saw my father step up to the podium.

"Ladies and gentlemen," he started, his face worn, "I have been called upon to come before you and make a statement about the horrors our capital faced today." His gaze dropped to the podium and he shook his head. "The truth is…there are no words to describe the horror of what happened today. For the first time in nearly a century, our country has seen a deliberate, hateful attack on the citizens of this nation. Only this did not come from an outside force…this did not come from other countries who were trying to undermine us…this came from within our own people…within our own family." My father sighed heavily and took a moment before he continued. "I come before you, not representing the Commission of the People, but as a proud American who is horrified at what has happened to our great country. This morning, we were attacked by something that was celebrated as a symbol of revolution, of change, and most importantly, a symbol of a revolution to dismantle the Commission of the People. The group known as Central Angels has given many rationalizations about the reasons they want the Commission of the People to be taken down. So I ask them, now, what is your reason for attacking every government building except the Commission of the People?"

He shook his head.

"There are over one hundred people from the Chamber of Regions that have been taken to the hospital. Almost all of them are in critical condition. I want to be sure that we thank and show our appreciation for the medical teams that rushed to their aid, to the people who came forward to help even in the face of such danger, and to the international community who has called to show their support through this terrifying time. As was shown on live television, Central Hall has been destroyed. Four hundred employees work in Central Hall, and of those four hundred, seventy-seven have been identified as alive. Leader Simon has been taken to the hospital for third degree burns and is in critical condition.

"When we were sure it was safe, I rode with Mr. Dana Christenson to the hospital and I asked him why our building had not been hit. Why? If we were the target of the Central Angels, why did they not attack as they claimed they would? Why did they involve the other branches of government, to which they raised no complaint?" He dropped his gaze again to his hands. "Mr. Christenson holds himself responsible for what happened today. The only reason I am standing here before you and not him is because he is staying at the hospital with Leader Simon to be sure of his health."

I wondered how many of my father's statements were true.

"Ladies and gentlemen, on behalf of the Commission of the People and Dana Christenson, I apologize for the horrors witnessed today. The Commission agreed to let the group known as the Central Angels protest and voice their opinions because we wished to understand their desires and what it was that they were advocating. We wanted to change things peacefully, but in the last week alone, that has proven to be a tactic they do not agree with.

"As I speak, the Commission of the People is working with the Domestic Defense Force, the American Military, and the Central Intelligence Administration to track down the winged man who attacked our city and bring him to justice. Our medical teams and doctors are working without rest to help those who have been devastated by this horrible tragedy. We will not fall to such scare tactics and underhanded attacks on innocent people, nor will we bow to the will of this terrorist group. We will stand strong against them. War is no longer acceptable, it is no longer needed in today's civilized world. And we will not let them make this a war."

The Commission agreed to let people know by the beginning of next week what their course of action would be.

My group, on the other hand, had no idea what our next move even *could* be.

"We can't jump up and deny that it wasn't us," Tori murmured. "There's no proof, and with how tender everyone is now, our statements would be ignored and make us look worse."

"I wonder how much of what my father said is true..." I mumbled. "I don't believe anything he says about Dana, but about the casualties...about the numbers..." I looked around the table in the strategy room. "Do you think it's accurate?"

"Hard to say," Griffin said. "Statistics change quickly."

"What should we do, then?" Clark asked.

"I would say keep a low profile," Griffin said. "We need to keep everything as calm as possible, stay in the shadows, don't make a scene. We can maybe post a video or two telling the people that we did not orchestrate the attack and see what kind of response we get."

"Dana is playing with loaded dice at this point," I growled. "An attack like that, on live television, there's no way the people won't support him."

"We just need to lay low," Tori assured. "We'll figure out the best thing to do if we just clear our heads and bide our time while this calms down."

* *** *

984

People were against us. That was the common sentiment. There were no protests about what happened, but people were flying the flag at half-mast, helping crews clean up the city and giving interviews about how furious they were, saying they always knew that the Central Angels were nothing more than a violent domestic terrorist group and should be eliminated as soon as possible.

Dana had managed to turn the tables so quickly that if we made one careless move, the entire country would likely hunt us down.

From all over the Regions people were voicing their anger at what happened in Central. They were relating it to earlier attacks against America, calling it an act of terror and explaining that it was a step backward rather than a progressive move to the future.

However, a lot of people were also angry at the Commission of the People. They were sick of the back and forth we were having with one another and told the Commission to take decisive action one way or another, wanting the conflict to be over before things escalated even more.

I called Becca on Wednesday. School had remained open, so I had to wait for her to get out of classes before I called her from the bus station payphone.

"Hello?" she answered, her voice strained.

"Hey," I murmured, keeping my voice low even though I was locked in the secure glass of the phone booth.

"You shouldn't be calling me," she gasped. "Do you realize how much the city is in panic? What were you thinking?!"

"It wasn't us!" I snapped. "Listen, it *wasn't* us. There is another experiment like Mykail—his older brother. I swear to you, Dana set him loose and tried to pin the whole thing on us."

There was a heavy silence on the other end of the phone.

"There's another one like Mykail?" she said skeptically.

"Yes," I said. "Do you think anyone would believe us if we told them that?"

"Is it the truth?" she asked. I was offended by the tone in her voice, but chose to ignore it.

"Yes."

"Then why not come out and say it?"

"I just asked you, do you think anyone would believe us?"

She fell silent.

"I don't know," she said. "There has been a lot of heated debate about what happened yesterday. After some of the students were killed last week…it only makes sense that they're getting nervous."

"Things are spiraling out of control..." I admitted dejectedly. I glanced around once more to be sure no one was nearby. "Listen, we're going to raid a convoy bringing food to one of the camps tomorrow night, can you make it?"

"Sorry, no," she said. "I'm grounded after my mother saw me on TV at the protest. And especially after yesterday, Mom's being super protective and keeping me in the house. I better not chance sneaking out in the middle of the night. She's been doing bed checks."

My heart fell, but I understood the parent factor, so I assured her it was alright and then told her I would call her another time.

Our raid had to be very precise. Due to the military involvement that came with the knowledge of our attacks on camps, we were in danger of being found out and apprehended before we could successfully steal.

But we were in need of food and medical supplies and had to risk it. Peter had used most of the salvaged medicine and bandages treating those who had been shot during the protest. There were a few who had also been trampled in the rush to get away and had needed more extensive treatment. Therefore, we needed more medical supplies as well. We knew that food was coming in the transport vehicle, but we were also hoping that there would be medical supplies.

Several of our gunners spent their time in the shooting range, practicing their aim. I also practiced with my own gun, though Mark told me I was not to be anywhere near the raid. I was going to be with him, on a hill, as he acted as a sniper, taking out some of the people in the convoy when we raided.

We lined up on the road leading to the camp three hours before the convoy was to appear. We placed nail strips in the road to blow the tires out, but we were sure to only place a few small ones that would not make it immediately obvious we were attacking.

I stayed with Mark, who was laying on his belly, the large gun in front of him, propped up on some stones we had stacked to hide our location.

I waited impatiently.

The longer I stayed still, the more I thought about what had happened through the week. I had become a ball of nervous energy. I was even surprised at my own feelings toward our revolution. Things were becoming unsteady, but rather than panic, I had to sit back and think very carefully about what I was going to do next. More than anything, I had to admit that I was impressed with the stunt Dana had pulled. While I hated the lives it cost and the horrific image it gave us,

I could not deny that it was a brilliant move to turn things back in his favor.

My job was trying to guess his next move before he made it.

When the trucks were heard rumbling over the dark road outside the camp, I saw many peek out from behind trees, waiting for the cars to hit the nails.

There were three vehicles—two smaller ones at the front and back of the larger truck with the supplies.

The first car spun out of control when it hit the nail beds, which caused the larger one to skid to a halt, not noticing their own tires had been punctured as they tried to slow the big vehicle. The third car did not come in contact with the nails, so I watched Mark carefully take aim at the front tire of the last car.

Everyone was getting out of the halted cars. There were three men in each smaller car and two men in the larger vehicle. I could not hear their conversation, but I watched the driver of the last car move forward to ask what was wrong.

Mark adjusted his shot and I watched with little emotion as he shot one man and then the other.

Carefully, a group of our people moved to the back of the largest truck.

"Now!" a voice bellowed.

The back of the truck flew upward with loud, rhythmic clanking and twenty men jumped from the back, their guns aimed at the revolutionaries.

Immediately, shots rang out in the dark. Mark remained where he was, taking careful aim at the people he could and shooting three before one of them yelled "Sniper!" and caused most of the men to turn their attention into the woods.

Mark grabbed my head and pushed me down behind the rocks, keeping me from seeing who was firing the shots. I could not even bring myself to worry about the wellbeing of the other revolutionaries. My only thought was figuring out how to safely get out of the situation.

Mark peeked over the top of the rocks, motioning for me to follow as he crept carefully along the side of the hill.

I was far too calm to be in my current predicament. It was not a normal response.

"Up there!" a voice shouted. Mark pushed me to the ground and then continued running ahead. The dark worked in my favor, concealing me while their shots were directed at Mark, the bullets buzzing over my head angrily, embedding in trees until they lost sight of their moving target.

I turned to look over my shoulder and saw several bodies on the ground. I could barely make out a burly figure I assumed to be Griffin violently banging one man's head against the side of the truck before dropping him to the ground.

Seeing that the action was calming, I stood and made my way down to the mess.

"Griffin," I whispered.

"Lily, what the hell are you doing down here?!" he snapped. "Others from the camp will be here any second! You need to get out of here!"

"Who's ours?" I asked, determined to drag someone back.

"Lily," a voice called near my feet that I immediately recognized as Cody's. I got behind him and hooked my arms under his, pulling him backward into the darker forest, not bothering to watch where I was going.

As I was pulling him off the road, I spotted a group of people running toward the scuffle from the camp, yelling, some of them stopping to fire shots before advancing again.

Everyone who was able was dragging one of our wounded comrades off the road, desperate to retreat. I struggled to pull Cody over the uneven surface of the forest ground and soon had bullets soaring my direction.

Thankfully, someone jumped in front of me, returning shots at the two people pursuing me before grabbing Cody's other arm and pulling him further into the trees.

"Keep going, keep going..." Josh said over and over again as we retreated, trying to keep from tripping over roots and other shrouded obstacles.

Finally unable to hear the sounds of the confrontation, I collapsed against a fallen tree, my legs shaking, breathing hard, unable to walk further. Josh was also trying to catch his breath.

"Are you alright?" he whispered.

"Yeah," I said. "Cody? Cody, where are you hurt?"

"My leg."

It was impossible to see with the canopy of the trees keeping the moon's rays from reaching the ground. I tried in vain to see something familiar in our surroundings, not sure where we were or how we were going to get back to the fort.

"Josh, do you know where we are?"

"No," he said. He took a deep breath and then grabbed Cody's arm, pulling the younger experiment onto his back. "But we can't stop moving. Someone must be around."

Forcing my legs to move, I followed Josh into the woods, not sure if we would find anyone in the impenetrable black.

I thought over the events. It should have jumped out at me that there were so few people protecting the truck considering the recent raids. It should have been obvious that we needed to stay away from this particular convoy and try to break into the camp instead, where we would have had more time to plan and see what we were up against in advance. And yet, I pushed to go after the convoy anyway.

Even upon reflection, I felt numb to the situation.

The statistics were taking over my brain. I needed to find a way to sustain my numbers safely while devising a way to counter Dana. It had been my turn to move a piece onto the board, and I had chosen poorly.

Chapter Seventy-Four

It took three hours wandering in the dark before Josh and I finally found someone else from our revolution. A few experiments had been sent to find people still lost in the woods. Candice was very thankful to find her brother, though she was terrified about his injuries. As we walked, Josh still carrying Cody on his back, I asked her how many were hurt. She told me that two were dead, and eleven came away with minor injuries. Three were in more serious condition.

I was not sure which category Cody was going to fall into.

My mind remained numb as I turned over the cruel irony of our attempt to get medical supplies ending with more of our people injured.

Dana was making moves to eliminate us. It was not possible for us to trust anyone or any event as being safe. The realization made my mind spin. I had always known that Dana had enough force waiting in the wings to tear us apart, but I really did not think that he would use that against us. It was hard to explain my reasoning, but I knew that he felt it would be cheating.

Thinking about our encounter in the park, remembering how Mark shot Dana in the leg, thus allowing our escape, I started to understand that Dana was still playing the game, still dancing, allowing the public to think that this was a war between a domestic terrorist group and the Commission of the People. Even I was pretty sure it was no longer that type of war.

Instead, it was seeing who could wait out more, seeing if we could hold out with our limited supplies while the Commission tried to keep the people from turning against either side too quickly and tearing the nation asunder.

I needed one decisive move on my side to swing the people back to me, and Dana only needed one well-placed act to turn us into public enemy number one.

Something had to give. Soon.

The fort was a mess. With the medical room out of commission, Peter and his team were treating everyone in the main bunker on sheets on the floor. There were two bodies that had been wrapped in makeshift shrouds and moved to the side, though no one was paying attention to them, focused entirely on the wounded. There were at least three people around each of the injured, taking instructions from Peter or Griffin as they worked hastily on those most in need of help.

Josh brought Cody to another group of people who spread a sheet over the ground for him. I watched the bloody chaos with little emotion, still wrapped in thoughts about how we were going to counter Dana.

This was a key moment in our revolution. To step carelessly again would mean the end of all of us.

For some reason, the thought that we could all be killed and that I would be brought into the Commission as an experiment did not seem realistic. It was a looming threat over my head, a dark thought that I pushed away and ignored because I did not want to see how close it had become. Even as I looked around the bunker, there was only the concern of how we were going to be effective as fighters with so many injured and so few supplies.

I glanced around the bunker to find Josh, seeing him with Mark, both of them looking over the others who were running at Peter's or Griffin's command to get more alcohol, or more sheets for incoming wounded, or to wrap wounds. A few were on a drip being held by one person near their heads as they cringed and cried out in pain during their treatment.

I thought back to Tara as she convulsed on the table, the way she fought so hard against her own pain that her arm broke, the way she screamed...Her pain sounded like the combined pain of all the people lying on the floor of Fort Daniels.

I weaved through the injured, observing how badly most were hurt. There were a few with bullets that had been close to vital organs, but only one had a wound that could quickly become fatal. Two had broken bones. Five had multiple gunshot wounds.

But no shots had been made center-mass. As I started to realize this, I began to understand that Dana did not have the intention of destroying us quickly. He wanted to make us destroy ourselves, strain our supplies, and force us into desperate action. That way, when we did fall, he would regain some of the people in the Commission.

I had to leave.

I went into the bunk room where a few of the younger humans who could not handle the carnage were also hiding. I sat heavily on one of the beds and ran my hands through my knotted hair, trying to get my brain into gear.

Not long after I had disappeared, Josh joined me, sitting on the bunk and looking me over. I stared at the floor, unable to make eye contact.

"Are you going to be okay?" he whispered.

I nodded slowly though I did not entirely understand what he meant by the question.

"Lily...listen," Josh said. "This is part of what happens. We're lucky we got away with as many as we did."

"We weren't lucky," I hissed. "Dana is playing us. He's trying to starve us out. It was my stupid idea to steal from the truck. Now we've got injured with no medical help."

"We're managing," he said gently. "We'll lay low for a while."

"Oh, Josh..." I groaned, putting my hands around my nose and mouth as I heaved a sigh. "I just can't think right now."

"Don't think, then," he murmured, putting an arm around my shoulders and rubbing my arm comfortingly. "You don't have to think. Feel whatever you're feeling. This is not a time to be rational."

"I have to be rational," I said. "If I get hysterical, so will everyone else."

"Do we need to go back to the store room?" Josh asked with a smile. I barked a quiet laugh, but shook my head, turning to him pleadingly.

"But will you sit with me for a while?"

"Of course," he whispered, pulling me over to rest my head on his shoulder as I continued to take deep, measured breaths.

* *** *

Josh had been right. We came away relatively unscathed from the incident Thursday night. The two that had been dead when brought to the fort were the only two we lost. We had one person who was still in need of constant care, even two days later, but she was alive.

Only three experiments had been hurt, which was a blessing in many ways, since they were the strongest fighters. The experiments who had been injured walked away with minor wounds and were able to help the wounded humans by the next day.

Griffin was working with Peter on treatments while Tori worked with Clark, Josh, Mark, and me to discuss our course of action.

Mykail, no longer trusted by the main strategy group, was unable to stay with us, and since most of the revolutionaries did not trust him either, he remained away from both groups, trying to help with the distribution of meals.

Clark and Tori were talking about other ways to get supplies, mostly medical and ammo, since we were dangerously low on both. The ammunition had gone quickly with the constant target practice and the two instances where handguns had been used. We had some assault rifles, but carrying those around in our type of warfare was impractical, so we had little use for them.

I was not interested in doing another raid. I was looking over at Josh and Mark, who were sitting quietly at the strategy table, both pensive.

It was obvious that they understood what I had realized about Dana's intentions. I could see it written on their faces. Mark looked at me for a moment, our eyes conversing the concern we shared in the five seconds we held eye contact.

Josh and I went for a walk in the dark along the river. Mark wanted to join me when I insisted I was going out, but Josh told him to get some sleep and that he would accompany me in his stead. Mark was hesitant, but agreed.

It was nice to have Josh with me, since we could have a conversation if we wanted, whereas Mark would get flustered when he could not articulate what he wanted to say.

However, the walk did not need conversation for the first stretch along the river. I crossed a bridge that I had always liked looking at, but had never been on. It arched over the growing spring waters, and the red paint was more chipped up close than I had noticed from far away.

I stopped at the top of the arched bridge and looked over the river, watching it bubble over the rocks as it moved between the banks, swelling every day from the melting snow as the middle of April brought warmer weather.

"Do you ever think about how spring is seen as the season where good things happen?" I murmured before I could stop myself. Josh, who had been leaning on the bridge beside me, turned to face me. "But the weather is the most turbulent in the spring, it seems like…"

Josh sighed and looked at the river as well.

"Change isn't easy," he told me, his voice quiet, deeper than I had ever heard it before.

"What if I'm the one changing?"

"What do you mean?"

"Do you think we can actually win against Dana?" I asked, my voice tight. "He turned everyone against us so easily…"

"I wouldn't say it was easy," he said. "To change the people's thoughts he had to crash a helicopter into a building. He had to kill a lot of people…"

I closed my eyes, bowing my head against the recollection of the number dead from the attack.

"You know, I still think about the pain on the table," he told me, running his thumbnail over the chipping paint of the bridge, refusing to meet my gaze. "I remember watching Hyunwoo being tortured…and in those moments…I thought we would die. It's been years and I still think about it. When someone as powerful as Dana does something good, it's seen as expected and then quickly passed over. But when someone as powerful as Dana does something horrible, people remember. People become afraid." He shook his head. "You can't expect people to always do the right thing," he said. "Survival is no longer man versus nature, as it was where Hyunwoo and I lived. Survival is now man versus man...and that brings a lot of bad out of people." He smiled at me gently. "What you are doing is trying to change things with good, and it's a lot easier to destroy good with evil than for evil to be destroyed by good. Don't give up. Eventually, it will happen."

I looked at Josh's gentle smile and felt a ball rise in my throat. I sniffed and swallowed it down, nodding as I averted my eyes to my feet.

Josh stepped closer, putting an arm around my shoulders.

"It's okay to doubt yourself," he assured, hugging me. "It's okay to be scared. But do you believe in taking down the Commission?"

I nodded, closing my eyes against the tears.

"Then that's all that matters."

Once again, I leaned my head on his shoulder.

We stayed in the cold for an indeterminable amount of time. I decided that I needed to try one more avenue to get supplies. With our symbol now associated with terror and death, we were in danger of being lynched if we were spotted. While I had no intention of demonstrating in the near future, I felt that it was important to have the means to defend ourselves.

So, going to another outside payphone, I called Becca.

"Hello?"

"Hey, it's me again."

"Oh, hi," Becca said, nervous. "Is everything alright?"

"Not really..." I admitted. "Listen, I could really use some help. You said your father was friends with Kirk Sterling?"

"Yeah."

"Would it be possible for us to get ammunition from him? We can pay," I added. She was silent before taking a deep breath.

"Well, Kirk is really conservative, and I doubt he supports the revolution..." she told me slowly. "Maybe his son, though..."

"His son?"

"Yeah, Greg," Becca elaborated. "We're kinda friends...my father keeps trying to set me up with him. You know how well that will work." I could not help but chuckle. "Tell you what, I'll send him a text and meet him for coffee tomorrow. Maybe I can get an idea of how he feels and we can arrange for you to meet him and discuss a deal."

"Could you do that for me?" I said, relieved.

"Of course," Becca said, a smile in her voice. "Can you meet me tomorrow? Maybe at the cinema on Lincoln?"

"Sure, what time?"

* *** *

Becca ran to me and Mark excitedly as we waited outside the theater. I still had a scarf on and a hat that was supposed to hide my face, but it was getting warmer. The weather had reported there would be a cold snap starting Sunday, but I had to pretend that day that I was not dying of heat under my layers already.

Becca looked like she had good news.

She told us that Greg was willing to meet us the following day in the industrial area close to their manufacturing warehouse. She assured me she would be there, too, and had told Greg that we were just suppliers for the revolution, not the main branch, and we were looking for ammunition. She had told him that we did not have any in order to make it sound like we were peaceful and that we had never fired a gun at anyone during our protest.

I thanked her and agreed to meet her the following day. Even though Mark had his eyes covered with sunglasses, I could see the tension through his entire body as he watched us plan the meeting.

Our designated meeting place was extremely close to one of the fort exits. For the sake of safety, and to be sure that we were not going to be followed, Mark wanted to take a small group of people.

He was extremely ill at ease for the rest of the night.

The following morning Mark was so on edge that it made my heart pound hard enough to make it difficult to breathe. The entire group of five was nervous, feeding off the tense energy of the leader of the Eight Group. All of us were looking around the old, dry sewer pipe, scanning for danger, even though we knew we were safely hidden. I blamed the sudden cold snap for the foreboding feeling.

I spotted the metal engraving near the next ladder that said "14th Street" and told Mark we had arrived. He hesitated, looking at the ladder as though contemplating whether or not to ascend. I could not understand why he was so nervous. I turned to Josh, who was standing in front of Paula and Dan, also looking anxiously at the ladder.

"Why are you two so nervous?" I asked Josh before turning to Mark, trying to hide my own anxiety.

"A feeling…" Josh muttered. "Do you have your gun?"

I tapped the holster under my jacket. Josh reached for his own gun and pulled it out, checking the magazine and the number of bullets. Seeing this, everyone did the same. While it was a smart idea to check our weapons regardless, it made me even more nervous.

"Do you think we should have brought more people?" I whispered.

"No." Paula shook her head. "We don't want to scare him off. It's just…with everything that's been going on…it's good to be cautious."

I knew what she meant. Griffin and Tori wanted to be the ones who accompanied Mark, Josh, and me to the meeting with Greg Sterling, but I wanted our two most powerful experiments to stay safely hidden, just in case we were followed back. I also wanted Mark to stay behind, but since it would be his money we were using to pay for the bullets, I did not feel right telling him not to join us.

Mark replaced his gun and started up the ladder, climbing to the top while the rest of us remained behind, watching him reach the cover and force it open. He pushed it to the side and scanned the surroundings. When he climbed out, I knew it was safe.

Josh went up first and I followed, Paula and Dan directly behind me. We came up in an alleyway full of dumpsters near the industrial edge of town. There was the sound of the nearby freeway and large trucks around the immense buildings, the backing sirens echoing off the buildings as the drivers worked on the loading docks. It was not an area I was used to. The unfamiliar territory frightened me a little.

There were no windows on the walls that faced the alleyway, which eased my mind that no one had seen us appear from the old sewer line.

Replacing the cover, Mark looked around again. All of us were scanning the area, wondering which way we were supposed to go, trying to find any indication of the Sterling Firearms building.

Mark walked further into the alleyway, away from the road, and we fell into position behind him, quiet, our eyes sharp, looking for danger.

Mark moved closer to the building on the southern end of the alley and pressed his back to the wall. Worried he had seen or heard something, we ducked to a similar position, waiting for him to signal an order, tense and acting on reflex. Mark was still for a few moments before he motioned us to wait. I watched nervously as he inched along the wall to the corner, my breath caught in my throat, feeling more anxious than I thought necessary for the situation. I tried to chalk the anxiety up to the memory of what happened at the failed raid earlier in the week.

Mark reached a hand into his jacket and kept it on his gun before he peered around the corner.

"Mark?" a voice called. I relaxed. Becca was there.

Mark stepped out and his hand dropped from his gun. I started to move closer, but Josh caught my arm. I glanced at him, confused and a little annoyed at the paranoia. Josh did not seem worried, but he was waiting for Mark to signal us closer.

"Where is everyone else?" Becca asked. "Is everything okay? Did something happen?" She sounded worried. Mark shook his head and then nodded his head in Becca's direction. "Oh, this is Greg Sterling, Kirk Sterling's son."

"It's nice to meet you, Mark," Greg's unfamiliar voice sounded around the corner. "I heard that you can't speak, so I'm wondering why you came here alone."

Mark was still for a moment, and then turned to us, dropping his head once in a nod. Josh released my arm and I stepped forward, walking around the side of the building and glancing at the people in the alley. Becca was standing next to a man in his late twenties, dressed in a suit though his tie was missing. No one else was there.

Becca smiled when she saw me.

"Lily, you scared me. I thought something had happened."

"No, I'm fine." I was still nervous. I told myself that if I was not wary, considering my situation, I was an idiot. I still glanced around behind her, noting that there were two windows on the buildings behind Becca and Greg, but they were dark and the door next to the windows was padlocked from the outside. There were two corners where people could be hiding out of our field of vision, but I chose not to consider the possibility.

Josh walked to Mark's side, both standing just slightly in front of me, shielding me. Becca looked at them and watched as Paula and Dan took their spots behind me. She let out a broken chuckle.

"Wow, quite the security detail you have..." she noted, looking at me skeptically.

"It's nothing," I said. "We just have to be careful."

"She's right," Greg agreed. "With everything that happened earlier in the week, it makes sense that they're traveling in groups." He turned to me. "Lily, right? I am Greg Sterling from Sterling Firearms. I heard that you were inquiring about some ammunition for your revolution leaders."

"Yes," I said. "But before we talk about anything like that, I want to know why you would even want to sell us ammunition."

"Simple," Greg said. "I am pissed that the Commission of the People has been taking people and making them into weapons." He looked at the four people around me. "All of these people have been taken into the Commission and tortured. The Commission assured us that everything they did with the people they obtained was humane and fair, but seeing the parade in January made me realize that they had been lying this whole time. We're going back to the days of Washington, and I hate it."

"And as for what happened earlier in the week?"

"Well, the Commission did a good job of pointing out that their building was not hit. I realized that if they had been attacked, it's likely we would have seen some of the other evidence of their testing surface. But they weren't attacked. If they were making weapons, of course they would also be able to have someone with wings. They probably ordered the attack to frame you."

I listened to him speak, trying to gauge if he was serious. I knew Becca would bring us someone interested in helping us, but I also had to be careful. With the failure of the raid, I felt compelled to be extremely vigilant.

And there was something about the man that was bothering me...

After he finished speaking, I remained quiet. He started to look nervous. Something was wrong.

"Let's get out of here," Dan hissed, also sensing something amiss.

"Not yet," Josh snapped quietly over his shoulder.

"Lily, what's wrong?" Becca asked.

Suddenly, I realized the problem. They had made no moves to approach us. We were speaking to one another as if we were in a standoff, over four meters apart. Even Becca, who had more or less earned the trust of Mark, was staying back, not going through her normal greeting of hugging me.

"Did you bring anyone else with you?" Paula called.

"No." Becca let out a nervous laugh. "Come on, guys, what's going on? Why are you so on-edge?"

Mark reached for his gun, Josh as well, and Becca gasped, turning and running down the alley, Greg in tow.

"Where are they?" Paula asked, grabbing her gun. My hand slipped into my jacket and rested on the handle of the gun, looking for what had spooked Mark.

"Shit! Go!"

Three men darted out from around a corner, but I did not get a good look at them, thrown off-balance by Mark shoving me backward, into Dan, who yanked me behind the wall in the direction we had come, Paula following.

Disoriented, I did not notice who fired the first shot, but a few shots after the first, I saw one of the men fall to the ground. I did not get a good look at him before I was pushed against the wall, listening to the commands of the people who had been lying in wait.

"Don't move!"

"Shit! They're getting away!"

"*Fuck!*"

There was pain in my arm, hot and sharp. I cringed, my hand going to my shoulder. A bullet had grazed me. I pressed my palm to the wound and took a deep breath, trying not to let the others know I was hurt, which was not difficult, since Paula and Dan were watching Josh and Mark.

Josh was pressed against the corner of the same wall I was against, peering around the corner and rapidly firing shots in short bursts before ducking back. Mark was across the intersecting alley, also pressed against the corner of a building for protection.

"We have to go!" Paula declared. She ran to the iron cover with Dan and both of them tried to lift it, though it would not budge, even with their combined strength.

I heard a shout of pain after Mark fired one shot and dared to inch closer to Josh, who was glancing around the corner, holding his gun ready, ducking back when a few bullets chipped the corner of the wall.

Josh cursed in his own language, opening the magazine and replacing the empty one with a new one. There were a few shots as Josh reloaded, to which Mark retaliated. I looked over Josh's serious expression. He was breathing hard through his nose, trying to concentrate.

"Josh, how many?"

"Six. One dead, two down," he answered. He took a deep breath and focused on Mark. Making a quick motion with his hand, Mark motioned for Josh to cover him as he went across the alley. Josh nodded and spared a quick glance around the corner. Gunshots sounded and the wall chipped away further. One shot came from Mark and then he ran across the alley as Josh stepped out from his corner and shot three times, firing his third bullet as Mark reached us. Josh did not move from his position after he stopped firing, which told me the other three were dead.

Mark stepped behind Josh and glanced over his shoulder at the people in the alley. I resisted the urge to go forward and see them for myself. I watched with Paula and Dan as Josh started to lower his gun.

"Okay," he said, turning, "let's—"

Josh's body jolted as several rounds of gunshots echoed through the alley. My heart stopped and my mind went white.

Mark stepped out from behind Josh and shot one bullet into the alleyway before grabbing Josh's shoulders and pulling him behind the wall. I rushed to Josh with Dan and Paula to assess the damage.

Mark's eyes were quick over his friend before he shook his head and pointed at the cover Paula and Dan had tried to lift.

"We can't lift it."

Mark darted to the drain cover and lifted it as I looked over Josh. The other experiment had slid down the wall, one hand around his stomach and the other hand still gripping loosely at his gun as he breathed heavily through clenched teeth, his body shuddering. I glanced down, seeing that his right thigh had a bleeding wound and there was blood pouring through his fingers as he gripped his stomach. There was another bullet lodged in his left shoulder, but even I could see that wound was not severe. The one in his abdomen worried me most.

Mark's hand was suddenly on my shoulder, pulling me upright and pointing to the drain.

"Lily, go!" Dan said, following as I ran toward the ladder. I glanced briefly back at Josh before I started down into the dark tunnel.

"Wait right at the bottom," Dan instructed.

I hurried down the iron rungs, my hands shaking with fear and my brain blank except for one frightened thought.

Is it fatal?

I reached the bottom and glanced up to see Dan close behind, but he had stopped on the ladder, looking up at Paula, who was also positioned just above him. At the top, Mark was carefully lowering Josh. Paula hooked an arm around his chest and under his shoulders, guiding his feet to Dan, who used one hand to wrap around the experiment and guide him the final way down the ladder.

My hands hooked under Josh's arms, finally getting his feet to touch the cement, though he let out a shout of pain before his teeth clenched and the labored breathing began pulsing out of him again.

Carefully guiding him backward, I helped Josh sit, holding the back of his head as I set him down. He let out another shout of pain that echoed through the tunnel hauntingly, though it was covered by the sound of Mark replacing the drain cover as he descended the ladder. Dan and Paula crouched next to Josh with me. Paula removed Josh's glasses, which allowed us to see the agonized expression on his face. His breath rushed through his teeth, his eyes tightly closed. Dan wrapped his fingers gingerly around the hand Josh was pressing to his stomach. As Dan pulled the hand away, Josh let out another cry of pain and his body convulsed.

Blood was pumping out of two holes, staining the white shirt.

Mark crouched by Josh's side and looked at the wounds, unbuttoning Josh's jacket.

That was when I saw the third bullet hole, lower and further to the side. He had been hit five times—three times in the abdomen.

Mark started to unbutton the shirt, but when he pulled the fabric, grazing it over the wounds, Josh let out another startled yelp and his body jerked, his other hand starting to reach for the wound. I caught the second hand, holding it as his fingers enclosed around my hand, tightening in a punishing grip.

"We have to get him back to the fort," Paula said.

"It's a forty minute walk…" Dan muttered.

Mark, who had also removed his glasses, looked at us with a purposeful gaze and nodded, taking Josh's hand from Dan and leaning forward, pulling the arm around the back of his neck before picking up Josh as gingerly as he could. The other experiment still let out a pained cry, turning his head toward Mark and pushing his face into the jacket, trying to hide his cries of pain as Mark straightened.

"We need something to press to those wounds in his stomach," Paula said.

Frightened that Josh was dying, I pulled off my jacket and handed it to her. She shook her head.

"Not absorbent."

I pulled my shirt over my head, balling it in my hands and walking to Mark and Josh. I wrapped my fingers around the hand that Josh, once again, had against his wounds. He muttered something, pained and pleading, before he let out a quieter shout of pain that escalated into a louder cry as I pressed the fabric of my shirt to his abdomen, placing his hand over it.

"Hold this there," I said. "Hold it tight."

His fingers curled into the fabric and I backed away, taking my jacket from Paula, slipping it on over my shoulders, the cold, slick lining making me shiver. Everyone was staring at me.

"What?"

"You're hurt…" Dan said.

"I'm fine." I had truly forgotten about my wound. "It's just a graze. Let's go."

Mark turned as soon as I said I was fine. I fell into step behind him, Paula and Dan covering our backs with their guns drawn.

I should have been thinking about how Becca had betrayed us. I should have wondered why she had done so when she had been so willing to help before. And I should have been wondering why there were so few people there to capture us, but all I could focus on was the labored breaths that were pushing past Josh's grinding teeth. I felt my heart skip a beat at the breaths that would shudder out of him with a whimper of pain that was only audible because I was so focused on him. I watched his hand grip at Mark's shoulder, fisting the fabric tightly as Mark walked as carefully as he could, trying not to jar Josh.

I had never felt so helpless.

There were tears in my eyes that I forced away, hating hearing the intense pain Josh was in and the way it made him breathe so irregularly. I continuously recalled Josh's body jolting when the bullets tore into him. Like all the experiments, Josh's tolerance for the pain was exceptionally high. Yet, there he was, in such immense pain he could not move other than to grip pitifully at Mark's shoulder.

What should have taken forty minutes took only thirty as we rushed to the fort, frantic.

As we turned the final bend that would take us to the main bunker, I darted ahead to look at Josh.

My stomach flipped over. His breathing was still very labored and pained, but his face was much paler and there was a sheen of sweat on his skin. His body was shaking violently and his fingers were clawing at Mark's shoulder and the fabric pressing to the wounds in his stomach. My shirt was saturated in dark crimson and some of the blood was dripping down Josh's wrist into his sleeve.

I ran and opened the door to the fort, holding it open for Mark and the others before sprinting ahead again and forcing the big door open for the main bunker.

"We need help!" I screamed hoarsely. The people in the main bunker leapt to attention, worried, and several others came out of the nearby rooms and hallways, watching Mark walk in with Josh.

There was a collective gasp when they saw Josh. Tori and Griffin ran forward with Clark close behind.

"When was he shot?" Griffin asked.

"About thirty minutes ago," Dan answered.

"We need water and alcohol!" Tori called. "Someone find the scalpels in the medical room! And someone get Peter!"

"Someone get a sheet!" Griffin ordered.

Almost as he finished the sentence, someone ran out with one of the sheets, laying it on the ground. I did not think it was possible to regret the mishap with the dynamite in the medical room more until that moment.

"Set him down, Mark…" Griffin whispered.

Mark lowered himself to his knees, which caused Josh to let out a yelp of pain when Mark's knees hit the ground, jarring his body. Tori and Griffin helped guide Josh out of Mark's arms and onto the sheet, though he cringed and cried out in pain, his hands clawing at Mark and the fabric against his belly.

Griffin grabbed Josh's hand and tried to pry it loose from the fabric, but Josh let out another agonized shout and yelled something. Mark claimed his flailing hand and held it tight as he steadied one shoulder to the ground. Hiroki and Rin ran forward and tried to steady Josh as he winced, grinding his teeth together, his eyes tightly shut, trying to move away from the hands and causing his pain to spiral higher.

Minsoo appeared at my side, looking over Josh, his eyes filled with fear and tears. He grabbed Josh's legs, pinning them as Josh let out a sob of pain, murmuring something I did not understand.

I watched as Griffin finally got the shirt away from Josh's skin.

"Here are some scalpels and alcohol," Jeanie said, running forward and setting them at Griffin's side.

"Where the hell is Peter?" Tori asked.

"Can someone get some scissors?" Griffin asked. Another person scurried away.

I looked over Josh's pale and pained expression as he tried to move away from the hands holding him. Mark's hand held his tightly. His eyes were locked on Josh, worried and filled with more fear than I had ever seen before.

As the man came hurrying back with scissors, Tori looked at those restraining Josh, holding her hand out for the scissors.

"Hold him still."

Even I tried to assist in holding him down as Tori cut away the shirt from Josh's body, revealing the gaping, angry wounds.

"This one hit his stomach," Griffin whispered. "This one is inside his intestine." He looked over Josh. "The other wounds can wait. His stomach might have ruptured…"

"What does that mean?" I asked.

"He was shot thirty minutes ago?" Griffin asked.

"About," I confirmed.

Josh murmured something, his body shivering violently. Everyone from the Eight Group turned to look at him quickly.

"What did he say?" Griffin asked. Rin shook her head, not knowing, but Hiroki, Minsoo, and Mark all shared a look with one another before turning to look at Ichiro and Keiko, whose eyes were wide and filled with tears.

"What did he say?!" Griffin repeated angrily.

"I'm here!" Peter called, running forward and falling to his knees next to Josh. He looked over the wounds as Griffin poured alcohol on the med-student's hands. Peter rubbed the alcohol over his skin as his eyes scanned the bleeding holes.

"When was he shot?"

"About thirty minutes ago."

Peter reached to the wound in Josh's side, further away from the two he had been trying to cover.

"That's in the large intestine," Peter deduced. He looked at the other two bullets and his gaze darkened. "Fuck..." he whispered. "Okay, get into the medical room and find anything you can. There must be some morphine shots that made it through. We can't treat him like this. We need to get him calmed down, maybe even put him under."

"We would need facilitated breathing..." Griffin said.

"See if you can find a mask!" Peter called to the people who were darting into the medical room.

Peter gently touched the edge of the wound. Josh's reaction was violent. His body bowed and his cry of pain echoed hauntingly around the bunker as everyone tried to steady him.

"...it's in his stomach..." Peter whispered under his breath.

"Is it..." Griffin didn't complete his thought. I looked between the two, frightened by the silence.

Josh murmured the same thing again and Mark bowed his head, closing his eyes. Josh's other close friends turned away. Minsoo lifted a hand to his face, swallowing hard as the tears gathered in his eyes.

"What did he say?" Peter asked.

Mark shook his head sharply.

Peter carefully pressed his hand to Josh's stomach again, causing the experiment to shout in pain once more, sobbing breaths heaving out of him. Peter backed away, startled and worried.

"We don't have a lot of time..." he hissed. He grabbed one of the scalpels and Tori poured alcohol over it. "Griffin, are your hands clean?"

"Yes."

"Good," Peter said. "I'm going to try and make an incision. Tori, hold him down as hard as you can."

1004

Tori moved to push on his chest though Josh let out a small choked sob and his eyes snapped shut.

"Hold on, Josh..." Tori whispered. "Please...hold on..."

Peter touched the scalpel to the skin below the highest bullet wound, cutting into the flesh and causing another river of blood to run down Josh's side. The experiment on the ground grit his teeth and turned his head away, breathing heavily through his grinding teeth. I heard the sound of rubble being moved from the direction of the medical room.

After an incision had been made, Peter placed the scalpel on the sheet, dipping his fingers into the wound to the last knuckle. Josh's cry of agony pierced my ears and his body convulsed violently. We tried to hold him down, but his altered strength had us struggling to keep him still.

Peter's hand slipped out of the incision as Josh writhed in pain on the sheet.

"Putting him under is the only way we're going to keep him still enough..." Peter muttered.

"What's the word on a mask?!" Griffin called.

"Can't find one!!"

"Can we do manual CPR?" Tori asked.

"With his wounds, that will do more harm than good."

My stomach was tying itself into knots with my lungs and made me a frightened mess. I glanced around, seeing that everyone was crowding around us. The bunker was quite empty with people out gathering food, but there were still far too many eyes on the situation. I felt claustrophobic, enclosed, angry at them for just standing there and watching Josh suffer.

Peter reached out once again and put one hand on the other side of Josh's abdomen, resting the other one just inside the area that had been shot, pushing lightly with his fingers. Josh let out a gurgled cry of pain and his eyes clenched tightly shut. Peter backed away, his gaze locked on Josh as the experiment fought tiredly against the hands holding him down.

Griffin looked at Peter and then they both turned to Mark. I watched the exchanged glances and felt the impending darkness settle over the group.

Slowly, Peter dropped his head and rocked back on his heels, standing and backing away. I watched, mortified, as Tori and Griffin also backed away. Rin moved away and Hiroki removed his hand from Josh's shoulder, sitting back on his heels and bowing his head. Minsoo released Josh's legs and sat silently, his hand over his nose and mouth as the tears began to fall down his face.

"No…" I choked. I glared at Peter, storming to him. "*No!* You do not just give up on him!"

"Lily—"

"*Help* him!!"

"There's nothing I can do…" Peter whispered. I couldn't hear the pain in his voice.

"Bullshit!"

"Lily," Griffin said, his hands on my shoulders, "it's too late. We can't save him…"

"You can't just let him die!" I cried, the tears choking me. Griffin held me close, though I tried to fight him. "No! Help him! He can't just die!!"

"There's nothing we can do…" he repeated quietly, his own voice choked.

I turned to Josh. I was completely helpless, watching him die in agony in front of me. I took a step forward, but Griffin's arms were around me again, holding me back as my eyes blurred from tears. The pain tore my body in half.

Mark took a deep breath, watching Josh cringe and breathe in labored pants as he held his hand. He was the only one still holding on to Josh.

Carefully, he reached down and pulled Josh toward him. Even though Josh let out a pained shout and his body was wracked with a violent shudder, his hands went to Mark's jacket, clawing at the cloth as Mark held him close, hugging him to his chest and bowing his head over him. Josh whispered something through chattering teeth. Mark's eyes closed and he cringed as though the words physically struck him.

Josh shuddered and his breathing started to sound choked, even as he murmured the same word over and over again against Mark's jacket.

Holding his head carefully, Mark held his dying friend, his eyes starting to well with tears, though none broke free. Josh's trembling hands moved down Mark's jacket and grabbed at his torso desperately. Mark flinched away from the touch and tried to grab Josh's hand as it went inside his jacket. Violently, Mark ripped away the gun Josh had grabbed and threw it angrily aside before his hand went back around Josh's head, holding him close, a few tears escaping.

My heart shattered into a thousand pieces.

Several people turned away, crying, unable to witness the death as it slowly happened. Josh was breathing hard, pain clear across his features. Every time his body shuddered, he let out a pained noise that made me realize how horribly he was suffering.

The tears blurred my vision, but I watched Mark hold his dying friend, his head bent.

It was twenty-three minutes later when Josh's labored breath stopped hitching in his throat and the shuddering of his body slowed from constant, to sporadic, to non-existent. His hands that had been grabbing Mark, anchoring him to the living, slowly relaxed and slipped from their position, limp, falling at his sides.

Mark curled forward, feeling the life leave his friend. The tears fell from his eyes, but his face did not contort in pain. He was trying to hold his composure, and even though his jaw remained clenched tight against the sobs and cries, his eyes showed more pain than should ever exist for one person.

Long after Josh had stilled, Mark still held him close.

Chapter Seventy-Five

Watching earth being moved by three shovels was the only thing I could focus on that dark day.

I glanced down at the sheet-wrapped body next to me, imagining the pale face underneath, my heart constricting as the pain ripped through me again.

Hiroki placed a hand on my shoulder, trying to comfort me. I smiled meekly at him before turning back to watch three shovels moving dirt and rocks away. I followed the spade of one shovel upward and saw the concentrating face of Mark as he focused on moving each shovel-full of dirt, like it was the most important task he had ever undertaken.

"I can't believe this happened..." I murmured.

Clark placed a hand on my other shoulder.

"Mark's handling it a lot better than I expected," I said. I heard a scoff next to me and turned to Hiroki, who was also watching his friend dig.

"If you think he's handling it," he glanced at me out of the corner of his eye, "then you really don't know him at all."

I turned back to Mark, worried by the intensity etched in his features as he widened the hole where Josh was to be buried. I wanted to ask Hiroki what to do to help Mark. I wanted to ask how to help him handle the death, but with the way Mark's close friends were watching him, it was clear that no one knew.

The Eight Group surrounded the widening grave. Griffin and Tori were helping Mark dig, but they would stop occasionally and throw glances at us, their gazes finally settling on Mark.

He was concentrating too intently to notice the audience.

Mark never stopped digging, jumping in and digging further down. He was joined shortly by Tori, but she eventually climbed back out.

"I can't stand to see him like this..." she choked, shaking her head, her hand over her nose and mouth as the tears welled in her eyes. My own eyes started to burn. I hugged Tori, who hugged me back, both of us letting tears fall as we embraced.

The overcast sky made the air colder, threatening rain, and fit the mood of the burial.

Tori and I stood with the Eight Group members, Clark next to me, trying to keep himself from crying again. I was trying to avoid looking at the covered body. There was a large part of me that felt guilty, thinking about the other stupid move I had made by contacting Becca, by not noticing something was wrong much earlier and getting away before it had a chance to take the life of such a dear friend.

However, in that moment, standing at Josh's unmarked grave, I could only recall my times with Josh, remembering when I first met him and he and Mark joking with one another. I remembered imagining how Josh had comforted Mark, and how he had always been the support for the strong leader of the Eight Group who helped so many others.

I remembered Josh standing outside my house, worried about my immature grudge against Mark, and the way he slipped on the ice on the way to the car. I thought about how he celebrated in the bunker, singing and dancing. I remembered the little times when he would talk with others of the Eight Group, smiling and laughing, always the loudest one. I thought about the way we danced together to the inappropriate radio music, both enjoying something so simple.

I thought about the recent times. I replayed the day he and Mark killed the Commission team to protect me and Clark...the way his expression had changed, serious and focused on his task...

Just like Mark, digging Josh's grave.

I thought about the store room, the way he had held me as I broke down, telling me that it was alright...sitting with me in the bunk room, his arm around my shoulders...

And the bridge.

I remembered his words on the bridge. His smile and his distant eyes that could see something better in the future.

I wished he would put his arm around my shoulders again and hug me, telling me that as long as I believed in what I was doing, everything was going to be alright.

Instead, he was lying on the ground, covered in the bed sheet he had died on while his best friend dug an unmarked grave among the many trees of the dense forest.

No one would know he was there. No one would be able to find his grave easily after today. There would be no one coming to pay their respects, no one bringing him flowers and telling him how much they missed him. He would fade into nature, unknown to everyone except us.

"It's not fair to put him in an unmarked grave..." I murmured.

No one turned to me, their eyes focused on the diggers as they moved the dirt to the growing piles.

"He should be buried with the same honors as a soldier," Clark agreed.

"Why do you suppose military graves are still marked with a cross?" I asked, my eyes focused on Mark working diligently. "Religion is banned...why would the military still use a cross?"

"Tradition," Tori said. "And maybe...with how gruesomely those men and women die, one still wants to cling to the hope that there is something better after death. That there is some higher power that is watching over them..."

"Even though they're no longer fighting for God?" I pressed.

"I think that it's not about the purpose anymore," Clark said. "Whether they were fighting for God or not, God is seen as the creator...the all-powerful and all-knowing." Clark cleared his throat. "We want to believe that He sees something better about the death of those who die for some greater cause."

Mark continued to move dirt rhythmically, like he was possessed. Despite the sweat that broke over his face from the work, he continued to dig. Griffin was working much slower, glancing at Mark before each shovel full of dirt to be sure that Mark was not about to hurt himself.

"And yet, Josh won't have a cross..." I whispered. "Does that mean God won't see him?"

"He sees him," Tori said, her voice breaking. "He has to..."

There was no more conversation while the final depth of the grave was carved out of the cold earth. Mark continued to dig until we could no longer see him, and Griffin's head disappeared not long after. The dirt was thrown out of the hole, and with the speed of each jut of earth, we could tell whose shovel had thrown the dirt.

Griffin's voice could be heard in the pit.

"Mark...that's enough."

Both shovels came out of the hole and Griffin climbed out, turning to help the other experiment, but Mark remained in the grave. Griffin stared into the pit and then nodded. He walked to the body in the stained sheet, carefully picking Josh up while we watched. He brought the body to the edge of the grave and lowered Josh's limp shoulders into the pit.

As Mark grabbed him, the rest of the body disappeared.

A few minutes later, Mark climbed out of the grave and turned to look inside. His shoulders were tense, his head low, and I could feel him desperately trying to keep his composure.

He lowered himself to his knees and pressed his hands to the ground in front of him, lowering his head to touch his hands as he bowed in front of the grave. A few members of the Eight Group lowered their heads. Minsoo's tears were streaming down his face. Hiroki took a deep breath and let it out shakily, the tears starting to fall down his cheeks.

When Mark straightened, he sat back on his heels and lifted one hand to his face, trying to hold the tears at bay. He stood and walked to the pile of dirt, grabbing a fistful and gently tossing it into the grave.

He folded his hands in front of him and stepped back, his head bowed, allowing the rest of us to come forward and bid farewell.

Rin went to the grave next, bowing at the waist before grabbing a handful of dirt. She held it in her hand, clenching the earth as she swallowed back her tears.

"You always had a way of making me smile, even when I really didn't want to," she said, her voice breaking as the tears began to flow. "Thank you, Woobin..." She tossed the dirt into the grave and stepped back, allowing everyone else to come forward and say their goodbyes. Some said silent prayers at his grave, a few others thanked him quietly, some only bowed, but everyone was crying.

Griffin said a silent prayer before throwing his handful of dirt into the grave. Tori thanked him for being who he was, for caring and loving so openly, and that she hoped to be at least half as loving of a person as he had been.

Clark could not say anything, but he bowed his head in silent prayer.

I was the last one to move.

I had been terrified to approach the grave, to see the sheet-covered body in the pit and realize it was about to be swallowed up. I slid my heavy feet forward.

Sniffing and blinking some of the tears out of my eyes, I grabbed some of the cool, soft dirt in the pile before turning to Josh.

The sheet was littered with spots where the dirt had fallen on him, his body turned on his side as though he was sleeping, tangled in the sheets of his bed. I could only hold the cold dirt in my hand, feeling it clump in my fist as I stared blankly.

I lowered myself to my knees, sitting back on my heels and sniffing as my tears fell.

I'm sorry...I said silently.

There was nothing else I could say. I remained on my knees, repeating the phrase in my head over and over again as I stared at the body. But finally, I released the dirt in my hand.

Pulling myself onto unsteady feet, I backed away from the grave.

Mark bent to grab a shovel. Griffin also moved forward, as did Tori, but Mark turned to them, placing the spade of his shovel on the other two and looking at the two experiments coldly. They stopped, staring at Mark before the leader of the Eight Group finally moved the blade off the other two shovels and began filling in the grave on his own.

Tori and Griffin backed away.

Many members of the Eight Group left the site, leaving Mark to fill in the grave as he wished, away from prying eyes. Clark turned to me and took my hand.

"Come on."

"No, I want to stay." I forced myself to smile thinly. "Go on, I'll be okay. I just…I want to sit here with him a little while."

Tori hugged me tightly. Griffin also wrapped his strong arms around my shoulders and held me.

But they left, throwing occasional glances at the two of us as they started back to the fort.

I sat on the ground, watching Mark take each shovel full of dirt and carefully drop it into the grave. I had no right to be there, not after everything that the two had endured together and the way Josh's life had ended. I knew I was witnessing Mark's painful goodbye to his best friend, but I could not bring myself to leave. There was something that made me stay.

As the grave was filled in, I found myself praying.

It took an hour for Mark to fill in the grave again. When he was finished, he gently smoothed over the dirt, bringing twigs and leaves over the fresh dirt in an attempt to hide the unsettled earth. He placed one larger rock over the top of the grave, and finally backed away, studying his work. That was when I stood.

I walked to the other two shovels, picking them up as I looked at Mark. His eyes were dark, filled with pain that no words could express, tears gathered around his bottom eyelashes.

Tenderly, I took the shovel from his hand. He let me remove it, his hand falling limply to his side as he continued to stare at the rock, the only marker that he could have made over his friend's grave.

I watched as, once again, Mark lowered himself to his knees and pressed his forehead to his hands, remaining there for several long moments. Some of his tears fell into the earth, absorbed into the grave.

When he stood again, he looked like he was barely clinging to his sanity.

"Mark…" I murmured, gently taking his hand. He did not move, even as my hand wrapped around his. I was sure that if he stayed at the grave, he would snap, so I tried to gently take him away from the painful place.

I gingerly pulled on his hand and he turned, following my lead as I walked with the shovels under my other arm, trying to keep the tears out of my eyes as I held onto his hand.

His eyes were focused low on the ground, his feet shuffling over the earth.

I stopped when his hand slipped from mine. Quickly turning, I spotted him pressing his forehead to the bark of a tree, his eyes closed tightly. I swallowed hard, not sure what to do.

He turned to look at his friend's grave again, the tears still welling in his eyes.

Mark reached into his pocket and sniffed once, pulling out his pocketknife and flicking it open. I was about to tell him not to do whatever he was thinking, but he turned the blade and lifted it to the tree, gently carving something in the bark, his eyes focused intently on the task.

I stepped over and looked at what he was carving.

There was a small cross in the tree, just in sight of the grave.

When he had the pocketknife stowed again, I took his hand once more, taking him back to the fort, both of us desperately trying to hold our composure as we left Josh to rest.

Once we were back in the fort, Tori walked forward to take the shovels. Mark started to walk further into the bunker, his hand leaving mine, his head down. Griffin saw him moving and walked up to him.

"Hey, Mark," he started, putting a hand on his shoulder to stop him, "why don't you—"

Mark violently jerked away from Griffin's hand, glaring at the taller experiment before moving toward the hall of the shooting range. Everyone watched him disappear, not wanting to disturb him but worried about leaving him alone.

Griffin sighed and then his brow creased in confusion. He glanced at his hand and his eyes went wide. I saw his palm and fingers covered in a line of dark red liquid.

"He's hurt..." Griffin muttered. "He must have gotten shot as well."

My eyes went wide as I began to panic.

"Don't worry, Lily," Tori said, spotting my expression. "If it was really a problem, he would not have been able to dig. Let's just leave him alone for now. I'll get a few medical supplies for him. We should just leave him alone, though. Let him grieve."

Everyone in the fort obeyed.

Tori gave alcohol, gauze, and tape to Mark, telling us that he was in the small recreation room, which no one ever used anyway.

1013

The entire fort was deep in mourning. Josh's death was much harder than Tara's, which only few had actually witnessed. It was harder to handle than the injuries received on our failed raid. His death was different. It felt like the entire mood of Fort Daniels had changed. Everyone was uneasy, anxious, and frightened.

I went to Eun, who had been trying not to cry out of respect for her older brother's mourning. I sat next to her as she sat against the wall of the bunker. She turned to me, her face looking much younger than she could have been and streaked with tears. I hugged her tightly, both of us crying together, not worried about the other eyes in the room.

Eun cried herself into exhaustion and Hiroki carried her into one of the bunk rooms. I had a horrible headache and felt the fatigue down to my bones, but my thoughts were too wound up to sleep. I sighed, rubbing my temples and trying to calm my mind.

Before I noticed him coming over, Mykail was at my side, sitting next to me.

"I'm so sorry..." he whispered, taking my hand. I sniffed and nodded before letting myself place my head on his shoulder, allowing myself to take comfort in him.

I looked at his hand holding mine as his thumb stroked my rough skin. Everything about me had changed. My skin was cracked and dry, my hair tangled and often pulled back because it was too difficult to tame. My health had obviously diminished as my diet had turned to the rations. I no longer cared about my appearance, too focused on the internal conflict I was constantly facing.

But I still thought our hands looked good together.

Several hours later, when everyone was getting their evening rations, their heads down and shoulders slumped, I slipped away, opening the door to the small rec room and peering inside.

No one went into that room because of the dissolving couches and bad lighting. Other than the couches, there was one table to the side of the room with a few chairs around it, but the light above the table had never worked. Mark was sitting at that table, ignoring the flickering of the faulty light behind him, his back facing me as he carefully pulled the sleeve of his shirt back over his newly-bandaged shoulder.

I closed the door, knowing that he heard me because the screech of the hinges set my teeth on edge. I approached hesitantly, looking on the table in front of Mark to see the scissors and tape, one more sheet of folded gauze on the table sitting next to the almost-empty bottle of whiskey used to sterilize after we ran out of sterilizing alcohol from the medical room.

It was obvious from the look on Mark's face that most of the alcohol had been ingested rather than used for medicinal purposes.

"Mark..." I started. "I won't bother you for long, but..." I carefully pulled on the knotted brown string around my wrist, removing the bracelet with the coin and holding it out to him. "I thought...I think you should have this."

He turned his head, looking at the bracelet that Josh had given me for my birthday, but he did not take it. I placed it on the table in front of him, allowing me to get a better look at his state. He appeared to be shut off, numbed by the alcohol and the pain of his loss.

"Please...let me know if I can do anything to help you..."

I turned to leave, sure he wanted to be alone, when his hand darted out, locking around my wrist. He was looking ahead, his eyes lost in the grain of the wooden table, but his hand was firm, asking me to stay.

I grabbed the chair next to him and sat, my back facing the table. His hand released my arm when I was seated. I studied the fabric on the back of the worn out couch, trying to see if I could make any patterns as the light flickered above, sparing short glances at Mark and pretending not to notice when he pushed a stray tear off his cheek.

* *** *

There was one matter of business I had to deal with that I could not tell anyone about. Mark, being drunk as he was, did not notice when I slipped out of the fort. Many of the others were asleep as I crept into the tunnel that led to the exit near the park, where we had successfully unloaded all the raided supplies on the night Becca had helped us. I glared at the parking lot for no particular reason as I started the long walk into town.

There was a feeling bubbling in my stomach that I could not put to words. It was a hot ball of lava that I had never felt before, rupturing the sides of my stomach to permeate into my bloodstream, down to the marrow of my bones, gripping every part of my being tighter than a vice.

I had never felt such intensity before. It consumed me to the point where I went into a hypnosis, walking along the sidewalks without noticing the cold or the landmarks that passed. I turned on instinct, weaving through the pathways of the city that I had come to know in the past months while my brain took turns in opposing directions, coiling the spring tighter, straining everything it could before I snapped.

I walked up the well-lit steps of the tall post office building and to the glass-surrounded phone that stood outside, the decrepit phonebook hanging from the chain at the bottom, graffiti of two wings painted on the left side with a sticker for Club Archangel on the other.

Picking up the receiver, I cradled it against my shoulder, fishing in my coat for the coins I had brought.

The phone rang seven times before the voicemail message sounded, the robotic voice of the woman infuriating me. I slapped the tongue of the cradle and inserted coins again, dialing the same number with angry fingers, grinding my teeth as I heard the shrill pattern of the ring.

Once again, seven times I endured the sound before the same voice told me I was being ignored.

But I was persistent, once again dialing the number, refusing to give up.

The fourth call yielded results.

Two rings and the phone clicked. There was a heavy silence for four seconds.

"Hello?" a familiar voice whispered, tired, weary, but obviously not from sleep.

"Why?"

It was a simple word, but apparently it stumped Becca, because she remained deathly silent for what felt like eternity.

"I…"

"You what?"

"I'm sorry."

"You're *sorry*?" I snarled, hot tears of anger rising to my eyes as the spring snapped inside me. "You're fucking sorry? That's what you have to tell me?"

"Lily…there's nothing else I can say."

"No, don't give me that bullshit. You can say a hell of a lot more. I asked you a simple question. *Why*?" I growled. "Josh is *dead* because of you."

There was a thick silence that followed the words. Saying that he was dead out loud was like admitting defeat to the universe, acknowledging that one of my dearest friends had been taken away.

"…no one was supposed to die…"

"What the fuck did you think would happen?!" I snapped. "I told you what would happen if the Commission caught us, and you brought them right to us! I trusted you! Mark trusted you! Why? *Why*?!" I demanded, the tears falling down my face. I did not care how weak and pathetic my voice sounded.

Becca's voice was just as wobbly when she answered.

"I had to…"

"You had to?" I gawked. "Well, guess what? I had to watch Josh die...I saw the life leave him. I watched people who knew him from childhood, people who loved him, bury him in an unmarked grave, and after all that pain we had to endure...you...you have the audacity to justify it by saying you just had to..."

"Look, the Commission knows about me," she said sharply, her voice nasal from the tears that had overtaken her. "They told me that I wouldn't be taken in if I helped them in apprehending you."

"What the *fuck*, Becca?!" I practically sobbed. "I have that threat over my head every goddamn day...that was when you should have called me, told me what was going on, and run to us for help. We could have—"

"I don't believe in what you're doing anymore, Lily," she growled around her tears. "You're attacking buildings, killing people to try and scare them...How can I stand behind that?"

"That was not Mykail!" I gasped. "I told you that!"

"I don't believe that it was his brother..."

I pressed my head to the cold side of the acrylic around the phone booth, the tears forming hot rivers over my face.

"I will never forgive you for this..." I snarled. "You and the Commission deserve each other, you heartless bitch!"

I slammed the receiver down, ignoring the change that clinked in the tray, and stormed away from the phone, wanting to scream though I refrained.

I walked along the river, past the couples enjoying the end of the weekend as the night grew darker. I ignored them, watching my feet enter and leave my field of vision as I walked, hypnotizing myself with the rhythm.

I looked up when I knew I was getting close and spotted the lonely bridge just ahead of me, arched over the river with its chipped red paint and painful memories. I approached the bridge slowly, stepping up the slope to the peak, where I stopped and looked over the rushing river below, leaning on the rail, entertaining with no serious devotion the question of how cold the water would feel.

I bent my head forward and was overtaken. Another spring had snapped, this one slicing open the part of my chest that I had tried to pull back together the previous day as I watched Mark wrap his friend in the shroud. I let out a pathetic moan and curled forward, pressing my head to the beam under the main railing as I crouched, trying to keep my body from splitting in half.

I turned around and sat against the same pole, bringing my knees into my chest and hugging them, dropping my head, the sounds of my crying covered by the roaring of the river.

* *** *

I had caught a chill and felt extremely sick when I woke from my forty-minute sleep. I had been lectured by Griffin when I got back to the fort. I pretended to listen, but when he stopped talking, I looked at him and asked a simple question.

"Did Mark notice I was gone?"

His silence was all the answer I needed. He did not scold me any further.

I carried my blanket around with me the following morning, trying not to look too much like death, but after glancing at myself in the showers I realized I looked a few shades worse than death.

I was not the only one, but the only person who looked worse than me was Mark.

Everyone fell silent when he emerged from the rec room he had made his bedroom the previous night to drink away his pain. He trudged across the bunker, head low, eyes bloodshot and face pale, toward the bathrooms. I watched him, surprised to see him so undone.

When he came out of the showers, he looked slightly better— about on par with how I looked once I was cleaned up.

Cody, sitting with his siblings and two other experiments, turned to him as he was walking toward the cases of water we always kept near the door of the strategy room.

"Mark," he called. The experiment stopped and turned, his shoulders slumped, his entire frame looking twenty years older. "The Commission is holding a press conference tonight to talk about their course of action. Do you have an idea of what we should do next?"

I understood Cody's effort to focus Mark on something else.

He stooped and picked up a bottle of water before shaking his head and walking away.

The action made me queasy.

Chapter Seventy-Six

"Ladies and gentlemen, thank you for joining us tonight," my father said over the live broadcast of the press conference. "People of America, I know you have been patiently awaiting this broadcast and I would like to thank everyone on behalf of the Commission of the People and Dana Christenson for being so understanding about the time taken to deliberate a course of action."

He looked down at the papers in front of him. Everyone watching in the communications room remained on edge, their gazes glued to the screen. I spared a glance at the others in the back of the room. Tori was leaning against Griffin, her arms looped around his, both looking torn and unsettled. Mykail was watching the broadcast with angry interest, just like Clark.

Mark was leaning against the doorframe at the very back of the group, his entire demeanor dark.

"Lately, there have been cries from the American people to stop the violence and find a peaceful compromise. The Central Angel group has spoken out against the Commission of the People, and while this group has been labeled a domestic terrorist sect, we at the Commission of the People remember the incredible support their demonstrations had from the American people.

"It is understood that the Commission of the People is an organization that has always been surrounded with controversy, even in times of peace. The population praised the Commission of the People during the restoration after the Second Revolution, and then became just as concerned about the power the Commission exhibits even today.

"Therefore, I would like to come to the American public today and explain that the Commission has never had plans to take over the country, and we have strict rules and regulations that are strongly enforced by Leader Simon and the Chamber of Regions, as well as the international leaders who were concerned about America becoming a totalitarian power. The claim that the Commission was researching the alteration of human performance in battle is not unfounded. I have been asked to tell you the truth today, and then make a very important announcement that will drastically change the power of the Commission of the People," my father continued, taking a deep breath before he pressed on.

"As was stated over a month ago, the Commission of the People did, in fact, have some research relating to altering the strengths of the human body in an attempt to help our soldiers, should they ever be needed for international conflict as happened two decades ago. This research was in the preliminary stage, and Leader Simon was meeting with the Regulators of the Regions to decide if it was a course that we wanted to pursue. After the research was approved about a year ago, Leader Simon took the idea to the international community, asking the other countries of the world for permission to peacefully carry out these tests, without fear of creating another nuclear race that would lead to a standoff across the globe.

"It would appear that the Central Angels terrorist group gained access to the preliminary information and created the abomination that destroyed Central Hall and the Chamber of Regions last week, costing hundreds of good American citizens their lives and reminding us of the terror that our country has seen in the past. This creature, and the others within the group, must be stopped at all costs to avoid such horrible tragedies in our future.

"But violence cannot solve violence," my father said. "And the American people have spoken, begging both the Commission of the People and the Central Angels to stand down and come together to discuss a peaceful treaty. The people of America came to fear the Commission of the People with the information that the Central Angels presented. Then, they became afraid of the Central Angels when they attacked our capital so violently. It is abundantly clear that the two groups cannot continue this war at the cost of the lives of Americans. The first step must be taken to resolve this conflict.

"This leads me to my announcement," my father said, looking at the press members before him. "Leader Simon is believed to be well enough to leave the hospital in the morning. Mr. Dana Christenson, who has been by his side through his recovery, has made a decision that will be monumental within the Commission of the People. Due to the horrific attack, he has decided that he is no longer fit to run the Commission and feels that he shares some of the responsibility for the attack on Central."

Try all of the responsibility... I growled to myself, grinding my teeth together.

"Therefore, Thursday, Dana Christenson will publicly resign his title as head of the Commission of the People."

That caused shock in the press as well as in the communications room of the fort. There was mumbling that rumbled through the speakers and around the room as the revolutionaries mused among themselves how true the statement was.

I looked at the people to my right, my eyes wide. They shook their heads, not believing the announcement.

Mark was staring silently at the screen as my father began speaking again.

"This will be the first time that the head of the Commission of the People will show his face publicly. He wishes to address the American people and apologize for the wrongs that the Commission of the People has been perceived guilty of and then he will resign his title. He will also plead to the Central Angels to come to the negotiation table peacefully, which will be his last act as head of the Commission of the People. Leader Simon will then decide our next leader of the Commission."

The press conference opened up to questions, but no one was interested in those, since they were asking why Dana had kept himself hidden for so long and if it would mean the end of the Commission of the People to have him resign.

I looked at Griffin.

"He has to be lying..."

"I agree," Griffin said. "I honestly don't know what to think about this move. I would have never guessed he would pull a stunt like this."

"But...no one outside of the Commission of the People has even seen Dana," Clark pointed out. "Dana will probably just put someone else out there to make a resignation and no one besides the Commission will know the difference."

"Except for us," Mykail added. "Why would he do that when he knows that all the experiments of the Commission have seen his real face?"

"How would we be able to prove it's *not* him?" I challenged. "We couldn't. We would be stuck."

"He says that the Commission wants to come to a compromise," Tori said, looking at the screen, her brow creased in thought. "Does that strike anyone as odd?"

"Not really." I shook my head. "It's a pretense. He'll just take us captive once he has us out in the open."

"It would have to be a very elaborate pretense," she said. "Think about it. If he pleads with us to come to a treaty with the Commission, then we're expected to follow that. If he tries to take us, then he violates the truce he decided to put in action. By making this statement, the people of America are expecting to see us make the truce. Our faces have been all over the news and the internet. The people know what *we* look like. How can he pull this off when he knows we're not willing to negotiate with him because we're sure that he'll use a decoy instead of himself?"

"Maybe that's the plan," Griffin mused. "He knows we won't negotiate, because he knows that we'll figure out he's lying. So we won't come to a truce, and he can keep the Commission in the clear. We'll be the villains."

"So, what? You want to go and try to reason with him knowing that he's just going to kill us?" Mykail asked.

"No," Griffin said, turning to us with an expression of realization. "That's just it. He has us in check. We can't move in either direction. We're stuck."

I sighed and rubbed my face, closing my eyes and trying to think.

I had to admit, it was yet another brilliant move on Dana's part.

"What do you think, Mark?" Griffin asked, turning to the silent experiment. Mark looked around at us, still leaning against the door frame before he sighed and turned away, disappearing.

"Damn it…" Griffin muttered, trying to figure out how to get Mark to participate in the revolution again. Mark had not even had a day to start grieving the loss of Josh before he was called upon to plan. I understood he was still in pain, but things were getting worse for us, and it was imperative that we had his strategic mind to help.

I left as well, going to the showers for the second time that day. There were two shower rooms, one for men and one for women because there was no privacy once inside the room. No one else was in the cold, tiled space, everyone fixated on what was going on with the press conference, starting to feel the pressure from the Commission of the People.

I stripped down, shivering as my bare feet moved over the tile and walked to the corner stall, stepping between the two half-walls and turning on the water. Usually, everyone was timed in the showers because of the limited hot water, but I decided to ignore that rule. I turned the water to hot, almost scalding, flinching when it hit my skin, but I welcomed the pain.

We had been backed into a corner.

Dana had manipulated everything so carefully that we had been forced into a corner without having to do anything. Our demonstrations only got violent when the people outside the revolution got out of hand. Then our very image was turned upside down. Mykail, our symbol, was now called the 'creature' instead of the angel…the 'abomination,' as my dad had stated for the press.

The only thing that could convince people otherwise was if we were able to storm the Commission of the People with cameras and reveal the true horrors. But now that Central had been attacked and so many were dead, the people were no longer supporting us. The few loyal followers we had were looking at us skeptically, not sure who to believe and hoping to see both sides come to a truce. Even someone I thought could be trusted had turned against us because of the attack on Central, and that was the reason I had spent the previous day watching Mark dig a grave.

But it was too late to act. Any action now would be perceived as violent. If we stormed the Commission after the announcement had come that the Commission of the People wanted to reach a truce, then we would be the violent party and we would lose what little support we still had. But going to the negotiation table peacefully screamed for a trap. Dana was far too cunning. There was something more, something else had to be in the shadows that would seal our fate.

There was a chance that if we didn't meet with the more-than-likely-fake Dana and remained completely silent in our fort, we could fade into obscurity and people would eventually forget about us, thinking we had gotten scared and disbanded. However, we had no supplies to sustain ourselves, and without Mark's connections and cunning, we would be unable to get necessities. There was no way money could buy the serums the experiments needed to survive. Mykail's wings were starting to bleed again. Maddy, who had a secondary spongy skin that could absorb liquid, was having problems with her outer skin starting to peel off. Sydney, who had a poisonous secretion from her skin triggered by higher adrenaline levels, had to remain completely covered at all times, including her face, because her lack of sleep was causing her adrenaline levels to run too high.

Almost all the experiments were having some trouble or another and we were in danger of harming the humans if the experiments got sick or accidentally attacked someone.

A realization came to me that made me pause and blink, ignoring the water running into my eyes.

Dana wanted me to go to him. There was some reason he wanted to acquire me and put me in his collection. I wondered if there was a way for me to use that to my advantage.

If I gave myself up to Dana, would he be willing to leave everything at that? If I agreed to give myself to him completely, would he let the others of the revolution go? Could that be the terms of our negotiation?

Would he even consider it?

The problem I faced was negotiating with him and actually having leverage. There would be nothing that would force him to listen to my terms. He had me in a corner and there was nothing I had to offer him other than myself, which he could easily take on his own. There was a chance that Mark would be able to put a gun to his head and make him pay attention, but with Mark's current mental state, I did not think it was safe to put him up against Dana Christenson.

Not only that, I doubted that Mark would let me try to negotiate with Dana, anyway.

Dana Christenson had the upper hand once again.

It made me wonder if there was ever a time that he had *not* had the upper hand.

* *** *

Thursday rolled around, and I knew I was not the only one holding my breath. It felt like the entire country was holding its collective breath, watching the mundane public broadcast program before the news. Every now and then, a commercial break would remind everyone of the coming announcement from the leader of the Commission of the People, showing live cameras at the curb, waiting for the car to pull up and show Dana Christenson—real or fake—walking to give his announcement, which had been moved to an outdoor amphitheater to keep more distance between the press and the head of the Commission.

There had been little change in the apprehension felt throughout Fort Daniels. I, along with the rest of the core strategy group, was feeling the pressure. If Dana really did call us to the negotiation table, we were going to have to think very carefully through our extremely limited options of survival.

And Mark was still deep in mourning, if the bottles he had been consuming over the past few days were any indication. He was unable to contribute to the strategy meetings.

Twenty minutes before the scheduled time of the announcement from Dana Christenson, the news ceased its talking about international affairs and moved to Leader Simon returning to office at a temporary location after recovering from his burns in the attack on Central Hall. Once they explained that he had returned and would be resuming his tasks to quell the anxiety of the people, they moved to the camera that they had waiting at the curb of the amphitheater. There were a few dozen big, burly guards that were keeping the press at bay, leaving an ample walkway for the leader of the Commission.

"Here is our live camera. We are still waiting for Dana Christenson to appear, though confirmation has been received that the convoy is en route to the venue," the female anchor explained. "The estimated time for his arrival is about five minutes." She continued to remind people why the head of the Commission of the People was coming to make an announcement and that this was the first time Dana Christenson would be seen in public after all his years running the Commission of the People in visual anonymity.

No one dared to move in the communications room as we watched and waited for the car.

"As you can see, the first car of the convoy has pulled up followed by two more cars," the anchor commentated. The press began heaving forward, extending their cameras to catch the moment Dana Christenson stepped out of the car.

A few men in black suits ran to the car, standing around the door as it opened and the man in the backseat stepped out. He was wearing a three-piece suit, his hair slicked back against his head, and his brown eyes were surrounded with wrinkles. He was an older man with salt-and-pepper hair around his ears.

"It's not him…" Griffin murmured.

"Shocker…" I groaned sarcastically.

Dana using a decoy was expected.

What happened in the following ten seconds, however, was extremely unexpected.

The fake Dana Christenson walked through the aisle that had been created for him by the security, his guards around him. One person close to the live camera of the station we were watching suddenly dropped his camera and reached for a metal water container, unscrewing the cap and pushing through the barrier of guards, managing to get past them for two seconds before they had their hands on him.

In those two seconds, he splashed the contents of the container on the fake Dana's face, as well as the guards close to him. The decoy screamed in agony, reaching for his face when the liquid hit, and the guards crumpled in pain.

"Die, you lying motherfucker! We won't stop until Central is *destroyed*!"

People were screaming and the guards pulled out stun guns, three of them hitting the man at the same time. He dropped heavily to the ground, his body locked as the waves of electricity pulsed through him. The other guards ran toward the three crumpled on the ground. There was a horrible hissing sound and blood was pouring over the ground.

"Don't touch it! It's acid!" one man yelled.

The chaos had the news station trying to explain what had just happened while the press members on the scene screamed, many covering their mouths with their cameras dropped while others were focused intently on the scene, recording as the horror played out.

I stared at the man who had used the acid to see if he was someone I recognized, even though no one had been let out of the fort in days for reasons of safety. I did not recognize the man at all, which made me realize that Dana had, indeed, thrown acid on his own decoy.

No one in the communications room could speak, stunned.

The camera cut away from the scene just as the decoy's bloody and contorted face could be seen. His skin was falling off, melting away from his bones as his eyes were shut tight, his nose sinking into the rest of his face, the blood pouring over his disfigured features. It was the most gruesome sight I had ever seen.

I completely ignored what the anchor was saying, the image of the man's melting face behind my eyelids every time I blinked.

"What the fuck was the purpose of that?" Tori hissed.

"There was no way Dana could have planned that." Clark said. "It doesn't make any sense."

"Whether he planned it or not, it helps him in the end," I sneered. "We attacked him when he came to resign from the Commission. In the eyes of the public, we reacted to his call for a peaceful treaty with acid." I finally tore my gaze away from the anchor who was trying to hide her mortification. "I would be surprised if Dana *didn't* plan that."

"He already had us in a corner, though," Griffin said. "This was overkill."

There was a two hour frenzy as the decoy of Dana Christenson was taken to the hospital for treatment. It was repetitive, aggravating, and more than anything, it made me more confused about Dana's intentions. It was true, it cast us in an even worse light in the public eye, and we lost what little support we might have had. But it was as Griffin said— overkill. Dana could have waited for us to actually make a move against him, knowing that we would never want to negotiate.

So why make such a horrific scene?

It was all over every news channel that Dana Christenson had been attacked and was in critical condition at the hospital. There were speculations across all media fronts about why the Central Angels had attacked when the head of the Commission of the People had agreed to step down peacefully.

We had officially become a terrorist group that needed to be eliminated rather than a revolution.

Griffin, Tori, Clark, and I gathered together in the back of the room to discuss what we could do to counter the damage that had been done to our image. Mykail even chimed in a few ideas, completely shocked at the cruelty Dana had shown to his own men.

Mark had disappeared.

When the news came four hours later that 'Dana Christenson' was in stable condition, I left to find the leader of the Eight Group.

I had to walk through the whole fort to locate him. I tried the bunk rooms, the strategy room, the shooting range, and the abandoned recreation room that he had been living in. But Mark was nowhere to be seen.

Finally, I moved into the smaller armory rooms further down the hall from the medical room. There was not much in those rooms, but there was some equipment to repair guns and a table with a light, which was where Mark was sitting, carefully cleaning the different components of one of the four guns in front of him.

I closed the door behind me, grabbing his attention and causing him to turn around. When he saw me, I halted, waiting for his reaction. He stared for a few moments before turning back to his task, picking up a rag and wiping down the gun.

I stepped forward again, approaching slowly but making sure he heard my footsteps, wary of sneaking up on the agitated experiment. I looked at the guns on the table, knowing that Mark only carried two. The other two had belonged to Josh. I saw the bracelet I had returned moving on Mark's wrist as he worked on the weapon.

"Mark?" He did not stop in his work, which shook my nerves, not sure if I should try talking to him. I took a deep breath and steadied myself. "Listen, I need to talk to you…"

Still, he continued working.

"Mark…Dana has us in a corner right now, and I don't know what to do. I'm really scared…" I admitted, my voice breaking. I cleared my throat, trying to be discreet about my anxiety. "And now…you're somewhere else and I don't know how to reach you."

Mark's hand stopped. His head did not move, his eyes going unfocused as he listened to what I had to say.

"I know you're in pain," I managed to choke out. "And I wish I could take that pain away. I know I have no right to ask you for more than you've already given me, but I…I need you. I can't do this without you…"

My voice broke and the tears tumbled out of my eyes, streaming down my cheeks. I lifted my hands to my face, trying to bite back the sobs that were threatening to rip out of me. I saw through my blurred vision that Mark had put down the gun and turned to me, staring at me through tormented eyes.

"I know how much you loved Josh…Woobin…" I corrected, closing my eyes. "And I can only imagine how hurt you are over his death. But please, don't bury yourself with him...don't disappear from me. Without you...I..." I trailed off, not sure how to continue.

"I'm so scared, Mark, that I'm going to lose you, too," I finally said. "Please, come back to us. Help us find a way out of this mess. I think you're the only one who can."

Mark sniffed and raised a hand to his face, rubbing his eyes to keep the tears back. Before I could stop myself, I lunged forward and hugged him tightly, crying loudly into his shoulder.

"Please, don't leave me!" I sobbed hysterically. "I'm sorry! I'm so sorry! It's my fault that he's dead, I know...but I'm begging you to forgive me."

Mark's arms went around me and he held me tightly.

There was a small glimmer of emotion in the hug that I understood immediately.

Don't blame yourself...

"I'm sorry, I'm sorry, I'm so sorry..." I continued to chant, blubbering incessantly into his jacket, repeating the only thing I could.

"I just can't do this without you... I *can't*..."

He held me close. I felt his own tears fall onto my shoulder and seep through the fabric of my shirt.

* *** *

"On behalf of the Commission of the People, I stand before you with news regarding Dana Christenson's well-being," Mrs. Markus said, standing at the podium of the press conference room. "Mr. Christenson and the three men who were also injured in the acid attack yesterday are all in stable condition. Two of the security detail will have permanent scars on their faces. Reconstruction of their noses and ears will take place in the next few days.

"Mr. Christenson, on the other hand, is severely scarred. His mouth was mostly destroyed in the attack, and he is now unable to speak, drink, or eat on his own. His nose will also need reconstruction and he is mostly blind due to the attack," she explained. "The doctors predict that he will be in pain for the rest of his life.

"The viciousness of this attack has stunned everyone," she continued, an angry quiver in her voice. "The Central Angels...these *terrorists*, have given their answer to Mr. Christenson's offer of a peaceful compromise with violence. We are appalled and horrified at what has happened, but we at the Commission of the People want the American people to know that we will not allow this threat to continue.

We will not allow a group to use terror tactics and get away with attacking people in the horrific practices that they have shown.

"We showed them mercy for attacking the government buildings, and we extended negotiations to them, but we will not show them such kindness after the horrific attack on Dana Christenson," she snarled, her voice dark. "It is true, they seem to have people who can act as weapons, people who can fly, those who are said to be able to fire a bullet without a gun. This is technology that came from the Commission of the People and we will now use it to defeat this group," she declared. "We will find a way to make a stronger weapon that can take down these threats before they kill more American citizens. We must protect ourselves and our country from such horrors in the future."

"That...son of a bitch!" I hissed angrily. "*That's* what this was about!" I looked at Griffin, my eyes wide. "This is his justification for the Machine of Neutralization," I said. "He's bringing it to the public eye now, saying that they're creating it to combat us. He's getting the public to support the project!"

"Mother *fucker...*"

"We will not allow these terrorists to run our lives, to threaten our government and then attack when we offer them the solution that they demanded. Instead, we will crush these terrorists. We will show them that the people of America are still strong and united against the dictators and terrorists who frighten us into a corner in an attempt to control us. We will triumph over them."

The entire country was at war against us.

Chapter Seventy-Seven

No one knew what to do.

It was impossible to rid the fort of the air of defeat. There was nothing we could do to fight Dana. He had swept the metaphorical rug out from under us, and with the country rallying to get rid of us, we were in twice as much danger.

No one really spoke to one another the following day.

Then, I took things into my own hands.

I called everyone into the main bunker, telling them to sit in a circle so we could discuss what they thought we should do. Most of the people said that we should remain where we were, while others said we needed to cross the southern border and get out of the country, even though that would not stop Dana from coming after us.

Some had no idea what the best course of action would be, and remained silent, their conflicted eyes averted to the ground.

No one said we should stay to fight.

Therefore, it was decided that we would try to make our way across the southern border into the Republic of Mexico.

Mark brought out a map of safe houses across the country. When I asked where the map came from, he told me that he had stolen it from Dana's office in a folder of objects that had belonged to the Coalition, the same group my uncle had been part of. All houses were approximately four days apart if a group walked along back roads and remained on foot. There were procedures for using the safe houses that I would have never believed, such as showing a particular sign and knowing a certain handshake. Griffin and Tori agreed that we should teach everyone the rules and send groups of four to five people every six days along a path toward the southern border. It was the only way we would be able to survive.

According to Tori there was one person who would be unable to follow the plan.

I thought there were *two* people who would never be able to leave.

I was one of them.

Two nights after the broadcast that declared us the national enemy, I pulled Mykail aside, taking him into the recreation room that Mark had used for mourning, hoping not to be disturbed. Sitting at the table, I sighed heavily.

"You know that we are trying to find a way to get everyone across the border."

"I know."

"I don't think it's practical that you go the same way as everyone else," I told him, my gaze focused on his feet, trying to avoid eye contact. "You have a tendency to stick out."

"I know," he repeated, chuckling sadly.

"Would it be possible for you to fly across the border?"

He shook his head. "I'm afraid not."

"Why not?"

"Because pretty soon my wings will no longer work," he said. "My right one is already going numb."

I shook my head, closing my eyes.

"What do you want to do?"

"You don't want to know."

"I do."

"No, Lily..." He shook his head. "Look...I've been thinking a lot about my life these past few days...and I don't see any viable option to continue."

"To continue what?" I whispered, horrified at what I thought he was trying to say.

"Lily, if I don't go back to the Commission and get treatment soon, the wings will kill me anyway." He dropped his head. "And I will be killed if I go back to the Commission."

"What are you saying?"

"I've been thinking about talking to Mark about killing me," he murmured. "I know he wouldn't be opposed to it..."

"*I* would!" I snapped, my eyes wide. "Are you fucking insane? You want to have Mark kill you?"

"I think it's best," he said, looking at his hands.

"How could you throw your life away like that?"

"What else can I do, Lily?" he asked weakly. "I think...after everything this is the best thing."

"What do you mean after everything?"

"After all the pain I caused you, after almost endangering the revolution..."

"...I think it was doomed from the start," I whispered. "Look at us now. The revolutionaries running with our tails between our legs to the south."

"You're saving lives, you've *saved* lives," he told me strongly, putting a hand on mine.

"And I'm also responsible for several deaths."

"What happened to Josh was not your fault. It was Becca's. You can't blame yourself for what she did."

"Josh is only one person," I said. "What about Tara? If she had had the medicine from the Commission, she wouldn't have died like that. And Francesca and Cooper? They died on the raid *I* rushed into. And all those people who died when Dana attacked Central…if I hadn't been stupid and challenged him, he would have never done that."

"Lily, stop," Mykail said, taking my hand in both of his. "The fault lies with those who did the action. You didn't think about killing all those people in Central, you didn't think of betraying Mark's and Josh's trust like Becca did."

"I should have realized it was a possibility…"

"You're only human, Lily," he reminded me, his fingers gently touching my cheek. "You can't know everything, or foresee everything."

I decided to bite my tongue. I could make a million arguments about how everything was entirely my fault, but I didn't want anyone challenging that belief. I knew I was at fault, no matter how many people told me otherwise.

"I can't go across the border, either," I whispered, my head low.

"What? Why not?" he asked, his hand falling away from my face.

"If I go, Dana will follow. *I'm* the one he wants." I sighed, shaking my head. "If I go, I bring him with me and I endanger everyone again. Dana is not going to give up on me just because I crossed the border."

"…what are you going to do then?"

That time, I was the one to reach forward and take his hand.

"You don't want to know…" I repeated his earlier statement. His eyes widened and his hand tightened around mine.

"Lily," he said, "*no*."

"And why not?" I challenged. "You're willing to throw your life away and you won't listen to me when I tell you no."

"That's different. I don't have a choice."

"And I do?"

He was silent, staring at me, conflicted.

"You know that Dana won't let a border stop him. This whole thing was about me, he said so himself." I lowered my head. "The best thing for me to do is to turn myself over to him and hope that he'll let everyone else go across the border."

Mykail looked at the floor before leaning forward and pressing his lips to my forehead, which caused me to look up quickly, surprised. I looked into his eyes and saw the turmoil, the mutual conflict we shared about our dark, uncertain futures.

"What was that for?"

Mykail sighed, looking at the floor again, as if searching for the answer on the dirty cement.

"I don't know..." he said quietly. "I guess...I still want to be the person who supports you when you're troubled." His thumb moved comfortingly over my hand and I smiled at the warm feeling spreading through me from the contact.

"I still care about you," Mykail breathed. "I still love you, Lily."

I swallowed hard and closed my eyes, taking a few deep breaths to contain the typhoon of emotions inside me.

"I would be lying if I said I didn't love you," I said. "But...what I learned...what Dana said...that can't be undone."

"I know," he said. "I thought that I just needed the right time to tell you the truth and to tell you that I wanted no part of Dana's plan, but I was a coward. I was too afraid of you hating me." He barked a laugh. "But I guess that already happened..."

"I don't hate you," I told him. "I don't. I'm starting to learn how to trust you again. But...I will never be able to forget the pain I felt when Dana told me he had sent you to basically trick me into doing the revolution." I dropped my head. "Especially now, when Josh is in an unmarked grave and Mark is...unreachable. I feel the blame for that...and every now and then, I think about what Dana said about your role in angering me enough to go up against the Commission." I shook my head. "...we can never go back to what we were."

"I know," he repeated. "I don't have any illusions about you forgiving me and resuming our relationship. I know the damage is too far done." He squeezed my hand. "But I do want to tell you that I love you. And that I don't want to see you in any danger or pain."

"Too late for the danger part, I think," I tried to joke. "I love you, too. Which is why it hurts me to think that you would be willing to throw your life away."

"There's nothing to throw away," he said. "I'm already dying."

Hot tears stung at my eyes and I sniffed, looking up at the flickering light to try and hold them at bay.

"I don't want you to ask Mark to kill you," I declared. "You've put me in a horrible position, you know that? I have to try and rationalize which horrible fate would be the least painful for you."

"Mark would be the best option," he told me with a strong nod. "He's an ace shot. He could make it quick and painless."

"I don't want you to ask Mark," I repeated. "He's barely holding on as it is. This will put pressure on him and he doesn't need that right now."

"He wouldn't mind killing me," Mykail said darkly.

"But *I* would mind if he killed you and he knows that."

"Have you told him that you want to turn yourself over to Dana?"

"Of course not." I shook my head. "I don't plan to, either."

"You don't think that will hurt him?" Mykail asked. "You disappearing? He'll know what happened. He loves you. He wants to keep you safe."

"I want him to be over the border before I go to Dana."

"So he can wait for you to never show up?"

I sighed heavily, looking at our linked hands.

"I don't know what else to do…"

We sat in silence, caught in the turbulent storm that surrounded us, looking at one another with fear in our eyes.

* *** *

The no-longer revolutionaries were packing things to take with them. While the first group was getting ready to start the trek through the country, the rest of us were carefully moving essential supplies to the same area where the van was hidden. I helped Clark and Tori move tents, ration boxes, and weapons to the van as well as some surrounding holes Griffin and Cody had dug and covered for us to store supplies.

Everyone moved with somber faces and slumped shoulders. We had been beaten by cheap tricks, leaving us feeling as though we had fought and sacrificed for nothing.

Mark was interacting with everyone more, but he also sported a defeated expression.

On the third day, we sent the first five people out of the fort to start their journey to the Republic of Mexico. We were sending the regular humans first with one experiment to protect them if they ran into any trouble. This did lead to a problem of some groups being left without an experiment, but we carefully selected each group based on strengths and weaknesses of the members.

Mark insisted that Eun was in the first group. I had no problem accepting that, knowing that Mark wanted his little sister as safe as possible, particularly after what happened to Josh. Because of that, Rin was assigned to go with the first group.

It was sad to say goodbye to Rin, knowing I was going to turn myself over to Dana without her knowledge. I hugged and thanked her all the same, telling her I would see her in a few months when I made the trip as well.

The lie almost stuck in my throat, but I managed to force it out.

And they started their journey.

One day later, as we were in the store room discussing what else we should take and what could fit in the holes we had dug, Mark jumped, startled, looking at his wrist.

"Mark?" Tori asked.

The leader of the Eight Group ran out of the room, the rest of us following. Other members of the Eight Group were also darting into the main bunker, not sure what the cause for alert was, though all of their wrist cuffs were buzzing, warning of danger.

When I counted all sixteen remaining members of the Eight Group in the bunker, my nervousness grew, wondering who had set off the warning.

Rin was the only one who could have.

Mark, noticing the same thing, motioned several of the others to move in different directions, giving silent orders before ascending the iron stairs to the spiral staircase that led to the Makay Power Plant.

He disappeared into the shadows and we heard a distant clang as he opened the door to examine what was going on outside.

"Gather everyone," Griffin ordered.

Tori and I ran into the various rooms of the fort, trying to calmly tell everyone that we were gathering in the main bunker. With the recent events, it was impossible for them not to be worried. They moved hastily, looking at one another with silent questions, though no one asked aloud what was happening.

"We should get ready to evacuate," Clark whispered. My stomach flipped over as I thought about what that meant.

Mark reappeared on the balcony. He lifted his right thumb and motioned it across his neck.

We had been found.

There was a dull roar of panic as people rushed to grab their bags, which had been packed the same day that Chris had attacked Central, just in case we were raided. I ran into the bunk rooms with everyone else and grabbed my bag from under my bed.

Darting into the bunker again, I saw Griffin with Mark and Tori at the base of the spiral stairs, pulling on the bent and warped structure, causing the metal to groan and strain. Finally, the bolts at the top gave way and the spiral staircase fell to its side, a third of it hanging over the edge of the platform. All three of them made their way down from the balcony and destroyed the next staircase in an attempt to slow the Commission.

I looked at those scattering to their particular exits. We had chosen six of the passageways to act as our escape routes, since they led to obscure areas where we were less likely to be spotted. We now had to crowd into five exits, since the one into the factory was no longer viable.

There were several people in the fort that I saw without their bags, standing in wait for the raid, having given up entirely.

Clark grabbed my arm and pulled.

"Come on!"

"What about them?!" I snapped, pointing at the people who were waiting for capture.

"There's nothing we can do!"

I wanted to protest but before I could turn around, Mykail had grabbed my other hand and was pulling me away.

I forced my feet to move, only having the chance to glance back once into the main bunker before I was pulled to one of the lesser-used tunnels that would lead us into the foothills.

The hustle through the passageway was crowded and panicked. Many were frantic as they tried to move faster only to be stuck behind more people. There was a small group behind us, terrified at being picked off from the back, trying to push forward.

My legs were shaking from adrenaline and fear as we started up the sloped tunnel toward the exit. I tried not to look back, listening to the frantic urges in front of me as people told each other to hurry. I did not hear any shouts in the tunnel behind us to suggest that we were being followed by those raiding the fort, but we could not take chances. We had to keep moving.

Ivo threw open the door leading outside when he topped the small ladder. While I was in the back of the group, I still saw the water pour into the tunnel from the torrential downpour outside.

We braved the weather and climbed the slippery ladder into the thunderstorm. Ivo helped everyone out as we crawled in the mud, struggling to get to our feet in the soaked field. Everyone followed the procedure we had practiced only twice before, running into the tree line and splitting up just enough to be able to see the person to the right and to the left.

Mykail got out of the fort and Ivo turned to him, nodding once as Mykail said something I could not hear over the wind. I followed Mykail, fighting against the stinging rain pelting my face and hands and the wind threatening to push me over as I got to my feet. Mykail spread his wings and let the gusts carry him upward.

"Where is he going?!" I yelled at Ivo.

"He's going to see if anyone is nearby!" Ivo answered, helping Clark off the ladder. "Go, Lily! Get into the trees!"

Pushing aside my worry, I did as I was told, moving through the muddy field into the thin tree line, trying to blink away the drops of rain that fell into my eyes. The wind sent my teeth chattering as I forced my muscles to move.

The spot it had taken us ten minutes to get to during our practice evacuations took everyone thirty minutes to reach. I found myself shivering against the rocks as we crowded around the bases of trees and the crevices of the hill's rock face to escape the rain.

My clothes were soaked and the canvas bag I was carrying was damp on the outside. I was not worried about the contents, since the bag was lined with rubber. I looked at the terrified and cold faces of the others who had escaped with me. We could only wait until the others showed up and the rain stopped.

After ten minutes of turning my back to the wind and trying to cram myself closer to the rocks, someone pointed upward and shouted that Mykail was back. Mykail was slowly descending into the trees, also soaking wet. He finally landed at a safe distance from everyone and searched for me and Clark.

When he saw us, he spread his wing over our heads to block the rain, his other wing being used as a brace against the howling wind.

"There are no Commission people coming this direction," he informed us.

"What about the other groups?"

"Griffin's and Mark's groups are making their way here. They should be here soon. Tori had a small group of Commission vans grab some of the people, but a majority of them got away."

"What about Cody?" I pressed.

Mykail lowered his head.

"When I flew over to their exit…they were being carried away in the vans."

"*All* of them?" I whispered, my eyes wide.

"I didn't see anyone along their path."

My chest ached at the thought.

The storm was still raging when the other three groups convened with us. Everyone was shivering, their teeth chattering, but with the wind and the rain, it was impossible to light fires. Yi Lin, Hiroki, and Minsoo risked going to one of the places we had stored supplies to retrieve a few tents. Everyone pulled out their emergency blankets and wrapped themselves tightly, covering their heads and huddling together to combat the chill. Clark and I were huddled close together with our blankets. Mykail held his wing over us until he got tired. He then joined us under another crinkling emergency blanket, shivering and wincing in pain.

The rain did not let up as night fell. Only a few of us were able to cram into the limited tents, leaving most to stay as close to the rocks as possible for shelter. Uneasily, I fell asleep against the rocks with the musky air under the emergency blanket pulling me into uncomfortable sleep.

Chapter Seventy-Eight

When I woke the sun was just peeking out behind the horizon, the departing clouds looking gray, silhouetted against the light, slowly being chased away as dawn grew brighter.

I glanced around the various huddled masses in the woods and against the rocks, trying to spot familiar faces to determine who was gone. I extracted myself from the blankets between Mykail and Clark, trying my best not to wake them as I stepped into the still-soft dirt, walking around the trees to count heads.

From one tent, Tori stepped out, holding canteens.

"Lily," she said. "I thought you would sleep more…"

I did not respond, looking around the disorganized camp.

"How many did we lose?" I whispered. She sighed and stepped closer, her expression sad.

"The final count we got was seventy-six people," she whispered. "Griffin, Mark, and a few others from the Eight Group went to look for any that might have gotten lost on the path. They're also going to bring supplies."

Seventy-six people…

That meant we had lost sixty-six in the raid.

I looked at the ground and nodded pensively. Tori put a comforting hand on my shoulder and I sighed, swallowing hard.

"…what do we do now?"

She pursed her lips. "I don't know. They drove us north…so we have to find another route to send the groups south while keeping the Commission and the military off our backs."

"I don't know if it's possible to send groups anymore," I said. "I was thinking about the signal we got from the bands of the Eight Group. If Rin made it all the way to where she was supposed to go, the signal would have been out of range. I'm pretty sure they were caught."

Tori sighed heavily.

"I've been thinking that, as well," she agreed with a defeated nod. "But don't say anything to Mark, okay? He's worried enough."

I looked among the sleeping groups, my thoughts jumbled and frightened. We were out in the open and the Commission was after us. There was no way that we could travel as a group to the safe houses. Any large movement would be seen and we would be attacked.

When the people had supported us, even if they were not with us physically, I did not feel such an overwhelming helplessness when I looked at the odds of our success. Now, it seemed that it would be impossible for us to get out of our situation alive.

"Lily?" Tori asked, calling my attention. "What are you thinking about?"

I shook my head.

"Nothing, just...trying to think of the best move from here."

Mykail was the only one who knew of my idea to turn myself over to Dana. Now that we had been chased out of the fort, it seemed like that time was even closer than I anticipated. As I was thinking over my plan, I began to wonder what exactly would happen to me when I was in Dana's grasp. He had said that he wanted to train me, that I wasn't going to be a slave. I had thought many times that that meant I would be an experiment, or part of the Machine of Neutralization project, but there was no telling what Dana wanted with me.

Since he had sent Mykail to seduce me, I wondered if he was at all interested in having sex with me, or if sex was just a tool he used to control people. I had been afraid of my attraction to Dana when I was in the Commission. Now that he seemed so far away, looming in the shadows, waiting to crush us, the attraction was nonexistent, merely a distant memory of a time that felt like a nightmare.

My reality also felt like a nightmare. There was a dark cloud hanging over me, fogging my thoughts with the fear that we were going to lose and everyone I knew and loved from my idealistic revolution would be taken into the Commission or killed because I thought I could overthrow the most powerful man in the world.

Dana said that the game was over when *he* said.

I was choosing to take the first opportunity I could to surrender myself to him in the naïve hope that he would let the others live.

"Lily," Tori said, grabbing my attention again. "There are a few things we need to be very careful of—"

"I would say more than a few things."

"We need to leave this spot. If we get discovered, we are pinned against these rocks. We need to find a better place we can defend while we think of another plan." She cleared her throat and looked at the faces of the people we had once rescued from the grip of the Commission only to put them right back in its palm. "And there is a big chance that we will start having deserters."

I looked at everyone, huddled under emergency blankets, their unconscious expressions mirroring their fears and concerns about the day to follow. Everywhere I turned, people were troubled, even in their dreams.

"Maybe we should just let them go," I whispered. Tori blinked at me, shocked.

"What are you talking about?"

"The bigger the group, the slower we are, the more strain on our resources, and the more likely we are to get caught. If they think they can make it alone, then we should let them go."

"Lily...these are people we're responsible for."

"And look at where we've gotten them."

I walked away, deciding to climb the rocks and look over the surrounding area to see where we could stay that would allow us to see if the Commission or the military were approaching.

It was good for me to hike up the hill, carefully making my way over the jagged, slippery rocks and getting to a higher point where I could see more of the area. The physical activity allowed me to clear my head and think of nothing other than where I was going to step next.

Unfortunately, the hill was mostly rock, which would not make it suitable, even if we could see what was coming our way. We would be exposed to helicopters on the hill. I glanced to the west and saw the tree line continue, heading further away from the bright lights of Central.

Maybe we could move in a wide sweep around the city and end up at the southern safe houses. I knew we could not go to the east, since that was where the national parks were and also tended to be where we got into trouble.

It took me an hour to make my way back down the side of the hill, the descent being far trickier. When I made it back to the camp, the group that had gone to search for our lost people had returned.

"We couldn't find anyone," Griffin said when I asked him how the search had gone. "We also went searching for someplace to set up a type of camp, but we're going to have to look west. There's nothing safe in the east."

"We'll send some scouting parties and move as soon as possible," I decided.

"We can't bring the van up here," Hiroki added. "The roads are mud. It'll get stuck."

"We'll bring it as close to our new camp as possible and trek the supplies from there," Clark said, having woken up while I was on my hike. "But we should move soon."

Tori turned to Mark. "I think the Eight Group is the best qualified to lead the scouting parties."

Mark nodded once and motioned for the Eight Group to gather around as he started ordering them. Tori turned to the experiments and strong men and women who were awake, asking them individually if they wanted to be part of scouting groups. Many were interested, supporting the idea of moving around rather than sitting and waiting for our next decision.

Griffin told Mark to stay with us and we disappeared into a tent, Clark joining us, waiting for the scouting parties to return.

"We are in trouble," Griffin whispered.

"The military is involved," Tori added. "I lost at least a dozen people in my group. They were put into army cars, not Commission vans."

"We can't go up against the American military. There are only seventy of us," Clark said. "What are our options?"

"We don't have any," I murmured. I heaved a deep sigh. "We can try and make a large sweep to the west of the city and drop into the south," I suggested. "But with a group this large, we're going to attract attention." I tapped my finger against the nylon floor of the tent. "I think it's only fair to tell everyone that they do not have to stay with us. If people do not feel safe, if they want to stand still and be caught by the Commission, or if they think they can make it alone, we should let those people go."

"Lily, these people are counting on us to keep them safe," Clark said.

"And I am saying that the best way to keep them safe is to split up," I said. "We are walking around with targets on our heads. If we stick together, we will be annihilated in one swoop." I sighed again. "We would be foolish to think that, right now, there is safety in numbers."

"What about the younger ones?" Griffin asked.

I hesitated. "We let each person decide what they want to do. We're not going to force anyone to stay or to leave, but we need to give them the option."

The tent was silent for many long, heavy seconds. Griffin turned to Mark.

"Do you agree with her?"

Mark nodded.

"As much as I don't like the idea of leaving everyone to fend for themselves, it does sound like the most viable option," Griffin said.

"When the scouting groups come back, we will gather everyone and tell them," Tori said. "They have the option to leave at any point in the next twenty-four hours. If we don't set a time limit, we run the risk of deserters leaving and giving away our location as we move."

"We might want to ask Mykail to fly around and see if he can spot the military anywhere in the vicinity," Clark suggested. "That should let us know where *not* to move."

"No." I shook my head. "Mykail's wings are rotting away. Flying last night really hurt him. I don't know if he will be able to fly again for a while."

"It will only get worse unless he receives treatment," Griffin reminded me.

I turned to him, trying to let him see that I understood the risks but did not know what to do about them.

The feeling inside the tent was one of mutual darkness that none of us could shake.

* *** *

"There is something that I think is very important to discuss with everyone," Tori started, standing in the lopsided circle everyone had made around her. Unfortunately, the scout parties had come back far later in the day than we had anticipated with no information on a safer location. Our only hope was to move further west. Before everyone packed up what they had taken out of their bags, Tori gathered everyone to talk about what we had discussed in the tent.

"Things look bad," she admitted, "and all of us understand that the future looks bleak unless we can cross the southern border. Therefore, we want to give everyone an option. If anyone feels that they can make it over the border on their own, and would rather try alone or with a small group, then we welcome them to go within the next twenty-four hours."

There was a murmuring around the battered revolutionaries. Tori had to lift her hands to silence them.

"This is not a ploy to tell you that you are safer in the group," she said. "The truth is that there is no safe option for us now. We have to do what we think is best. That is why we are extending this option to you. We are not forcing you to go or to stay, but we want to make sure that you understand the risks of both options.

"Trying to cross the border on your own will mean it will be difficult to survive on your own. While we don't have a lot of rations with us, being in the group does mean a better chance for a successful hunt. However, being in the group has a greater risk of exposing all of us together. Moving in this large group makes us easier to spot, and easier to capture if someone makes a mistake. Ultimately, this is a decision you have to make. We want everyone to do what they feel is best for them. Please do not feel pressured one way or the other."

She looked up at the sky.

"We will have to stay put for tonight and move in the morning," she said. "By the time we pack everything, it will be dark and it will be difficult to not walk into a trap. You have tonight to decide your course of action. As of tomorrow evening, we will expect everyone to have made their choice and acted accordingly."

Everyone in the camp was in debate. Some were debating in small groups, trying to decide what their close friends and family were going to do. With others, the conflict could be seen in their eyes as they listened to everyone around them talk.

Night fell, and while some packed their bags and left the group, Griffin, Tori, Mark, Mykail, Clark, and I were sitting silently, pondering how we could evade capture and death long enough to get across the border. Mykail and I shared secret glances with one another, thinking about our own plans.

As soon as it became dark, we put out the fire to avoid being seen and kept close to one another, trying to stay as inconspicuous as possible.

My eyes were drifting shut as I leaned against Clark, both of us starting to doze into an uncomfortable sleep when Tori gasped and stood, grabbing our attention. Mark also stood, pulling out his gun and using his thumb to click the safety off. Griffin turned to me and mouthed something.

"Get everyone and go!" He pointed to the west.

Clark scrambled out from under the blanket. Several of the other experiments, who had also heard something we could not, were moving around to the humans, waking them and telling them quietly to run. I shook a few of those near me, pointing for them to flee.

I glanced around the trees to be sure everyone knew to run, and then pulled out my own gun, taking a few deep breaths.

But a shrill scream to my left made me jump out of my skin.

"Go! Go! Go!" an unfamiliar voice bellowed. There was movement all around us. Screams were heard in the direction we had sent people and Tori followed their cries. Clark pulled out his gun and both of us held our weapons at the ready, scanning for movement. My hands were shaking. I could hear everyone moving, but I could not see them in the dark.

Griffin backed up and ran toward a tree, turning his shoulder and slamming full force into the trunk, causing a sharp splintering sound along with the rustling of higher branches as they started to crash into the other trees. There were terrified screams as the soldiers who had been in the area around us scattered to avoid being crushed.

"Let's go!" I snapped. I grabbed Clark's hand and started running toward the rock face that I had climbed earlier in the day, deciding that defending a hill was a lot easier than trying to see in the darkness of the surrounding trees.

We both stumbled over the loose rocks, trying to find our footing in the dark. Mark and Griffin followed, also hoping to see lights from vehicles and locate different groups of soldiers.

Of course, with their enhanced vision, Griffin and Mark could see far better than me and Clark. Griffin grabbed and pulled me into his arms, carrying me to the top of the rocky hill.

My eyes went wide when I saw what was at the edge of the trees. There were dozens of lights shining, stationary, fixed to the sixty or seventy cars lining the woods we had made our sanctuary.

"Holy shit..."

Everyone was trying to catch their breath from the steep hike, staring at the military vehicles of the night raid. There was a surreal feeling, seeing the lights just beyond the tall trees we thought sheltered us.

"There's a helicopter!" Griffin barked, pointing his gun into the air. It took me another ten seconds before I heard the beating of the propeller blades as the aircraft approached.

All four of us pointed our guns to the sound of the helicopter. A sweeping, blinding light passed over the hilltop next to us, and I followed the beam up to the black machine, barely darker than the night sky.

Mark inhaled deeply and took careful aim.

"Mark...can you get the gunner?" Griffin asked.

Mark's answer was a gunshot.

Judging from the lack of bullets that came our direction, I knew he had succeeded.

The helicopter turned.

"Shit, the copilot's—" Griffin stopped immediately.

A figure passed in front of the helicopter's spotlight and rose to the side of the aircraft. I had flashes of the previous two times a winged experiment had taken down a helicopter. I was thrilled to see Mykail come to our rescue.

We watched the battle for control of the helicopter in the sky, until we heard a gunshot and the helicopter suddenly turned again. My stomach flipped, wondering who had received the bullet.

My question was answered when the helicopter, as it was making a turn to come back to us, began to nose dive into the trees. Mykail leapt free of the aircraft and flew high into the air, speeding toward us just as the explosion occurred. The bright flames lit up the night and the bark of the trees surrounding the crash ignited, the heat from the fire drying the remaining rain water off the timber.

Mykail stumbled as he landed near us. We rushed to him as he collapsed onto the rocks.

"Mykail, talk to me," Griffin ordered.

"I...I can't...m-my wing..."

"Okay, I got you," Griffin said, picking up the collapsed experiment, maneuvering him onto his back while Clark and I helped situate Mykail's wings.

There was a sound from the west side. Mark turned, shooting the soldier who had come up the hill. When Mark turned back to us, he pointed the other direction, which would lead us further away from where our comrades had run, but could keep us safe from encroaching soldiers.

I followed Griffin as he picked his way down the hill with Mykail on his back, the large wings dragging over the rocks. Mark picked up the rear, his gun at the ready.

When we reached the bottom of the hill, Griffin laid Mykail down against a boulder and told me and Clark to remain there, Mark protecting us as Griffin disappeared.

I crouched next to Mykail's side, holding his sweating hand as I looked around, keeping my own gun ready just in case.

* *** *

Griffin found where the military had set up base and came back to lead us through the trees in the dark, taking us to where he had found Tori and the others who had managed to survive the attack. The group had gone over a hill and dropped into a clear valley, staying in front of another rock face.

Griffin brought Mykail into the area just as the survivors were digging a trench at the base of the boulders. It was as much to defend ourselves as it was to hide. Mykail was carefully placed against one of the larger boulders. It was difficult to see in the dark but I could tell from the slight reflection off his forehead in the moonlight that he was sweating profusely.

"What can I do to help?" I whispered, pressing my hand to his face. His skin was burning hot.

"Nothing..." Mykail shook his head, his eyes sliding shut. "Just...just let me rest..."

Tori walked to Mark.

"We lost another twenty-nine," she whispered. "There are groups of soldiers all over the place. They took a lot of them and shot them on sight. I don't know if any survived."

I looked back at Tori, horrified at the numbers.

"Twenty-nine?" I whispered. "Who? Who did we lose?"

"I don't entirely know," she said. "I'm waiting to search the woods until it's almost dawn and we have a safe place to hide," she motioned to the trench.

"How long until dawn?" Clark asked.

"Maybe three hours."

Clark moved to the trench and looked for shovels, but there were only seven. Experiments were using their hands to move dirt and large rocks, some of the other humans were using flat rocks to move the earth out of the way.

"What about supplies?" I asked.

"Hiroki, Minsoo, and Ichiro are going to get more," Tori said. "They'll be careful. After everything has settled and we know what the military is doing, we'll send smaller parties to get more supplies."

"We can't fight them," I said.

"We just need to keep ourselves safe," Tori said. "We'll send a few at a time in openings that we find in their line and they can flee. It's the only thing we can do right now."

I stayed with Mykail until he fell asleep, holding his hand as he shuddered.

When the middle part of the trench was deep enough that Griffin could stand straight and be completely hidden, those digging worked on widening the area, fueled by the time limit of the approaching dawn. The three members of the Eight Group returned with supplies, including alcohol and bandages for the injured, who were treated using gruesome, primitive means.

I could not stand to watch the trench being dug, so when Tori said that we needed to comb the surrounding area for survivors and see where the smaller groups of soldiers had set up camp, I volunteered to go with Mark.

He looked like he was about to protest, but I started walking in a direction before he could find a way to tell me no. Keiko also joined, following as Mark picked up the lead. All of our guns were ready, our hands by our legs as we moved quietly through the trees. The sky was beginning to lighten, which cast a blue tinge over the woods.

My eyes were constantly sweeping through the brightening trees, trying to spot anyone who might be hiding to either kill us or find where we had taken shelter. There was nothing but a cold fog in the trees as we moved in a large sweep.

I was relieved and terrified that we had not found anyone.

Mark slowed, debating whether or not to return to the trench. He nodded to go a little further. We moved another thirty meters before we stopped, hearing a muffled and off-tune singing float to our ears, reverberating off the trees.

We shared nervous glances and Mark led us forward, toward the singing, to see if we had found a camp of soldiers.

I moved cautiously, keeping my eyes on Mark's back as we got closer and the drunken singing got louder. They were celebrating, and had clearly been celebrating through most of the night. The bitter taste of anger took over my tongue and I wanted nothing more than to shoot them for finding joy in the horrible chase.

Mark pressed himself to a tree and motioned for us to do the same. Taking cover behind the nearest tree, I waited a few moments before I peered around the trunk to catch a glimpse of the people in the forest.

There was a camp not far away. I could see cars and there was a fire crackling as the soldiers drunkenly stumbled around.

I turned my eyes to Mark, who made his way even closer, trying to find a place where he could count the number of soldiers. Taking a deep breath, I moved to the tree next to Mark's. Keiko followed, her gun ready at her side.

I peeked around the trunk, much closer to the camp, able to see the soldiers as they huddled around the fire, passing a bottle around and singing drunkenly.

"Fuck! Don' 'member the rest!"

"Who cares, you drunk sonovabitch? You can't sing for shit!"

"Fuuuck…" one of the men groaned, his head rolling back. "What the fuck is taking those assholes so long? They said fucking two hours, tops."

"It's been eight hours," another agreed. "I'm bored as fuck."

"We're out of Jack," another snapped, smashing the empty bottle against the rock where he was sitting.

I glanced at Mark, who was taking only three seconds to look around the tree at a time. He turned to Keiko and me and motioned for us to back away. I nodded, spotting the next tree I wanted to hide behind. I turned when I was around the tree and waited for Mark to make it to his hiding spot next, holding my gun around the tree to shoot anyone who saw him.

"How about this one?" one of the men laughed. A shrill screaming snaked through the trees, causing all of us to halt and peer out from our hiding spots.

"She's not bad," another said. "Wha'd'ya think the Commission wants with these fuckers, anyway?"

They pulled a struggling woman to their circle by her hair. I could not see her face, but judging by her hair, I guessed it was Paula. My heart was in my throat.

"Who gives a fuck?" another growled. "This little slut and all the others are going to pay for what they've done."

"And who's gonna teach 'em?" One of the men barked a laugh. "*You*?"

"Hell yeah!" the second snapped. "Here, give the bitch to me."

"No! *No!*" Paula screamed.

"You can't say no," the man laughed coldly. I saw her tossed roughly to the ground, almost landing in the embers of the fire. The second man grabbed her hair, pulling her close. "You're just a Commission criminal. You don' have the right to say anythin'. So be a good little whore for me."

She began screaming and kicking at the drunk soldiers as they laughed, two other men holding her down. I was about to start forward but Mark shook his head sharply. I stopped, turning to look at the camp again, chilled by the horrific screams that chilled me to my core.

Mark motioned me to him and, taking a deep breath, I crossed the distance to his tree. He grabbed my arm, motioning for Keiko to follow as we turned to leave.

There was a rancid smell in the air that caused me to wrinkle my nose and Mark to stop as we retreated. Both of us scanned the trees, Keiko stopping when she came upon the stench. It was sharp, stabbing the inside of my nostrils and causing my stomach to flip.

Keeping an eye on the camp of soldiers, even though they were preoccupied with their horrific torture, Mark stepped in the direction he thought the smell was coming from. I followed.

Paula let out a scream that caused me to shiver, closing my eyes and trying to keep myself from being sick at my own inaction.

I took two more steps forward, following Mark, when he suddenly stepped back and wrapped one hand around my mouth turning me around quickly and standing completely still. I almost let out a choked cry, shocked at the sudden movement, but I held the sound back, trying to glance at Mark over my shoulder, confused about his behavior. I looked at Keiko and saw her eyes wide with horror, her hand over her mouth as her face went pale.

I understood.

The smell was dead flesh.

They were trying to keep me from seeing the horror.

I could call it morbid curiosity, or something I simply needed to see to understand what our friends had suffered, but I angrily pushed Mark's hand away and whirled around, coming face to face with the gruesome sight.

Sydney was hanging from a tree by her ankles, her blonde hair drenched in blood, dripping into the earth as her intestines lay down her body, draping her front in a tangled, bloody mess. My stomach heaved at the sight, my eyes following the gore down to Jared, a nineteen-year-old who had been a quiet and gentle person. He was tied naked to the tree below Sydney, his eyes and face contorted from a broken jaw and the shattered bones in his face. His body had been bleeding from the ropes that were cutting into his flesh, his genitals also cruelly twisted in a bloody rope. There were stains on his body that were obviously not mud.

Next to him was a stack of four dead bodies, slumped over one another, naked and bloody, their eyes glassy and their faces forever locked in expressions of terror.

Mark came up behind me and turned me around again, taking my head and pulling it to his shoulder, trying to shield me from the horrific sight of our mutilated friends as the angry bile rose in my throat, getting hotter and hotter. Every time I blinked, the image flashed before me, carved into my mind with razor sharp precision.

* *** *

"Dana! You son of a bitch!" I bellowed into the dark woods. After being sure that Mark and the others were fading into sleep, I had slipped into the woods, getting past Clark by saying I was going to dig a hole for a toilet.

In truth, I had decided that that was the night the game would end.

I stood in the dark trees, unable to see anything around me, my gun holstered at my waist. I spun around, looking for any movement, knowing that someone nearby would hear my screaming.

"Are you satisfied?!" I screeched. "You've torn us apart! You've tortured and killed people I loved! How could you do that?!"

Somewhere in my mind, I heard his voice.

"You were the one that did this...not me."

"You said that you wanted me to come to you!" I screamed into the shadows. "You wanted me to give up so that you could do what you wanted with me!" I spread my arms wide. "Here I am! You want me? Come and get me and get it over with!"

Silence followed my bold challenge. There was no way that no one heard me. I was screeching at the top of my lungs, hoping that someone would hear, even if it was the people who had raped Paula and tortured my other friends to death. At least they would be able to end the twisted game.

I wondered if Dana had ordered them to kill everyone, including me, or if there were special instructions for my capture.

Either way, I wanted it over.

"*Dana*!" I bellowed. "I know you're out there, you fucker!"

There was nothing but silence.

"I'm giving up!" I yelled. "I'm ready for you to take me to the Commission and do what you want with me! I don't know if that will make you stop, but I am telling you now that I am giving myself to you!"

The silence was as heavy as the darkness surrounding me. I listened carefully for noise of anyone, believing that at any moment I was going to be shot, or tackled to the ground by the soldiers around me. There was someone waiting around the trees…waiting for me to turn my back so they could pounce…Dana was holding his hand up to everyone…telling them to wait until I was frantic before they fell upon me…

Any moment now…

The silence made me fall to my knees. The quiet invaded my senses, absorbing my words into the trees and strengthening the shadows around me. It knocked me down, forcing me to confront the reality of my situation.

I was insignificant.

I was unheard.

I was nothing.

Chapter Seventy-Nine

I stumbled back to the trench as the sun was coming up, unable to keep my balance and feeling as though I was drunk from lack of sleep and sobbing pitifully. My throat was raw from screaming through the night, demanding Dana to take me then and there. I felt sick, physically, mentally, and emotionally.

When I got back to the trench, there was panic.

Mark pulled me into the muddy depths of the corridor in the earth. I was confused by the mud until I recalled that it had rained the previous night as I was trying to stumble back to the others.

It took me a while to register the sense of panic in the trench. Mark pulled me along behind him, passing others who were loading the weapons we had brought with us and tying some long strings together, though it escaped me why they were doing so.

Finally, I saw Griffin and Tori, though Griffin was just lifting Tori up out of the trench and she ran as fast as she could across the open field somewhere.

"What's going on?" I asked.

"Oh my God, Lily, where the hell have you been?!" he gasped, grabbing my shoulders. "Minsoo saw the main camp send a bunch of troops our way, even some tanks. We're preparing to fight."

I felt sick.

"*Fight*?" I squeaked.

I knew what was about to happen.

"We don't have any other option," Griffin said. "We took a vote, and decided that if we were going to die, we would rather die fighting then be taken back to a camp and tortured to death, or worse, taken to the Commission."

Oh… He was talking about Sydney and Jared…

"Lily!" Griffin said, shaking my shoulders. "Snap out of it! What is wrong with you?!"

I could not answer, opening and closing my mouth uselessly.

We were going to lose.

That was what I wanted to say. I wanted to tell him that no matter what, we were going to lose and then we would be nothing apart from a blip in the great history of social unrest.

There was no way to fight against Dana Christenson and win.

"Griffin," Clark called, coming to my other side. "Tori's gone?"

"Yeah."

"What's she doing?" I asked.

"She's going to go around and try to take out some of the tanks," Griffin explained. "She should be able to at least take a good portion of their men out." He looked at Clark. "Is the line planted?"

"Yes."

"Good." Griffin turned back to me. "Better get some ammo…"

I looked back in the trench where I had helped bring the ammunition in the previous day, lining it up depending on the size of the bullets. I ignored the running of everyone else in the trench as they prepared for battle.

Prepared as if this was a battle in a war rather than impending annihilation.

For all the quick preparation we made in the early morning, we were sitting and waiting for a long time, waiting for Tori to destroy what she could of the approaching army.

The anticipation was painful. A few of the people who were scouts were watching out of the trench, standing on empty ammunition cases to see over the edge. Others were leaning against the front wall of dirt, holding their guns and taking deep breaths. Some were praying, others were crying. The feeling of fear was ricocheting off the walls of earth, bouncing back to hit everyone left in our little revolution.

I was looking at Mykail, who was standing next to me, his face pale. He had insisted he would help. He had bombs strapped to his body and two guns that he would shoot from the air. I had asked him not to fight or fly, knowing that it was going to kill him, but he just smiled at me, stroked my cheek, and ignored my pleas.

It was early evening when we finally heard the sounds of distant crashing through the forest.

Our lookouts did not report seeing anything, but everyone could hear the noise, and it made our hearts knock angrily against our ribs.

This was a real battle.

I had always watched war movies with my father when I was a young teenager. He was a fan of war movies. It didn't matter if it was about the World Wars or the Revolutionary Wars, he just liked following the stories of the heroes that half the time died, and the other half made it through to be reunited with their loved ones.

My loved ones were in the trench with me. I wasn't sure how that boded for my survival.

"We have five jeeps!" one of the women with binoculars said.

My heart picked up speed.

"And following them?" Griffin called.

"Several walking soldiers," a man announced. "At least fifty so far!"

My stomach turned over and I closed my eyes, trying to keep myself from passing out.

"What the hell do they have there?" Griffin murmured. My brow furrowed, worried by Griffin's confusion. Several others in the trench looked at one another, not sure what it was that Griffin saw.

"Oh my God..." the woman next to me gasped, crouching, her hand over her mouth and her eyes wide with horror, the binoculars loose in her other hand.

"What?" I demanded.

"...it's Tori."

I snatched her binoculars and stepped on the case. If it had not been for Griffin's confusion, I would have thought Tori was kicking ass. That was not the sight I was greeted with when I put the binoculars to my face and focused on the approaching jeeps and soldiers.

Tori's head was raised high above the first jeep on the antenna. Her arms were tied between the lead jeep and the second jeep, stripped naked, her legs extended behind her to the two jeeps following the first two. She was decapitated, drawn and quartered, and the army was showcasing the cruelty as they charged forward, ready to destroy us.

Our strongest experiment had been killed before the battle even began.

I understood from the horrible torture that her body had endured that the long delay into the afternoon was likely due to Tori actually causing damage to the military forces. Seeing them come at us so strong with the Ward Ten experiment dead, made us all realize we were staring at our own fate.

Griffin was livid.

"Clark, when those motherfuckers get close enough, blow them to hell!"

We watched with nauseous stomachs as seventy-five foot soldiers, a tank, and five jeeps came toward us, intent on their mission. By all respects, the group was small, but it looked as terrifying as thousands of soldiers to the tired, frightened people in the trench.

Griffin raised his hand, watching the jeeps get closer. When they were in range, he motioned his hand down sharply. Clark yanked the tied-together strings and, a few seconds later, there was a boom that resonated through the walls of the trench. Dirt was sent flying high into the air and came showering down on us.

I climbed back up on the empty ammo case and looked at the two front jeeps. One of them was turned on its side and the other was on fire in the front. Most of the people in the jeeps that had been hit were dead, but one or two climbed out, limping over the bodies of the soldiers that had also fallen prey to the buried grenades.

There were many who were still charging. When the soldiers got close enough, Peter pulled on the second string on the other side of the trench, setting off the second, and more powerful, row of grenades. This time, the dirt came flying into the trench to cover us in a blanket of earth.

"Go!" Griffin ordered.

People clambered out and ran toward the soldiers while I, and many others, fired from the trench, poking our heads out just enough to aim. I pulled the trigger fifteen times on my gun, pointing at the soldiers whose faces I could not see despite their close proximity. I saw a few of them fall, others collapsed when I hit them in the leg. I replaced my magazine and fired again, watching more uniformed men fall to the ground meters away from the trench.

After my third magazine was empty, I dropped into the trench to reload them. There were only a few boxes left, and already people were scrambling to reload, grabbing bullets and taking them to other ends of the trench. I grabbed one box and sat in the mud to reload my gun.

Mykail looked at me and nodded, spreading his wings and taking flight with a powerful stroke, soaring into the air as I protected myself from the displaced air.

Seconds after I turned back to my task, there was a loud boom that nearly ruptured my eardrums while several in the trench screamed. I heard a commotion that I could not relate to anything I had heard before and turned to my right, where Mykail had been moments before. Several large portions of the rocks above our trench had tumbled down and crushed two people.

I holstered my gun and ran to the hand I could see sticking out of the rocks.

"Lily! Look out!"

I turned around quickly and saw a soldier standing at the top of the trench, pointing his gun at me. He stopped and blinked.

"Lily?"

The man's head snapped to the side as a bullet hit his temple. He went limp, falling into the trench in front of me as I turned to see who had fired the shot. Clark nodded once and I smiled weakly back.

I had been correct.

There were special rules regarding my capture. My name had been passed through the ranks.

I grabbed the dead man's weapon, stepping over his body and handing the gun to a person looking for bullets.

I peered over the edge of the trench to see that the people, mostly the experiments, were being surrounded by many soldiers, and were still able to hold their own very well. I was shocked to see Mark use one of the soldiers as a shield while he shot everyone surrounding him before picking up one of the guns from the dead soldiers and shooting a straight line across the soldiers approaching the trench.

I looked at Griffin, who was making his way to the tank. The tank explained the booming and the shattered rock in the trench.

Many of the bigger guns were focusing on Mykail, who was dropping bombs on the large groups of soldiers trying to surge forward. He avoided most of the bullets, but his attention was suddenly diverted up the hill in the distance where the military forces had come from.

There were more jeeps making their way down the slope and into the darkening valley. The coming night heightened my concern, knowing that we were not going to be able to defend in the dark.

In Mykail's distraction, one of the gunners on the back of the jeep that had crashed into the overturned jeep turned his gun upward and shot several rounds.

I saw Mykail's body jolt and his wings snapped in several places, causing him to spin in the air and then plummet to the ground. I watched in horror as he fell to the earth, making contact with an audible thud on his shoulders and mangling his wings further.

I let out a horrified cry and, before I understood my own actions, I scrambled out of the trench and ran to him, shooting as I moved, though I was sure I did not hit anyone. I crouched next to Mykail, failing to rapidly determine whether or not he was dead. I grabbed onto his arms and pulled him along the ground, dragging his body with more strength than I should have possessed.

My arm snapped to the side and an incredible pain surged through my body, causing me to fall to the ground and grab at my bicep.

I had been shot.

Fighting the pain, I reached to my gun, shooting the soldier as he was approaching.

Seeing the trench nearby, I grabbed Mykail's arms and pushed my way along the soft dirt with my feet, finally tumbling into the deep trench, which jarred my arm and made me inhale a mouthful of mud and dirty water.

Choking and spluttering, I reached up to Mykail, teetering on a box as I grabbed his arms again.

My eyes went upward, seeing Griffin charge the tank and try to lift it with his altered strength. The man operating the tank opened the lid, shooting Griffin in the chest, though all that did was startle the experiment.

Griffin grabbed the man's gun, ducking the spinning turret as he attempted to pull the man out of the tank. The man grabbed onto the experiment's clothes and pulled him closer before screaming one word.

"Forward!"

The tank lurched forward, the tracks hitting Griffin's legs and pushing him to the ground before covering him completely, his bones shattering under the weight of the weapon.

I watched in horror as Griffin's body was flattened.

Grabbing Mykail, I hauled him into the trench, though he landed on top of me and caused more pain in my arm.

After a few moments where I caught my breath, I pushed myself upright, the tears forming in my eyes as I fought against the pain in my arm and the pain of my chest being ripped apart.

I pulled Mykail closer, cringing and groaning as the pain tore through me. When he was next to me, I rested my hand against his neck, feeling for a pulse as I looked over the mangled bones and white feathers that had once been his wings.

To my shock, there was a slight pulse.

I leaned closer, hearing the pained breath trip over his teeth.

I leaned my head against the wall of the trench and let a few tears spill down my cheeks.

Gradually, the sounds above the trench decreased.

We had been defeated.

Even though there were some who still stuck their head out of the trench far enough to shoot at the soldiers, we understood that we were finished. The realization hung over us. I clutched at my arm, trying to keep the pain from overwhelming me, but the pain was intense as I sat in the muddy trench, trying to keep myself from curling up and crying next to Mykail's unconscious form.

I looked over the experiment in my arms, his wings badly mangled with bullets and broken bones. I wasn't sure he would ever wake up.

But for now, he was alive. *Barely*.

Night fell, and the dark trench became encased in impenetrable black.

I could still hear the sounds of the fighting and the angry voices yelling above us, but I could not do anything but sit next to Mykail, hearing the sounds of fighting lessen as we were systematically annihilated. Bullets flew over the trench to embed in the rock. There were shouts and cries as people were mowed down. In the trench itself a lot of people were sitting against the side of the muddy walls, shivering, *waiting*.

It had been foolish to think that we could ever defeat Dana. It had been delusions of grandeur that made us think we could ever stand a chance against him, or that we could work without his knowledge and mange to topple the powerhouse that was the Commission of the People before he found a way to retaliate.

And we were going to pay for our naiveté.

A body dropped into the trench, barely avoiding a round of bullets. He looked around the narrow space, his eyes frantic and wild, realizing he was trapped.

"Mark?" I whispered, my voice weak.

He whirled around and ran to me, dropping to his knees and placing a hand on my face.

He wrapped his arms around me and held me for several long moments as I cried. He was trying to find a way to get us out of this mess, as I had pleaded for him to do, but with the way he was holding me I could tell that he had run out of ideas.

There was a triumphant shout above me and I yelped, startled, but Mark pulled out his gun and shot the soldier in the head, causing him to fall into the trench with a gurgle and a thud.

I was hyperventilating. The soldiers were getting to the trench now. The battle was over.

Mark opened the magazine of his gun and rotated it to see how many bullets he had left. With the way he stared at the magazine, I knew it was not good. He took my hand and squeezed it before darting back across the trench and moving to the ammunition. I could not even raise my voice to tell him that there was nothing left, so he continued to rummage around in the muddied supplies.

The sound of bullets died down and the sound of voices could be heard moving steadily closer.

This is it...

I sniffed back my tears and held Mykail closer, my brain frozen, waiting to see what they would do to us. I was not sure if we were going to be taken prisoners or if we were simply going to be executed. I did not know how many were still alive or how many had already been captured. All I knew was that my fate had already been sealed by Dana, and I could not begin to imagine what he had planned.

I glanced at Mark, who looked at me and held up his hand, telling me to stay still.

There were beams of light that shone around the trench and the voices began to get louder as people approached.

"Take the dead out and identify them!" one man ordered.

"Any of them that look like they'll survive, load them into the Commission van. Put the others out of their misery!" another voice added.

I swallowed hard, feeling the sick, twisting fear in the deepest part of my gut. Their footsteps sloshed closer in the mud, the beams moving over the huddled people in the trench. Two gunshots caused me to jump, wondering who they had killed.

I could see Mark's silhouette further down the trench as the lights drew closer. He was watching them, his eyes hard and defiant despite the crushing defeat.

When the footsteps got even closer, the light fell to the ground, allowing my eyes to focus on the faces behind the beam. Horrible nausea caused me to feel light-headed as I studied the man standing next to the soldiers, dressed in his impeccable three-piece suit, eyes uncovered and locked on me as I held Mykail.

Dana took another step forward, his eyes holding mine when he stopped, slowly turning to Mark, who was crouched on the ground, glaring at Dana. For three agonizing seconds, the two shared the most intense glare I had ever seen in my life—the look of a furious dictator and a defiant subject when both had come to realize who was going to win their battle.

Dana's mouth curved upward at the corners and he reached into his jacket.

He pulled the gun out, pressed the barrel to Mark's forehead and, without blinking, he pulled the trigger.

My heart stopped, my eyes focused on the way the bullet ripped through Mark's skull, exiting through the back of his head with a torrent of blood. His head snapped back and then rolled forward as his body fell limply into the mud.

Dana replaced the gun in the holster as I stared at Mark's dead body, the tears caught somewhere between my churning stomach and the agony that ripped through me.

Dana stepped to me, crouching with a heavy sigh as he shook his head.

"Poor Little Lily," he whispered. He reached a hand out, which finally caused me to pull my eyes away from Mark's lifeless body. "Don't fight me anymore...just come with me." His voice was dark, commanding, showing that he had total control over me.

I stared at him for a long moment, scrambling for any way I could defy him. I looked at Mykail's pained expression, at Mark's dead body, and then back to Dana's piercing gold eyes.

"Come with me, Little Lily."

It was then that the gravity of the situation settled over my head. I was trapped. There was nowhere else to go...

I took his hand.

Chapter Eighty

Dana carried me up the hill, through the forest, and to his car, where Sean was silently sitting in the driver's seat. I had no will to fight Dana or ask him to spare the others. I was petrified of the coming repercussions. No one would be able to help me. My parents had abandoned me, the rebellion had failed, and the Commission had been sure to spin our deviant behavior so that the public believed we were dangerous, painting anyone who sympathized with our movement as traitors to the nation.

It was over.

Dana slid into the backseat after me and closed the door. I flinched, frightened, understanding the finality of the sound.

Sean pulled away from the dirt clearing where the other vans were busy loading others who had survived only to be taken back to the Commission—some were going to be in the back of the Commission for the first time.

Dana wrapped an arm around me and pulled me to him. I followed, my brain numb and tired. He turned my body, holding my shoulders to his chest as both of his arms wrapped around me, as though to provide comfort. My head remained pressed to the smooth fabric of his tie.

Everything moved around me. I could hear Dana's steady heartbeat and feel his chest rising and falling as he breathed but, otherwise, I did not feel movement, or register the scenery changing. I replayed Mykail falling to the ground, hitting with a sickening thud, the pain that shot through me as the bullet pierced my shoulder, the way Mark and Dana stared at one another before Mark was shot in the head so unceremoniously.

Dana scooped me back up in his arms and walked me through some hallways in the Commission that I had never recalled seeing before opening a door to a bedroom. I blinked slowly, confused, unsure how I had gotten to the room.

Dana gently set me on the bed and went to his knees in front of me, pushing the jacket from my shoulders, hesitating when I cringed in pain.

"Daniel, get one of the doctors in here," Dana called to one of the guards who had, apparently, followed us.

"Yes, sir."

Dana extracted my arm from the jacket and grabbed the hem of my shirt, moving my uninjured arm through the sleeve, positioning my useless limbs as he wanted, pulling the fabric gently from my body, being mindful of my injuries.

He looked at the wound, carefully pressing his fingers to the blood dripping down my arm as I winced.

We were silent even when the doctor got there, treated, and wrapped my shoulder.

I could only stare at the carpet meeting the wall as I sat on the bed, replaying the memories of the past few months and how quickly, and violently, everything had ended.

The doctor pushed some pills past my lips and then held a glass of water to my mouth that had magically appeared in his hand. I swallowed mechanically, my eyes never wavering from the spot I had found on the floor.

He left and Dana stepped forward again. He gently pushed me back on the bed, reaching for the button on my jeans and shimmying them off my hips. I was still, not registering the possibility of being raped.

Dana stripped me down completely, my body deadweight, before scooping me up in his arms once again and stepping to one of the doors. Toeing it open, he turned on the light with his elbow and walked to the bathtub, carefully setting me down on the cold porcelain. The tears began to fall down my face and the sobs rose in my throat, though they only rocked my body back and forth as Dana turned the silver knobs of the faucet, slipping his jacket off and rolling up the sleeves of his somehow-still-pristine white shirt.

He went to his knees next to the bathtub, reaching for a washcloth and rubbing some soap on it.

His hand, wrapped in the cloth, moved over my entire body as I cried, cleaning the mud, sweat, and blood from my skin. The urges I had in my body would have frightened me if I had been in my right mind. I had half a mind to grab the cloth and rub my skin completely off, trying to get rid of everything I had done over the year I had been in Central. I wanted a razor to slice at my skin, bleed me dry, and wash everything away down that drain so I was left hollow.

Instead, I was being washed like an infant, turning over violent thoughts.

I was crying, though I could only tell because the water on my face was hot and the droplets of water that clung to the other areas of my skin made me shiver from the cold.

Dana cupped water in his hand and poured it over the soaped areas of my body, cleaning me and unplugging the drain to let the browned water swirl away as I watched through blurred eyes.

He waited for the tub to empty completely before he started on my oily, matted hair. He took a bowl out from under the nearby sink and used that to rinse, using his fingers to massage the shampoo and conditioner through my hair, taking great care to be sure I did not get any in my eyes.

When the drain was, once again, unplugged, Dana's large hands hooked under my arms and pulled me upright before hauling me out of the tub, setting my feet on the cold tile. He grabbed the towel hanging on the wall and wrapped it around me. Just as he had done when he washed me, his hands passed over every area of skin, drying me before placing the towel over my head and rubbing my hair to dry it.

The tears were still falling steadily...

We had yet to speak to one another.

Tossing the towel over the sink, Dana placed an arm around my shoulders, guiding me as I walked with heavy steps back into the bedroom, ignoring my naked state and the tears spilling freely over my face.

He turned me around and sat me on the bed, grabbing some folded clothes from the top of the dresser. Setting the clothes on the bed next to me, he fell to one knee and grabbed my wrists, pulling me to stand and placing my hands on his shoulder, allowing me to step into the panties he was holding for me. He slid the soft cotton up my legs and placed the elastic band around my hips before grabbing the baggy blue pants and holding them open for me.

He then wrapped the big, button-up shirt around my shoulders and fastened each button carefully, starting from the bottom and working his way to the top, where he fixed the collar before lovingly placing a hand on the side of my neck and kissing my forehead, which only caused my tears to fall faster, fear rocketing through me.

He gently pushed me back on the bed, grabbing my ankles and lifting them before adjusting my head on the pillow.

Dana ran his hand over my wet hair, down my neck and over my shoulder before leaving the room, closing the door behind him.

That was when I broke down violently, crying from every cell in my body, my chest heaving and my stomach turning sickly as I came to the realization of how many different directions my fate could go.

For three days, I did not see Dana.

The only people I saw were the guards who brought me food and the doctor who came to treat my wound. My arm was not broken, and the pain lessened with pills, but the pain I felt was so much deeper than anything physical. Even though my brain had gone in a million different directions about what Dana could do to me, the actual reality had not hit me. I was still in the trench, holding Mykail as Mark tried to comfort me while I cried.

The replaying memories turned into nightmares, making it impossible to differentiate when I was asleep or awake. The pain radiating in my ribcage made me feel as though I was constantly awake, but my constantly-changing positions on the bed made me believe I was drifting in and out of sleep.

On the third night, my food was brought in and set on the desk in the corner of the room as usual. I turned to look at it as the guard exited, locking the door behind him. Like the other times food had been brought to me, I was not interested in eating. However, I was very thirsty. I crept over to the tray and grabbed the paper cup of water that had been in the same place every time the tray was brought in. Sipping the water through the straw, I savored the cool liquid, glad that it brought some relief to my burning throat from my violent sobbing.

I crawled back on the bed, curled on my side with the paper cup in my hands.

I drifted to sleep.

My eyelids were heavy when I woke and I groaned, feeling a soreness in my shoulders. I forced my eyes to open, cringing as I tried to move my arms and assess the source of the discomfort.

Only my arms would not move from their position above my head.

My eyes shot open and I craned my neck to look at my hands, which were fastened to the headboard with padded cuffs with long leather straps. Fear bolted through me at lightning speed. I pulled myself further up the bed and tucked my legs under me, trying to pull my wrists out of the restraints, burning my skin and straining my muscles and joints. My body was weak, and I shivered from the cold air against my exposed skin.

The door opened and Dana stepped inside. My eyes focused on him as he walked forward, unbuttoning the buttons on his suit jacket.

"You're finally awake."

His voice sounded foreign. I shivered from the sentence, but shifted to defend myself, preparing to kick at him, even though I knew there was no logical way I could escape.

Dana was slow, meticulous even, measuring his steps as he approached the bed. My heart was threatening to break my ribs and my stomach knotted. I knew what was coming.

"Stay the fuck away from me...." I warned, baring my teeth.

"Now, Little Lily," he said, finally reaching the bed and looking me over, shaking his head, "you caused quite a mess out there. It's going to take years before the people will be able to simmer down, and it's all your fault." He wagged his finger at me with a wicked smile.

"Fuck you," I bit back. "If the people actually agreed with what you were doing, that revolution would have never gotten off the ground."

"True, but there will always be that group of people that you will never please, who think that they are higher than everyone else and that their opinions are close to that of God's will." Dana leaned forward on his hands, his weight pressing into the mattress. "Allow me to let you in on a little secret," he whispered, leaning even closer as I tried to back away, hoping to melt into the headboard and through the wall behind it. "God would have approved of what the Commission was doing, if he was still alive. In the past everything was open to interpretation and governments said that the laws that were supposed to be absolute, ordained by God himself, served their political agendas."

"...aren't you doing the same thing?" I asked. "Saying God would approve?"

"Up to your interpretation," he said. "That's not the point I'm trying to make. I'm telling you that the Commission of the People has become the new bible—the new all-powerful law that people acknowledge even though they choose to ignore the parts that make their skin crawl." He smiled. "You went and threw all those nasty little bits in their faces and, at first, they were angry and wanted change...until they realized that you were the one who brought all this dirty information to them, and their anger turned to you." He shook his head. "You should know better than that, Little Lily...never make a society realize that what they're doing is wrong. It's too uncomfortable to change."

He let out a laugh before standing straight.

"Now, because of the trouble you've caused me, I think it's time we start your punishment."

"Don't you fucking touch me," I snapped, though my voice was trembling.

"Where are you going to run, Little Lily?" he whispered, smiling dangerously. "I don't see your little army of rebels or that sneaky fuck of a chink around anywhere to help you out of this one." He cocked his head to the side. "I told you long ago...one day, I would take you and there would be nothing you could do to stop me."

Fear turned into desperate panic.

His hands were lightning fast, grabbing my ankles out from under me. I screamed loudly, trying to thrash my weak body as he climbed onto the bed, maneuvering himself to lay on top of me, my legs around

1065

him. Even though I had no strength in my kicks, I tried as best I could to get him away from me.

He struggled only slightly with my flailing limbs as I began screaming.

"No! No! Let me go!!" I screeched, hoping someone would come to my rescue. I knew that no one nearby would stand against Dana, certain that even Sean had been ordered away. "Stop it!!"

One of Dana's hands pressed flat against my chest, nearly pressing hard enough to break my ribs as he shoved me flat to the mattress. I felt my straining bones under his strength as I struggled to breathe and scream. His other hand went to his fly, unzipping it.

The terror consumed me.

"*No!!*"

"Come now, Little Lily," he chuckled, grabbing my thighs with both hands and pushing my knees to my chest, his fingers digging into my flesh as my body was forced into the painful position. I cried out as my body protested the movement. "Don't pretend you didn't know this was going to happen." He positioned himself against me. "You were the one that gave yourself up to me."

At first, the pain was so horrible that the scream remained stuck in my throat, unable to break free, choking me as my body trembled. The agony was almost enough to take me out of the room entirely. My eyes were locked on the ceiling, focused only on the pain, my other senses dulled. Dana's movements were nothing compared to the anguish of realizing that I had put my hand in his in that trench knowing, somewhere deep in my mind, that this would be my reality. I was Dana's prize and no one would save me.

"You brought this on yourself, Little Lily…" he said. "The chase was fun, but now it's time for you to learn."

Even when he was finished, the pain did not end. It seemed to radiate deeper, past the cells of my skin and muscles to the very marrow of my bones, splintering every part of my skeleton that was still intact.

I flinched as Dana unbuckled one of the padded cuffs, sighing as he brought my arm down. I should have attacked him then. I should have leapt up and beaten him with all the strength in my body, but at that moment, the only strength I had was used to keep myself from pleading with Dana to kill me.

He released my other hand.

"Little Lily, allow me to explain how this is going to work," he started, sitting down as if he was about to explain some fact of life to his child. I glared at him tiredly.

"Fuck you…" I murmured under my breath.

Dana leaned forward, taking my face between his hands.

"That's my girl," he whispered. "After all that, you're still biting." He pressed his lips to mine, though I refused to reciprocate. "Here is what will happen. From now on, I will be the only one who can enjoy you. Unless, of course, you need to be punished for being a bad girl, in which case I will bring in one of my men to show you how bad it can get."

He tucked some hair behind my ear, ignoring how I flinched away.

"I'm going to break you, Little Lily…" he breathed. "And from the pieces, I will build you into everything you've always wanted to be." He trailed the backs of his fingers over my cheek. "Nod to tell me that you understand."

I remained still, staring at him as though looking through water.

"Do you understand?"

I nodded, the tears creating hot rivers over my face.

* *** *

Dana took me into the bathroom and washed me again. I was in too much pain to move, and while I desperately wanted to get clean, I hated having Dana's hands on my body, wiping my skin with another damn washcloth. I wanted him to push harder, to scrub away everything, but I also wanted him to be gentler with my abused body.

I remembered pleading with him at one point to leave me in the bathtub, but he did not listen, finishing washing and drying me before chaining me up again on the now-clean bed, naked and cold. He paused as he turned away when he saw my shivering. He hooked an arm under me, lifting me off the bed with ease and covering me with the blankets.

He kissed my forehead before he left.

He left me for a very long time.

Being alone was even worse.

I was sure hours ticked by as the constant panic and pain exhausted me further. I felt lifeless, powerless…as though I didn't exist at all. I began to wonder if I was already dead, but was certain even death would be more merciful than my situation.

I lost track of time—not that I really had track of it to begin with—and it seemed like weeks until Dana returned.

I jumped when the door opened, terrified. Dana smiled at my reaction.

"Very good, Little Lily."

And then, with me kicking and screaming, he violated me again. I could not tell if the pain was worse then or the previous day but it still shone brightly behind my eyes, pulling me down to some cold place I never knew before. When it was over, he walked out the door, returning with food, where he tried to feed me, though I refused, my stomach twisted sickly.

I could not tell if it was day or night. I counted each time Dana came to torture me as a day, marking the end of a horrible time of waiting for the leader of the Commission for the People to rape me before tenderly washing me clean and trying to feed me.

The pain was constant and common, so after the fifth day, I felt that I could move even with the intense pain. When Dana picked me up and took me to the bathroom to wash me, I scrambled out of the tub, shouting like a banshee, my hands going for his neck.

We both fell to the tile, my hands squeezing his neck, trying to choke him. He smiled and turned me over, pinning me against the cold tile, his knee against my lower back as my face was pressed to the floor.

"Very good, Little Lily. Right on schedule."

I struggled whenever I could. All the while, I was starting to wonder if I was ever going to leave the room. I was entertaining the idea that I might die in that room. I did not know Dana's goal, or what he said I was doing 'on schedule.' As much as I spent my quiet, waking moments thinking over what he had said about breaking me, I could not understand what he wanted.

One day, the torture changed.

Dana stepped into the room and I flinched, turning my head and clenching my eyes shut, waiting for him to yank my legs apart as he had done for the past six days.

When I heard his footsteps move but no change in the mattress, I opened my eyes and turned to watch him. He walked to the desk, reaching into his jacket pocket and pulling out his gold pocket watch, setting it next to some files and a thin book before removing the jacket from his shoulders. Curious, I watched him fold the jacket over the back of the chair and then toe off his shoes.

My heart pounded and my brain raced at watching him undress. It was when he turned to me, slowly unfastening the cufflinks on his shirt that I realized I had never seen Dana's skin apart from his forearms and face.

He climbed on the bed wearing his white shirt and suit vest with his belt and trousers, unbuttoning the other sleeve as he straddled my waist.

I could do nothing but stare at him, confused.

Dana reached to my right wrist and unbuckled the restraint, allowing my arm to drop loose and causing my worry to swell.

Freeing my other hand, he placed one hand on each side of my head and leaned down, pressing his mouth to mine, opening his mouth to lick my lips.

"What..." was all I could manage to say.

"Undress me."

My eyes shot wide and focused on the three buttons on his suit vest. I stared at them as though they were red hot, ready to burn my skin if I touched them.

"I...I don't..."

"You heard me," he said, sitting straight, settling all his weight on my hips. "Undress me."

"No..."

The prospect of undressing Dana terrified me. It was a very intimate act, revealing the skin I had never seen before, and I felt as though I would be giving my consent to his torment.

"Little Lily," he said with a dark smile, "that was not a request, it was an order."

"No," I protested, a little stronger.

"Whether you undress me or not will not change what happens," he informed me, his eyebrows high, expectant. "If you're a good girl and you obey, I will be gentle. If you don't...well, you know what happens."

"I can't...I-I *can't*..." I shook my head, chanting the same two words over and over again.

He took my wrists in his large hands and moved them to rest against the fabric of his vest. I cringed away, but he held my hands close, leaning down so I could reach the first button.

"Please...d-don't..." I pleaded pitifully. "I-I can't..."

"Last chance, Little Lily."

I shook my head violently.

"Fine."

With incredible speed, he moved his hips off mine and grabbed my legs. The panic ripped through me like lightning.

"No! No! Please! Okay! I'll do it! I'll do it!"

To my surprise, he stopped, settling back over my hips and waiting. I opened my eyes, crying as I turned my attention to the three buttons.

My hands were shaking as I lifted them to his vest, once again flinching at the touch of the smooth black button. I struggled, my fingers shaking too much to skillfully push the button through the buttonhole. Dana remained still, watching, allowing me to take my time.

Eventually, the first button gave way.

The sobs overtook my chest, heaving my entire body under him and my hands left his vest, covering my face as I cried.

"Two more, Little Lily," he told me, his voice calm but with a touch of darkness that reminded me of what would happen if I did not finish the task.

Crying and blubbering, I worked the second button open and finally the third.

When the vest was open, I raised my hands to my face again, crying into my palms, sobbing.

"You're not finished." He had not removed his vest, allowing it to sit open over his white shirt and tie, looking at me expectantly. "Go on."

I was starting to sicken myself. My fingers wrapped around the open edges of the vest and pulled at them uselessly, unable to move the fabric from his shoulders. Sniffing my tears back, I used my grip on his vest to lift myself off the bed. With the way he was sitting on my hips, this put my face next to his collarbone, where I froze for several moments.

I pushed the vest from his shoulders and down his arms. It was only then that he shifted, extracting one arm and then tossing the vest aside with his other hand.

"Tie."

I hooked my fingers in the knot, pulling at it uselessly. If my brain had been functioning, I would have thought to strangle him with his own tie, but my mind was racing in too many different directions to consider the plot.

When I was having no success with the tie, Dana chuckled and his fingers wrapped around mine as he ducked his head, kissing my forehead.

"I forgot, this is your first time undressing a man." I did not miss the way he enunciated the word "man."

His fingers worked around mine, pulling the tie loose and finally over his head to join the vest on the floor.

"And the shirt."

That time, my hesitation was for an entirely different reason. While I was still crying over how frightening it was to undress him, I was also intensely curious. I remembered seeing my mother reach to undress Dana before he stopped her. It felt as though I was uncovering something forbidden.

Working slowly, I unbuttoned the stiff collar.

I had never taken note of Dana's scent before, or the way his breath sounded moving over his teeth. As I unbuttoned the shirt, I saw the expanse of his smooth skin revealed, spread over the rounded area where his collarbone met his neck. His scent drifted to me, gently, as though carried on the kindest of breezes. His scent was cold, a little metallic, like ice sitting against the roof of my mouth, but there was a wood musk to it as the heat from his skin rolled toward me, making the smell intoxicating.

There was a light dusting of hair across his chest that was revealed as I unfastened his shirt. My eyes, cleared of tears to sate my curiosity, traveled down the smooth muscles of his abdomen.

My hands still trembling, I pulled the fabric free of the waistband of his trousers to unbutton the last two buttons.

Once the buttons were free, I nervously grabbed the collar, pushing it away from his skin and over his broad shoulders. He swooped down to kiss my forehead once more before tugging the shirt off his arms and tossing it to the side.

My breath was heavier now and I sniffed again. I looked him over, my hands barely touching his chest.

"Are you finished?" he whispered.

I turned to look at him, staring into the bright, golden eyes, horrified at the prospect of removing his pants.

"Okay," he whispered, his voice turning to honey. "You did very well. Baby steps," he said, one arm wrapping around my back and lowering me to the bed.

He leaned over me and kissed me a few times as I remained still and stoic, tears leaking from my eyes as he moved his mouth to my neck and down the middle of my chest, one of his hands resting over my right breast while his mouth went to the other one, kissing under it before trailing his mouth upward toward my nipple.

I felt sick.

I closed my eyes and waited for it to be over.

When he was finished, he tucked himself back into his trousers and refastened his belt before moving to my side.

"You did very well," he told me again, his hand tracing up my belly.

"I fucking hate you..."

"And I hope you continue to do so." Dana placed his hand against my stomach, spreading his fingers to cover the expanse of my skin. "Don't you understand, Little Lily? This is all a part of it."

"A part of what?"

"A part of your transformation into something more than what you are." I stared at him for a long moment before he drummed his fingers on my skin, hopping off the bed and moving to the desk.

"Your parents found some interesting things when they were cleaning out your things, like the sketch of the angel with the flag." He turned to me and smiled broadly. "Also, they found this under your mattress." He lifted the file with a stamp across the front that read "TO BE TAKEN OFF RECORD."

"It's a good thing that they didn't look in it," he chuckled. "Otherwise, I would have had to explain a few things." He raised an eyebrow at me. "But you looked through it, didn't you? You know whose file this is?"

I hesitated before nodding.

"I was wondering where it had gone," Dana said. "Not that I really needed it. You see, the file is a book of reference for this," he held up a familiar book. I blinked at the diary of Bryant Morris as Dana brought it to the bed, crawling to sit against the headboard and opening the diary.

"Four-eleven forty-one..." Dana clicked his tongue. "What a tricky son of a bitch. Your uncle really caused a lot of trouble when he came to the Commission. That's why he received so much attention from Bryant Morris."

He turned to a dog-eared page and began reading.

"July seventh," he read. "Four-eleven forty-one is a fascinating subject indeed, and I must admit to a certain amount of special attention that I have been giving him. I have never seen a subject so resilient to the basic testing and manipulations. Despite the pain that he is put through on the table, he insists on acting out against the guards, causing him to be beaten down repeatedly, often until he is unconscious. Yet every day he's as defiant as ever.

"I am beginning to imagine possibilities for him that I could never have imagined for any of the other experiments. Rather than create a weapon, why not test the limits of the human spirit? See how much physical, emotional, and mental pain we can inflict on a man before he finally breaks? And when he does, what becomes of him? What if the human spirit cannot actually break? There are so many fascinating avenues we can take with him that I can hardly decide the best course of action."

He turned to me as he flipped through more pages.

"Is it sickening to hear?"

"This is probably your bedtime story," I groaned, but I did not say anything else. I was curious and I wanted him to continue.

"I will admit to having Sean read a few pages to me every now and then when I was feeling particularly uninspired," Dana said, stopping and reading more of the handwritten pages.

"September twenty-third," he began again. "After much deliberation with the doctors and my assistants, it was finally decided that four-eleven forty-one would be made audience to an interrogation torture of his partner and mother of his child, Katherine Laughton," Dana glanced at me briefly as my eyes shot wide. "Of course this was off-record, but what a fascinating afternoon it turned out to be. The subject was guided into the observation room under heavy sedation and when he was secured, we waited for him to come to completely before beginning.

"When he first saw her, he went completely silent, and as we began the torture he became increasingly agitated. His heart rate increased and his respiration doubled...but he never made a sound through her entire session. It was clear to me that it was not an act of keeping her safe, but rather an act of defiance against me. He was still so aware of my presence even as his lover was tortured in front of him.

"Later, one of my assistants euthanized the girl after hooking her up to a reader to allow four-eleven forty-one to watch her heart stop. That was the only time he showed a reaction. He managed to break free of his restraints and nearly succeeded in breaking through the observation glass. When she was dead, the subject was taken back to his cell. He did not cry or scream. He appears to be in shock. Starting tomorrow, we will pipe in a recording of a heartbeat monitor to see if his reactions hold true to someone suffering from post-traumatic stress disorder."

Dana turned to me, his eyebrows high as I looked away from the book.

"I know that wasn't in his file."

"Why are you so happy?" I growled. "Does that not make you sick?"

"No."

"Did you watch this happen?"

"Yes," he said. "I have to admit, and I'm sure you agree...it's quite fascinating." He closed the book and tapped the cover. "No one understood what made him so different. No one could have predicted anything he did..." He glanced at me out of the corner of his eye. "What a fascinating creature your uncle was."

I stared at him, unsure what to say in response.

"Enough of that for tonight. Time to wash you up."

Dana returned the following day with the book again.

But before he continued my uncle's story, I had to get through the horrible task of undressing Dana once again. I was also forced to remove his belt. He was gentler than before, but I still hated every painful moment.

When it was over, he smiled.

"Something tells me you want another chapter of your bedtime story."

He did not bother to tie me up as he grabbed the book from the desk. Before I could think that it was an opportunity to attack him, understanding flashed through my mind. He was purposely putting opportunities in front of me, because that would give him another reason to harm me and take away any kindness he had been giving. He had control over the entire situation—over my entire life—and I had to be very careful how I worked with him, now more than ever.

With the tone of the past two days, I was beginning to think that I could get out somehow, that I could get close enough to Dana to make him lower his guard and then run and live my life in some remote area of the globe, far away from him and the Commission of the People.

Dana resumed his position on the bed, flicking through the entries quietly as I waited, genuinely interested.

"Ah," he said suddenly, "this is where it gets really fun. September twenty-ninth. Subject four-eleven forty-one has responded most peculiarly to the recorded heartbeat. At first, he screamed and ran around his cell, trying to smash the walls but then collapsed in the corner, rocking back and forth.

"We have played this recording at random intervals for the past six days and nights, seeing if the reactions remain the same. During the seventh time the recording was played—September twenty-seventh—the subject fell to the ground and grabbed his chest. I called for him to be brought to the table and assessed by the doctors to be sure of his health. Upon being strapped to the table, he bid everyone goodbye and went completely still.

"His reactions to pain are now extremely fascinating. His muscles flinch and his brain fires accordingly, but his facial expression does not change.

"It has been two days since the subject has spoken, eaten, or shown further reaction to social interaction with other experiments, doctors, or even me. I discussed with my assistant that he was currently playing with us and seeing what gave him attention. This was his strength over us since we all continued to fuss over him and keep him from going back to his cell where he would be subjected to the heartbeat recording again. The idea was brought forth that his masculine identity should be taken.

"Two of my doctors and one of my assistants sexually assaulted him and broke him out of his coma-like state," Dana read on. I closed my eyes, feeling the bile rise bitterly to my mouth. "His reaction to the assault was to plead and cry, finally ending with him begging for death. When the assault was over and the doctors took him back to his cell, he snapped one of their necks. He was shot with sedatives to keep him from harming others."

"Over the next week, the team plans to perform seventeen different tests on him, several in one day, to test the physical limits of his body, since he seems somehow immune to the testing thus far."

Dana turned to me.

"What's your critique? I think this man likes to talk to himself far too much in this narrative."

"How can you possibly...you were there for all of this and *that's* what you have to say?"

"Little Lily, this man is dead," Dana said, lifting the book for emphasis, "both of them are dead. Generally, when a writer is dead, that is when his work is analyzed so that it is impossible for the readers to ask the writer what he meant by his work of art."

"Work of art? Are you fucking kidding me?" I snapped. "He was a horrible, sadistic jackass! And this was not a fictional character! This was a living, breathing human being!"

Dana shrugged, getting off the bed.

"It made for good material."

I groaned and rolled my eyes.

"You are fucking impossible."

Once again, he washed and restrained me. But as he was redressing in his pristine suit, I dared to ask him a question.

"What time is it?"

He glanced at his watch before righting the lapel of his vest.

"Three."

"In the afternoon?"

"In the morning," he clarified. "I'm busy cleaning up your mess through the day," he teased, tying his tie, glancing in the small mirror on the desk, his hands quick and skilled. "I don't have time to play with you during the day. I see Eina and then I come to see you."

I let out an indignant snort.

"You sure went through a lot of trouble to get me only to put me second," I snarled. He turned to me, grabbing the book and slinging the jacket over one shoulder.

"Then do something that will make you first."

He left.

More hours passed as I fumed, trying to wrap my mind around what Dana had seen my uncle endure under the orders of Bryant Morris.

How could a man sleep at night when he had ordered that a human be tested on just to see if, and when, he would break? While Dana had often talked about changing people and how he was fascinated by the change, he had never said that he tested on someone just to torture them.

Did that mean that Dana was a better person than Bryant Morris?

I shook my head violently, trying to dislodge the thought.

Even though Dana had been a test subject himself and had been tortured by Bryant Morris as well, he had stood by and watched as my uncle was tormented and raped. That made him far, far worse.

Several hours and one forced meal later, it was time for the third round of undressing Dana. That time, I unbuttoned his pants and unzipped his fly, but still, he did not remove his pants.

He grabbed the book and sat on the bed easily, excited to continue reading the horrors of my uncle's torture.

"You seem a little too excited about this," I noted dryly.

"You're interested, too. You can't deny it." He flipped through the pages. "Otherwise, you would be using this time to try and kill me."

I blinked at him before my eyes hardened.

"But if I do that, then you go back to being even more of an asshole. It's not interest, it's self-preservation."

"You're starting to catch on." He lifted the book. "October eleventh. After worrying we were going to lose four-eleven forty-one, he has started to make a recovery. His heart rate is back to normal levels and he has shown signs of consciousness and comprehension of our voices, though he has yet to speak.

"Once again, his body has shown no change as a result of the tests. His muscles show no measurable change, nor does the composition of his blood, apart from the anomalies first noted in the study of this subject. The components of his brain seem to be firing at an extremely rapid pace over extended periods of time, and the areas in which there is activity are far larger than an average man his age."

Dana turned the page.

"October fourteenth," he read. "One of four-eleven forty-one's compatriots had their first turn on the table today. In an attempt to gauge a reaction, I had him brought to the lab to see his friend be tested on.

He had the most unusual reaction when he saw his friend. Rather than tense up or glare at me, as he had done before, he began comforting his friend, telling him that he was about to be reborn and that he should not be frightened.

"Then, the subject attacked Dr. Bowers by slashing his carotid artery. He studied the blood as Dr. Bowers bled out, playing with the blood before he was removed from the lab and taken back to his cell. He was beaten and electrocuted as punishment. His testing will be postponed for ten days for his shattered arm to heal."

"Fuck…" I whispered.

"Indeed," Dana agreed. "He certainly killed a lot of employees…" Dana sighed, shaking his head. "Of course, a lot of the male scientists raped and mutilated him, so I guess it made sense that he would want revenge."

"And you did nothing?" I whispered. "You didn't interfere during any of this?"

"I tried." Dana shrugged, his eyes distant as he closed the book. "He wouldn't let me. He was stubborn as a fucking mule, that one. He insisted that he would do everything himself and that he would die before he allowed any of the tests to affect him."

"You think it was willpower that kept him from being affected?"

"No." Dana shook his head. "His blood showed anomalous composition. Willpower can have some effect over the testing, but the body always gives way at some point."

"But none of the tests affected him."

"Not true," Dana corrected, offering his hand to me to lead me to the bathroom. "They did not affect him in the way everyone expected, but he changed. He became stronger, started breaking through the cell walls and even broke the restraints in the lab. He changed, just not in the way everyone expected."

Dana washed me and was rinsing my hair out when I finally asked my question.

"Did you really try to help him?"

"Of course," Dana said. "I hated Bryant Morris and I wanted him dead. I kept telling him to let me help, but he refused. He wanted that revenge for himself." Dana sighed and pulled the plug on the drain. "So I sat back and watched the fireworks for a while."

"What do you mean?" He took my hands and stood me up before grabbing the towel.

"You'll have to wait and find out."

I thought it over the entire time I was left on my own. For some reason, nothing seemed out of the ordinary with my conversations with

Dana. Nothing was weird about him bathing me after violating me, or discussing what happened to the fabled experiment of the Commission of the People. It was not normal, nor was it routine, it was simply reality.

Which was why I was surprised when the door opened what seemed like several hours before Dana was due back.

It took everything in my power not to shout in relief when I saw Clark run into the room, carefully closing the door behind him.

"Clark," I whispered, watching him dart to me. He was dressed in the Commission holding cell blue jumpsuit with his number on the left side of his chest.

"Shh..." he said, standing next to me. "I only have a few seconds before the guard comes back."

"What are you doing here?"

Clark reached behind him and pulled a gun from the waistband of his pants. I stared, wide-eyed, as he shoved it under the mattress.

"It's Sean's," he answered my startled gaze. "I stole it. Listen, take whatever opportunity you can. Shoot Dana in the fucking head. We might not be able to take the Commission down, but we can at least kill him."

"Are you insane?!"

"Just do it!" Clark snapped. "I'm going in for blood work tomorrow to start my testing. I hope I don't see you back there."

"Clark..."

"Just kill Dana and get it over with," he whispered. He turned to look at the door before sparing me one tear-filled glance in his bloodshot eyes. "I'm sorry..."

And he ran out. I was too stunned to move or call out for someone, wondering how he got Sean's gun and how he had managed to slip past everyone to get the weapon to me.

For the next several hours, I could feel the gun under the mattress. Dana had left me untied so often and I had told him that I was not stupid enough to try anything because I knew he had the upper hand. However, if I was quick enough and he was far enough away...

The problem was catching Dana off-guard while my hands were free.

I spent my time waiting for him combing through all the memories of each encounter, trying to find the perfect moment to shoot him. Perhaps when he was reaching for the book...or when he was leaning over me to refasten the restraints...

He was almost always in close proximity, which made it harder for me to get the gun pointed at his head for the one shot I would have.

Remembering the planning that went into breaking out the experiments, in our parade reveal, and in the different attacks throughout our revolution, I began to feel that same set of nerves fire, preparing me for something dangerous.

Dana walked into the room, his eyes pensive, focused on the ground as he walked to the desk and removed his jacket, setting the book and pocket watch in their normal spot before he hesitated, his eyes distantly staring at the ground.

He was still for several long, tense moments.

"Dana?" I finally whispered.

He shifted his eyes to me and then reached up, unlinking his cuffs and then pulling his tie from his neck. He took off his vest as well, laying everything meticulously over the back of the chair with the jacket before kicking his shoes off as he undid his belt.

I watched, confused, as he undressed in front of me, moving easily, fluidly, without a stumble in shifting his weight as he pulled off his trousers, standing naked, folding them over the chair as well.

My eyes could not stop traveling over his body as he climbed onto the bed. He did not sit on top of me as had become his normal routine. He unhooked my wrists before sitting next to me, folding his legs casually.

"There are eighteen scars on my body," he said. "Find all of them, and I won't rape you today."

"You want me to find eighteen scars on your body?" I blinked, stupefied by the request. I had studied his chest on the last three occasions, but I did not find a flaw on his skin.

"Yes."

I briefly wondered if he was in his Dormant State. He seemed quiet, almost sedated. I sat up and moved to him, my eyes dropping to his neck and looking around his collarbones and pectoral muscles, but there were no scars. My eyes drifted over his left shoulder and then down his arm. I thought I saw a small bulging of skin on the inside of his elbow, so I carefully reached out, moving slowly so as not to startle him—or myself. I turned his arm and saw the dotted scars over the vein inside his elbow.

"Track marks..." I whispered. I looked up at his eyes, confirming he was in a Dormant State when I saw the tender, soft look. "Were you a drug addict?"

"No," Dana corrected. "That's what happens when you fight the needle on the table."

I blinked, barely remembering my knowledge of his resistance as an experiment. I glanced at the needle-made scars and ran my thumb over them.

"How many scars does this count for?"

"One."

I picked up his arm and turned it over completely, where I saw two long scars that ran from the bottom of his wrist to half way up his forearm. It was clear the injury had been self-inflicted.

I ran my fingers over the bumps, my mouth opening to speak though no words came forward.

"You asked if I was willing to be an experiment," Dana whispered, looking over the scars. "I was extremely unwilling at first. Unfortunately for me at the time, I missed the major veins and they were able to stitch me back together before too much damage was done."

I grabbed his other wrist and turned it over, seeing one similar scar on his right arm. Then I looked up at him, expecting to see pain and torture in his eyes as he recalled the suicide attempt. There was none. There was calm, a deadly quiet in his eyes as he watched me.

"Two...three...four..." I said, running my fingers over the scars. He nodded slowly, his hands dropping to rest on his thighs, my eyes following the motion. I saw the large, wide scar that ran along the inside of his right thigh.

"Five..." I breathed, touching the warm, rough flesh before my fingers retreated quickly.

"That was from Mark," Dana said.

I felt my chest crack in two at the mention of Mark.

"During his first little rebellion. He was the only experiment to ever attack me and draw blood." He shook his head. "Such a pity he had to be put down. He was something special..."

I swallowed hard to keep my tears back before my eyes fell to the next small scar, not far from the large slash on his thigh, clearly made by a bullet.

"Six."

"You know what that's from," he said with a chuckle. "Same damn chink."

Ignoring my thoughts of that day and how that had put Mark in Dana's sights, leading to his death in the trench, I searched for other scars on his right leg, bending my neck to look at his knee and calf as he remained cross-legged.

"Two more bullet holes..." I whispered, touching the small, round scars on his left calf. "Seven and eight."

"Sean," Dana said. "The first and only time I truly frightened him. He put two bullets in my leg and then avoided me for months." Dana chuckled. "That was at the beginning of our relationship."

"Relationship?"

Dana smiled and waved his hand distractedly.

"We're not in love," he said. "I just enjoy teasing him."

Ignoring the questions I had always had about Dana's bizarre interactions with his head of security, I searched for more scars.

"I…I don't see any more…" I whispered, my voice trembling.

"You haven't looked at my back, yet," Dana said, chastising me for not thinking to look there before.

Crawling around him, my eyes watching for any movement that he was about to grab me, I rounded to his back and my eyes widened, positive that the other ten scars would easily be found across his broad back.

The first ones I touched were the two long, jagged scars along his right shoulder blade. "Nine…" I whispered, tracing one. "Ten…"

"My father was fond of the belt," he elaborated. "When I was sixteen, he became a fan of using the buckle side."

My stomach turned again and I closed my eyes, my hand resting against the skin. There was another jagged scar running very close to his spine that I traced.

"What's number eleven for?"

Dana chuckled.

"Oh, that one. Believe it or not, Bryant Morris sent me on a few assassin jobs before he was killed. I got that when another assassin was trying to kill me before I killed his client."

"…obviously, you won."

"He did surprise me, though," Dana chuckled. "After I had shattered his femur, he still managed to leap after me on one leg and drag that knife down my back. Barely missed my spine which was very lucky for me."

"And then you killed him?"

"He was in so much pain. I put two bullets in his skull and put him out of his misery."

Trying not to think about younger Dana acting as an assassin, I looked for other marks. There were three small, crescent-shaped burn scars on his lower back near his left hip.

"What the hell happened here?" I asked, pressing my fingers to the shapes delicately.

"Numbers twelve through fourteen?" he asked with a smile in his voice. "Every experiment had their own form of punishment. When I went after Bryant Morris, he grabbed the poker out of the fire and hit me three times with it. The hot part connected there."

Swallowing hard, I scanned his lower back, seeing a large scar running from just above his tailbone across his left buttock.

"Dare I ask?" I asked, touching the top of it.

"Number fifteen happened before I was taken in by the Commission," Dana explained. "I tried to flee over some concertina wire from a deportation camp, and the camp decided to keep a chunk of my flesh as a souvenir."

"What were you doing at a deportation camp?"

"Sneaking people out so I could get them across the northern border into Canada."

"Smuggling people out?" I repeated, something cold settling over my body as I spoke.

"I was apprehended by the Commission for helping criminals across the borders," Dana said, looking over his shoulder. "Incidentally," he reached behind his head and moved some of his longer hair away from his neck, showing me a scar that ran into his hair, "that was how I got scar sixteen," he lifted his right arm and pointed at another small scar on the side of his ribcage, "and seventeen. Seventeen is from the stun gun. Sixteen is from the billie club I took to the back of the head, both from when they finally caught me."

I stared at the back of his head for a long moment, surprised and a little annoyed that the man who had broken up our rebellion had once aided Commission criminals as well.

I looked over his back, trying to find the final scar, even moving around to his front and looking him over again when I was unsuccessful at locating it. After I had studied his face, I shook my head.

"I...I don't see the last one."

Dana looked thoughtful for a moment.

"Alright," he said. "It's not exactly a scar, but it might as well be. My Commission number tattoo." He moved his left foot out of the crossed position and set it on the bed, heel on the covers, facing the bottom of his foot toward me.

My stomach flipped.

41141.

Almost frightened to look, I moved my gaze back up to Dana, who smiled wickedly, showing all his teeth, his eyes crinkling in the grin.

"Come on, really? You didn't even *suspect*?"

"No..." I whispered, shaking my head and backing away from him. "It's not possible...you-you *can't* be..."

"Why not?" Dana challenged. "Because the experiments all told you that four-eleven forty-one was a myth? Or because I'm your long lost uncle?"

"No…it's not…" I shook my head, frightened tears rising to my eyes as I tried to process what those numbers meant. "It's not true…you…you did that…just to fuck with me…"

"I can think of a lot more ways I'd rather fuck with you than tattooing my foot," he chided. I could feel his eyes watching my every reaction, but I could not lift my head, my tear-filled eyes focused on the five numbers. The mark was older, worn and faded with a blue tinge, showing that it had been there for quite some time.

His foot moved and suddenly his hands were on my wrists, pulling my hands away from the side of my head, which I had no recollection of moving there. He then took my chin.

"You…you said you…didn't r-remember…"

"I don't," Dana confirmed. "You were born after I was brought into the Commission. Tommy was eight when I left the house and ten when I was captured. But your name rang a bell in my head, and I did some research into where I came from and who I was before I was Dana."

I broke down slowly, my walls crumbling as the realization crashed through my thoughts like a freight train.

"You…none…none of the tests…"

"None of them worked on me," Dana completed my thought. "They beat me and tortured me and did things to me that you can never imagine, but that's all part of it." His voice sounded excited, thrilled even. He ducked his head to look me in the eye, though I could not focus through the tears and the churning in my stomach. "I still rose above it. I grew stronger. And you will, too."

I finally looked up at him and he smiled at me, a smile that would almost be considered comforting if it weren't for the bright look in his unnerving eyes.

"Wh…what?"

"You're going to join me, Little Lily," he whispered. "I'm going to turn you into more than you ever dreamed. You're going to be able to do and take whatever you want. I'm going to give you that freedom. I'll give you everything you want."

"You're…you'll…kill me…"

Dana kissed my forehead, wrapping his arms around me and pulling me into his chest as I cried.

"Only a part of you…"

My eyes snapped open and were burning immediately. I was frozen, my eyes wide as I stared into the chest in front of me.

Dana.

He was holding me.

He was also lying very still.

Was he asleep?

I dared to look up at his face and saw his eyes closed, his head resting on a pillow as he breathed slowly and deeply.

Afraid of waking him, I also remained completely still, assessing where I was and what state I was in.

Everything seemed like a blur, the way I had searched Dana's body for scars...the numbers tattooed on the bottom of his foot—what numbers were they again?—and the way he held me as I cried, promising me all the power I could have ever wanted. All I had to do was kill a part of myself to achieve it.

The tears came back with a vengeance.

This was my uncle, the experiment I had admired and strived to imitate if I was ever brought into the Commission. The irony was not at all laughable. Now, Dana was going to force me to walk down the same path, force me to become like him.

I no longer had someone to look up to. The one I had seen as a hero, as a pillar of strength against the corruption and terror of the Commission for the People, had actually turned into the man running the entire circus.

There was a click at the door and I jumped before forcing myself to be still in fear of waking Dana.

The door slowly opened as I watched, trying to crane my neck to see who was there. Sean's worried and pale face poked into the room. I blinked, surprised to see him. When his eyes met mine, he bowed his head, his gaze apologetic as he walked in, closing the door behind him.

"Dana," he called.

"Whatever it is I'm supposed to do, I refuse," Dana said simply, not even partially asleep.

"Leader Simon needs you at Central Hall," Sean continued, walking to Dana's side of the bed. He placed a hand on Dana's shoulder and tried to pull him onto his back, away from me. "Come on, get dressed. We need to leave in twenty minutes."

"I said, no," Dana snapped, swatting at Sean distractedly, still keeping his eyes closed.

"Dana, you've been in here for four hours."

"Really?" He finally cracked an eye open and turned to look at Sean, still keeping his arms around me. "Four hours?"

"Yes," Sean groaned, exasperated. "Now, will you please get dressed so we can go?"

Dana sighed heavily and released me, rolling over the side of the bed and to his feet, stretching his arms above his head before donning his clothes. Sean's eyes turned to me and he placed one knee on the bed, reaching over and placing a hand against my cheek.

"I'm sorry…" he whispered.

"Don't be sorry, Sean," Dana said. "She's going to go through an amazing transformation. She's going to become like me."

"That's why I'm apologizing," Sean growled, fixing Dana with a harsh glare.

The leader of the Commission narrowed his eyes playfully as he stood straight from grabbing his socks and took a step forward, flicking his wrist and using the socks to hit Sean across the backside.

"Don't be naughty or I'll have to spank you," Dana warned with a playful tone. He was out of that Dormant State and back to his normal, electric self.

"You would do that if you wanted to, regardless of my behavior."

"Don't give me ideas," Dana said mischievously, drawing his shirt across his shoulders. "It distracts me from my work."

"*You* distract you from your work."

"Restrain her for me," Dana ordered. Sean turned to me—the look in his eyes nearly broke my heart.

"Dana, why not just let her back into the holding cells and—"

"No." Dana cut him off. "She can't go into the holding cells."

"Why not?"

"Because if she goes back there, she will meet with all her little revolutionary friends and they will organize a riot during Free Hour."

"What makes you think she would do that?" Sean pressed. "She needs to be around other people."

"I know she would do it because that is what I did." Dana smiled thinly. "And if you're worried about her social interactions, don't worry, she'll be on the table soon enough. She'll see plenty of people, then."

"That's not what I meant…"

"Just tie her up before we're late for this meeting you insisted was so important," Dana droned, annoyed.

Sean threw one more apologetic look at me and then took the raw skin of my wrist in his hand, moving my hand to the cuff, tightening the restraints as carefully as possible. I watched him, trying to school my expression to assure him that I understood he was not the one to be angry at. I watched Dana fix his tie and grab his jacket, but I could not find it in my heart to be upset at Dana either. My brain had not recovered from the shock I had received four hours previous.

My brain and body were frozen, trying to process information into memory and understanding. But there was too much going on in my mind, too many thoughts buzzing around my already-pounding head to organize.

Sean finished fastening my second wrist just as Dana placed the pocket watch back in his pocket.

"Alright," Dana said. "Little Lily, I will be back later."

"Sean," I called. The head of security turned to me. "Feel free to crash the car."

Even though I had no way to tell time in the room, I could tell that it was far longer than normal that Dana was gone. I was beginning to think that Sean *had* crashed the car.

If he hadn't, I had every intention of shooting Dana when he returned.

My uncle…

There was a small part of me that still did not believe that Dana was William Sandover, the man who had been on the domestic terrorist list since he was a teenager for sneaking more than three hundred people over the different borders and having one of the most extensive networks of safe houses ever known in the history of America.

I continued to remember how much I had admired 41141. In life, my uncle had been unyielding in his belief that the cleansing of America was the worst thing that ever happened to the country, believing that people were equal. And then the Commission changed him into a monster living under the name of Dana Christenson.

If William had been changed into Dana, there was no one the Commission could not break. The strongest experiment that they had ever had—the one who had been immune to all the tests—was now running the tests. He was breaking people who had been much weaker than him on the table as if he was filing paperwork. It was thoughtless, easy for him to change a human to be something else. He must have been able to see into people and change them the way he did because he had found that same part of himself when he was going through the same tests.

Dana knew all the results before testing even started.

And he had taken those skills to dealing with people who were in the government, strapped to a different kind of slab, more metaphorical than the tables in the labs of the Commission of the People. He found what little weaknesses he could exploit simply by meeting the person and watching the way they reacted to him.

For some reason, I thought of an ad I had once seen in my first school's counseling center when I had been waiting for my turn to talk to the counselor after punching Tommy Barker in the nose. The poster was a cooking sheet of gingerbread men, perfectly shaped to match one another, except that all of them had a different edible ornament attached. Some of them had a gumdrop sitting on top of their chests, while others had a light sprinkling of sugar, a few had little cracks in them that were filled with a thin line of red icing. The caption had read: "Not all scars are visible. Be kind to all."

Only, rather than thinking about the emotional scars people in the Commission had to bear, Dana was the edible ornament on those gingerbread men. He enveloped people like batter, hardening around them with something as simple as a handshake so he could find their cracks and bumps, filling them and completing their flawed beings by changing himself to match them.

He was not a man.

He was not a monster.

He was what everyone wanted.

He was an idea. An empty vessel that people filled and took from as they wanted.

He had told me this before.

"I'm absolutely nothing. People read into me however they wish...They can turn a blind eye to everything else because there is that one thing that I can give them that nothing else can: a sense that they have accomplished something, fulfilled something, had power over their own lives..."

Before I could stop the thought from forming, it was there, wrapped in a sense of awe and amazement and lined with fear.

What an incredible creature...

* *** *

Dana finally returned, wearing the same suit and looking annoyed.

"I swear, have to run the entire country on my fucking own...no one is competent enough to do anything," he mumbled. He turned to me. "I'm sorry, you must have been lonely."

"No," I said as strongly as I could manage.

For some reason, I felt very small and weak in front of him in a new way. I had felt helpless several times—increasingly so since the end of our insurrection—but the feeling that night was different. It did not make me defiant. My brain understood that I needed to be afraid and be quiet. The creature in the room was far more powerful than me and there was no way to know what it would do next.

"Oh," he started, remembering something as he unbuttoned his vest. "You got your number today."

I could only wait silently for him to continue.

"88911," he told me. "Tomorrow, you get your tattoo and tracer and then we start you on the table as soon as your blood work clears."

"A-Already?"

"Yep." He kicked his shoes off. "No time to waste. I'm going to need you by my side as soon as possible."

"Why?" I asked, watching him tug his shirt off and then his pants. He smiled mysteriously and stalked to the bed, climbing on top of me and grinning with a cat-like quality that frightened me.

"Rehan is almost finished."

"Who?"

"Eina's sister," he chuckled. "She's almost done. The testing is going seamlessly. She's responding just as her brother did. When she's complete, we'll impregnate her and see if she can give birth to another Machine of Neutralization." He shuddered with excitement. "It's incredible. Just imagine being able to breed an army of these warriors."

"They'll destroy everything," I barely managed to breathe.

"I know."

He kissed me hard, crushing his lips against mine, his teeth nipping at my lips as his body settled heavily over me. I had never realized just how much larger he was until he was resting over me like a blanket, warm and soft, but weighing down on me.

He bit my bottom lip hard enough to draw blood and I flinched from the pain. He backed away, licking his lips with a predatory grin.

Then his head dropped to my neck, kissing and biting the skin, one of his hands running from my hair down to my breast, cupping it completely in his large hand, remaining gentle. He pressed on my ribs, his mouth sucking a mark to life on my neck as his hips pushed forward, grinding him against me and causing me to cringe, afraid of the inevitable pain.

Confusion swirled in my head and a terrifying set of thoughts came to me.

Dana was more dangerous than anyone I had ever known. Unlike the television villains in horror films and late-night programs, he was terrifyingly real and currently laying on top of me, gently touching me with his mouth locked around the pulse in my neck. He could kill me so easily as I was laying there, chained and helplessly at his mercy. But he had not made any effort to end my life. There was something he wanted from me, something carnal and dark, and because of that, he was being gentle with me despite his overwhelming power.

That made me feel surprisingly powerful, even in my vulnerable state.

My resistance made me powerful. I could drag this on and on. Dana did not want me to submit to him, to enjoy sex with him as everyone else did. He wanted the challenge, the tease that whet his pallet for more.

And I could control that.

As his mouth moved down my belly, his lips locking just under my belly button, I thought back to the previous interactions I had had with him. The times he had touched me and lit my body up like dynamite, the gentle whispers against my ear, the way he had promised to change me from a virgin into a powerful woman who could get what she wanted.

Without me knowing, he had already changed me. He had hardened me and made me unafraid to stand up against something. He had pushed me to grow into a woman, willing to fight for what I believed.

Did he know he had changed me? Did he mean to do so? Or had he been chasing me and waiting to see how I would change on my own before he picked the right moment to capture me, knowing the precise moment when it would break me the most?

What had my flaws been? What had I needed from him? What had I taken from him?

Or maybe I was the one person he could not mold to. Perhaps my wounds and flaws matched his, and no matter how he tried to encase me to fill anything that was missing, it was the one thing he could not give me.

When he entered me, the fear that rocketed through me was more painful than the penetration.

We were the same.

That was how he knew he could break me. Our connection to one another was much deeper than blood. Young and stupid, we had both fought for the idealistic world we had imagined the globe to be, only to be caught, ripped from the ones we loved and torn down. I was on one side of the transformation and he was the mirror looking me in the eye, showing me what I would become.

"Are you afraid?" he whispered, seated inside my body, connecting us.

I nodded, my gaze locked with his.

He smiled and began moving, slowly but with strength and power that I could see and feel from the flexing of his muscles and the intensity of his eyes as he looked at me.

Was there any way to fight his influence?

I had tried to go against the Commission, tried to rally the people behind me, but the Commission proved much stronger. It was a living, breathing organism that shifted to overcome the opposition, crushing anything that dared to get in its way. It was far too large to be toppled, just like Dana.

Dana was the Commission of the People, and the Commission was Dana Christenson.

The tears fell from my eyes as I felt the walls closing around me, the room spinning as he moved above me, staring into me. Everything was moving as I stayed in one spot, helpless and overwhelmed.

My eyes shut and I pulled against my restraints, my body bowing under him as I let out a choked sob. He stilled for several long seconds before he pulled out and took my face in his hands, his lips pressing to mine, causing a small sting to radiate from the cut in my lip.

The tears tumbled down my cheeks.

It was the end.

No words needed to be exchanged. He knew that I understood my situation, and I knew that he could see my horrified realization.

I opened my eyes again when his weight lifted and dipped the bed next to me. He unbuckled my wrists and then rested his head on the pillow next to mine. I looked at him, sniffing and trying to clear my blurry vision, though my tears refused to shake free from welling against my eyelashes.

He closed his eyes as I continued to cry.

If I was weak against him, succumbing to what he wanted and what the tests did to me when I was on the table, then I would be surrendering everything to him. It was possible that he would simply lose interest if I stopped providing entertainment for him and I would rot away in the back of the Commission. If I fought against the testing…then I would become like Dana.

Could I fight even more and avoid both?

My eyes snapped open.

I turned my head to look at him. His eyes were closed, his breathing even and slow. I supposed he really did sleep, maybe in the same way Mark did, only twenty minutes or an hour a day, just to rest his body.

I watched him intently, looking for confirmation that he was completely asleep.

He did not shift, even as I counted each second for five full minutes. His breathing remained at exactly the same pace.

Moving so slowly I was certain it would take an hour to get out of the bed, I slipped my legs over the side of the mattress, watching Dana with unblinking eyes.

He did not stir.

I moved at an agonizingly slow pace, rising to my feet, standing next to the bed, watching the motionless leader of the Commission of the People. As I watched him, I reached down to touch the cold metal that was wedged tightly under the mattress. Having to pull harder than I wanted to, I finally freed the heavy gun from its hiding place, holding it in both hands, glancing back at Dana to be sure he had not moved as I had struggled freeing the weapon.

He had not moved.

I glanced back down at the gun, not even moving my head, worried that the sound of my muscles shifting under my skin would be loud enough to wake him. My fingers gently pressed the safety switch, being sure to keep my gaze on Dana when the switch actually slid to the other end, unlocking the trigger.

I dared not open the magazine to be sure there were bullets. I should have put some thought to the original possessor of the gun, but for the moment, I was intensely focused on the sleeping figure on the bed.

My whole body was shaking with anticipation, making my aim worse. I had one shot and I needed to steady myself to make that one shot count.

Lifting my left knee, I pressed it into the bed, steadying my weight and extending the gun, one hand supporting the other, remembering how Mark had taught me to aim. I took a deep breath to steady my shot, aiming directly at Dana's forehead.

My hands were shaking too much. I tried to draw in another breath to center myself, but the air was suddenly thin and the deep breath only made me light-headed and caused my shaking to worsen.

I swallowed hard and forced my hands to still as much as I could, taking aim.

Dana's eyes opened, locking on me in an instant. My body went weak with terror. I let out a small sound that could barely count as a pathetic whimper, but my arms did not waver from their position, still pointing the gun at the leader of the Commission of the People.

Five seconds passed like years where we both stared at one another, silent, the gun between us.

The corners of his mouth curved into a confident smirk and he closed his eyes once again, laying his head back against the pillow, resuming his apparent slumber.

The actions spoke for themselves.

I know you're not going to shoot.

I had never felt so insignificant.

The terrified sobs rose in my throat and I looked frantically around the bed. My arms were weak, the heavy gun was slipping from my hands as I began hyperventilating.

Dana's eyes opened again and he took a deep breath, the smirk fading from his face as he sat up and reached out to take the gun. The panic grabbed at me and I steadied the weapon, pointing it at his forehead again and pressing the barrel to the spot between his eyebrows, the tears falling free from my eyes as I shook like a leaf in the wind.

He hesitated only for a moment, his eyes calm and understanding as he looked further than into my mind. The golden color reached to the deepest pit of my stomach, to the core of me, and held me there.

His hand went to the gun and he pulled it from my fingers, moving slowly as I panted, my eyes wide and frightened, caught in his stare. The gun dropped to the bed between us and, as soon as I heard the sound, all the tension in my body released, moving out of my toes and into the floor. I collapsed on the bed. He gathered me in his arms, holding me tightly as I sobbed and cried out loudly, nearly screaming as I broke down, only feeling the warmth of his body against mine and the small bite of cold metal as the gun pressed between my hip and his.

* *** *

Dana returned only an hour after he left me dazed and frightened on the bed. He secured me in my restraints again only because he left the gun in the room. I stared at the cold, black metal, not sure why he had left it.

When he returned, he had brought some folded red clothes. It was my uniform, symbolizing I was an experiment.

Dana released my restraints and slapped my hip.

"Get dressed."

I could not move.

"Do you really want me to dress you again?" he asked.

Two seconds later, I finally rose from the position I had fallen into and reached for the clothes, pulling them on slowly as Dana supervised. When I was covered, he offered a hand and led me out of the room.

My head was low as I walked. I did not want to see where I was going. I already knew.

Holding my hand, Dana led me, barefoot and shaking, through the front security of the Commission. I ignored the snickering of the guards when they saw me. The tiles beneath my feet were very cold and caused my toes to tingle as I walked through the hallway of the termination cells...through the middle of Ward Three...then Ward Six...finally turning to the lab.

There was a group of three men and two women in the lab, all wearing their white coats and looking over a single clip board.

"Mr. Christenson," one of the women greeted.

"Jeanie," he said, stepping further into the lab with me in tow. I dared to look at Jeanie, who had dark blonde hair that was tied neatly out of her face. Her brown eyes were looking at Dana with adoration that made me wince.

"Is this her?"

"Yes, it is."

"Alright," Jeanie said. "Barry, put her on the table." As the man named Barry took me away from Dana, I heard Jeanie continue speaking with him. "Will you be staying?"

"I'm afraid not," Dana said. "I have some business to attend."

I was picked up and set on the table as I heard Jeanie make some show of pouting that Dana wasn't going to be there for my first time on the table. He chuckled.

"I was there for all of her other firsts." My head snapped in his direction, ignoring the way Barry was rolling my right sleeve up. Dana's eyes glanced in my direction and he smiled as if to say 'yes, I was there. You should have been paying more attention.'

"Oh, Mr. Christenson," Jeanie giggled. "You shouldn't say such things!"

"What can I say?" Dana teased, leaning down to her, playful. "Sometimes, I kiss and tell." Jeanie giggled again and it took everything I had in me not to roll my eyes.

Dana ran his thumb over the scientist's cheek, still smiling.

"I apologize, but I really must run."

"Alright," Jeanie consented. "But it really has been too long since you were present for an experiment that wasn't Eina."

"Eina's fascinating. I can't keep myself away."

"But he's not my project," Jeanie pouted. Barry grabbed my ankles and moved them onto the table, strapping them down with metal cuffs. The cold metal barely hit my skin, allowing me just a little bit of room to move if needed. Pushing me down, he strapped my neck and arms as the other scientists moved toward me, pulling on blue, latex gloves.

"I know, darling, but the last time I watched one of your projects on the table, you and I got distracted," Dana teased, pretending to scold her.

"That was a good day."

"A very good day," he agreed. "Take care of her."

"Will do." I heard the door open and close as Dana left the lab.

"So, this is one of the little terrorists of the Central Angels," one man mused, shaking his head as he looked me over.

"Apparently," another sighed. "She looks pretty dull to me. How could she have gotten all those experiments and people out?"

"You cost us millions of dollars," the other female scientist told me as if she was scolding a five-year-old for breaking a toy. "There's a lot of money that goes into each of those experiments and you took over twenty of them, not to mention you got the Eight Group killed. They were expensive."

"If you count all the work we've had to do calming the people down, it's over a billion," Jeanie said, stepping to a rolling table and pulling two gloves out of the dispenser. "She's quite the busy bee."

"She seems pretty tame now," Barry chuckled, grabbing a swab of cotton and soaking it in something before rubbing it on the inside of my right elbow. "Seeing all her friends killed must have calmed her down a little."

"Either that, or Dana has tamed her," the final man said darkly.

"She only entertained him for two and a half weeks," the woman pointed out. "She must not have much to offer if he's already had his fill of her."

"You mean filled her," the man laughed, causing a round of taunting to surround me before I caught sight of the needle coming toward me. Barry laughed when he saw me flinch away.

"What? Afraid of a little needle?" he leered. He pushed the needle into my skin and I turned away, clenching my eyes shut and biting my lower lip. "Don't be a wimp. We're just drawing blood."

"What if she's pregnant?" one of the men asked. "Wonder if Dana will want to keep it. It will slow down testing…"

"Dana is infertile."

"You would know," the other woman laughed.

"Don't be a bitch," Jeanie teased back. "You were the one who freaked out when he fucked you in Ward Seven because you thought you were pregnant."

"That gossip rocketed around in no time," Barry recalled with a laugh.

Their voices floated to me gently, barely brushing my ears as I tried to ignore the needle drawing blood.

"Fuck you, Barry," the girl laughed. I heard a sound and then Barry let out an indignant snort.

"Watch it, Tamara!" he snapped. "I'm working with a needle here!"

"Oh, who cares?" Tamara groaned. "Corbett," she said to one of the men, "ready for a vitals read?"

"Yep."

"We might as well check her for internal injuries, too," the final man said.

"Smooth, George," Tamara chuckled. "You say that all the time. Anything to see a girl naked."

"That's why I love my job." George was an older man with a large, rounded belly and a salt-and-pepper beard surrounding his thin lips.

"The boys, too," Corbett added.

"Fuck you," George snapped. "I'm not some fucking homo."

"Except when you want to suck Dana's cock," Corbett corrected.

"To be fair, who doesn't want to suck Dana's cock?" Barry said, removing the needle and taping something over my elbow. His eyes moved from my arm to my eyes and he smiled sickly. "I'm sure even this little whore did it at some point over the last couple weeks."

They moved around me, halting their conversation as Corbett and Tamara took note of my vitals, feeling my pulse, checking blood pressure and a bunch of other things that never happened when I went to the doctor normally. I could not take note of everything, slowly slipping in and out of consciousness.

Sleep was easier than reality.

When they suddenly began fastening my left foot into a vice, I began to pay attention. I was about to be marked with my experiment number.

"Are you going to do it?" Barry's voice asked near my feet.

"Yeah," Tamara's voice responded. "Greg is busy right now."

"You know, Jake wanted to get a tattoo," Barry said. I could not lift my head to look down and identify the mechanical noises at my feet.

"Did you let him get one?" Jeanie asked.

"I told him when he was twenty, he could do whatever he wanted," Barry sighed. "Denise told him that if he got a tattoo she would never let him back in the house."

"I wouldn't mind if my children wanted tattoos," George said. "I mean, unless it was a really stupid one, then I would have a problem with it."

A wet cloth rubbed the bottom of my foot, cleaning my skin. I shivered at the thought of the little needle going in and out of my foot, tattooing the number that would seal my fate.

"One of my classmates in med school got a really stupid tattoo, a tramp stamp," Jeanie said.

"What was it?" Tamara asked.

"It was a really elaborate design, like a letterhead, and the text read 'Connor Was Here' right above her ass."

The scientists' booming laughter echoed around the lab.

"Was Connor her boyfriend?"

"No!" Jeanie laughed loudly. "She meant Connor North, the actor! She had never met the man in her life. She was high as a fucking kite. In the end, she married a man named Paul!"

The scientists shared another round of laughter before Tamara turned on the needle for the tattoo. There was a buzz from the little machine and I flinched at the sound, my heart thumping in fear.

"Hey, you. Just so you know, we're starting," Tamara called to me. "Don't struggle too much because you're only going to hurt yourself in the process."

Her fingers pressed into my foot, pushing the skin taught as the needle found its way to my skin. I let out a choked scream, my anxiety causing me to feel the pain more acutely. It was sharp, a small point that touched my skin with a hot, vibrating motion.

"Do you have a tattoo, Tamara?"

"Yeah. Just a little snake on the back of my neck."

"I was always curious about tattoos," Corbett said. "I had a lot of friends who went into the military and came back with all kinds of ink."

"What would you get if you got a tattoo?" Jeanie asked.

It was amazing that I could focus on their conversation while there was the hot, vibrating feeling against my foot, disappearing every now and then only to return all too soon.

"I don't know," Corbett mused. "Maybe something simple...I can't think of any reason I would want to be on the table for hours and hours."

"I know what I would get," Jeanie said. "I would get paw prints across my shoulder and collarbone..."

"Why?" Tamara asked.

"That's where my cat always walks on me to get me up in the morning."

Cat? Did they have animals in the basement of the Commission? I was pretty sure that the scientists lived in the Commission. And did Barry and George say they had kids? I don't remember any of the Commish Kids being the children of the scientists...

As the tattoo continued, I calmed down, becoming more accustomed to the strange feeling that dragged over my skin, a cloth occasionally passing over the area before starting again with more ink. The conversations of tattoos continued with stories of friend's tattoos and their own thoughts on their children getting tattoos or what they would want on themselves.

I had never wanted a tattoo.

When the needle was turned off, Tamara wiped the area again and then cleaned it before wrapping something over the bottom and slipping a soft boot over my foot as the other scientists released me from the vice.

"Okay, 88911," George addressed me, coming back into my line of sight. "We're going to take you to your cell. We will see you back here tomorrow." He grinned as though it was an appointment I could look forward to.

I was led out of the lab in cuffs fastened to my wrists, a long chain running from the cuff around my neck to the cuffs on my wrists, and finally to the two cuffs around my ankles. I cringed every time I stepped on my right foot, the fresh tattoo leaving me even more sensitive to the cold floor.

I wondered where my tears were as I was led through Ward Seven. The tears had not come at all since my breakdown when I failed to shoot Dana. My emotions were in recovery time and the response to any emotional stress now was to simply slip into an alternate state of mind similar to unconsciousness.

I shuffled into the room connecting Wards Eight, Nine, Ten, and the Dome, a place I had only been in once before, when it was littered with bodies of the men and women who had been killed during our great escape.

Jeanie led me to the second door on the right wall—a door I knew from breaking out Tori. My heart fell into my stomach at the recollection of her smiling face.

Punching in the new code, which I didn't bother to memorize, Jeanie and three guards walked into the east section of Ward Ten, leading me silently. We turned down the first hallway, just as I had before, only this time, I could see the experiments in the cells. I kept my head down, glancing at them discreetly.

They moved forward, gazes locked on me, following me to the furthest corner of their cells, their eyes raking over my body. It was even worse than I had imagined.

I was fresh meat.

We stopped at the dead end and turned to the right, walking the familiar path to the cell that Tori had once occupied.

Something told me it was Dana's idea to put me in her cell.

The guards punched in the code into the electronic lock and ran their keycard over the top, the door sliding open. I hesitated, looking around the white walls in fear, but Jeanie's insistent hands and the final push between my shoulder blades from one of the guards caused me to finally set foot in my new prison.

As my chains were removed, I looked around the square space, seeing the toilet that had a small wall to barely conceal the area from outside view. There was a metal slot at the bottom right corner of the glass wall where I assumed food was given. Otherwise, there was nothing breaking the starkness of the cell.

The cuffs were gathered and the entourage left.

For several long moments, I could only stand in the middle of the cell and look around the plain, white walls and the hallway. There were two cells across from mine, one of them dark and empty and the other lit with a female experiment studying me. She only looked a few years older than me with black hair and dark eyes. She was deathly thin and her skin was pale and chalky, contrasting with the sharp red of her clothes.

Feeling uncomfortable with the scrutiny, I walked to a corner and sat, hugging my legs to my chest and setting my face on my knees, taking deep breaths, my brain buzzing with static that led to no thoughts at all.

I must have fallen asleep for a few hours, despite the bright light of the cells, because the next thing I knew, there was a clank that startled me and a tray of food was pushed through the slot. I craned my neck from my position laying on the cold floor to see who was giving the food, but they walked away, rolling the cart with them.

I turned onto my stomach and then rose to my hands and knees, crawling to the food, though I passed it and pressed my face to the glass to see who they were. There were three people dressed in white suits followed by an incredible amount of black-clad men in heavy gear, guns pointed forward as they walked closer to the cell Eina occupied.

It only occurred to me then that I was in the same ward as the completed Machine of Neutralization.

I quickly slinked to the other corner of the cell, pressing my face against the glass, barely able to see the cell where the entourage halted.

The guns were pointed at the door as one of the people in white crouched down, pushing the tray of food into the slot.

The woman leapt away. I thought I saw a movement of red against the glass, but I did not have a good view of the cell and, therefore, could not see enough to determine what had happened.

The group of people retreated down the hall. I shrunk away from the glass when they passed, feeling very small and fragile.

When I saw the group round the corner, I went to my tray of food and picked up the paper bowl, pulling off the lid and sipping the soup, huddling near the tray, hungry, cold, and terrified.

I finished my food, though it was bland and I was still hungry afterward. I then paced along my cell, nervous and unsure what the scientists had in store for me.

The lights never went out, never dimmed. There was no way of knowing what time of day it was, or the weather outside. I wanted a window. I wanted to see outside just to have a sense of time.

The experiment across from me was watching me again. I shifted nervously, looking away from her unnerving stare. I was thankful that the other cell across from me was empty, otherwise I know I would have had a panic attack with two experiments staring me down through the window of my cage.

I moved around the cell lazily, sitting down when my legs were tired, bored and unable to hear anything apart from the humming of the lights and the streams of air that blew in from the two slats in the roof of the cell. There was a camera placed at each corner that I would look up at and count each time the little red light flashed, losing count and starting over repeatedly.

I fell asleep again and woke up not long after for no reason.

I began pacing again.

There was nothing to distract my thoughts. The pale, blank walls and glass offered no form of entertainment for my wandering mind, which made me think back on the revolution. I remembered the joy and thrill of having everyone out of the Commission...I remembered the tears as we went around in the circle and told our stories...I remembered the tender looks and touches of families and lovers as they rejoiced in their freedom...I remembered the laughter and the way we teased one another, like a family of over one hundred people...the silly moments when we were preparing for our battles and no one could hit the target...the funny songs and dances that passed cold nights...

It didn't seem real. Maybe they were only illusions. Maybe I had really been trapped in this cell, caught when I tried to break the experiments out, and ever since I had been imagining the glorious fight that we had all dreamed about.

The walls were sucking away all feelings and thoughts, playing them on every wall, the ceiling, the floor, reminding me of those times like a movie on repeat.

But the tears still did not come.

There were people outside my door that drew my attention. I watched Jeanie and Tamara walk into the cell, Tamara holding my restraints. I remained seated, watching them approach as the three guards remained stationed at the door.

"Stand up," Tamara ordered.

I was not sure if it was the bright lights of the cell, but I noticed then that Tamara was particularly unattractive. Jeanie was beautiful in her own way, but Tamara looked as though she had endured a very difficult life. Her skin was dark and creased with wrinkles, dotted by sun-made freckles. Her blue eyes were small on her face and her light brown hair sat in crinkled curls around her face while the rest of her straw-like hair was held behind her head in a clip. Her hands were knotted like a tree and her nails were painted a horrible shade of red.

I stood and held my hands out as instructed.

I did not move as they chained me up, but I was still reluctant to put weight on my right foot. The tattoo had stopped feeling hot, but it was itchy.

I was led out of my cell, out of the ward, and to the lab marked with the sign I barely registered as reading "Lab Two."

I was startled to see one experiment sitting on a table, surrounded by another group of scientists dressed in their pristine white coats. The experiment was swallowing some pills as I was led to my table. I looked him over, wondering what ward he was from and what he was being altered for.

Jeanie ordered the guards away as Tamara released me. I dared to glance at the experiment again, who was now being cuffed by one of the scientists. A familiar scientist turned away from the other group and approached me.

"Ah, the little terrorist again," Barry said.

"Her blood tests came back with some interesting results," Jeanie started, looking over the file she had picked up from the cart where a case labeled S.I.D.-3 sat next to some syringes. "I tried to find out what these mean," she said, pointing to the something in her folder as Barry looked over the charts with her, "but nothing showed up."

I heard some clanging and whirled around to see the male experiment being led out of the room by George and Corbett.

"Did you notify Dana?"

"Yes. He said to go through with the first round and report exactly what happens."

There were anomalies in my blood. Just like in Dana's blood.

"Alright," Barry said. He walked to me and grabbed the front of my shirt, unbuttoning it. I gasped and tried to back away, pushing him. My voice wouldn't come out. It was stuck in my throat.

"Hold her for me," Barry growled. "Quit making a scene."

Tamara grabbed my arms and held them steady as Barry finished with the buttons and then worked the shirt from my shoulders, which Tamara took and dropped to the ground as Barry pulled the pants from my hips.

I started kicking, feeling my knee connect with his jaw.

"Shit! Barry! Are you alright?!" Jeanie gasped, running to the other scientist. I felt the smile pull at my lips.

Barry looked at me and I glared back.

Before I could register his movement, his hand struck me across the cheek, causing my face to explode with pain.

"You bitch," he snapped. "Quit struggling, or I will have to teach you what happens when you disobey."

I spit in his face.

"That's it." Barry grabbed my shoulders, turning me around, my arms ripping free of Tamara's grip. He bent me over the table, slamming my head into the metal and stunning me as I tried to scream. My voice was still trapped.

Barry held my hands behind my back as he yanked the pants off my ankles and then his hand came in sharp contact with my skin as he spanked me with a dark laugh.

"Trust me, next time I will actually rape you."

"We never checked her for tearing or bruising," Tamara noted, as though there was nothing unusual about the rape threat. "Let's do that now while we're waiting for George and Corbett."

Barry held my arms behind my back and Tamara's hands enclosed my ankles, spreading my legs as I was held in the humiliating position, bent over the table, naked, without seeing who was touching me.

Jeanie's hands were covered in cold latex as she touched me, spreading my skin to look at the damage.

"There's some bruising between the inner and outer labia on both sides," she noted. Something cold pressed into me and I gasped, shaking and trying to move my hips to avoid the metal, though it caused a pinching inside me and made me still immediately.

Then there was a pressure, a small clicking sound, and finally enough pressure to push me open.

"No signs of tearing, though," Jeanie said. "Looks a little irritated, but otherwise, everything looks fine." The pressure eased and the metal slipped away, though that did nothing to lessen my panic. "We'll be sure to give her supplements before we put her back in her cell."

The door opened and my heart nearly leapt out of my throat.

"Ooh, this looks like quite the party," George's voice chuckled behind me. "Look at that pretty sight."

"You want Dana's sloppy seconds?" Corbett asked skeptically.

"Actually, she seems to be in distress," Barry said with an annoyed groan. "Let's just get her on the table and get going. We're behind schedule."

"Fucking buzz-kill. That's what you are, Barry," George said pointedly.

Tamara released my ankles, but only after she had lifted them onto the table and strapped them down with the metal restraints.

They moved around me, getting their gloves and putting masks over their noses and mouths. I looked around, frightened, unsure what was about to happen.

"What are we running?" Corbett asked, fixing his mask over his nose and mouth.

"SID-3," Jeanie answered.

"That's pretty low-level," Corbett murmured, sounding disappointed.

"Dana's orders," Jeanie said, setting my file down and grabbing her own gloves, being the last one to get ready. "He was very specific about what he wanted."

"Why did he put her in Ward Ten?"

"Take a look at the list of what he wants done." Jeanie nodded to the folder. George picked up the folder, his eyes scanning down the page rapidly.

"*Shit*," he groaned. "This is a lot of tests…" His eyes narrowed and he looked more intently at the paper. "Fuck, if we do this, we'll likely kill her."

"That's what I said," Jeanie agreed. "But he insisted she'll be fine. He told me that I would understand after this test, so it must have something to do with those anomalies in her blood work."

They placed tacky pads on the skin of my neck, forehead, biceps, forearms, belly, thighs, and calves. One of them clipped something onto my finger while another one started an IV that almost made me pass out from my phobia of needles.

Barry then swabbed my other arm. I heard the case on the rolling table click open.

"All monitors are running," Corbett called.

"Okay," Barry said. "Someone call time for me." He reached to the rolling table out of my line of sight and grabbed a packaged syringe, tearing it open and grabbing a vial of clear liquid from the case marked with a black number one. He filled the syringe as my panic became all-encompassing, dulled by whatever was pumping through my IV. The drug made it impossible for my body to panic. My brain raced, watching as the plunger on the syringe moved up, pulling in more of the clear substance.

Barry put the vial back on the table and his hand went to my arm, pushing the syringe under my cold skin. I opened my mouth to let out a pathetic sob of panic and fear, but no sound came out.

"Time, 16:17," Tamara started. George wrote something in my folder.

The serum was cold as it moved into my arm, trapped in a puddle under my skin where the syringe had left it. As the needle was removed, Barry's thumb trapped the wound and the other hand pushed the liquid up my arm, rubbing to get my circulation moving.

When he was satisfied the serum was moving, Barry moved his hands away from my arm and reached for another syringe and the second vial in the case. I watched, trying to ignore the cold feeling in my arm as it spread toward my chest.

"Time?"

"16:20," Tamara answered when the room had been still for what felt like three hours.

"Still a little early..." he sighed. "We'll give it some time."

And again, we waited.

I tried to tell myself to stay calm, to not be frightened by what the serum now pumping through my veins could do to me. But there was no way I could remain calm. My breathing was erratic and the air in the lab was cold. My shivering only heightened my panic.

"Okay," Barry said, lifting the new syringe, which had a liquid with a golden color to it. It reminded me of Dana's eyes.

There was a pinch and the serum was pushed into my arm.

"16:23."

The feeling was not cold this time. It was hot, burning like molten lava moving through my veins. I pursed my lips against the pain, turning my head to the side and clenching my jaw.

1103

Barry pushed the fire up my arm, working it toward my shoulder. I could feel my body sweat, my muscles tensing. I was breathing heavily through my nose as the heat moved across my collarbone and then curled down my ribs, wrapping around them individually while simultaneously curling up my neck.

Then, without warning, iron-hot needles stabbed through my ribs and into my lungs and heart.

I screamed.

It was the first sound to come out of me in what felt like years, and the breath it took to scream did nothing more than hurt me more as the fire ravaged my lungs and caused me to scream again in a vicious circle of intense pain and agony.

The fire was fast, moving like electricity, lighting each blood cell aflame. My hair stood on end and my muscles locked painfully. My bones trembled. I screamed and choked as my throat constricted. I was completely unaware of the panicking scientists surrounding me.

The fire enveloped me, devoured me whole, and still the agony did not end. I wanted to move, to get away from the pain, but I was held down by metal so cold that, when it contrasted with the lava in my body, the pain quadrupled.

It was never ending.

It pervaded all thoughts and emotions, permeating into memories of my childhood, making it impossible for me to remember when there wasn't such pain, destroying my brain as the serum destroyed my body. Everything about me was strung tight as the fire ate away at my being. I wanted to beg for death. I wanted to scream at them to kill me and put me out of my misery, but the screams that ripped from my raw throat were lost to me. I might have been pleading for death. I might have just been screaming. For all I knew, I was screaming from joy and excitement.

All the lines blurred. I could no longer tell where my body was, I could not tell where my neck was in relation to my head and everything beyond was lost in a shadow of black flames that destroyed me from the inside. I could tell I was convulsing...or maybe the earth was shattering. It was possible that it was not the serum, but that it was actually the end of the world, when fire would rain down and destroy anything it touched...

Thoughts of fire and blood, pain and agony, death and destruction...those carried me through the end of the torture and into blackness.

* *** *

From the intense blackness that had pulled me under, the bright lights of my cell were too much to bear.

I screamed again, but the echoing sound split my aching head open and my hands went to my ears, my eyes closed tightly.

There was no way I was dead. Everything was too agonizing for me to be dead.

I pressed my forehead to the cement floor of my cell. The cool feeling against my heated skin was a welcome relief, but it was not enough. I longed to encase myself in the cement until my body stopped burning.

Moving my hands away from my ears, I pulled uselessly at the red fabric that covered my body. I tried to pull it over my head, whimpering pathetically. All I wanted was to remove it.

I managed to get some part of it over my face, but I was distressed and tangled in my clothes and it made me let out a sob of frustration and pain. Everything was so hot...so painful...

My back and belly were free of the clothes, and when I collapsed to my side in exhaustion and distress, I felt the cold against my skin. Gasping in surprise, I lowered to my belly, letting the cement leech the heat from my body. Moving my heavy, lead-filled arms, I pulled the fabric further, finally managing to get it over my head, leaving only my arms entangled as I pressed my front entirely to the cool slab.

A few minutes—or hours, I didn't know—later, I managed to shake the fabric from me. I did not dare to open my eyes, knowing that the piercing light would make my head explode. I moved my hand down my side, trying to find the other piece of fabric trapping heat to my skin.

I weakly shimmied my legs out of the pants, whimpering when my strength would give out and I was left tangled, confused, and pained, waiting for the smallest sign of strength so I could move the fabric a few more millimeters.

Finally, when the pants were around my ankles, I used only my feet, the boot around my tattooed foot making it impossible to rid myself of the clothing completely. They remained locked around my left ankle, holding me down, but as long as the cool cement was against my skin, I did not care about my foot.

When the cement heated from my body, I rolled onto my back and let a new patch absorb the heat.

I did not open my eyes, even when the food came or the door opened and people walked in to grab me.

Their hands were like barbed wire, cutting into my flesh with every touch. I screamed, the sound splitting my head open and tearing out of my throat with painful claws. I tried to fight, but I was too weak and tired and their hands hurt too much. I was crying. I had to be.

But they pulled me, without redressing me, back to the cold metal table for another round of the horrific torture.

Time had no meaning. I did not know if everything was happening within the expanse of a day, a year, or if I was already dead and this was my eternal punishment. There was so much pain that I could not remember who I was, my name, my parents, or why I was even there.

Three times I was submitted to the torture before I finally opened my eyes again.

When I did, I was back in my cell.

I felt so weak and helpless that dragging myself to the toilet was the most arduous task I had ever undertaken. Even then, I could not lift myself up to the toilet to use it. The sounds of the people coming in and cleaning the cell were so overwhelming that I would beg and plead for them to stop.

The lights were too bright...

The sounds were too loud...

Everything was just too much.

I could only count how many times I had been on the table based on the amount of times that the pain eased enough for me to move on my own. By the fifth time, I could start to remember who I was and where I was. The pain was still intense and it made everything in my head go white when I was on the table, but when I was in my cell, I had managed to recall memories, remembering faces of other experiments.

Is this what they had all endured?

The seventh time on the table was not nearly as painful. When I resurfaced from the pain, I was still in the lab and there were two other tests going on around me, or at least I assumed so with the way the groups of scientists were talking on either side of me.

I listened, recognizing one voice.

"...he's going to go abroad next semester," George said. "He's going to go to study the new medical technology in the Greater UK."

The Greater United Kingdom? That must have been Connor, George's oldest son who was in his second term of medical school.

"That's fantastic."

How did I know that?

"Have you checked on her? She's awake," an unfamiliar voice called from my other side.

"Oh, shit," Jeanie said. "Here, Corbett." Her heels echoed as she walked to me. I blinked at her. Actually, she wasn't that pretty. Her face was not proportionate and her pores were quite large. I wondered why I hadn't seen it before...

"Yep, she's conscious," she announced. "I'll get Dana."

"Look alive people, the boss is coming," another voice called with a laugh.

"How alive can that guy you're doing the autopsy on look?" Corbett quipped.

There was a dead person next to me.

Which meant I was still alive.

Fuck.

I remained still, feeling the cool air sweep over my skin as I listened to George talk about the scholarships Connor had received to go abroad. I listened, surprisingly interested though I did not know how I understood who they were talking about.

The door opened and conversation ceased immediately.

I heard another voice.

"...but no change to her muscle mass?" Dana's voice floated to me on air.

"No," Jeanie answered. I heard them both, but I could feel Dana drawing closer. My skin sparked and my hair stood on end. His presence was electric.

"I see."

"It's all very strange," Jeanie continued, stepping closer as Dana walked to my other side. I saw him first and I was a little startled to see him with his dark glasses. I wanted to shout at him to take them off. I needed to look into his eyes, but could not yell at him with the raw feeling of my throat. "There is no change in her muscle mass, but she can strain the restraints on the table. Her reflexes are much faster as well, but her brain has not changed and her blood composition remained the same. It's like her liver processed the serums and removed them. There's no trace."

"Perfect."

"What do you mean?" Jeanie asked. "The tests failed and she was left in agony for ten days."

"I know," Dana said. "That was to be expected."

"It was?"

"Back when I was an assistant to Bryant Morris, we had a very similar person on the table with almost identical anomalies in the blood. I am running the same tests we ran on him."

"Where's his file?"

"I have it," Dana answered mysteriously. "You just follow the instructions I gave and we should have a very strong warrior when she's finished."

Jeanie was hesitant, but she agreed.

"A few things," Dana continued. "I want her put on rotation now. She should be allowed Dome time."

"Alright."

"Also, halt her testing for a while," Dana said. "Her period should start any day. Once she's finished, go ahead and perform tubal ligation just to be safe."

"Of course, sir."

Dana ran a hand over my head. I shivered in response. "Give me a few minutes alone with her."

"Dana, we have an autopsy and an experiment—"

"The dead one is not going anywhere, and I will be sure the other one doesn't wander off," Dana cut her off sharply. Even through his dark glasses, I could feel the power of his eyes as he glared at her. "I need a few minutes alone with her."

"Yes, sir," Jeanie acquiesced. She called for everyone to leave the lab and, as they filed out, Dana removed his glasses. Filing them neatly in his pocket he turned those amazingly powerful eyes on me. It had been years since the last time I had seen the gold color...

"How are you doing, Little Lily?" he asked me as the door closed behind those leaving the lab.

"Fuck you..." I croaked around my sore throat.

"Oh, I wish I could say that it will get easier, but it won't," he sighed, continuing to run his hand over my dirty, knotted hair. "The first test is actually the...third hardest one to get through."

"I hate you."

"The fifth testing round will be a really nasty fucker," Dana continued, ignoring me. He leaned close. "That's when you'll be closest to death..."

"Just kill me now..."

"No, you can't give up," Dana said, getting even closer, leaning over me as he took my face in his hands. "I know it feels like hell, but you did beautifully. The test went exactly as I expected."

"I want to die..."

"The part of you that wants to die will slowly die, I promise. And the part that is left will be the stronger part of you," he told me. "Just remember that. Realize that each time you go through this, you get closer and closer to being one of the most powerful creatures you could ever imagine."

"I don't…I don't want to…be…like you…"

"You say that because you're afraid of what you feel when you're with me," he explained. "You're afraid of the desire, of the pleasure, of the absolute gluttony you can partake in when you're around me." His fingers brushed across my lips. "I'm breaking those walls down. I am letting you feel for the first time in your life."

I said nothing, the tears burning my eyes.

"Don't cry…" he cooed. "Don't cry. This is a beautiful thing."

I could not stop crying.

* *** *

The following day I was led into the Dome for the first time.

While there were still stabs of pain from my first round of testing, I was too interested in seeing the Dome to notice the twinges. I was barefoot, not recalling when the tattoo healed enough for them to remove the boot. I hardly noticed the difference until I was walking to the Dome and the cold hallway bit into the tattoo that still itched.

The four guards had not chained me, but the two behind me kept their guns pointed at my back as we walked, telling me what would happen if I tried anything stupid, like running.

I had no such plans. I wanted to see the Dome.

The door opened and I gasped at the heat that rushed into the cold hallway. My eyes shut briefly against the bright light, but I forced them to adjust, eager to see the place I knew to have grass and water.

The two gun barrels pushed me forward and I stepped into the warm, bright Dome, looking around in wonder.

The structure was massive, paneled with bright squares that shone light from all sides. The artificial light almost looked natural, as though I was standing in a huge greenhouse and the sun was shining through the glass panels. I looked back to the door, where the panels nearer the ground were dimmer, growing in intensity as they reached higher and higher into the apex of the ceiling. I could not see the center point of the domed roof, since there were large trees that towered into the light, blocking the view of the far edge of the enclosure.

My eyes, which had been traveling up the lights, fell over the expanse before me. It looked like a beautifully maintained garden, with flowers and trees, abundant with color. The stream that had so many memories flowed peacefully. There was a small bridge—with extremely high walls to keep experiments from throwing others over the edge—that crossed over of water. The grass was soft and tickled my ankles. There were boulders that provided places for experiments to sit and talk to one another. I saw nine experiments, all dressed in red, which contrasted with the green and white environment. Two were talking while resting under a tree as if it was a warm spring day. Three others were sitting in the grass not far from where I was standing, holding a conversation, ignoring me entirely. Another experiment was explaining something to a younger boy, sitting on a boulder while the younger male sat in the grass, engrossed in the story. One experiment had climbed into a low branch of one of the nearby trees and was watching me. Another was sitting on the edge of the stream, her feet dipped into the water, looking into the flowing water as she sloshed her feet back and forth.

It felt too peaceful to be part of the Commission of the People.

Not sure what I was supposed to do, I started forward, looking for a place to stand or sit, wondering if any other experiment would talk to me.

I walked across the metal bridge. The experiment in the tree shifted to watch me, her eyes sharp as she followed my movements, causing my hair to stand on end.

When I reached the other side, I walked to the far wall where the stream left the Dome, putting my hand on the warm light and turning to walk the perimeter, deciding to explore.

There was a grove of trees that sat in the middle of the Dome and my heart caught at the sight of a butterfly moving through the grove to rest on one of the large flowers nearby. I could have stayed in the Dome forever. It made me forget the pain of the table, of where I was and what Dana wanted to make of me. Somewhere in my mind, I knew that this was fake, but it filled me with such joy that I could push the thought away. There were a few trees that rested close together near the wall, bent to fit the curve of the ascending light panels and creating an extremely dark area that I stepped into carefully, worried I would disturb another experiment. The area was empty.

Moving out of the grove, I followed the back curve of the Dome, finding myself among a meadow with small, rolling hills. I climbed up one of the small hills along the back and looked over the Dome from the top. The grove of trees in the middle of the Dome blocked my view, but I could see the large tree near the entrance to the Dome, where a little red figure was barely visible on one of the higher branches.

Was that experiment still watching me?

I was half tempted to roll down the other side of the hill, but decided against it, walking down the grassy knoll, strolling along the flower beds until I reached the stream again.

I looked at the wall next to the stream, seeing the water bubble out from underneath. I barely remembered being pulled through the frigid water and out of the Dome, but I was sure that the area had been improved to keep experiments from escaping again. I did not know if Dana had discovered our method for achieving the breakout, but I assumed he had figured it out and wanted to test me, to see if I would try it again.

Of course, now that the Dome was on, the fans would be going so I could not attempt an escape.

"I wouldn't try that again if I were you," a voice called.

I whirled around and saw two experiments under a tree stand and walk to me. The man was older, maybe in his thirties with brown hair and eyes and a sharp jawline. The woman was extremely beautiful, in her mid-twenties with a thin waist but voluptuous breasts and wide hips. Her blonde hair framed her light face and her green eyes were large, but sharp.

"What?" I asked.

"The fans in there will rip you to shreds," the man informed me. "Besides, the last time you did that turned out badly if you ended up here."

"Do I know you?"

"No," the man said. "But we all know who you are, Lily Sandover."

I knew I was in danger.

"How do you know who I am?"

"Hard not to," the woman scoffed. "You were the one who helped get experiments out of the Commission." She stalked toward me. "Tell me, what made you leave some of us behind, huh?"

"I-I didn't choose…" I defended nervously. I glanced around and saw that the younger male and the man he had been talking to were also walking to us. The woman who had her feet in the stream was watching silently from her position. The three talking on the other side of the stream were turning to watch the confrontation.

"No?"

"Stacie," the man started, "Mark and Griffin chose."

"So…this is Lily Sandover," a dark voice said. Everyone turned to the approaching woman. She was also beautiful, but obviously foreign. She had an accent and her thick, wavy brown hair with her wide brown eyes set into dark skin gave her a very exotic look.

The other experiments backed away. I figured she was the experiment in the tree who had been watching me with fire in her eyes.

1111

Even though I had no idea who she was, it was obvious that she knew me and she hated me.

"I have something I need to ask you," she started sharply. "Is Griffin dead?"

I hesitated, but nodded reluctantly.

Her hand was lightning fast across my face and I fell to the ground with the force of the slap.

"You bitch!" the woman screeched. "You decided to come in with your plan to take down the Commission and you kill the best people we had in this dump!"

"Maria!" the woman sitting in the stream called. "Don't do this! It wasn't just her!"

"I don't care!" Maria snapped. "She survives, but Griffin, Mark, Tori," she listed with a growl, "they're dead because of her! Why did you survive?!" Maria turned her attention back to me, falling to her knees and grabbing my hair violently, pulling my head up. "If you hadn't stuck your hands into this place, they would still be alive!" She smacked me again and as my face snapped one direction, her hand in my hair increasing my pain. "It may have been some kind of game for you, but for us and for them, it was survival!"

I kicked her in the side, pushing her away roughly and scrambling to my feet.

"You think it wasn't survival for me, too?!" I snapped. "I loved them! I loved Griffin and Tori and Mark, and all the others..." my voice broke as I listed their names. "I thought we were going to win!"

"You were playing with fire!" Maria said, grabbing my ankles and pulling me heavily to the ground before grabbing my hair again and slamming my head into the ground repeatedly. "It wasn't a fucking game to win!"

"Stop it!" the younger boy cried. "You're going to get us in trouble!"

"Get off me, bitch!" I snarled, moving my leg to push her away by kicking her chest. She fell backward and I wasted no time jumping on her and punching her across the face before grabbing her hair as well, slamming her head into the grass once, angry and hurt. "You have no idea what I've had to go through!"

"Boo-fucking-hoo!" she growled, spitting at me. I dug my nails into her scalp and pulled her upright before dragging her to the stream and dunking her head into the rushing water, pulling her up again.

"What the fuck did you say?!"

"You think you're the only one who's suffered?!" Maria spluttered angrily, trying to reach back and grab me. I pushed her hand away, putting my knee in her back. "Griffin was the only one who gave a damn about me and you got him killed!"

Her hand finally latched onto my shirt and she pulled me down. I tumbled into the river, but not before I grabbed her, pulling her with me. The other experiments were yelling at us to either stop or to kill one another. I ignored the rushing water that made it harder for me to keep my stance and clawed at Maria, who was clawing back, her nails scraping open wounds across my face. Using my position upstream, I kicked her ankles, causing her to collapse further into the water where I pushed her head under. One of her flailing hands connected with my face, punching me in the jaw, making me see stars.

I let her go, holding my jaw and cringing in pain.

She leapt on me and pushed my head underwater. I tried to struggle, pulling on her clothes in an attempt to pull myself to the surface, fighting on an adrenaline high.

Just when I was starting to panic from lack of oxygen there was a hand on the back of my collar, yanking me out of the water and dumping me on the grass as I gasped for breath, taking in precious oxygen as orders were shouted.

"Don't you two fucking move!"

I blinked the water from my eyes and saw seven men in black uniforms pointing their guns, ordering us to remain still as we choked and spluttered.

"She started it!" Maria snapped.

"Don't fucking talk!" another man ordered. "Get your asses up slowly."

Raising my hands, I got to my feet, wobbly as my oxygen-deprived limbs quivered. Maria did the same, glaring at me hatefully.

"Alright, both of you, walk," one man said, poking me with the barrel of his gun in the shoulder. I began walking as two of the men led us out of the Dome. Maria looked ready to kill me, but she was not suicidal enough to try something with the guards so close.

We were led toward the labs but we turned into a small hallway just before Lab One where four smaller cells remained empty. One of the guards opened the door to the nearest one and motioned with his gun for us to get inside. I walked in, shivering and frightened, but also very angry.

As if I didn't feel guilty enough over the deaths of everyone in our revolution...I still did not know who survived and who was taken back in the Commission. I had purposely tried not to dwell on the question. Maria's words had struck a deep wound inside me.

"Don't you fucking move," one of the men snarled.

There were gloved hands on me and my wet clothes were pulled from my body. When we were both stripped naked, we stood, facing the guards, shivering and exposed, petrified about what was to come next.

"Turn around, put your hands on the back of your head, and get on your knees," the same man ordered. Slowly, wary about turning our backs, both of us obeyed, getting to our knees, our hands clasped against our wet hair.

"Punishment is ten strikes," the man announced.

As soon as I realized what was happening, the blunt club connected with my back and I fell forward, catching myself on my hands as the pain radiated through me.

"Sit up!" the man behind me ordered, grabbing my hand and pulling me upright again, holding my hand in the air as he hit my back again. I let out a choked scream. Maria let out a sob too when her second strike was delivered, barely able to keep her hands on the back of her head. She had clearly endured the punishment before.

The fourth strike immediately followed the third and hot tears spilled down my face. I fell limply, but the beating did not stop. The man hit my sides and shoulder, putting so much force behind the strikes, I was sure he was going to break bones.

I did not count the strikes. Even when the ten were finished, I flinched and shivered, waiting for the next punishing blow, curled on my side, crying, my body throbbing.

"Don't fucking fight in the Dome," the man warned, finally dropping my hand and walking away. My back was turned to Maria, so I did not know how she was faring but I could hear her breathing hard and crying behind me.

"Really? That's it?" one of the men asked. My fear returned stronger than ever.

"Yeah, you don't want these cunts," one of the others chuckled brokenly. "The Latina has been had by way too many and the young one is Mr. Christenson's sloppy second. There are better pussies to be had."

"Eww," one of them groaned, spitting into the room. "Fuck that."

"Get them some dry clothes," the one who had been giving commands ordered. "You two, stand your ugly asses up and get ready to be put back in your cells."

I heard the sound of boots walking away from the cell. When those had faded, I weakly pulled myself to my hands and knees. My body throbbed at the movement, my ribs trying to recover from the clubbing.

I pressed my head to the floor to support myself as my hand gently touched my protesting ribs.

Hearing a whimper of pain that mimicked mine, I turned to see Maria trying to straighten, her face creased in pain.

Taking a few deep breaths, I finally pushed myself into an upright position, panting heavily through my nose at the pain.

I got to my feet as Maria stumbled getting to hers.

"Maria," I said slowly.

"*What?*"

"I'm sorry…"

"Fuck you," she sneered. I sighed, understanding that I was not going to make her believe that I was legitimately sorry. If I could trade my life to save Mark, Griffin, Tori or any of the others the revolution had doomed, I would have without a second thought.

"I know you hate me, and I'm sure that you loved Griffin and the others, but Dana is the one who killed them, not me."

"You stuck your nose where it didn't belong," Maria said. "Dana will kill all of us eventually, but at least we could have been together. You tore the family apart."

I remained silent.

The sound of boots returned and dry clothes were thrown to the floor in front of us.

"Get dressed," the man in charge ordered. "You're both going back to your cells."

We did not look at one another as we pulled the clothes on, silent and angry. I wanted to scream at her that at least she had not watched Griffin die in front of her, or any of the others who perished. But in the Commission, there was no sympathy for pain, no regard or empathy for emotional scars as it existed in the outside world. Everyone was suffering. It was not a petty contest to prove who had endured the most. It was a struggle to get through the current pain and to help others who were enduring it as well.

Be there for one another…Don't take what the others couldn't give, including pity.

* *** *

My period started as Dana had predicted. Because I wasn't given anything for it, I spent most of the time sitting on the toilet, in pain from cramps and hating having to lay on the floor when sitting on the toilet became too uncomfortable.

I fell asleep on the floor which meant that I was covered in blood when I woke. The cleaning crew that always managed to get the cell back to pristine white also cleaned me up. On two occasions, the same man took the opportunity while wiping down the backs of my thighs to violate me with his fingers.

There was nothing I could do but endure it, worried about worse if I made a fuss about his actions.

During the four days of my period, I came to understand why the experiment in the cell across the hall always stared at me. It was boring to wait in the white cell. My thoughts could only occupy me for so long before I began to go stir-crazy.

On the third day of my period, eating the hard bread and drinking the soup, I saw movement up the hall. All the experiments I could see in the cells were grabbing their trays and darting to the backs of their cells in fear.

Confused, I remained where I was, watching.

Through the glass walls of the cell of the woman across from me, I saw what appeared to be over twenty armed guards following four scientists, two holding rifles themselves.

There was only one experiment that would draw so much attention.

As the entourage moved past my cell, I moved to the other corner, eager to catch a glimpse of Eina. One scientist without a gun stepped in front of a dark cell, opening it while the others continued down the hall.

The small hallway was packed with black-clad guards, so it was difficult to see what they were doing, but through their legs I caught a glimpse of a man lying on his belly, readying his gun outside the food slot.

All the guards and scientists jumped as a flashing red movement sped across the front of the cell, disappearing as quickly as it appeared.

The scientist emerged from the dark cell with a set of chains and cuffs I remembered being called "The Teeth."

The guard laying on his belly pushed the barrel of his gun through the food slot and his entire body gave a jolt when he pulled the trigger.

I gasped and fell backward at the sound that radiated through the ward. It was not a shout or a roar of pain, but some sonic mix of the two that had an animal-like quality, leaving me shaking, my chest rattled by the sound.

Several of the other experiments also jumped, their faces pale and eyes wide with terror.

I thought the cells were soundproof.

The roar sounded again and left a dull ring in my ears as the echo died away. I assumed they were tranquilizing Eina so I was also very curious as to why they still needed rifles.

Resuming my position in the corner, I watched the scientists wait for the drugs to take effect. They were studying the cell, their eyes locked ahead as my gaze remained glued on them.

I was scarcely breathing when the group opened the cell, filing in to retrieve the Machine of Neutralization.

I spared a glance at the experiment across from me. She was hiding in the back corner, crouched with her arms pressed to her chest, her eyes wide with fear as she stared at the wall next to her, listening to the sounds of the group extracting Eina.

I looked back down the hall, pressing my face against the glass.

Two men backed out of the cell, both of them pointing their guns. My heart sped up, thinking Eina was breaking out.

Two more people backed away, holding the thick chains attached to the cuffs around Eina as he was guided out of the cell, stumbling, his head low. The others filed out of the cell, blocking my view. I craned my neck, though I knew it would not change what I could see. The group moved awkwardly and slowly through the narrow corridor, their guns ready, pointed at the chained experiment.

When they had fallen into their ranks, I slinked away from the corner, waiting for Eina and the others to pass the front of my cell so I could get a good look at the Machine of Neutralization. My heart was thundering in my chest, excited and frightened. I didn't blink, worried I would miss him.

The first guards that walked past were facing forward and I jumped a little at their hard expressions, my nerves on edge. The guards behind the first three were facing backward, their guns aimed at the Machine of Neutralization over the shoulders of the people who were holding the chains to his brutal restraints.

I watched, fascinated, as the most powerful creature ever created by the Commission of the People stumbled past my cell. His head was bent and his hair hid most of his face, long and unkempt. His frame was not broadly built, but there was a strength in his presence that I could feel through the thick glass. His skin was pale, but not chalky or unhealthy. It was smooth, pristine, without flaw or hair. His baggy shorts hung from his hips, stained with blood, though I could see no open wounds on him.

I stared at the cold gray metal of The Teeth that held him, unable to see puncture wounds. Carefully, I inched forward, but as soon as I shifted my weight, I was startled by Eina falling to his knees, his head almost reaching the ground as his arms remained useless at his sides, held by the chains.

The party stopped. My eyes followed a single bead of blood trail down Eina's side. It was dark red, sharp against his pale skin, and slid with no resistance down his ribcage. The sight was fascinating, beautiful, captivating, the bead of burgundy staining his side, slipping over the curve of his ribs and reaching the fabric of the shorts.

Before I knew it, I was close to the glass, staring at the line of stained skin.

His back rose and fell as he breathed, labored, fighting the drugs coursing through him.

There was a sharp tug on his restraints, causing him to flinch and tilt his head to the side as the neck cuff hit his chin.

His eyes lazily focused on me.

Every instinct told me to run, but another part of me was warning me that if I moved too fast he would pursue me. I could not turn my back on him and I could not move a muscle or he would pounce, like a lion waiting in the grass, watching his prey.

His eyes were a light hazel, bright with power and fire, even through the fog of sedation. Even as his eyes rolled, unable to focus, I could see that there was power there, like a wildfire, uncontained and dangerous.

We locked gazes and my breath left me.

He's beautiful...

Another painful tug on the chains caused me to cringe with him. I wanted to scream at the guards for harming such an incredible creature. Even though I knew he was more dangerous than anything that had ever walked the earth before, I could not stand how they were treating him. He had an air about him that called for worship.

I saw the muscles flex under his skin as he pulled himself to his feet unsteadily, his gaze leaving me to drop to the floor as his head rolled forward once again. I watched as those muscles moved his body forward, taking him wherever Dana wanted. He rounded the corner with the entourage, the other experiments averting their eyes or backing into corners as he passed.

There were conflicting emotions running through me when the Machine of Neutralization disappeared from sight. I understood the fear the experiments had of him, but I also did not see why they felt the need to avert their eyes, as though they would be scolded for looking at him.

Eina did not come back for a very long time.

I entertained the idea of seeing him return while I sat in my cell, wondering when they would bring him back and what they were doing with him in the meantime. When he did come back, he was just as drugged as when he had left. I watched him stumble past my cell, looking him over again, trying to study every detail.

He did not look at me.

He was dumped unceremoniously in his cell and the group of guards left, looking relieved to have him contained again.

From that point, I would spend at least a few hours of my day pressed against the far corner, trying to see if I could spot Eina in his cell down the hall. He did not come forward to eat. Sometimes, I would see his hand reaching across the floor and pulling the tray out of my limited field of vision, but not for every meal.

Two days after Eina had been taken out of his cell, I was taken to the lab and promptly knocked out.

I woke up in my cell, stiff and sore, particularly in my abdomen.

After pulling myself upright, I lifted my shirt to see what was itching so badly and found cotton taped over my belly button and lower on my torso, just above my pubic bone. I could only stare at the wounds in confusion for what felt like hours before I remembered that Dana had asked the scientists to perform tubal ligation.

It was a term I had never heard before, but it did not take me long to figure out what it meant.

Even though I had never thought about having children and I knew that it was impossible to lead a normal life and have children now that I was being tested on by the Commission, realizing that I no longer had the biological capabilities of bear children filled me with a profound sadness. It was just another thing Dana had taken from me, proving his complete control over my life.

That left me with much to mull over the following four days while I was left alone to recover from the surgery, only being removed for short periods of time to be sure that no infections were setting in as the wounds closed.

Being left alone, my thoughts began to spiral downward, leading me deeper and deeper into darkness.

Considering everything I had seen, it made sense that I had a pessimistic outlook on the world. Not many teens my age had seen a failed revolution, had seen their friends—family, really—die in front of them in some of the most horrific ways possible. Recalling all the media I had seen depicting the atrocities of the Second Revolution, the images seemed distant, watered down, almost imaginary compared to the memories that seared through my mind when I thought about our failed rebellion.

I could not help but wonder if the people were shown the evidence of the cruelty that had quashed our revolution. I wondered if the people reveled in the brutality, since I was certain very few felt empathy toward us after Dana's smear campaign.

I had pondered my revolution so much while locked in my bright white cell that I had started to wonder if I had imagined the entire ordeal. But the memories were too painful to be imaginary. I had not imagined Tara convulsing, Josh bleeding out, Sydney and Cooper's mutilations, Mykail's feverish infections, Tori's decapitation, Griffin's body flattening under the tank, Mark's head snapping as the bullet ripped through his skull...

They were memories that were going to be branded in my brain until the day I died.

I just hoped that the day I died was fast approaching.

Perhaps it was best that I was no longer able to have children. Even if I had managed to escape the Commission, if I had lived a normal life and had children, I would raise my children in a country where anything out of what the society deemed 'normal' was not only deviant, but dangerous, and those people would disappear without a trace into the Commission of the People.

I wondered how many experiments in the Commission knew that the 41141 experiment they considered to be a legend had actually come to be the one who tested on them, who ran the Commission as the horrible institution it had evolved into.

The Commission really did change anyone that fell into its clutches.

Dana came to visit me the fourth day after my surgery.

He opened the cell door as I stared at him, leaning against the side wall, lost in thought as I watched the horrible memories play out in front of me on the pristine white walls yet again.

"Good morning, Little Lily," he said, closing the glass door behind him as he walked inside, crouching in front of me with a smile. I turned my head to look at him, shivering at the intensity of his golden eyes. The color seemed sharper in contrast to the white walls.

He reached toward my stomach and I flinched, my eyes closing tiredly as I waited for any sort of pain.

He lifted my shirt and slowly pulled the tape around my bandages. I barely managed not to wince, even when his thumb passed tenderly over the aggravated skin.

"They healed nicely," he noted, removing the other bandages. "That means we can continue your testing."

I could only stare at the floor. Dana chuckled quietly, turning to sit next to me, leaning against the wall, his legs bent like mine.

"Nothing to say?" he pressed.

"What do you want me to say?"

"Whatever you want to say."

"I hate you," I murmured.

"It's hard to start a conversation from that."

"I don't want to have a conversation with you," I sneered.

He sighed and looked around the cell as I watched him from my periphery.

"Are you sure?"

I rolled my eyes, turning to face him.

"*Why* would I want to talk to you?"

"Because it might be a while before you see me again," he said. "You'll miss me."

"*Hardly.*"

"We'll see…"

He still did not move. We sat awkwardly next to one another for an eternity, not speaking as we stared at the opposing wall. The silence was agitating, becoming worse the longer it continued. Finally, I groaned, exasperated.

"Can you get the hell out of here?" I snapped, standing, uncomfortable in his presence.

"You really don't want to talk to me?" he asked in that annoying tone that told me he was expecting something very specific. I stared at his expectant expression and waited for him to speak again. The Commission was his domain, and I was determined to stay as far away from the rules as I could possibly endure, including trying to figure out what he wanted from me.

"No."

He also stood, shaking his head.

"Let me ask you something, Little Lily…what are you so afraid of?" he said, undeterred by my pathetic attempt at a defiant expression. "You've been on the table, you've been raped, you've fought and faced death in the Dome…what are you still afraid of?"

"…I'm afraid of what you want to turn me into," I choked.

"I'm not turning you into anything," he said. "I'm merely speeding up the evolution of what you already were."

"What the hell does that mean?"

"You have everything you need to become just like me already inside of you…you were born with it. And you followed the same path as me so precisely that there was no way you would not become me...in due time."

"Never," I growled. "If we had won the revolution—"

"Who would have been in power?" he demanded. "You?"

"No."

"You would put someone else in power?"

"Yes."

"Who?"

"Whoever was best qualified to clean up this mess," I snapped.

Dana nodded slowly, his expression pensive. "Clean up the mess and replace it with what?"

"I don't know," I snapped. "There are people a lot smarter than me that could figure that out."

"Really? You would just take your hands off the wheel of your so-called revolution and let the people that accepted and understood the purpose of the Commission of the People clean up the mess?" He looked at me skeptically. "No...you didn't like what you were seeing and you sought to change it. If it had not changed, you would never be able to leave it alone. That's just who you are."

"Don't tell me who I am!" I sneered, pushing him, though he barely took a half-step back. "I actually *cared* about people. You just see them as toys and dolls to play with."

"I started out just like you, Little Lily," he said. "But I went through a transformation so grand that you could never comprehend what it has done to me." He stared at me for a long moment. "You really don't see it, do you?"

"See what?"

"Who I really am," he said. "I am the one who cared and gave everything of myself to everyone who needed it. I am the one who put other's needs before my own. I was the one who helped people escape from the Commission. I opened my home and heart to them, gave them food and safety...I was the promise of a new and better future away from laws that had become too constricting and too horrible to bear. Do you see any similarity between me and someone else?"

I stared, unsure what to say, my mouth opening and closing uselessly as I tried to form a coherent sentence, trying to follow his train of thought as I pertained it to myself and my own actions in the revolution.

"America." His head tilted to the side in that dangerous manner that always made my hair stand on end. "I am America. I entrusted everything I had to people who were considered outcasts by the government and by society. I gave them an escape. I gave and gave...and yet, despite the good I believed I had done, I was taken, stripped of everything that made me who I was, plundered and raped and warped into something that is now unrecognizable—an altruistic idea that no one can touch, change, or reclaim. Just as humans did to this country."

"That...That doesn't..."

"Oh, Little Lily." He stepped closer, placing a hand on my face. I shivered, frightened at the touch, yet unable to move away, terrified to see that his bright golden gaze held no pain at recalling the torment he endured. He didn't feel anything for what had happened to him. He was not traumatized, he was not in pain anymore...he had completely accepted and embraced it. That was who he had become. That was the danger I had always seen in his eyes.

"You...you d-don't...care..." I barely managed to breathe.

"No, I don't." He leaned forward and kissed my head. "And soon, neither will you."

His hand dropped from my skin and he brushed past me to the door of the cell. He turned back to me as I stared after him, cold fear gripping my entire being. "I'll see you in about two weeks, depending on everything pans out."

At first, I thought he meant depending on his schedule until I remembered his expectant stare earlier. He meant what happened with *my* schedule, with my testing. My stomach twisted into knots, dreading the next round I was set to endure. I still remembered all too well the pain of the previous round, and knowing that was only my first of many, panic swelled in my chest.

But I refused to let it show on my face.

Within a few hours, another group of people had come to my cell composed of scientists I had never seen before. I stared at them warily as they walked into the cell and grabbed me, slapping the cuffs around my wrists and ankles before leading me out.

I studied the strangers worriedly but did not fight them, assuming that they were going to lead me to my normal group of scientists.

Despite the pain that I had endured at their hand, I felt more comfortable with the scientists I already knew—at least I knew what to expect of them.

The lab was empty when we walked into the cold room. Dread sat heavier inside me as I realized that a new group was going to run tests on me. I bit back my whine of fright.

Surprisingly, the new group was far kinder than the other group. The scientists were younger, and the young man who looked to be only in his late twenties, offered his hand to me when the shackles were removed.

"Could you lay here, please?" he asked.

I was wary of his smile. Hesitating, I looked between his gentle smile and the hand offered to me. No one behind me forced me to take his hand, one of them waiting to be sure I did not run while the other two moved around the table, preparing trays on the rolling tables for the tests they were going to perform.

Slowly, I took his hand, suspicious of his courtesy.

"Thank you," he said as I climbed onto the table. "My name is Randy, by the way," he introduced. "And this is my team. That's Amanda and Tiffany over there, and back there is Andrew."

I looked around at the younger group of scientists, extremely skeptical of Randy's kindness. They did not act hard and callous like the other scientists, and I briefly wondered if they even understood what they were doing in the Commission.

"We're going to be administering your next two tests," he continued. "They're pretty close to one another, but they should only take about a week to complete."

I wanted to ask about the other team of scientists but could not find it in me to speak.

"Alright, just lay back." He guided me to the cold metal of the table, gently placing my wrist in the cuffs. "This is just to keep you from accidentally hurting yourself."

The others moved around me, fastening the restraints with consideration. They spoke quietly as they looked over what I assumed was my file, discussing my odd reaction to the previous test and that Mr. Christenson had ordered them to administer these tests at exact intervals.

"So, 88911, this first test is going to hurt, but I promise you will survive," Andrew explained, stepping up to my side and wiping the skin covering the large vein in my arm. "Just trust us. It will hurt, but the pain should pass within twelve hours."

Clearly he did not understand that it did not matter if the pain lasted twelve hours or two minutes. It still felt like an eternity when every cell of your body was ripping itself apart.

"Take a deep breath," Amanda instructed, gently placing a hand on my leg, as if comforting me.

I could not do so. I remained with my eyes locked on the needle progressively making its way to my arm. Andrew looked at me and stopped, staring at me for a long moment before turning to Randy.

"Hey, are you sure this is what Mr. Christenson asked?"

"That's what he said," Randy said.

Andrew turned back to me, his hand resting over my forearm as the needle came closer. My heart picked up pace, remembering the intense pain I had endured during my first round of testing. It should have eased my mind that the ten days I had been in agony before had passed quickly with nothing to distinguish hours, but I could not shake the queasiness brought on by the sight of the needle.

"It will be alright," Andrew assured. I felt the prick and bit back a scream. Nothing hurt yet, but I knew it was coming.

The serum filled my vein, cold and sharp. It felt like ice. I shivered and my eyes closed, waiting for the incredible pain to overwhelm me.

Despite the way the serum moved up my arm and through my chest, the pain only started after my entire body was shivering from the icy liquid in my veins. My left side began to cramp. I was focused on the pain, on the way it was building in my body, until it became overwhelming. It seemed like a short time before the pain that was growing inside overtook me and made my back arch off the table.

The pain was not at all hot. It did not burn my body as it had before. That time, it was frigid. My muscles tensed as if they were straining harder than ever, pushing on the bones and quivering with effort. But despite their contracting, the ice took them over, covering them in frosty crystals before penetrating into each fiber and freezing it to the core, making the muscle brittle and sharp as it moved under my skin.

My lungs were heaving, trying to find a way to take in air around my shivering teeth and the freezing of the muscles around my ribs.

My back was arched off the table, my muscles frozen. As the cold stopped spreading, the panic took over. If I moved, I was certain every muscle in my body would shatter. My eyes snapped open and focused on the bright lights of the lab above me. I let out a scream, trying to find a way to plead with the scientists to keep me from moving so that my muscles would not splinter.

But the scream was intelligible and my body fell limply to the table.

As soon as I felt the jolt of my body stopping on the smooth surface, it was like every bone and muscle in my body shattered, splintering apart and sending shards of ice all around me, like an icicle falling off a roof. I could not even scream, my mouth and jaw frozen completely as I tried to gauge what muscles remained.

None...

Nothing was moving.

I willed my body to move, but when no movement came, I began to believe that my body had shattered to a deflated mess of frozen muscles, torn skin, and broken bones. My brain was only functioning because it was slow to realize what had happened around its own frozen cells. The pain was very different. It was all-encompassing, powerful, but I was still coherent. My understanding made me panic. I could not look down my body to see what had become of it. There were sharp, stinging pains that brought to mind images of my skin being cut to ribbons. I was convinced I was a blink away from death.

All I needed to do was blink and I would be dead.

At first, the thought terrified me, made me panic more that I was going to die on the table from my body shattering into a thousand pieces. Memories bubbled to the surface of bodies being crushed under heavy machinery, but I could not place the time or person of the memories.

And then...I thought about what I would escape if I could die.

I tried to blink, but my eyes would not close.

I was stuck in a limbo of being in between painless death and unimaginable pain, leaning one direction but being chained back. I wanted to let out a sob, the tears rising to my eyes, but the hot water of my tears was searing my frozen flesh, causing the pain to heighten.

I had managed to convince myself that I was just a head laying on a table while the scientists moved around me, picking up pieces of my body and collecting them, trying to decide how to tell Dana what had happened.

I was further convinced of my dismemberment when I started to feel pain in my right leg. Then I felt a sharp stab in my right hip, cracking heavily as if the socket had been popped back into place.

They were reassembling my body.

Finally, I could hear what they were saying...around the same time that an ache began to move from my neck down my spine.

"She's showing regression..."

"*Finally...*"

"Mr. Christenson said this would probably happen."

"Yeah, well, it was worse than I expected. I thought he was exaggerating."

"He said to give her J5, right?"

"Yeah."

My eyes finally closed, but death did not claim me. Sleep was reaching up to engulf me. I was exhausted. The panic of having my body dismembered and then slowly put back together took its toll. I fell deep into unconsciousness just after I felt another needle in my arm.

* *** *

I woke sore and exhausted, cringing under the bright lights of my cell. As soon as consciousness took hold, my stomach flipped at the searing pain in my head. Nausea overwhelming me, I found myself clawing toward the toilet and dry-heaving into the bowl.

Choking as my body tried to rid itself of the non-existent contents of my stomach, I became certain I would pass out from lack of breath in the toilet. I moved away, head pressing to the cold cement in front of the toilet, my body convulsing as I coughed.

Slowly, the spasms ceased, I remained in my position near the toilet, breathing hard, acutely aware of the aching in my body, feeling as though I had just slept out in the winter cold.

"Lily?" a voice whispered.

My eyes shot wide, my heart stopping at the familiar voice.

"Lily?! Oh my God, are you alright?!"

There was a hand on my back, warm and gentle, but it made me recoil as if it had branded my skin. I fell backward, my elbow striking hard against the cement as I stared in horror at the woman in front of me. Her blonde hair was just as perfect as I had ever seen it, and her bright green eyes were wide with concern, her hand suspended in mid-air.

"No...no, you c-can't..." I babbled. "You're not here!"

"Lily, it's me. Don't you recognize me?"

I vaguely remembered a head raised on a pike...a body drawn and quartered...

"No...no, no, *no*...you're dead."

"Lily, I'm right here."

"Stop it!" I screamed, shoving her backward. She fell back and we both stared at each other, eyes wide with fear. "You're not here."

"I'm here to help you, Lily," Tori whispered. "You're barely holding on by yourself..."

Oh my God...this can't be happening...

I curled forward, shaking my head.

"Please...go away..."

"Lily, you need help!"

"You're *dead*!" I screeched.

"No, Lily...I'm right here." Her hand rested on my shoulder again. "All you need to do is fight a little harder. I know you can win."

"We already lost..."

"No, here," she clarified. "In the testing. You need to keep fighting. Don't succumb to death. You can beat Dana."

"...you think I can?"

"Absolutely," Tori whispered. She grabbed my arms and pulled me into a hug. I remained still, not sure what to make of the incredibly realistic hallucination. "I'm here to help you."

"How can you help?"

"When you're back on the table I'm going to sneak up and attack them. Then, we're going to hijack a car and get the hell out of here."

"Where will we go?"

"Away, far away," she told me. Her arms tightened around me and I found myself hugging back. I was sure she was a hallucination, but it gave me a glimmer of hope, a small anchor in the stark cell around me. But the memory of the last time I had seen Tori resurfaced in my mind...

"Tori..." I pulled away from her. "I thought you were the strongest experiment made here...besides Eina."

"I was."

I sat back on my heels, my eyes on the ground, unable to look at her.

"Then...how did you die so easily?"

"*Easily*?" She barked a laugh. "It wasn't easy. First, they had to drag me behind the jeeps by my neck to suffocate me enough so that I wouldn't fight back when they tied me between the cars."

I had to close my eyes against the words and the images they brought up.

"Then they took their knives and continued to stab me as I was suspended, laughing, telling me how stupid I was for thinking that they didn't know how to take me apart. Like I was just another machine, like their cars. Then they took a little wire and wrapped it around my neck, tying it to the bumpers of some other cars, and having those cars slowly pull away from one another...until my head came clean off."

My breath had stopped, pain threatening to break all my ribs.

"Come to think of it...they kept asking me if I was you. And when they discovered I wasn't the precious Lily Sandover, they said they were going to kill me nice and slow." I looked up quickly to see that her normally smiling face had set in an angry expression. "Why should I help you? You're the reason I'm dead."

My heart stopped and my stomach flipped over again.

"I...I never thought..."

"What? That we would lose?" Tori scoffed. "Then what were you doing screaming in the woods the night before we were killed? You should have found Dana and thrown yourself at his mercy!"

"I tried!" I bellowed, tears rising to my eyes. "I tried...I didn't want anyone else to die..."

"Why were we all so willing to kill and die for you?"

The words struck my core.

"I...I don't know..."

"What was so special about you that we were willing to die for it?"

"Tori...please, I'm sorry. I don't know what else to say."

"You're sorry?" she chuckled darkly. "*Really*? I'm dead...I was torn apart...and you're sorry."

My eyebrows furrowed. It wasn't Tori. Even my hopeful hallucination was contrary to Tori's personality. I shook my head slowly.

"What?" Tori snapped.

"I want you gone," I growled, trying to keep my voice strong as I held back my sobs. "I'm paying for what happened now, but if you're going to bitch at me, then I want you gone!"

"Well, good news for you, I *am* gone." Tori snarled, standing and walking to the cell door. "And you sure as hell haven't paid for everything, yet!" she snapped as she walked through the door that magically opened for her and slammed shut when she was gone.

I stared into the hallway, studying the wall between the lit cell and the empty one across the corridor, expecting to wake from the bizarre dream. I was sure it was a dream until I had remained in the same position for an eternity without waking or falling asleep.

The tears rolled down my cheeks. I moved to the wall blocking the toilet, banging my head lightly a few times on the wall, trying to regain myself.

It was not long before Randy came to collect me again. He led me to the lab and told me to sit on the table.

"Don't worry, nothing bad today," he said, rolling my right sleeve up. "We're just going to check your vitals and then give you a shot and take you back to your cell," he explained. "You might feel a little stiffness in your muscles, but it will pass with time."

They did exactly as he said. They took my vitals, gave me the shot as I turned away from watching the needle, and after they had waited the twenty minutes to be sure I did not have a negative reaction, they returned me to my cell.

I watched the ground as I walked, thinking back to what Tori had said about me not yet paying for what I had done. I wondered if I ever could. With Dana's promise to make me like him, I would be treading further away from what we had fought for. They would have died for nothing.

I was just as curious about what they had seen in me that made them die protecting me.

I was praising myself too highly, thinking that they died for me. They died *because* of me.

Randy opened my cell and I turned to go in obediently. As I lifted my head, I saw someone standing in the cell and I stopped in the doorway, back-pedaling.

"It's okay," Randy assured, gently pushing me forward.

"No..." I whispered. Clearly they could not see the tall, broad figure with his tattooed muscles and kind eyes. I tried to back up again, but the four scientists pushed me into the cell.

"I've never seen an experiment want to stay with us..." Amanda whispered as they left.

I was completely still, staring at Griffin with my back pressed to the locked glass door. I knew I was hallucinating. Griffin was a figment of my imagination, something to break the monochromatic white walls.

"Not even a hello?" he chuckled.

"Griffin..." I whispered. "I..."

"Surprised to see me?"

"Of course," I said. "Because...you're not real."

"I'm not? That's not a nice thing to say."

"I mean, you *were* real...but...I saw you die."

"Yes, you did," he agreed. "I'm left wondering, then, why am I here?" He shrugged. I took a deep breath, staring at him for a long moment, my heart constricting painfully in my chest as I recalled the horrible event and everything surrounding it—the whole battle that had been the end of us as a revolution.

"I don't know..." I admitted. "It's obvious I'm hallucinating."

"Of course," Griffin laughed.

"I'm not sure if the fact that I recognize that I'm hallucinating is a good or bad sign."

"You're interacting with your hallucinations," Griffin pointed out. "That's a bad sign."

I lifted a hand to my head and closed my eyes, trying to gain my bearings.

"I don't know what's going on with me...I wish you were really here..." Tears burned in my eyes. "I really need someone to help me get through this."

"I think you just answered your own question." Griffin stepped forward, stopping when he was in front of me. "What is it that you expect me to do for you?"

Anything.

I could only blink at him, unable to bring the word forward.

1130

"I can't fix anything for you," he said. "You knew this was coming."

"I-I know, but—"

"But nothing. I tried to help you, I really did. But there was nothing I could do that would change the fate coming at you. And there is nothing I can do now. There is no one left to help you."

"But you're here..."

"No, *you* are." Griffin shook his head. "I've paid my dues in this hell hole. And look where it got me."

"Griffin, please," I whispered, grabbing his hand. "You always had a way of making me feel safe, of making everything better...why are you so indifferent now?"

"Because I accepted reality," Griffin said. "And you should, too."

I sniffed my tears back, shaking my head. "No..." I breathed. "I know there is a way I can fight Dana. You're supposed to help me."

"How?" he challenged. "We tried and we failed. That's all that can be said. Dana is too powerful. We can't win. The best we can do is accept his rules and try to survive with them." He nodded to me. "You have to try. You're not dead."

"Griffin, please, help me. Tell me everything is going to be okay, that I can find a way to escape Dana and what he wants to do to me..."

"I'm not going to lie to you. He's already won." He gently placed his hand over my face, covering my eyes. "That much should be obvious..."

My eyes closed as his hand moved over my eyelids. His hand was warm, calloused as I remembered, and when the pressure was gone from my face, I opened my eyes to find Griffin gone.

I sat in the back corner of the cell and curled around my knees, crying pitifully.

Tori and Griffin had left me, somehow leaving more pain in my chest than their deaths had. Tori was enraged at her fate, Griffin was indifferent—the strong experiments who had managed to endure testing and Dana's horrible whims, and yet they felt helpless for my situation...angry and indifferent...

No...I felt angry...and then, indifferent.

Why were they appearing before me? What was it that I gained from seeing these faces from my past, faces that I felt responsible for erasing from the world? What were the drugs doing to me? What was I doing to myself?

I could not eat the next two meals. Before long, Randy returned to take me to the lab. I was hesitant to follow him obediently but, with an insistent push and a gentle 'please,' I stepped forward. If I had had two meals delivered…it meant that it had been about twelve hours since I had last been in the lab. After Griffin had disappeared, I was expecting all sorts of other hallucinations, monsters coming out of the walls, other members of the revolution coming to blame me for what happened, or telling me to give up…

But nothing else happened. The stagnant walls remained as they were.

That was far worse.

I sat on the table, nervously looking at the box that had been set on the rolling table next to me. *J5 – 88911.*

My blood pressure, pulse rate, and reflexes were noted as my attention remained focused on the box, looking over the five digits that made up my new name.

"We're going to take some blood, now," Randy said, wiping the inside of my elbow. I did not acknowledge that I heard what he said, staring at the box, imagining what the vials of serum looked like under the lid. Even as the needle pricked my arm, I was focused on the box, dreading what horrible hallucination was going to greet me next.

Randy talked me through the rest of the appointment, short as it was. I did not notice that he had not bothered to tether me to the table. I remained obediently sitting on the edge, docile, humbled by the horrible images I had seen in my cell.

That little vial was able to make me see faces and figures from my past…and it was so realistic that I found myself interacting with them without thinking twice.

When I returned to my cell, no one was waiting for me.

My next meal was delivered and I stared at it for an indeterminable amount of time, trying to decide if I should force something down. I was not at all hungry, nor was I nauseous with the pangs of my ignored stomach. I was simply disinterested.

Figuring it was still best to keep my strength, I moved closer and took a bite of the bread, sipping the water.

I flinched at the horrible taste that filled my mouth and replaced the bread on the tray, spitting it out and gulping down the water in an attempt to rid myself of the disgust.

The water sat heavily in my stomach and it made me cringe, my body cramping, unable to remember what to do.

I curled near the tray and closed my eyes, realizing I had not slept in what appeared to be nearly three days, based on the meals I had received. I tried to let sleep claim me, but every time I felt myself start to go under, I would jump awake, expecting someone to be in the cell with me, or waiting for me in my nightmares to continue the torture of the mind-altering drugs.

I decided that had to be the effect of the J5. The other two tests had morphed my body in ways that I could not see but could feel. That test was doing the same to my mind.

A part of me wanted to see another hallucination, wanted someone to appear who was willing to support me and help me through my time in the Commission.

I had never felt so utterly alone.

Even seeing Dana would break the horrible banality in my mind.

Finally, sleep claimed me. I knew it because when I woke, the tray of food was gone. I sighed and sat up, hugging my knees and staring out the glass wall of my cell.

A man in a simple black suit started to walk around the corner of the hallway in front of me and the movement caught my attention. He stepped closer, slowing to a stop in front of the door to my cell, smiling.

The tears were immediately in my eyes.

"No...not you, too," I pleaded with my brain.

Josh shut the door behind him as he entered my cell.

"Lily." He greeted, crouching and hugging me tightly. The tears spilled down my face like rivers. I did not care that it was a hallucination. The hug felt real. It felt like Josh. I buried my face in his suit, crying into his shoulder. "It's okay...I'm here, now."

Those few words sent a feeling of warmth spiraling through my body, chasing away every ache and pain. I smiled into the fabric of his suit, holding him tightly.

We stayed like that for hours.

Finally, I broke the hug, pushing the final tears away from my eyes.

"I'm so happy to see you," I hiccupped. He thumbed a stray tear off my cheek.

"I wish I could see you happier."

"I wish I could be happier...but there's nothing to be happy about," I whispered. "I'm here being tested on, turning into Dana 2.0, and...you're..."

"...you can say it..." he assured with a gentle smile.

"...you're dead."

Josh put a hand on my face tenderly.

"But you're not," he reminded me. "So, don't lay down and give up like you are."

"What else can I do?"

"What happened to your fighting spirit?"

1133

I stopped. There had been many thoughts about our revolution since I had been captured. I had so much time to myself that I had tried to figure out the turning point of our rebellion.

"Everything changed when you died..." I choked. "No one...no one really felt right after that."

"I guess I should be happy that no one was celebrating my death," he tried to joke.

"I'm so sorry..." I whispered, ignoring his playfulness. "If I hadn't rushed into things...if I had thought about how wrong the whole situation felt..."

"Lily," Josh said, his hand going to mine and squeezing it. "Don't. There's nothing you can do to change it."

Feeling the tears come again, I leapt forward and hugged him once more.

"I never got to say thank you..." I murmured. "You were like a brother to me...and I can never thank you enough."

He held me tightly and, for the first time in what I was sure was several lifetimes, I felt safe.

He finally moved to my side and I rested my head on his shoulder, holding his arm, drawing comfort off him.

When Randy and his team came to collect me for another round of testing, I turned to Josh as the scientists opened the door. He looked between the scientists and me and then slowly stood. I stood as well, wondering what Josh was planning. My eyes were darting back and forth between the approaching scientists and Josh. The former member of the Eight Group did nothing. He remained where he was, watching them approach.

The others did not see him.

"Come on, 88911," one of the guards said, fastening my hand in the typical restraints for traveling from the cell to the table. As Randy had done before with the guards, he told them that he could handle me and led me out of my cell. The guards followed silently, but they stopped at their respective posts as we moved toward the lab. I studied them, wondering if they were members of the Eight Group and if they were letting Josh follow me because they knew Josh's plan. I felt my heart quicken in excitement, wondering if Josh would be able to find a way to get me out of the Commission and back to the fort...or wherever it was that the survivors—if there were any—were hiding.

We walked into the lab and I was moved onto the table again, sitting quietly as Tiffany removed the cuff from my right wrist to test the mobility and reflexes of my limbs.

I looked around the four scientists' faces, wondering how Josh was going to get us past them.

Josh stared at me, took two steps forward, and then he retreated the two steps, nervous and worried.

I was confused, my heart speeding up and slowing with every movement I saw.

"Everything seems normal," Andrew noted over the hissing of the blood pressure reader deflating. I looked at Josh expectantly, waiting for him to make his move.

"What are you waiting for?" I whispered. The scientists turned to me and Amanda sighed behind me.

"She's showing trauma related to the testing," she mused. "Better not give her this dose. She should have had enough of it anyway."

Josh turned and began walking toward the door, leaving the lab.

I panicked.

"No!" I screeched, lunging off the table and trying to make a run for Josh. Randy grabbed me, but he was knocked off balance and both of us crashed to the floor. I let out a sob as I tried to wiggle out of the scientist's grip, reaching for the door. "Don't! Please! Stay!"

There was more yelling around me as I struggled against the vice grip. I kicked and screamed unintelligibly, my feet connecting with one of the rolling tables and sending instruments and the case of J5 serum clattering to the ground. I turned to the case, seeing the broken contents.

That was what was keeping Josh with me.

I changed the angle of my struggling, kicking someone in the jaw as I clawed at Randy, clambering to the shattered glass, my hands slicing open as I went to the ground and tried to drink up the serum, desperate to keep Josh near. Tears were flowing down my face as I slurped up the remnants of the J5 from the dirty cement like a drug addict in withdrawal.

The sharp pain of nails in my scalp as my hair was pulled, removing my head from the puddles, made me cry out in pain, and another sharp sting was felt in my shoulder, followed by a cool spread of liquid over my shoulder blade, continuing up my neck.

My vision blurred and I barely heard the echoing of the people around me, screaming something about detox and fluids. My eyes turned heavily to the door, seeing Josh with tears streaming down his face as he remained where he was, his hand on the handle, watching me fall unconscious.

* *** *

I woke up cold and terrified, turning my head from side to side to see if there was any sign of Josh. There were so many white coats around me that I knew more people had been brought into the lab to handle my outburst. They were mumbling, maybe even speaking a foreign language.

I groaned and, suddenly, there were hands all over me. I tried to move away, but the burning around my wrists and ankles proved that I was strapped into those rarely-used fabric cuffs on the table.

Josh...

Where was Josh?

"...J-Josh..."

"What did she say?"

My eyes flew open. Corbett was standing to my right. Andrew was on my left. Both the teams that had tested on me were in the room, crowding me.

"I don't know."

I looked at the faces, trying to identify everyone. Two of them were wearing surgical masks. I let out a pathetic sob and tried to move my arms again.

"Great, she's having a fucking breakdown," Tamara groaned, annoyed. "Did she show any negatives on the J5?"

"None," Randy answered.

"And security didn't see anything in her cell?" Amanda asked, looking at the first group of scientists.

My Group-A and Group-B were arguing over their joint project.

"Nothing unusual."

"What should we do, then?" George pressed.

"I say we turn her files over to Dana and tell him to deal with her," another voice snarled as she lowered the surgical mask from her face. I gasped, seeing the painfully familiar green eyes and blonde hair.

"Agreed," the other one wearing the mask seconded, also in a familiar voice. I turned to him, seeing Griffin's face appear from behind the white fabric, standing across the table from Tori. "He said that she would probably start hallucinating, but she seems to be losing her fucking mind."

I screamed. The scientists jumped, surprised, but Tori and Griffin continued to look at me, smiling darkly.

"Get away from me!" I bellowed. "Josh! Josh! Help!" I screamed, the tears choking my voice as I thrashed on the cold table, pulling at the restraints until I could feel my skin split and bleed.

"Who the fuck is Josh?!"

"Who gives a shit?! Sedate her, damn it!"

Another sharp pinch in my shoulder and I was, once again, pulled under, my eyes turning to the side to see Josh behind Jeanie, looking at me with tears streaming down his face, falling onto his dirt-covered suit.

I was not under for long, coming back to consciousness with a heavy head and a weak body. My eyes rolled uselessly in their sockets as I tried to take in where I was, recognizing the bright lights above me surrounded by the dark walls of the lab.

I was still on the table.

I was much colder, my bare skin pressing into the metal surface. My wrists were still fastened to their spots, and my ankles were locked in place.

I groaned, trying to force my foggy brain to create a solid thought.

My eyes finally began to focus, and I saw the line attached to my arm leading to an IV bag. I could only stare at the tubing and watch as each drop of the clear liquid fell into the top, feeding the long passage to the needle in my arm.

There were four scientists sitting at the table in the corner, looking over papers and talking among themselves. My senses were not sharp enough to hear the words, so their voices came to my ears as a dull rumble.

I moved my head to the other side, a stab of pain in my neck making me hesitate before I turned to the darker half of the room.

Josh was there, sitting in a chair, looking at me morosely.

I moved my arm as much as I could and reached out to him, holding my hand for him to take, making pathetic whining noises that I barely heard.

He stood and walked to my hand, closing his fingers around mine.

The tears burned hot in my eyes and I squeezed his hand, though my grip was weak with the drugs coursing through my body.

"I'm sorry…" I choked.

He looked me over before reaching out and tugging on the restraints on the table. I looked at the chains supported by the leather straps and sniffed, trying to help him by struggling against the restraints. He sighed and let go of the strap, moving to my ankles, also tugging weakly. I knew he was stronger than that. Why wasn't he trying harder?

He moved to my other side and pulled on the cuff around my wrist but it did not give way.

He moved around my head and to the left arm again, once again pulling on the restraint, silent, as I watched him in confusion and concern.

He rounded the table three times, tugging weakly on the cuffs as the tears streamed steadily from his eyes.

"What is wrong with you?" I murmured. "You're stronger than this..."

There was a man in a white coat beside me in no time.

"You're already awake?" Randy asked.

"He-help me..."

I was talking to Josh, choosing to ignore the scientist at my side.

Josh walked to my other side, his hand passing over my hair as he leaned down to kiss my forehead. I panicked. I knew he was saying goodbye.

"No," I begged. "No, don't leave..."

Josh's hand slipped from my hair and he walked to the lab door, not turning to look back.

"No! Don't leave me! Come back!" I bellowed, fighting against the restraints again. It was only then that I noticed they had been tightened, that I did not have nearly as much mobility in my flailing.

"There she goes again..." Amanda sighed, also coming to my side. My eyes were locked on the door. I heard the latch snap into place as if it was a gunshot and the pain tore through me. I screamed and bellowed, the pain tearing into my chest.

As soon as I began screeching like a madwoman, the door burst open again and everyone in the room jumped. My screaming ceased, my eyes wide and my breath heaving from my struggles.

"This is the little psycho?"

"What are *you* doing here?" Amanda growled.

"We're taking over from here," the man declared.

"The hell you are," Randy snapped.

"Dana's orders, kids," another male voice laughed. "Here's the transfer. Don't worry, you'll have her back shortly. We're just taking over for the next two tests."

"You're not supposed to get involved until later," Tiffany said.

"Again, Dana's orders," a third man said. "If you have a problem, take it up with the boss."

"Maybe we will," Amanda snarled at the approaching five men. For some reason, they all looked the exact same to me. The five new faces had nothing to distinguish them from one another, or from any other face I had seen in my life. I was not sure I would ever be able to recognize them.

"For now, we've been instructed to take over," the first one said. "Where are her charts?"

Randy hesitantly retrieved the folders from the table, bringing them to the man who was apparently the leader of the next group that was going to run tests on me.

One of the men smiled darkly, and his hand crept over my leg, running up my ankle and over my knee as he stared at me hungrily. I shivered in grim understanding.

"You're not fucking serious," the leader groaned, looking up from the papers. "You wasted time with the J5? She's fine. She's not atrophied or having spasms."

"She had severe psychological reactions," Amanda pointed out. "We had to give her recovery time."

"She can have recovery time during POLE-8," the leader groaned. "That test is nothing."

"We wanted to be sure of her physical and mental health."

"Do you not know who this little cunt is?" One of them barked a laugh. "This is one of the leaders of the damn Central Angels. After what happened to her little friends, her mental health is going to be so far gone, you shouldn't even spare a thought about it."

"That's the difference between you and me."

"No, the difference between you and me, Randy, is that I've got twenty more years than you under my belt when it comes to working with these things."

"Your gut definitely shows the extra years," Amanda snapped.

"You want to say that to my face, little girl?"

"Enough," the leader snapped. "We're taking her for now. We'll turn her back to Jeanie and her team after we have completed our work." He closed the file and tapped Randy's shoulder with it, flashing a condescending smile. "You can go now."

Begrudgingly, the other four scientists left. With their departure, a sickening fear settled deep in my stomach.

"Her detox done?" one of the men asked, stepping up to the needle in my arm, his hand clasping my forearm sharply.

"Yeah."

He yanked out the IV, ignoring my cry of pain. He then reached for a syringe that was being handed to him, sticking that into my arm and lowering the plunger to empty the contents into my system.

"Alright, 88911," the leader said, leaning over me as I tried to squirm away, "I want to show you something." He lifted a small device out of his pocket. It looked like a USB drive. "This is something you will get well-acquainted with."

He jabbed the device into my side and I let out a shocked yelp at the pulse of electricity that rocketed through my nerves.

"If you do anything stupid," he said, jabbing me again and walking around the table as I flinched away, "like leap off the table and destroy valuable equipment," he pressed the device into my right collarbone and I screamed, "or start screaming for people to help you," he jabbed my other side again, eliciting another cry, "this will be the response."

I yelped again as he jabbed me in the thigh with the black hand-held device.

"Am I understood?" he snapped, hitting the same spot again. I let out a sob and nodded quickly. "Say yes, sir!" he ordered, shocking me once again.

"Yes, sir!"

"Good girl." He yanked one of the restraints open around my ankle as the others unfastened the other restraints. Without allowing me to redress, they violently hauled me off the table, one of them pulling me by my hair.

"Let's get you back to your room now," one of them said with a sick smile as he tightened the last cuffs around my wrists and pulled me to follow him.

I was forced to walk naked through the halls of the Commission, passing surprised experiments and shocked guards. It was sickening and humiliating.

When I got to the cell and the door was opened for me, I had just enough time to look at Josh standing in the middle of the cell waiting for me before I was shoved violently in the back. I stumbled forward, falling on the ground, breaking my fall with my elbows. I turned quickly onto my side, watching the leader of the group approach me, crouching and unfastening the cuffs, looming over me, his eyes scraping every inch of my skin.

He pulled the restraints away and flipped them over his shoulder as he stood, snorting in contempt with a cocky smile pulling at the corners of his mouth. He left. Another man, the one who had been touching me before, threw my balled-up clothes into the cell, causing them to hit me hard in the chest and face.

"Cover yourself. You'll get raped parading around like that."

The door shut and I remained still, holding my clothes to me, staring at the glass wall in fright as my new scientists disappeared from sight.

Finally, I turned to Josh. He looked different. His face was paler, his suit was covered in dirt and he looked at me with a cold sadness in his eyes.

"Why didn't you help me?"

"What could I do?" he asked. "I'm useless. I can't protect you."

"What are you talking about?" I clumsily pulled on the scratchy pants of the red uniform. "You are a member of the fucking Eight Group."

"I was." He shook his head, looking at the ground. "I'm nothing now."

"Josh," I said, yanking the shirt over my shoulders and pulling myself to my feet, buttoning up the shirt with shaking fingers. "How can you say that? It was because of you and Mark that we even got as far as we did."

"No, it was because of Mark," he said, shaking his head. "I should have never tried to help. I messed everything up."

"No, Josh, no," I said strongly, grabbing his face. "That's not true. You were the soul of the group. That's why no one could recover when you were gone. You had a light about you, a strength that helped so many of us—helped *me*—get through the hardest times." Tears blurred my vision. "Don't you remember what you told me? Do you remember the bridge? You said as long as I kept fighting, as long as I believed in what I was doing, that I would be okay. You said that it's harder for good to destroy evil, but you believed in it! You made me believe in it!"

He took my hands from his face and held them in his.

"Do you know what evil looks like?" He took one of my hands and began leading me to the front of the cell. "Do you know how powerful it is?" He pushed the door open and led me out of the cell, turning down the hall and walking me toward the front of Ward Ten.

When he opened the door that should have led to the room joining the wards to the Dome, I was confronted with a completely different scene. There were trees everywhere, their canopies full of leaves, blocking the little light that shone down from the overcast sky. It was colder and there was something artificial about the scenery, something about the lack of smells or noise that made everything even more unsettling.

Josh continued to pull me through the trees, eventually dropping my hand when he pointed to the ground.

"*This* is evil."

There was a large hole dug in the ground. Inside the hole bodies were piled on top of one another, bodies with barely-recognizable faces. I saw Griffin with hair cut to the military style in his military uniform. Tori was in her school uniform, her backpack under her causing her back to contort in a disturbing way. A young blonde boy resembling Mykail was lying across several other bodies. Someone who looked like Josh, but with longer hair and simpler clothes, was laid over another body in similar dress, with longer hair and a painfully familiar face.

I was hyperventilating, my eyes rapidly flicking over the familiar faces, remembering how well I had known the people in the grave.

"I said good can destroy evil?" Josh said. "Good doesn't exist...whatever scrap of goodness was in the human race was destroyed by Dana...by everything Dana is. Evil didn't destroy good...it never let it come into being."

I turned to Josh, my eyes wide with fear.

"That's something you're going to have to accept."

He moved quickly, seizing my arm and pushing me violently into the pit. I screamed, feeling the weightlessness of falling before jolting suddenly on the cold ground, pain radiating through my arms and shoulders as they broke my fall.

I stared at the cool cement under me, my eyes blurred with tears that were falling to make splatters on the floor.

I could see the white walls of my cell through my tears, finding myself near the back of my cell. I turned and saw the half-wall concealing the area of the toilet just behind me.

That must have been where I had fallen.

I clambered to my feet, frantic, waiting for Josh to appear. Every ill-timed heartbeat sent my body on edge, expecting Josh to suddenly step out of the walls.

But he never did.

I had lost Josh once again.

*   ***   *

There was a feeling in my stomach that I had heard of and had experienced a few times before, but I was unable to act on. It was the feeling that grabbed at my core and told me to run as far away as I could, telling me to get away from the five approaching men because they were dangerous and they had every intention of harming me.

I backed away from them as they entered my cell, but when I backed myself into the wall, their leader grabbed my wrists and fastened them in the cuffs. He pinched my skin in the metal and then grabbed the connecting chain, pulling me to my feet again.

"Come on."

I unwillingly followed, seeing the various smirks on the faces of the other scientists.

Once we were in the lab and I heard the door closed, I felt the sense of doom fall over my being.

"We're going to start your fourth test now," the leader said, leading me to the table. He began unlocking the cuffs around my wrists. I was shaking in fear as his fingers moved over the cuffs and placed them on the nearby table. He grabbed my shirt, pulling the buttons open angrily.

I screamed and tried to run, my hands raising to defend myself. Another set of hands pulled my arms to my side, locking them in an incredibly strong grip.

"Stop it!"

"Hold still, you little bitch!" another snapped, helping with my struggling arms as they removed my shirt, leaving me half-naked.

"Don't flatter yourself, you little whore," the leader said coldly. "We were just going to undress you for the test, nothing more."

I thrashed, kicking my legs in an attempt to keep them at bay. Even though I knew there was really no escape, I wanted to at least hurt them back.

"Hold still!" the man repeated, grabbing my hair, pulling my head to the side. I reacted without thought, opening my teeth and feeling them sink into flesh as the man pulled away, his skin breaking, leaving the taste of blood in my mouth.

"You bitch!" he bellowed, his hand striking my face. The force of the hit sent me reeling. My legs went weak as my eyes closed to keep from exploding. Before I could recover from the first strike, the hand returned on the same path and hit me again. This time, the man behind me let me go and I fell to the ground, where I was greeted with feet kicking my exposed ribcage, leaving indents in my bare skin.

My breath was knocked out of me. I tried painfully to take in air, only to be greeted with more feet and insults. I could not hear the words they were yelling, trying to keep my ribs from breaking and keep a sense of myself amid the blows. I choked and spluttered, trying to grab the legs as they came at me, but I was never fast enough.

The kicking stopped and I was able to catch my breath, though not for long.

"Fine, that's the way you want it..." the one I had bitten growled. He grabbed my hips and pulled the pants from me, turning me over. The sudden pain ripping through me caused me to lose focus once again as he violated me. I screamed and clawed at the ground, trying to find the strength to fight back.

"Is that what you were expecting?" another laughed, crouching in front of me and grabbing my hair, lifting my head. I tried to keep myself from vomiting, knowing that there was nothing in my stomach and the dry-heaving would only inhibit my labored breathing. "We wouldn't want to disappoint, would we, gentlemen?"

He dropped my head to the ground and I went still, intent on letting them do whatever they wanted so that it would be over as quickly as possible.

It felt like hours that all of them passed me around on the floor of the cold lab, laughing and jibing, calling me a slut, a whore, and a cunt. The words were just as bad as the actions themselves. I felt worthless, helpless, as if I was no longer a person but an object.

I had to be moved by their hands onto the table and strapped down for the next round of testing. They roughly fastened me to the table as I cried and babbled incessantly, pained and tired.

I was in such pain from the beating and rape that I barely noticed the pinch in my arm as another serum was pumped into my bloodstream.

Then, the pain quadrupled.

At first, it was radiating from each heartbeat. I did not feel any particular sensation with the serum in my arm. The injection felt like a normal shot. But my heart was pushing a sense of dread through my veins.

Then the serum reached my lungs.

It felt as though the liquid from the shot had permeated into my esophagus and moved down my windpipe, causing me to choke. It slipped into my lungs and grew, spreading through all the areas of my chest, suffocating me.

That was when I was sure that it was not the serum I was drowning in, but my own blood. I had images fly through my mind of the serum moving through my bloodstream, popping veins along the way before it hit my windpipe and poured blood into the passageway, flooding my lungs and drowning me. By the time I realized I was suffocating, it was too late to tell the scientists what was happening. My lungs were wracked with spasms, my muscles were cramping, my head was going light as I fought the panic and the liquid trying to drown me.

My arms and legs jerked and flailed, burning and ripping the skin around my ankles and wrists. I choked and gasped for air.

"They always make the worst sounds on this test," one of them groaned, disgusted.

"Turn on the music," another agreed. "I don't want to hear this."

I couldn't believe it. I was drowning and they were putting on music. I tried to grab at one of them, trying to call to his attention to the fact I was suffocating, but none of them were within my reach. My fingers splayed out in the air as my head turned to the side, seeing the sharp lines of my hands as they contorted and twisted against the restraints, trying to find something to hold to keep me alive, to pull me out of the water.

I was choking, my throat constricting…

Upbeat music sounded over the speakers of the nearby audio player and I faintly heard them talking about how much they hated the music the female scientists played. The conversation ensued about changing the peppy pop song.

It was too happy, too fast, and made me feel as if I was drowning that much faster.

There was a pressure in my throat that made me want to vomit, but the suffocating blood angrily latched out with claws, refusing to leave my esophagus, pushing harder and harder against my trachea. I felt my neck arch as I tried to dispel the angry blood.

My lungs pushed the sloshing liquid around, trying to find room for oxygen.

My eyes rolled, unfocused.

My fingers flexed like claws into the air, my body jolting and gyrating against drowning.

The worst part was that I did not pass out. I listened to the song repeat twenty-nine times, blasting loudly over the speakers to drown out my gurgled pleas for help. As the song was playing through the thirtieth repeat, the scientists were around the empty table next to mine, playing cards and smoking, even though there was a no smoking sign near the lab door. My whole body suddenly relaxed and I took a deep breath.

My eyes shot wide, shocked and relieved at the sudden ability to breathe. The water evaporated from my lungs and I was able to catch my breath within seconds.

"Finally," one of them groaned, throwing the cigarette on the ground and stomping it out before stepping over to the speakers and quickly shutting off the annoying song. "Jesus, that took longer than usual."

"Dana did say the bitch had unusual reactions, which was why we couldn't deviate from the administration schedule," the leader said, gathering the cards and piling them together.

"Fuck…we gotta clean her up. She's been leaking blood and jizz over the table this whole time."

"That's fucking gross, man. I'm not touching it."

"I didn't tell you to clean it up with your hands. Get some towels," the first one groaned. "Fucking moron…"

I closed my eyes, not wanting to see them as they gathered around me, their hands cleaning my legs and hips as another two read my vitals.

I was surprised at my sudden calm. There was a darkness in my thoughts, an anger and a depression rolled into one that I could feel sitting heavily in my gut, occupying my being. The feeling disappeared, however, when they stood me up. I looked at my clothes on the ground and started to reach for them, offering to clothe myself, but the leader of the group pressed a hand to my chest, pushing me upright again.

"No, your clothes are torn," he said. "We'll have some brought to you later."

I blinked in horror, realizing that, once again, I would be paraded through the Commission naked.

With my head low and my eyes focused on the ground, I moved with the group of scientists through the halls of the Commission, ignoring the eyes on me from the nearby cells.

When we entered the room connecting to the Dome, one of the scientists turned to the guard.

"Frank, can you go get another set of clothes for this one?" he asked, jerking his thumb to me.

"This is the second time you have her walking through here with no clothes. You know Mr. Christenson doesn't like it when the experiments are paraded around naked," the guard groaned, though he was smiling knowingly.

"I know, but her clothes are all torn," the man said with the same faked innocence.

"Oh, I see," Frank chuckled. The other five guards present also chuckled. "And how did that happen?"

"She was struggling and fell into a bunch of scalpels," the scientist laughed.

Frank smiled, looking me over. "She's not bad..."

"No, not at all, quite enjoyable, really."

I turned my gaze to the ground, ignoring the eyes traveling over my skin.

"Fine, I'll get some clothes for her," Frank said. "But next time, you have to let me know when she's struggling."

"Deal," the leader laughed. They pushed me forward, all the guards in the room looking me over and laughing as I passed.

They returned me to my cell—my empty cell—and tossed me in. I fell onto the ground, being pulled onto my back as my cuffs were released.

"Shall we try again tomorrow?" the leader sneered. I closed my eyes and turned my head away. He laughed, walking to the door and closing it behind him, passing his card over the lock to seal it. I curled on the floor, shivering and trying to keep the tears at bay. My eyes were burning, trying to cry, but there was nothing left in me. I was drained of tears.

I was drained of everything.

I did not react when Frank, the guard, threw new clothes at me, snorting in contempt as he left. The clothes lay in front of me, bright red against the cement.

I did not have the energy to put them on.

Instead, I closed my eyes and let sleep claim me.

For once, it was a dreamless sleep, dark and quiet, away from the nightmares I had been enduring for what must have been an eternity.

I realized that my sleep was dreamless because I woke up in another reality.

I was awoken by the soft draping of fabric over my body, tickling me as my arms and shoulders were covered.

That was when I felt a hand gently set my wrist on the ground, achieving the task of pulling my arm through the sleeve. I was terrified to open my eyes and discover the identity of the person in my cell.

Taking a deep breath, I forced my eyes open and focused on the wall of glass in front of me. There was no sight of the person currently pulling the collar of the shirt around my shoulders. The person was behind me. No guards were outside the door…which meant only one thing…

I turned around to see who was taking care of me and my heart soared.

I lunged upright and threw my arms around his neck. I didn't care that he hated to be hugged, I was too thrilled to see him right when I needed someone the most.

"Y-You're here…you're actually here…" I sobbed into his shoulder.

His arms wrapped around me. Just as before when he hugged me, the world was blocked from my mind. I was completely safe in his embrace.

I broke the hug to push away the tears that had fallen down my cheek. He reached behind me, pulling the rest of the shirt around my shoulders and allowing me to feed my arm into the sleeve. When he pulled it closed, I started doing up the buttons as his dark eyes turned to my face. I hastened to button the shirt, but was slower in progress as I stared at him in shock. He was there, he was sitting with me, a smile tugging at his lips…

"I am so happy to see you," I said, my voice breaking.

1147

He gently touched my face before withdrawing his hand.

I finally got my shirt buttoned up, shaking my head in disbelief.

"Are you here to help me?"

He nodded. I smiled and, before I could stop myself, my arms were around him again, hugging him as if my life depended on it.

In my mind, my life did depend on him.

It had always depended on him, ever since our first strike when we broke everyone out of the cells of the Commission. And there he was with me as he always had been, my last hope to fight against Dana and the Commission and what I was to become.

For an indeterminable amount of time, the two of us did nothing but sit in silence, my hand in his, taking comfort in him, telling him only every now and then that I admired his ability to bear up to the torture of the Commission, now understanding what it entailed.

I had no idea how long we sat until I finally asked him a question. "What should I do?"

He held his finger up to his lips, telling me to be silent, and then pointed to the door of my cell. I turned. The five scientists of the horrible team torturing me rounded the corner.

I turned to Mark.

"Do something," I whispered. "They're going to hurt me."

He shook his head, motioning again to remain silent.

The group of scientists opened my cell and I nervously watched the one I had attacked last time approach.

"Here we are again," he said. He lifted his arm, pulling back his sleeve to show me the bandage around his skin. "This is what you did to me. Don't think I've forgiven you for it."

He slapped me across the face, and my bruised cheek cried in protest, my eyes immediately welling with tears.

As I was trying to recover, he grabbed my wrists and slapped the restraints on. I turned to Mark, who was sitting silently next to me, watching what was happening indifferently.

"Come on," the man snarled, yanking me upright. Mark's hand went to my shoulder, and helped push me up, though he stayed in the cell, looking at me with his expressive, dark eyes. I wasn't sure if he was pushing me to go through the torture again, or if he was trying to tell me to be strong.

As I was pulled away, I figured he was telling me to be strong. After all, it was Mark and I could trust him. As we walked away, leaving Mark inside my cell, I knew it was best he did not follow. I did not want him to see what was going to happen to me.

He likely already had a vague idea and was worried enough.

But he did not want to get me in trouble. Those were the scientists who had likely harmed him when he misbehaved. He did not want me talking to him on the table and getting shocked with the disciplinary device whenever I spoke.

I knew he would be waiting for me when I was brought back.

When I walked back into the lab, my whole body began shaking. We were back in the horrific room where the terrors from yesterday still lingered.

I needed to get out.

There was another figure waiting, one that I recognized.

"Here she is," Frank said, hopping off the table and rubbing his hands together excitedly.

"Yes, of course, she was struggling the whole time we were walking here," the leader said. "As you can see."

"Yes, I can." Frank grinned. "Here you are." He reached into his pocket and pulled out two packages of cigarettes. I watched numbly as I was bought for two packages of low-quality cigarettes.

"Even though I've seen everything she's got already, I got to admit, I really like her tits…" Frank said, unbuttoning my shirt as I tried to back away. As soon as I stepped back, two of the scientists seized my shoulders, holding me in place.

The shirt was pushed from my body, falling back on my shoulders and tightly trapping my upper arms.

"Perfect…" Frank said as the shirt was removed entirely. The scientist I had bitten grabbed my restraints, forcing my hands painfully over my head, bending my elbows so my hands were stuck behind my head, forcing my chest forward, causing Frank's pupils to dilate.

"Take her pants off, too."

The fabric was pulled as I struggled, though they forced the pants to pool around my ankles, effectively keeping me from moving as they tangled with the restraints.

"Those bruises make her fucking hot," Frank said, his teeth toying with his lower lip. "I love it when they're defiant and need to be shown who owns them."

"Well, Frank," the leader said, pushing me forward and bending me over the table. "Go ahead and show her."

Much to my relief, it didn't hurt as much as the previous day.

The others did not waste the opportunity. I tried to block it out, tried to ignore what was happening, letting it take its course, knowing I could come back to reality when they were done.

That also did not take as long as the previous day.

Frank left, spanking me once as he zipped himself up, telling me: "Thanks for the fuck."

That was my cue to return to the present.

Which I promptly wished I had been absent for.

It was just the same as the previous day. The drowning feeling made me think that every moment was going to be my last, that I was about to collapse and die on the table. While death would have been a welcome relief from what was going on in my body and the pain of my pitiful existence in the Commission of the People, the panic that gripped me at every moment was animalistic instinct. I was unable to breathe, my body and brain were fighting to function, and there was nothing I could do to calm down and accept what was happening.

And the entire time, that damn song was playing again.

That time it only played twenty-three times.

I was led back to my cell, dressed, but exhausted and cold.

Mark was pacing in the back of the cell, waiting for me.

He ran forward and hugged me as I fell to my knees, trying to ignore the men as they locked the door and walked away.

I looked at Mark, who was watching the men leave through the glass. When they were gone, his gaze turned back to me, worried and confused.

"I need to get out of here," I choked, clutching the front of his suit. "You have to get me out of here. I was just sold for two packs of cigarettes..." His eyes went wide and he stared at me in horror. "And I...I'm starting to get used to this torture," I whispered, shaking my head as I stared at the floor of my cell. "I-I just s-shut down when they were raping me."

It took me a while to gather myself enough to talk to Mark sensibly.

"You said you were going to help me, so help me," I pleaded, staring at him expectantly. He took a deep breath, as though fighting with himself about how to tell me bad news. "Don't you have a plan? You always have a plan!"

He looked sheepishly away, keeping his gaze low. He gently guided me to the wall and sat next to me, taking my hand in his and holding it comfortingly.

"Please, Mark, I really need to get out of here...I can't take this anymore."

He sighed again and shook his head, giving me a sad smile.

I was losing him just as I had lost Josh, I could feel it. I leaned my head on his shoulder, desperate to keep him close, refusing to let him slip away.

1150

I did not pester him, hoping to give him time to think up a brilliant plan. Three times, I did look at him, asking him if he was thinking of a means to help me. I was getting tired of his silence. I needed stronger confirmation that he was going to help me, that he was going to get me through that hell…

I could not do it alone.

Each time I asked, he would nod and smile mysteriously, but I was getting upset at his avoidance. It made me nervous and angry.

Mark was so good at thinking on his feet. Why was he acting this way?

Once again, the group came to retrieve me. I had decided on a name for them in the silence I shared with Mark. Since they were only interested in torturing me, I was going to call them the T-Team, to separate them from my Group-A and Group-B scientists, who I knew the individual names of.

Every member of the T-Team was molded into one face. They were indistinguishable shadows, sharing the same form, face, and voice.

I went with them, leaving Mark behind again.

They took their fill of me as before, but as soon as I saw the door of the lab coming closer, I felt my brain shutting down. I did not need to be present for any of the torture. I remained unmovable, unshakable as they tried to get me to scream and cry. I did not give them the satisfaction.

The rape was over far quicker.

As was the testing. The song only played twelve times. I knew all the words now, though I could not recall them as I was led back to my cell.

Because of my lack of comprehension of my own situation, it took me at least three hours before I finally managed to talk to Mark.

"I need to know your plan, Mark," I whispered. He remained where he was so I stood and fell to my knees in front of him. "Are you going to help me or not?"

Mark sighed, looking at the floor again.

"No, no," I said strongly. "Do not just stare at the floor and avoid the question. I need you to talk to me!" The words stuck in my throat and the tears began to overtake me. "I don't know what's happening to me…I'm losing everyone. I-I'm forgetting the people I loved and cared about…I'm…I'm even forgetting how you used to be able to think so quick on your feet and get us out of situations." I sniffed and tried to swallow the lump in my throat. "I need you to come back to me, Mark. Help me get out of here…I don't want to become like Dana…"

Mark stared at me for a long moment before swallowing hard and closing his eyes in pain. My heart fell.

"You...you don't know how to help me..." I murmured. I fell to my knees and shook my head. "You always know..." I began crying, curling forward, holding myself around my bruised middle.

"Please, Mark..." I pleaded. "You're the only one I have left! You have to help me out of this! I'll die without your help! I'll end up in the pit like everyone else! *Please*, Mark!"

Mark tried to touch my shoulder, but I shied away, slapping his hand and turning another direction, trying to clear my vision of tears and get rid of the embarrassment I felt at begging pathetically like a child.

His hand found my shoulder a few moments later. I looked up slowly, pushing the tears away with the heels of my hands and trying to focus on him. His hand came up and gently brushed some droplets away from my cheeks, his eyes looking into mine, reading my agony.

"Please...*h-help* me...tell me...just tell me everything is going to be okay..."

He averted his eyes. I waited, my heart beating loudly in my chest, waiting for anything. I wanted him to tell me something. To tell me that everything was going to be okay, that he was sorry, that he was going to help me, that all I needed to do was stay strong...

I needed his support.

"Mark...please..."

He turned back to me and opened his mouth. My breath caught in my throat, my eyes wide. He was going to speak. He was going to tell me what I needed to hear and it would renew my fighting spirit. He knew me better than anyone...he knew what I needed to hear...

He hesitated, trying to find the right words. I hung onto each heavy second, waiting for him to speak.

He took a deep breath, his mouth opening slowly.

"Here's the truth," he whispered.

His voice was wrong. There was something painful and cold about his voice.

It wasn't Mark's voice. It was too familiar...too frightening...

"This was all part of the plan. This was everything that needed to happen. It's only going to take one or two more things...and you'll fall right into your role."

I knew that voice. I knew who was really talking around Mark's façade.

"Really, Little Lily, you're so silly. You were *weak*. Everyone was weak. Griffin, Tori...they were the weakest ones you had. Griffin flew into a rage seeing his lesbian dead, and Tori gave up fighting as soon as she was strung behind the car. They. Were. *Weak.*"

I stared in horror at Mark's mouth, certain that the words were striking me like bullets.

"And Josh?" The voice barked a laugh. "He was pathetic. Sniveling and wandering around, trying to make sure everyone was happy so no one would see how useless he was. I never could stand him."

"No…"

"He wasn't worthy of the love you gave him," the voice said. Mark's face was cold, unrecognizable, dark and evil. I was terrified, staring into the dark eyes, trying to find any semblance of familiarity, any sign that Mark was still there.

"But then again, you always cared too much about people. That was how Mykail got you in the sack so quickly. You opened your heart to him and your legs followed shortly."

"Shut up…" I said, turning away. The words were worse than knives and bullets. They felt like acid ripping holes in me. The pain was too slow, too precise.

"But you were just so naïve and precious. You cost everyone their lives. You should have just been captured in the Sweep and saved everyone the trouble of trying to keep you alive."

"Shut up!" I yelled, turning back to him. "I tried to give myself over! I was going to give up and let everyone else live!"

"Then why are you begging me to get you out of here?" he challenged. "You were going to give yourself over to him, so why don't you just take what you deserve?"

"Shut up!" I lunged at him. "You took everyone I loved. You either killed them or turned them against me, and now you're taking Mark and destroying him in front of me!"

"You did all of that on your own," Dana's voice snarled through Mark's face. I was sitting on top of him, pushing him to the ground, watching as he leaned up to taunt me. "You did everything all on your own…I'm so proud of you."

"Stop it!!"

I reached for his jaw, shoving my fingers through his teeth, sticking them further and further down his throat, my nails scratching along the surfaces of his mouth as he choked.

"I won't listen to you anymore! Give me Mark back! He's all I have!!"

I was crying, forcing my hand further into the mouth, trying to rip the voice out, trying to free him of Dana's hold, knowing that it was not

Mark talking. Just as Dana had taken away Mark's voice, I was going to take away Dana's.

We had all suffered too much because of him. Lives had been lost and people had been stripped of everything they knew because of him. There was too much pain in the words, too much pain in the voice, too much pain at seeing him consume the one person I knew to be infallible...

There was blood spilling out of the sides of his mouth, shooting upward as they were forced between my hand and his lips as he choked and suffocated, his voice fading in echoes around the cell. I knew I was almost at his voice...Dana's voice was almost gone...

When everything went still, I knew I had succeeded. I felt myself relax, knowing that the words were no longer there to hurt me. They were gone. I had destroyed them.

I moved my hand, but was startled by a warm, stickiness on my fingers. Carefully, I looked at them and saw the thick, burgundy blood that soaked my skin. My stomach flipped and my panic swelled. I turned to the figure below me and saw Mark's face, pale, blood pouring from his mouth as his eyes stared, glossy with death, but filled with the emotion he had in his final moments.

I fell off him, sitting awkwardly at his side, my leg still over his abdomen as I stared at the expression.

Fear...

He was afraid...

...of *me*.

I was not staring at Dana. I was staring at Mark.

I had just killed my strongest support, my best friend and big brother...

...I had just killed him again.

My breath was short, staring at the expression, the blood on the cement, and the blood on my hand.

Lifting my hand to pull at my hair, I let out a scream that echoed through the cell. I pulled at my hair and face, grieving the loss of Mark and the battle I had lost with myself. I screamed and screamed, wanting my throat to bleed so I could lay on the floor and die with Mark.

I screamed until I could scream no longer.

* *** *

There were sores all over my body. I knew they were there despite the fact I could not see them. I did not bother to look more than once.

My eyes had been deceiving me for weeks. It was no surprise that I could not see the horrible, weeping sores.

I just had to wait for infection to set in, or for me to bleed dry, and then I would finally die.

For three days, I sat in my cell, my meals delivered and taken away without notice as I stared at the dead body in my cell. Sometimes, the corpse moved, turning the dead, fear-filled eyes on me. But regardless of where it was looking, I saw the terrified countenance every time I blinked.

When a group of guards came to get me, slapping the restraints on my wrists and hauling me to my feet, I put up no fuss, unable to find the energy. Maybe they had seen the sores and were taking me for treatment. Or maybe they were taking me for another round of testing.

Perhaps they were going to 'take me out back and shoot me.'

Did it really matter what they did?

It was over. There was no hope. Dana was either going to kill me, or turn me into the next leader of the Commission of the People—his clone.

The guards walked me through the halls and to the offices that now seemed unfamiliar. They then led me into a hallway I vaguely remembered from a distant past.

We walked into a room that was very different from any room I had ever seen in the Commission. There was a chair covered in restraints facing a wall of glass. I was going to be electrocuted. They must have brought me there for execution.

I followed their lead as they brought me to the chair, sitting me down and strapping my ankles and wrists into the tight restraints. My skin was still raw from the restraints on the table and the tight hold of the leather hurt more than it probably should have.

But I did not say anything in protest.

They moved my head into place on the back of the chair, strapping my forehead into another restraint, making it impossible for me to turn my head. I heard their boots stop as they positioned themselves behind me. Only two remained behind my chair. The other four left the room.

After the door closed everything remained very still.

I looked at the glass wall in front of me and saw a large, dark space beyond. There was one table, similar to the ones in the lab, but it was positioned upright.

There was something sparking in the back of my mind. A memory of a story, the one that Dana had told me…

This was what had happened to Liam…to my uncle…to Dana…

His lover was tortured to death in front of him. Following the script of his own testing, Dana was going to torture mine.

I was about to see Mykail again.

Of course, it would be the last stab to my heart after the horrible hallucinations and what had happened with Mark in my cell. I found myself rather weary of being hurt so badly. There was something about it now that was no longer sharp…it was too much for me to even take notice of…I was too exhausted.

I was already hurting. What was a little more pain?

But when the door opened behind the glass, I did not see a winged man with the guards. It was a much smaller person, slight of frame and clearly a woman. I stared at the bag over her head, watching the guards and men in white coats lead her to the table, pushing her down heavily and strapping her in the same fashion I was secured.

I stared, waiting for the bag to be removed so I could see who was in front of me. Despite the fact I had already come to terms with what I was about to see, I found myself exceptionally nervous.

The bag was removed sharply, pulling her long black hair over her face as she slumped, her shoulders shaking.

One of the guards tangled his fingers in her hair and pulled her head up.

My eyes went wide.

"Eun…"

Mark's little sister was across from me, about to be tortured, all for the sake of making me like Dana. Still thinking clearly about how I had murdered Mark, I now remembered his sister, the last tie that he had to my life. She was at Dana's mercy, about to be part in the horrible experiment to turn me into a Dana clone.

"No…"

How could I not be affected by seeing her? How could I not be terrified realizing that Eun, my final tether to Mark, was going to be tortured in front of me? She was what Mark had endured so much for. He had been obedient to Dana only because of Eun. Now that he was gone, she was without protection.

A voice piped over an intercom system reached my ears.

"Can you hear us?" one of the scientists in the room asked as the guards exited, leaving the three scientists clad in white coats with the petite woman.

"We can hear you," one of the men behind me responded, clicking the button on the side of his personal radio.

We could hear them, but they could not hear us.

"Alright, then we're going to get started," one woman said.

"No...please, don't..." I whispered.

I saw two of the scientists go to a table and pick up an iron that came from a fireplace set. They walked to another stationary table and lit a fire, placing the iron over the bright blue flame. I pulled on my restraints, trying to get out of the confines of the chair and stop the torture before it began, but the leather straps cut into my wrist, pain weakening my muscles.

The third scientist, the woman who was leading the torture, grabbed Eun's jaw, pushing her fingernails into her face, forcing Eun's teeth open, at which point she shoved a wad of cloth in her mouth to keep Eun from biting her tongue. The action was frighteningly similar to what I had done to Mark.

"Don't touch her!"

How was it that Dana knew using Eun would get more of a reaction out of me than Mykail? How could he have possibly seen what happened to Mark? How could he have known? It wasn't possible.

The tip of the iron was glowing white as they pulled it away from the open flame, bringing it to the terrified Eun. Her eyes were wide as she stared at the approaching poker. Mine were also wide, frightened, trying to move the chair and wiggle my limbs out of the restraints.

When the scientist reached his position next to Eun, I watched, petrified, as the poker descended to Eun's knee, pressing into her flesh, melting the cloth of her blue pants and searing her flesh in a bubbling hiss that I could hear over the intercom. The hiss was covered by Eun screaming in agony around the cloth. She coughed, screaming and trying to breathe as she panicked, twisting to get away from the burning iron.

"Stop it!" I bellowed.

No one in the other section of the room gave any indication that they heard my desperate plea.

They moved the iron up Eun's leg, pressing it just above the first injury. She screamed again, the sound shrill and loud despite the fabric in her mouth. I flinched at the noise, trying to turn away from the sizzling flesh, but my head would not move, strapped against the back of my chair. I could only close my eyes tightly, desperate to escape the horrific sight.

When a far more painful scream sounded, my eyes snapped open and focused back on the room where Eun's body was arching, fighting against the poker pressing another horrible burn to the upper part of her thigh.

The scientist with the poker moved away and the woman who was running the horrible exercise in torture reached to the table she had

1157

uncovered after Eun's third burn. She picked up a bottle with a nozzle, spraying the liquid over the gaping burns. Eun's scream dislodged the cloth from her mouth and set my teeth on edge, rattling my bones.

I pulled at my restraints, watching the bubbling of Eun's flesh on her leg as the burns were further aggravated by whatever solution was in the bottle.

"Stop it!" I jolted my body, trying to overwhelm the joints of the chair. "Dana! I know you're watching this, you sick fuck!" I screamed. "Call it off! If you want to torture someone, torture me! This is pointless! All you're doing is pissing me off!!"

I had a feeling that Dana was chuckling. It sounded down my spine in a shuddering crescendo...

It was exactly what he wanted.

The poker returned. They pressed it to Eun's collarbone. Another scientist forced a strip of cloth between her teeth, pulling tight and locking her head in place on the back of the chair. Eun screamed again.

I pulled and pulled at my restraints. The chair was jumping as I tugged, trying everything in my power to get free. I was sure that I could use the chair to break the glass and, therefore, get to Eun. The tears were streaming down her face, which was contorting in pain even when the poker was not against her flesh.

The woman with the poker laughed and moved the iron further down Eun's chest, pressing it to the top of her right breast with a horrible smile, relishing in Eun's tormented cries.

I jerked my legs violently and managed to break one of the legs of the chair. Stepping firmly on the cement, I pulled my wrists with all the strength in my body, feeling the wood of the right arm strain and finally give way, the metal plate that held the leather strap to the chair ripping free.

I heard another scream and looked up quickly to see Eun's other breast being burned, the women teasing her about how they could not have her asymmetrical.

"Grab her!" one guard snapped, starting toward me. I turned the back of the chair to him and backed up awkwardly, blocking him from getting to me. As the other was approaching me from the front, I kicked at him, hitting his knee and causing him to fall to the ground in pain. The attack made me lose my balance and I found myself on the ground, breaking the other leg of the chair and twisting my ankle horribly.

Forcing myself up and using the chair as my shield against the other guard, I hobbled to the glass.

The guard grabbed the chair to hold me still. I reached up with my free hand, clawing at the side of his head and tangling my fingers in his hair, pushing his head with all my strength into the glass. There was an audible crack and the man let out a gurgle of pain, though Eun's scream drowned out the noise.

"You think you're in pain?!" I bellowed, pulling the guard by his hair away from the glass and slamming his face back into it. "Look at her and tell me if you think I care about your pain!"

I slammed his head once more into the glass, watching his eyes slide shut.

Dropping him to the ground, I turned to Eun, seeing the scalding, red wound on her neck, surrounded by burnt flesh and blistering skin.

The poker was being heated again.

Angrily, I grabbed the chair, which was still attached to my left wrist, and hurled it viciously into the glass, though it bounced back harmlessly, dragging me down with the force of the rebound. I was about to throw it once again, but I caught sight of the other guard hobbling towards me.

He grabbed the chair, dragging both of us to the ground as I tried to scratch in retaliation.

He lifted the syringe in his hand and plunged it into my arm angrily, emptying the contents as I tried to escape.

My limbs turned to lead. I teetered as I tried to stand, falling to the floor and hitting my head on the overturned chair, causing another jolt to my system before I blacked out.

When I opened my eyes, I was in my cell, staring at the concrete under my face. Groaning, I forced myself to my hands and knees, breathing hard and sweating from the drugs they had used to knock me unconscious.

I took a few deep breaths and then slowly turned, wanting to see if they had finally cleaned the corpse out of my cell. Peering over my shoulder, I glanced at the middle of the room.

There was no one there.

Relieved, I took a few more deep breaths, running my hands over my head, pushing my hair back as I sat up. I cringed as the torn skin around my wrists was agitated by the cuffs of my shirt.

It took me a while to remember Eun's torture. I hoped that they had stopped after I had been knocked out. It was painful to think that she was only tortured because Dana somehow knew it was going to get under my skin. She had done nothing to deserve what had happened. Her only crime was being someone I cared about.

That hurt more than anything.

She probably did not even know what she was being tortured for. She probably thought she had done something wrong, or that she was being punished for escaping the Commission of the People.

I felt sick at the thought of her innocent ignorance.

When the food came several hours later, I could not think to touch it. Not only did it not look appetizing, but my stomach was turning and twisting, doing flips and tying itself into knots with my intestines. Everything felt disgusting.

I was focused on Eun, wondering if she was still alive, or if Dana had used her for what he needed and killed her without regard.

There was something building inside of me, sharp as nails and hot as lava, running through my organs and my veins, building to an almost intolerable heat.

I closed my eyes and took a deep breath, trying to regain control of myself, but there was nothing I could do to stop the growing pressure in my chest. Pretty soon, I was sure that my whole body was going to explode, coating the pristine white walls in blood and bone.

Every time I filled my lungs to capacity—which I found to be much more than I recalled before—there was a flash behind my eyelids of searing flesh and screams that pulled at the lowest part of me and made me feel like my spine was being ripped out by my tailbone.

Without warning, the flashes became reality.

There was a scream that echoed through my cell, a scream I recognized, recalling the circumstances for that horrid sound from memory unwillingly.

I leapt to my feet, listening to the final echoes of the scream reverberate through the corners of my cell. My eyes were wide, my breath short as I tried to find where the sound originated from. The vibrations died away and I was left in the middle of my cell, looking around the walls frantically, terrified.

Assuming that I was hallucinating again, I slowly relaxed, deciding that I was not going to let my own brain trick me as it had previously. I dropped my shoulders and stood straight, walking to the glass wall and looking outside, glancing back and forth along the hallway. The experiment in the cell across from me was asleep. Even she had lost interest in watching me. A few of the others were quietly eating the food that had been brought to them. None of them seem disturbed. They had not heard anything. The scream must have been in my head.

I sighed and stepped back from the glass wall.

The scream resonated again and I jumped, whirling around, expecting to see Eun in the cell with me, being burned with the poker. Her scream was so close, I was certain she was there with me.

But the cell remained vacant apart from me.

I counted the seconds before the cell fell silent again, glancing at each corner.

My heart was starting to thud a frightened rhythm against my ribs. There was a constant prickling of my skin as I waited for the sound to return.

It's coming...

I stayed still, my whole body anticipating the return of the sound. Even my blood had slowed to stay as quiet and still as possible in anticipation. I was a deer that had heard the snapping of a twig and was scanning for the predator lying in wait.

To my surprise, I was able to stay in the tensed position for hours, waiting, expecting each moment to be the one when I heard the scream again.

But the thing that made me jump first was the sound of the food slot opening and the tray sliding into the cell.

I spun at the noise, turning and finding myself snarling at the young man pushing the meal into the cell. He looked concerned but not frightened. He let the door slide shut, clicking the latch into place before he moved on with the rest of the group to give food to Eina.

I approached the tray, sitting next to it and staring at the contents, trying to muster some sort of appetite.

Instead, I reached for the cup of water, deciding that it was better to try and quell the hot lava tossing in my belly.

I sipped quietly, my eyes focused on the ground.

Once again, the water was hard to swallow. It felt like trying to force down rocks that sat heavy and hard in my stomach.

The screaming returned.

Shrill and sharp, the sound pierced through the quiet air and I jolted from my seated position, furious.

"Shut up!!" I screamed, throwing the rest of the water onto the floor as I hurled the cup into the vastness of the cell. The screaming sounded again, not allowing the first horrific sound to disappear into the walls. And, for a third time, the screaming continued.

"Shut up! Shut the fuck up!!!"

There was nothing I could do. I had to destroy the noise.

I ran to the walls around the room, pounding on them with my fists and screaming madly, trying to drown out the noise of the repetitive horror as I attempted to tear down the walls of the cell. Either I had to find a way to get out, or I had to find a way to destroy the one who was making the horrible screeching noise.

I yelled and ran to another wall, slamming into it with my entire body, ignoring the pain in my shoulder, clawing at the wall before kicking it and pounding at it with my fists.

Again, the screaming pierced the air.

I ran to the half wall that concealed the toilet and tried to break it down. I had to destroy anything I could. There had to be a way to get out, to break the noise and break the walls containing me.

I was going to find a way.

The wall would not budge. I covered my ears as the screaming continued.

"Stop it!!!"

I fell to my knees and curled forward, trying to drown out the horrible noise, my eyes about to explode, my teeth rattling, the sound shredding every nerve in my body. I hit my forehead against the ground once…twice…three times…until I clawed my way to the toilet and shoved my head in as deep as I could, the water doing little to drown the horrible cacophony, my ears pressed against the cold metal of the rounded seat. My throat was being pressed by the front edge of the oval, and even though I knew it would not be long before I was yanked out of the water by the ever-vigilant guards, I entertained the thought of killing myself before they arrived.

The scream flew above me, bombarding my back with its vibrations. I mirrored the sound, letting all the air out of my lungs as I pressed my throat harder against the metal.

The nails scraping my scalp told me the guards had arrived.

They yanked me back by my hair and the back of my neck, tossing me to the ground as I choked and spluttered, my eyes wild around the room, unable to focus.

The echoes were dying, fading into the room. I looked around, trying to see what had changed in my surroundings. There was a black figure in the white colors of the cell, standing near the half-wall, blocking my way to the possibility of drowning.

Just as I had when I was drowning from testing, I recovered quickly, but crawled into the corner and rocked back and forth, my hands covering my ears from future attacks as I waited for the next bombardment.

The attacks continued the next day.

Not long after the next ignored meal entered my cell, the screaming resumed. I was not the only one who jumped. The guard stationed directly outside did as well, cringing against the noise as I began to panic, my eyes going wide and my breath coming in pants.

"No, no, no, no, no, no..." I chanted aloud, trying to cover my ears, or even rip them off so I would not hear the horrible sounds of my failure.

That was what the screaming had become. Failure. Failure to protect, not just Eun, but everyone from the Commission of the People. A constant reminder of bullets ripping through wings and foreheads, tanks crushing bones and organs, and jeeps pulling apart limbs.

I was painfully intact physically and crumbling mentally.

For twelve meals I endured the screaming, sometimes running around the room screeching and bashing at the walls until I rounded on the black spot that was standing against his white background, the guard having been stationed inside my room to keep me from causing myself too much harm. The stain of black frightened me, and I would back away, crouching in the corner and staring at him, expecting him to open his mouth and let out that horrid sound.

A few times, I was sure he did.

The stain changed once in-between meal deliveries and once at every meal time. There were four black spots that wandered in and out of the cell, making me uncomfortable and unsettled. I did not use the toilet, instead staying in the other corner of the room. That was when the blue stains would come into the white room and clean up the mess I had made while avoiding the black stain.

For three days, the four faces were the same, until three of them changed. I had seen their faces grow paler each day as they hesitantly stepped into the cell. It was obvious that even the guards were being horribly afflicted by the constant screams.

Finally, when the screaming sounded, that hot ball of lava and nails ripped out of me.

I was no longer screaming when the sound rolled around the room like thunder. I was hiding, shying away from the noise, sometimes crawling along the walls in an attempt to escape. That time, I was crawling toward the glass, my head bent low to bear the attack of the noise, and I turned to look at the black stain. He had been very pale the last time I had seen him, and now he looked just as sick and terrified as ever. Staring at him then, his face was different. It was not pale, it was chalky, dead, even. His eyes were darker, his hair had changed. And there was a constant stream of blood rolling over his bottom lip and down the front of his shirt, sliding along his chin and his neck, where a jagged scar could be seen marring the skin.

I screamed at the same terrified and agonized pitch as Eun, both of us seeing her brother standing, eyes focused ahead of him, blood from his torn throat pouring out of his mouth.

The thread snapped.

I reached up to my hair and pulled, my broken and torn fingernails ripping hot gashes in my scalp, my fingers coming away tangled with fine rope as I bellowed and screamed into the room. I ignored the rope around my fingers, turning my nails on my own body, tearing at my chest, pulling at the fabric as the threads caught in the broken crevices of my nails. My neck soon was searing with hot gashes that allowed the lava to pour out of me, finally giving release to the pressure that had been building inside me.

Relieved by the feeling, I clawed at my neck, moving down my chest and pulling at the buttons to reach more of my skin. I had to release the lava or it would burn me from the inside out.

The stain turned, and I saw the horrific face of the man I had killed in the cell a week previous.

Ripping the sleeves away from my wrists, I bit deeply into my flesh, ripping the skin and muscle away to allow the gaping wound to release the lava. I could feel the heat eating away at my flesh, causing those gaping sores that were festering with yellow pus to erupt with blood and magma.

I bit into my other arm, allowing the blood to splash into my mouth as I tore the flesh.

There were hands on my shoulders, pulling me backward and throwing me to the ground as I screamed, covering the recorded scream with my own symphony of cries. I was flipped onto my stomach, my face pressed into the concrete as my arms were brought behind my back. The man was yelling hurriedly, ordering for help, though my screams drowned out most of his words.

I felt something force its way between my teeth, opening my jaw and keeping me from closing my mouth entirely. Then, a musky smell surrounded me as my world plunged into black.

Hands were guiding my body upright and ushering me away, two hands locked around my bleeding wrists, stopping the flow out of my body. I fought them. I had lanced the wound and they were not letting the pressure drain. It hurt. Everything hurt.

I felt each turn, knowing where we were going, and smiling to myself when I succeeded in determining that we were in the lab. They strapped me down and began bandaging me as I thrashed and fought. The bag was still over my head, keeping me from seeing the faces that the voices belonged to, but I recognized some of them.

1164

Jeanie came in frantic...

Randy was too shocked at what he was seeing that he had to be screamed at to participate in sewing me together...

...the others were unknown to me.

They calmed as the final wounds were treated, though someone reminded the doctors that I had scratched at my head and hair as well.

The bag was removed, my eyes adjusting frighteningly quick to the surroundings. There were a lot of unfamiliar faces that had worked on stitching me back together. I felt better, surprisingly. I was lighter, not as bogged down with the heat and nails that had been slicing through my organs for days.

But I was still covered in wounds they had not treated. I could feel them growing on my body, peeling away at my dry and cracked skin...

When the man came closer to press the cotton seeped in antiseptic to my face, I lunged, teeth open, ready to bite. In my sudden movement, the restraint around my left wrist snapped free and I moved close enough to him to bite his nose, sinking my teeth in deep.

A blunt blow to my shoulder caused me to let go of the howling scientist, and another smack with the metal ruler drew my attention to the other person. I growled, and he quickly backed away, as did everyone else.

For several long minutes, no one moved.

Until the door opened and three men that I vaguely remembered walked into the room. I quickly fell back onto the table, feeling nausea wash over me at their appearance.

"Well, she certainly caused a scene..." the leader of my T-Team laughed.

"What did Mr. Christenson say? Did you show him the footage?"

"No," the leader said. "I didn't have to. He saw the whole thing from the beginning."

"And? He agreed that her testing should be halted?" Jeanie pressed. "This is going too far..."

"No, no, quite the contrary," the man laughed coldly, walking to my side and looking at me with a sick grin. "Everything is going according to his plan. He said he was very pleased with her reaction."

"Pleased with her reaction?!" Randy repeated angrily. "She tried to kill herself! How could he be pleased with that?! If we let her go, she'll do it again."

"No, she won't." He looked at me knowingly. "Dana says to leave her here alone for three hours and she'll calm down. Then we can resume."

"Resume?" Jeanie snarled. "I refuse."

"It's not your decision. The next test is mine," he snapped.

"At least give her some recovery time," one of the others hissed.

I saw the leader of the T-Team look down at me darkly.

"Dana said two days was all she would get. Then, she's back on the table."

* *** *

My feet dragged over the ground, my head low as I lumbered down the hallway with the guards toward the Dome.

I felt as though I was no longer human, as if I had mutated into something horrific and disgusting.

I needed to die.

There were no illusions in my mind about being able to kill myself. There was no way for me to achieve such a thing in my cell where I was under constant surveillance. After I had calmed and been led back to my cube of Commission property, guards were posted nearby, just in case I had another "outburst," as they called it. I was sure that even if I tried to break free of the restraints on the table and grab at one of the scalpels or needles and endlessly hack at myself, someone would stop me before I could accomplish any real damage.

And unless Maria was in the Dome at the same time as me, I doubted any of the other experiments would kill me.

I hardly noticed the sheer number of guards lining the halls with rifles. I didn't remember the Dome being so heavily guarded before...

I stepped under the bright lights of the panels that made up the fake sky. It was warmer in the Dome, which brought some relief and comfort, though it also made me feel disgusting. Even though there appeared to be no marks on my body, I could feel the oozing and angry pus-filled sores that littered my skin. It was clear that my skin was hanging off the bones of my face, stripping everything down to the bare structure. I was a hideous sight, and the heat made my wounds fester and bake, as though I was a walking carcass in the desert, a monstrosity of torn flesh and infected sores.

I walked further into the Dome and looked around, trying to decide what to do with the boring surroundings. There were seven other experiments crowded near the door, looking petrified and eager to leave.

The guards at the door began yelling harsh orders that hit my ears like battering rams, telling the other experiments to get back, even as they pleaded with the guards to let them out.

I found myself chuckling without smiling.

The door slammed shut and I turned over my shoulder to the experiments who were sharing worried glances. Sighing, I decided to go off on my own into the Dome. I would save them the pain of having to look at what I was certain was my disfigurement.

"Don't go in there!" a woman gasped as I started walking. I halted.

I turned, not bothering to open my mouth and ask her why. My eyes would be enough to get her to tell me an answer.

"He's in there..." she whispered, her eyes wide.

He?

I blinked, slowly, trying to process who was denoted in the pronoun.

He...

Sure that Dana would not waste his time in the Dome, I had to conjure up other options.

He...he...

...the Machine of Neutralization.

A glimmer of excitement could be felt beyond my discomfort. I turned to the bridge and, only hesitating for a second, I left the entrance, ignoring the protests behind me.

It was possible that if I went to him and asked, Eina would kill me and that would be the end of it. Dana was stupid to set up a time in the Dome with me and the Machine of Neutralization. Surely he understood that I would go to him and he could kill me...

If Dana wanted to keep me around, he should have kept me far away from his most prized experiment.

Finding Eina was no easy task. I walked around the perimeter of the Dome, climbing on top of the grassy knolls to see if I could spot the other experiment. Finally descending the other side, I slipped into the trees where the dark and cool clearing rested.

That was where I found him.

As I ducked into the trees, I heard a growl and stopped, raising my eyes to scan the area for the Machine of Neutralization. I could not see him as I scrutinized the shadows, so I looked into the boughs. Still, I could not spot the hazel eyes or brown hair that I knew to belong to the Machine of Neutralization.

"Leave," a voice warned.

That was Eina's voice...it was the first time I had heard him speak but I could tell it belonged to him with the incredible power that came from the single word. I almost did leave, but the thought that he could kill me and get rid of the disgusting feeling in my body made me stay, deciding that if I did not do what he said, he would kill me quickly.

I took another step forward.

There was a quick displacement of air next to me and I jumped, turning, but saw nothing other than a blur. I turned back around and saw Eina, free of his chains and crouching in front of me, his teeth exposed in a snarl.

For several long moments, neither of us moved. I stared at him, at the incredible power of his muscles, at the way he looked at me...I could have sworn I was staring at a lion waiting for me to move so he could pounce.

"You..." he said slowly, his expression softening. "I know you..."

"Uh..." I started stupidly. "We've seen each other a few times."

"Tori's cell...you're in Tori's cell." He tilted his head, standing straight and, suddenly, his composure seemed approachable, albeit dangerous. "You were the one who broke the experiments out."

"Yes..."

"Why didn't you break me out?" he asked, suspicious.

I hesitated, remembering that my goal was to anger him.

"Everyone was afraid of you," I said. He blinked, tilting his head to the other side ever-so-slightly. "All the other experiments were sure that you would kill everyone if we let you out."

"I would kill everyone," he agreed. "Which is why I was surprised that you *didn't* let me out." He turned away and moved through the clearing. He turned back to me before sitting on the ground. "I'm not going to hurt you."

"You're not?"

"No."

"You just threatened to kill everyone," I reminded him, taking a slow step closer.

"Everyone in the Commission, yes." He agreed. "The scientists and the guards, Dana and Sean and all those people who come to those stupid meetings every six days..."

"But not the experiments or the prisoners?"

"Some of them."

"Have you ever killed before?"

"Yes," he said. "I've killed any scientists I could."

I was finally standing next to him, though I was looking around the cove of trees.

"Why do you hide in here? Everyone is around the door wanting to be let out, but you're in the back of the Dome..."

"They hate me," he whispered. "They show compassion and understanding to everyone else who was on the table...but not to me." He looked up. "Sit down," he motioned to the ground. I lowered myself, sitting with my legs crossed and my hands on my ankles. "I sit back here because the lights are too bright everywhere else," he murmured. "And if I can keep everyone else away, that's good, too."

"Eina..." I started asking if he would be willing to kill me, but stopped when his eyes became confused.

"That's not my name."

It was my turn to be puzzled.

"It...It's not? But...that's what Dana calls you..."

"It's not my real name...It was the name I had when I was a child, when I was still human." He had a strange look in his eyes, somewhere between disbelief and total shock. "I have a new name now."

"You do?"

"Hyreyna..." he whispered, looking at me intently. "My name is Hyreyna."

There was nothing I could say. Finally, I cleared my throat and took a deep breath.

"Dana gave you a new name?"

"No, no," he corrected. "The earth did."

That testing has really gone to his head... I said to myself.

"I know it sounds crazy..." he said desperately, seeing the disbelief on my face. "But I started having dreams when my testing was finished. I-I-I started seeing things, things I should have never been able to know. I knew of other worlds, of different types of people living in alternate universes, of dragons..."

"Eina," I murmured gently, reaching my hand out, trying to calm him.

"That's not my name," he growled.

"Hyreyna..." I corrected. "The testing makes you hallucinate. Your brain can't handle everything that's happening."

"My brain can handle everything and more...Do you have any idea what I'm capable of?" he asked, leaning close. "I don't even know your name...but I can see that you were loved by an angel..."

"Loved by an angel?" I repeated in a choked whisper.

"Yes. The red dragon has told me that if I keep practicing—"

"The red dragon?" I asked, cutting him off.

"Yes. The red dragon...he's good, and powerful, and...*sublime.* He's going to help me escape..."

There was nothing I could say. It was obvious that he was hallucinating, just as I had. My only hope was that he would get excited enough to attack me if I disagreed with him. Maybe then he would kill me...

I was about to open my mouth when he stopped me.

"Why do you want me to kill you?" he asked, his expression becoming mortified.

His eyes were not nearly as wide as mine. I was baffled by his question, certain I misheard him. We blinked awkwardly, as though we had never seen creatures like one another in our entire lives.

Was he really asking me that question? How could he not see the gaping wounds on my body that were killing me slowly?

His mouth opened and before I could register that he had moved, his hands grabbed my shirt and ripped it open, the buttons flying on different trajectories as I fell back, surprised. I tried to push him away on instinct, but his body did not even flinch at my shove. His eyes were sharp over my skin, looking me over before he retreated, disturbed and confused. Our eyes met in mutual surprise.

"I-I'm sorry..." he whispered. He released my shirt and his hands went to his head, his eyes distant. "It happened again..." He slowly leaned forward, his forehead pressing into the cool ground in front of my feet. "I'm sorry..."

"What happened?" I asked, grabbing the ripped fabric and covering my chest again.

"I thought...I-I could have sworn...there were holes a-all over your body...not those ones," he pointed to the bandages taped over my scratches, "but...others that were infected."

I was dumbstruck. While everything he had said and the way he had been talking sounded like ravings from the poor creature who had suffered too much under the influence of the Commission of the People, I was beginning to wonder if he had some kind of power that was beyond the realm of what would be considered possible. He had been able to see the wounds around the exact same moment I had thought of them.

"How did you see..."

"I don't know," he groaned, shaking his head. "I don't know myself anymore...I see things I never should...I-I-I can't stop it."

Before I could stop the question coming out of my mouth, I asked. "What else can you see?"

He slowly straightened, his eyes wide with horror.

"Dragons," he whispered.

"The red dragon?"

He nodded. "He tells me that things are going to get really bad...He says that there will be a revolution...a bloody revolution."

I lowered my gaze.

"That already happened."

"...how?" he asked, puzzled. "It was my revolution."

"Your revolution?"

"Dana is going to mass-produce Machines of Neutralization. He's going to sell them all over the globe, and when we're numerous enough...we're going to take over the whole planet. That's what the dragon told me."

And...we're back to the ravings of a mad man.

I sighed and shook my head.

"I think you're hallucinating."

"I want to get out of here," he said, his eyes filled with tears. "Can't you feel how much pressure weighs on this place? How little the air moves? I want to be among real trees and grass...I think...if I were to get out into the outside world a little...I...I might be able to understand what is going on in my head."

I could only stare.

"I'm dying in here..." he breathed.

"...me, too."

* *** *

Thankfully, the screaming was no longer piped into my cell, but I was so convinced that it would sound at any second that I became jumpy and paranoid, sometimes standing up and screaming around the cell, telling them to sound the horrible noise just to offer me some relief from the anxiety of waiting.

It never did.

Admittedly, I smiled when I saw the scientist with the bandages over his nose leaving the lab I was entering for my testing.

The T-Team was waiting. I felt no particular emotion other than defensiveness. I had to find out what made them wince, what made them fear me. Seeing the way everyone was backing away from me after my outburst, I knew I could regain control if I had the right type of reputation. Right now, my reputation was that of being unpredictable, dangerous, and able to cause pain. I just needed to find a way to extend that control to my T-Team.

"Well, here we are," the leader announced with a dark smile. He reached to the table next to mine and picked up one of the white pipes there. I looked it over, wondering why he was tapping the pipe against the palm of his other hand and why the others were also picking up pipes.

"This is punishment for the other day," the one I had bitten said. "And, lucky for us, it actually has to do with your fifth test."

Fifth test...there was something about the fifth test...

Three guards were still holding my restraints, keeping the chains tight so that I could not reach any of them. I glanced around, seeing some of the guards flinch away from my stare. I hid my smile.

"Prepare yourself," the leader warned.

He took the pipe in both hands and swung hard at my stomach. I doubled over around the pipe, but I made no sound despite the pain. I had to be silent. If I screamed I would revert back to the image of the weak little girl that they could take advantage of and rape. I had to show strength. I had to prove that they held no power over me.

Another pipe struck my shoulder, causing me to bend further to the ground. I forced my foot forward to keep myself from falling to my hands and knees, even as another pipe made sharp contact with my back.

I was able to stay standing through most of the beating, but my body was quivering from the strain of not folding under the blows. Eventually, I did fall, which allowed them to hit the other areas.

Their goal was clearly to hit every portion of my body.

I could only imagine what the fifth test was supposed to change about me that the beating had to precede it.

While in the silence of my cell, I had pondered how the tests had altered me. When I had calmed down and thought about my actions on the table, such as biting the scientist, I was horrified by the instinctive response. Never in my wildest ideas would I think to randomly bite someone who was treating wounds. The recorded screams had changed my mind drastically. I no longer had the burning ball of hot nails in my belly. I was better able to notice differences within me.

I had not eaten in four days. I had sipped water, but I had been unable to touch the unappetizing meals. My eyes adjusted very quickly to light and dark, and I was able to see details that I had never been able to see before. My eyesight had gotten so impressive that I was even able to see the freckles on the face of the furthest experiment in my field of vision.

My hearing was more sensitive but my sense of touch had become dull.

Each test was supposed to alter the strength of a human, or make them able to do certain things. I was unsure what tests I had undergone, but I knew that they did not have the usual effects on me, just as they had not had the usual effects on Dana. I had spent hours mulling over how each test had altered me, contemplating what would happen next.

Once every major portion of my body had been hit with pipes, I was moved to the table and strapped down, naked.

What had Dana said about the fifth test?

The guards left, telling the T-Team that they would stand guard outside the door to be sure that we were not disturbed.

That had never happened before.

"Alright, let's get started," the leader said, pulling on surgical gloves and donning a mask. "Go ahead and start playing the song."

The first thing I noticed when the song started playing was that the table they were working from had a huge case on it, and when the top was opened, I could see twenty vials of yellow liquid. It was going to be a long test, dragged on for days and days, probably...

I closed my eyes, trying to mentally prepare myself.

There was a sharp pain in my leg, as though a hot knife had pierced my skin. I opened my eyes, looking at the lights surrounding the table, confused and unsure of the purpose of the incision.

And then it happened.

It felt as though a cold, metal chain entered my body from the wound—at least the first link did. It felt like something smooth and cold slipped around my bones, growing on its own, carefully encircling each component of my ankle. Whether those components were bones or muscles or even nerves, I was not sure. The feeling crept upward, growing the chain link after link, circling my leg and reaching my knee, where it stopped.

"Five, four, three, two, one..." the leader counted.

Something else cold pressed to the incision and worked like a magnet, ripping the chain out of my body—and everything attached to it—in one sharp, overwhelming motion. I could not stop the scream that tore from my throat. My back arched and my body convulsed at the feeling. It was like my leg had been turned inside out, the muscles and veins exposed to the world, waiting to be sliced away, the nerves aggravated and raw.

Three times, I was certain my leg was turned inside out, ripped and stripped, tanned and shaved of everything that made it my leg.

By the end of the third time, the pain was so intense, my brain blocked it.

I lost track of how many times the song had played as my leg was being turned around, and I was sure I would not survive that test. I was certain that I would bleed out from the testing, despite remembering that there were twenty vials of serums and no one had picked up a scalpel.

A pressure fastened itself around my upper thigh. I flinched, wondering if the T-Team was going to turn the upper part of my thigh inside out as well.

They did.

It started with the small incision near my knee, and then the first link of the frozen chain moving up my leg, surrounding all major functions of the limb. The anticipation grew in me. Once again, the chain was ripped out through the same incision, turning my insides to the world.

My vision turned white from the pain and my back arched.

Three times this happened.

Two incisions were made in my abdomen, just above my hip bones. I was nauseous. First, the right side felt the chain wrap around my stomach, over my organs, wrapping everything in a tight hold, ready to rip free of my body and bring the gore to the outside for everyone to see. I shivered, feeling the chain climb past my belly and over the right side of my ribcage, wrapping three or four times around each rib, and hitting the sternum before finding my collarbone. There was something pushing into my neck, something that kept the chains from going further up, so they moved to the left. Wrapping down my collarbone before starting their journey down the other side of my ribs, coiling and snaking like a thousand metal serpents. They grabbed at the lower floating ribs, moving in and out of the folds of my intestines, heading to my left hip.

It was eternity that they were wrapping around my body. I tried to stop the ropes and chains, or even just slow them down. They would rip my entire body open once they had everything in their grip. I tried to will my body to fight back, but it refused, allowing the chains to move over every internal function.

When the countdown happened, I was ready to scream.

What I was not ready for was the inability to do so.

The two magnets were placed at the two openings above my hips and the chains pulled sharply on everything, ripping my ribs apart, grabbing my lungs and esophagus, pulling them apart and squeezing them through each small incision on my body.

At least that was what I felt, unsure that a serum could have such a devastating effect.

I was unable to scream. I no longer had lungs. I was dying, I was going to suffocate, my body would be unable to function without my heart. My esophagus was no longer there to carry air to my throat to scream. Every organ was gone.

My brain was desperately trying to understand how to breathe without lungs, how to pump blood without a heart...

Every part of me was disoriented when the process happened two more times.

The scream would not come out. My vision was going black. I was dying. Over the loss of sensations in my legs, a cold, creeping feeling started from my ankle, encompassing my foot, and moving toward my knee.

There were so many sensations that my brain decided to shut off.

There was still pain, intense and spiraling, that moved over my body, starting at my right arm and stopping just before my neck.

When my neck was skinned and emptied of nerves and bones, I was certain my brain had been torn out as well. Everything was overwhelming. My vision was gone, I could not hear, and I could not feel the injections, unable to tell when they were going to turn my body inside out.

After completing the horrible process on my other side, I was begging for death to claim me each passing second.

Sporadic and unexplainable pain tore through me. It was the only proof I was not dead.

After the last injection, there was silence and stillness for eternity. I wondered if the song was still on, if the scientists were still in the room, if I had finally slipped into the hands of death...

Then, it started all over again.

Only that time, I was laying on my belly. My spinal cord was ripped open and the nerves were yanked out by my tailbone.

It happened over and over and over again...

I would have begged for death, but there was nothing I could say. I had no lungs, no breath to cry for help or scream in pain...I was empty. I was not even sure how my skin was still on my bones. I was sure that even my bones had been stripped, the marrow gone, leaving nothing but brittle calcium ready to be powdered.

Again, I was left for an eternity.

I was dead.

This was death...

It wasn't as bad as I had come to believe from watching all those people die. It was quieter, darker. The only complaint I had was that it was cold.

Then, a flicker of something.

In what I thought was my leg, there was a flicker.

Right there! There it was again!

Was something...growing?

Muscles began to twitch, forming and growing but not in an organic way. It felt like a craftsman pouring molten metal into a mold to make a statue. The molten silver moved through my ankle, forming a muscle in the same position as the old one. Then it wrapped around my knee joint, forming tissues and cartilage. My leg was growing back, throwing new connections to my brain, reminding it of its purpose to move my limbs.

And then it moved through my hip, molding around the area where my intestines and stomach used to be, cooling as the rest of the liquid spread upward, falling into place around where the ribs used to protect my chest, forming malleable metal lungs and a heart that began to pulse.

My breath came back as my throat was rediscovered and my collarbones were put back into place. My arms were reset, strong, yet still so small. I could have sworn I had more muscle than that...

And there was a feeling of pressure as I was turned back on my stomach and the same metal reformed my back. The liquid moved up my spine, hardening in the mold of my spinal cord and carefully reforming the shoulder blades.

I was whole.

But I was still unable to see or hear.

I felt the metal cool under my skin, felt the way my brain sent test fires to various parts of my body, causing them to jolt in response.

Eventually, red was noticed behind my eyelids and my brain reacted violently, eager to see again, pulling at me to open my eyes.

I did.

My hearing followed shortly and I heard a constant snapping that bombarded my eardrums and caused me to flinch.

"And auditory is back," the leader's voice declared. He had been a smoker for about sixteen years. I could tell. The way his voice moved out of his throat suggested sixteen years—maybe sixteen and a half years—of tobacco abuse.

"Finally, damn," another groaned. He had never smoked. I was surprised, remembering the cigarettes that had passed between the members of the T-Team after they had sold me to that guard...

"We're not done, yet," the one I had bitten said shortly. Ooh...he had been smoking for years and years, at least thirty, by the sound that pushed out of his throat.

They moved my right leg, lifting it and bending it at the knee. It should have hurt to have the metal pinching and grinding against itself, but there was no pain. Just intense relief as the metal morphed into muscle, or some combination of the metal and skin...it was hard to tell.

My arms were stretched and then the scientists rolled me up and allowed me to lay back down before telling me to stand and perform basic tasks, like counting with my fingers, standing on one foot, touching my nose...They took their hammers and checked my reflexes, they shined a light in my eyes, telling me to watch their finger...

I performed perfectly.

And they allowed me to dress as my final test of dexterity.

I had perfect balance.

As I was being guided back to my cell, the scientists began groaning, talking about how no test should ever be allowed to take four days.

Four days?

I was left in my cell, completely alone with a brand new body that felt familiar and yet so completely foreign that I knew I would have to get used to it, like a newborn taking their first steps.

* *** *

My first steps came in leaps and bounds. I found strength that I had never known before. I did laps around my cell without breaking a sweat or running out of breath. My muscles didn't cramp, nor did they tremble from weariness. Rather than be thrilled about my new abilities, I felt even more restless.

I tried various balancing exercises, constantly falling, though I was never hurt, and then trying again until I was able to stand on the half wall and lean backward, put my hands on the edge of the toilet, flip my feet to touch the other wall and walk down to stand.

Food was fascinating. I could see every hole in the composition of the bread and the fibers that bound together to make up the crust. I studied bread for hours, intrigued.

I dared to take a bite, but the food turned to ash in my mouth and I spit it out, vowing never to eat again.

I was left alone with nothing to do but learn about my new body and think.

Fourteen meals passed, and there was no moment I was not thinking about the leader of the Commission of the People.

The grace and elegance he possessed when he moved, the perfect posture and balance that he exhibited in his stance...it all made sense. Not only did I understand it, I knew I felt nearly the same. I longed to see him again to compare how we moved, how we commanded this body of metal and flesh.

My brain was also operating differently. I registered every movement around me. Every yawn, every itch, every stretch caused me to focus with laser attention, like it was some sort of beacon. I thought it would get exhausting and tried to ignore the need to document every twitch, but it was enthralling to witness. After some study, I was able to predict many of the mundane moves of the other experiments. I had gotten to know so many of them in ways I had never thought possible just by observation.

I knew how each one of them felt about the testing they were going through, how everyone viewed those who brought them food, and it was completely obvious when they were bringing Eina out by the way everyone would cower in corners, trying to look away from the strongest experiment.

I watched Eina pass in front of me, drugged, with a newfound fascination and appreciation.

He was even more beautiful than I remembered.

I understood why Dana loved him so much.

I tried to imagine what else Dana could do that I would learn as time progressed. I thought about how he formed around people, how he could control their desires…I wanted to watch him again, eager to learn how to do the same.

I had some plans for my T-Team.

Dana occupied my thoughts entirely. It felt like years since I had seen him. How long had I been in the back of the Commission, anyway? It had been long enough that even the testing seemed mundane.

Ironic. Excruciating agony had become boring.

Every now and then, my muscles would twitch and ache as though I was going through a growth spurt, and with those small pains, concern of higher levels of agony came instinctively. However, there was no more fear.

What was the point of fear?

It had been a long time since I saw my A-Group scientists. When I saw Tamara and Barry, I was surprised to find that I recognized them after the extended absence. I never really had a chance to look at the T-Team through the last round of testing, and seeing faces that registered in my brain was a shock to my system.

Everything about their appearance was far more acute, stronger in a way and, yet, so very weak.

Nothing about them caught my attention other than the fact that I recognized them.

But their recognition came with annoyance as I rolled my eyes. I knew exactly what those people could throw at me.

It was going to be another boring day.

As I walked to the lab with them, my eyes focused on the way Jeanie's ass moved under her lab coat—it sort of swayed side to side, but there was no volume under the skirt. It was more of a circle that just shifted ever so slightly without any definition. What did Dana see in her body that compelled him to have her occasionally? I recalled vague memories of a distant time when Dana's touch used to spark something overwhelming through my whole system.

What had that power been?

What would Dana's eyes look like now that my vision had improved? Would I be able to see flaws in the amazing golden color or the face that held the brilliant eyes?

I held so many questions about the man who had ordered the tests on me. I was beginning to think of him as a mythological creature that I needed to seek out. He was so far from my recent memory, I wondered if I had dreamt him up in one of my many hallucinations.

I was placed methodically on the table. Before they went to any testing, talking among themselves about Barry's recent trip to the Western Region, they checked my reflexes, moving my arms and legs and looking for any sign I was in pain.

I was bored, desperate for anything to break the routine.

Amazingly, something did.

"Hey, Jeanie," a voice called as the door opened. Everyone jumped in surprise and turned to the newcomer, except for me. I had heard him walking to the door before he entered the lab.

"Vince," Jeanie said. "I thought this was your sleep block."

"It is," he groaned, rolling his eyes. "We got a problem with Goliath."

"Goliath?" she gasped. "What's wrong with him?"

"He's complaining about his back again." Vince sighed, rubbing his eyes. "My new fucking intern came to me all frantic because he was in pain, so here I am." He jerked his thumb out the door. "He's your project."

"Watch her," Jeanie told Vince, pointing at me as I watched the interaction play out. "Barry, grab the bag." The appointed man went to a shelf and extracted a black bag that looked like the cases doctors carried in old movies for house calls. I almost laughed at the sight of it.

"Fine, you want me to take her back to her cell?"

"No, just leave her there and watch her," Tamara said as my A-Group began to file out.

"Fuck that, I want to sleep."

"Fine, you fucking baby," Barry growled. "Just sleep in here. She's not going to do anything. She's been pretty well broken by Greg and his team."

"Great," Vince groaned, walking in further and sitting at one of the chairs at the corner table, glaring. "Like I want to be stuck in here with you, you little psychopath."

I listened to the words come out of his mouth as an observer rather than the subject of his anger.

I watched him, remaining still as a statue. I was not even sure that I was breathing.

I wondered where Dana was. Was he in the Commission? It was impossible to tell what time of day it was, so there was no way to determine the probability that he was there.

I watched Vince look around the room, trying to avoid eye contact as I watched him. He was tired. I could see that through his whole frame. His eyes slowly closed and he fought sleep for as long as he could, but every time his head dipped forward and came back up, like a bird drinking water, I saw sleep dig its claws deeper and deeper. Finally, his head didn't rise.

Getting off the table as slowly as possible, I moved closer, glancing at his wrist.

It was six in the morning.

Surely Dana was there.

I looked around the lab, my eyes settling on the door where the scientists had exited. Then, I looked at the other door, the one at the back of the lab.

I needed to see him.

I moved to the door and opened it, peering through the crack to see what was beyond. A hallway leading to another closed door lay ahead. Slipping into the dark passage, I closed the door behind me and moved to the next one.

A familiar sight greeted me. I saw the massive room with rows and rows of glass-front cells. I could see some of the humans in the holding cells moving restlessly, newer to the Commission. Others were out of sight, likely sitting or lying on the bunk beds that I had seen when I had broken out prisoners an eternity ago.

I cast glances in all directions, searching for guards. There was one to my right, his back turned as he patrolled the other direction.

I moved out of the hallway and gently closed the door behind me, my eyes forward as I crept along the cold hallway, ignoring the incredulous looks of those in the holding cells.

A feeling stopped me as I approached one of the hallways. After one moment used to analyze the sensation, I ducked into the hallway next to me and pressed myself to the corner of the cell, peeking around the edge.

I was acutely aware of all the people gathered close to me, banging on the sound-proof glass, trying to get my attention.

Ignoring them as best as possible with my hyper-sensitivity, I spotted one of the black-clad guards leaving the hallway I had almost passed. He turned, walking to the next hall, his back to me the entire time.

Finally paying attention to the four humans in the cells I was pressing against, I took note of their expressions. They looked horrified, desperate, begging and pleading with me through the glass to release them, even though I could not hear their cries.

They looked ridiculous, silently yelling, begging to be set free, their faces contorted in terror...it was a funny sight.

I smiled, turned, and left, ignoring the other cells who were repeating the silly dance against the glass wall of their cages.

Moving as silently as a breeze, I made my way to the end of the room, keeping my senses open to where the guards in the holding cells were likely hiding. My bare feet moved effortlessly over the smooth cement.

When I was at the last row of cells, I stopped, carefully peering around the corner and seeing the guard posted at the door into the car elevators.

It was six in the morning. I somehow knew that the Sweeps teams were asked to report back at five-thirty, which meant that the teams had had time to clear out of the car elevators and were probably sleeping.

I lifted my fist to the wall and angrily pounded on the thick concrete five times, attracting the attention of the guard and causing him to run closer. With a smile, I danced around the other side, running up the aisle, through the gallery of comical startled faces in the holding cells and to the door, sliding through it easily.

When the door was closed behind me, I remained still, my back facing the hallway that led into the room with the car elevators. I listened intently for any movement in the next section of my course.

Positive I had heard nothing, I turned and, just as quietly as before, moved through the larger hallway, not caring if the cameras caught my movement. I located the shelving unit I remembered in remarkable clarity from a distant dream.

Ah, there you are...

I pulled the shelves away from the wall and slid behind them, entering the small, dark, cold hallway, sealing myself in as I pulled the shelves back to the proper place.

I could not stop the smile pulling at the corners of my mouth.

It was too easy.

I moved to the other door and pushed it, looking into the dark Records room. It looked exactly the same as it had before but I still did not entirely recognize it. I remembered flashes of faces and information, files pulled from dusty cabinets in my memory, but the room itself had etched no particular images in my brain.

I pushed the filing cabinet back into place, looking at the rest of the room, trying to recall the path.

Barely seeing a door around one set of shelves, I tilted my body to get a better look. There was a door across from where I was standing, so I moved closer, looking it over once before reaching for the handle.

I stopped, feeling a pulse from the metal. It was alive...

The door was pulsing with the electric sensors that would trip and send an alarm through the entire building if opened without proper clearance.

I retreated.

Taking my time and acutely sensing for any changes in temperature or air movement, I moved around the crowded space. I vaguely remembered another passage...

I stopped, turning to another filing cabinet. With a smile, I reached to the floor, pulling a latch on the back of the cabinet, releasing the door and opening up another hallway.

Giggling like a child, I moved into the dark corridor, sealing it, and finding the latch on the other door at the end of the hall with no trouble, and sliding the book shelf to the side on its tracks.

I stepped into the huge library of the Commission of the People and could not help but look around in awe. There was something beautiful about it. I did not realize it was a library. I felt as though I had stepped into a work of art, as if someone had gone through and painstakingly arranged the stripes of colors in each of the outlined boxes on the walls, creating a masterpiece of colors.

Enthralled, I left the open passageway and walked through the ground floor, studying the book spines. There was a type of feeling I had never experienced before when looking at physical books. Libraries were almost all electronic now, apart from some universities and government libraries, but looking at the physical copies, I felt something far more profound, something deep, filled with various emotions that clashed together just outside the spines.

The room was electrifying.

I got a spark of something in the back of my mind, and I remembered that I needed to track down Dana.

I started toward the door that I remembered when I caught sight of the gaping black mouth I had left open. Unsettled by the blackness in a room filled with such intense colors, I closed the passageway, nodding in satisfaction when the black abyss had been covered.

I continued on my mission, trying not to be distracted by the adorned shelves.

I opened the door leading to an empty hallway and smiled. It was familiar territory.

I had to see him.

If it had been another time...if I had not been on the table so often...if I had never been submitted to the T-Team...I might have been frightened by my desire to see the man who had captured me and promised to break me, but I was not frightened. I needed to be with him.

I could not explain it.

It was a longing for someone to understand me. Like on school trips in my other life as a child and the only thing I wanted to do was go home, back to my parents and to those who felt comfortable.

That was the desire I felt in needing Dana.

As I approached his office door, my pace silent on the carpet, I halted, feeling something off about the situation.

Dana was not alone.

Someone was in there with him.

I dropped to a crouch, inching forward, wondering who was with the leader of the Commission. I pressed my hand to the cold door handle, feeling the metal slide along the latch and release the door. I pushed the door inward and pressed my face to the opening.

There was no one in sight, so I pushed the door further, maneuvering myself to peer around the other area of Dana's office. Dana was walking toward a woman. She caught my attention immediately.

She was beautiful, and it was not just her vibrant auburn hair, or the perfect curve of her hips that were hugged by the pencil skirt, or the way her back dipped slightly at the waistband before curving into a beautiful slope ending at gentle shoulders. It was the entire feeling she had about her. It was warm, comforting, yet powerful and intoxicating—like Dana's presence, only not as electric.

"Fascinating, isn't it?" Dana murmured, a smile in his voice. He was dancing with her. He was practicing that seductive waltz that no one could refuse. I shivered in anticipation, eager to watch.

Dana stood directly behind her as she remained by his table, his hands not touching her. She lifted a picture—Eina's picture.

"It is," she admitted. Her voice was pure, powerful, and beautiful, rolled into a symphony of sounds that caused me to shudder.

She turned to face Dana and my breath caught in my throat. She was as radiant as the sun. Her skin was smooth and perfect, her wide eyes a light hazel, dancing with a fire that matched Dana's intense gaze. She was alluring, and surprisingly composed considering her close proximity to the leader of the Commission. She was staring directly into his eyes and no part of her was overwhelmed.

"But don't you think you are messing with something you shouldn't?" she asked.

"Like what?"

"You've created an entirely new species, stronger than man and animal," she elaborated. How was she not affected by him? I looked over her body, over the curve of her beautifully round breasts under the blouse to the tight cinch of her waist and out over those hips that led down into toned, smooth legs and back up to her perfect face, mirroring Dana's movement as he looked her over. He was trying to dominate her, loom over her, make her react. But she was a rock, staring at him as though he was doing nothing out of the ordinary.

"You're playing God," she finished.

"I would never think to do something like that," Dana said with his voice of honey. "Merely testing the limits of humans...seeing how powerful they can become."

His hand rested at her hip and my body jolted at the touch, knowing that she would do the same. She did not. She was still and silent, watching Dana, at ease and still completely in power. It was exciting to watch them. She did not seem surprised or even concerned when Dana's hand moved from making circles over her hip to snake around her back and pull her to him, almost crushing their pelvises together. My breath caught in my throat and I bit back a whine.

"It's...intoxicating."

"You're addicted to power," the woman stated matter-of-factly.

I blinked at her, intrigued. The woman was very strong. If she did not find Dana attractive and was not responding to his sexual advances, I would assume she was a lesbian, but even a lesbian would have felt overpowered by his presence, dominated and weak...this woman was in complete control and Dana was enjoying the challenge.

"What about you?" he purred. "What gets your engine going?"

I watched his hand move from her back to her hip again before tracing down her right thigh to the bottom of the skirt, his eyes locked on hers as she remained still and silent. I saw his fingers brush her thigh. Was her skin as smooth as it looked?

"You're very warm, Miss Harris," Dana whispered, his voice wet with seduction.

Still, she did nothing. She was silent, impervious to his powers of seduction and dominance. His fingers stole under the skirt and my entire body reacted, my back straightening, watching each new patch of skin revealed as his fingers continued on their path, pulling the skirt up. But that flawless, taught thigh became marred with dark ink, swirling over her skin. I blinked, surprised to see her with such a large tattoo. Dana seemed just as fascinated as he pushed the skirt up to reveal more.

It was a serpent-like tail…

And back legs…

A red dragon spiraled over the expanse of her taut skin, the head and wings most likely spread over her ribcage. Dana smiled when he recognized the animal and glanced at her eyes, his hand moving further to bunch the skirt at her hip. The tattoo was very bright and I longed to rip the clothes off of her and see the dragon in its entirety. The tattoo was meticulously done. It looked real, as though there was a dragon resting against her thigh, spiraling up her side, hiding under the confines of the fabric still covering her body.

I heard the air move over Dana's teeth as he opened his mouth to speak, his eyes focused on the tattoo, but the breath halted. From his profile, I could see his eyebrows furrowing in confusion. I blinked, wondering what he was seeing that I could not. His hand moved away from her, quick, as though he had been bitten. He backed away three steps.

His entire demeanor changed.

Dana was afraid.

He was overwhelmed. There was something about the woman that made Dana's instincts react and tell him to get away. He looked like a cornered animal, desperately looking for a way out without upsetting the approaching predator.

The woman watched, unwavering, knowing the effect she had on him.

"The power you have is over a very small world, Mr. Christenson," she whispered. "In the grand scheme of things, you are very small indeed."

"What do you want?" Dana snapped.

There! That was fear in his voice!

"I want to follow the progress of the Machine of Neutralization project," she said, standing straight from her leaning position on the table and pushing the skirt to cover the bottom of the vibrant tattoo. "I want to see what you have created because I want to try and stop the destruction you will unleash on this world."

1185

"Humans have already done a good job of that," Dana said.

"It's true, and perhaps there is nothing I can do to stop what is about to happen." The woman took a step forward and Dana immediately retreated, his shoulders stiff, alert, ready to defend himself. "So, Mr. Christenson, at most, I will be sure that when humans escape to the new planetary system, *you* will not join them. You will stay and be prey to what you have created."

Both were still, staring at one another. The woman nodded to the door, her gaze never leaving Dana.

"You have a visitor."

Dana turned slowly and I shied away from his gaze, expecting him to be angry. However, he looked surprised and slightly amused.

"Well, if it isn't Little Lily." He walked to me, the woman also turning her attention to me. I shied behind the door further. "What are you doing here?" Dana asked tenderly, as if I was a small child who had climbed out of bed in the middle of the night to see a parent. He extended his hand and I took it, following his guide as he pulled me to my feet and into the office.

As I stepped in, I let go of his hand and wrapped my arms around his waist, holding him and pressing my head to his chest. He chuckled, and I heard the rich sound move through the cavity of his ribs.

"Veronica Harris, meet little Lily Sandover," Dana introduced, moving us to the middle of the office, across from Veronica. I was closer to her and all I wanted to do was explore everything about her. Until I was standing in front of her, with my arms around Dana, I did not realize that her presence in the room was overpowering Dana's influence. It was incredible to feel the clashing of such intense energy.

"It's a pleasure to meet you, Lily," Veronica greeted. I shivered. With that voice directed at me, I felt myself go weak in the knees. I pulled myself away from Dana and moved closer, looking her over carefully, fascinated by something I could not see but could feel acutely. There was something about her that was otherworldly, far too powerful to be described in words.

I did not take into account her puzzled expression as she watched me. She looked between me and Dana, her hazel eyes revealing confusion that only could be seen along the edge of the vibrant energy in her eyes.

When I was right in front of her, close enough to feel the heat rolling off her body, I stopped and shivered again in anticipation of touching her.

Slowly, my hand rested on her arm. I was surprised by the incredible warmth of her skin. She did not flinch from my touch, though her body language suggested uncertainty about how to react.

I pressed myself closer, my hand running up her arm and to her shoulder, pulling her even closer as I pressed the length of my body against hers. The warmth that engulfed me made my eyes close in bliss. There was something calming about her presence, but even in that calm, I found an intense excitement at being so close. Dana had a feeling of energy and movement, while Veronica was energetic and stable, like a fire, contained, controlled, and necessary for survival.

My hand moved up her neck to her face, gently tracing the contours of her high cheek bones as I looked at her long eyelashes and perfectly-shaped nose. There was no way a human being could be so perfectly crafted...Her beauty even overpowered Dana's.

My other hand reached to her shoulder and I rose onto my toes, my body sliding along hers. Even with the fabric covering both of us, the sensation was surprisingly tactile.

My hand went to her soft, full auburn hair, pressing it to my face and drawing in a deep breath.

The hand on the back of my collar pulling me away was the most horrific thing I could have experienced in that moment. I whined, eager to return to my exploration of the powerful woman.

"You'll have to forgive her, Miss Harris," Dana said, putting his arm around my shoulders and keeping me at bay even as I looked her over longingly. "She's just starting out. You know how they are when they're young."

"I'm sure I don't," she said. "She seems to be very similar to you." There was a spark of fear in my gut at the words, but I could not place what about the statement worried me. I cocked my head to the side, trying to understand the meaning behind her observation.

"We're working on it," Dana said. He looked at me and rubbed his hand over my shoulder. "However, we're making great progress if she managed to get all the way here without detection."

I looked up and saw him smiling. I returned the grin.

"She's another project?"

"Yes. Just as I said the bloodline has something to do with the success of the Machine of Neutralization, the bloodline for this project has an effect on its success."

"I see," Veronica responded. I could tell by the tone of her voice and the glance between us that she knew we were blood related. "You certainly have your hands full down here."

"I'm never bored."

"Well, Mr. Christenson, Miss Sandover, I will leave you now," Veronica said, standing straight and tucking her hair behind her ear again. "I will have my secretary call you and let you know how often I want updates on Eina and Rehan."

"We value your interest in the project." Dana bowed his head to her. "My head of security, Sean, will lead you out."

"No need," she said, grabbing her jacket from the back of a chair, her statement stopping Dana as he reached back to call Sean. "I will see myself out."

She swept from the room gracefully, moving on air, her curls bouncing as she walked with a long, confident stride.

Both of us watched her leave silently.

I turned to Dana when the door closed behind her.

"Who is she?"

Dana released me and moved around his desk to his phone, pressing a few buttons.

"Yes?" Sean's voice sounded over the speaker.

"I want you to look up everything you can on Veronica T. Harris," he ordered. "Find out where she was born, any family, and any connections she has to the international community. Use all the tricks we have. I want to know absolutely everything."

"Will do," Sean said. "Lily is missing from the lab. We're searching for her. We know that she did not leave the Commission."

"Call off the search, she's with me," Dana said, annoyed, picking up the phone and placing it back in its cradle to hang up. He slumped back in his seat, staring distantly at the papers on his desk. I remained where I was, unsure if I should approach. He was somewhere else, listening to confused thoughts, intent on figuring out everything about the woman that had managed to shake him up.

Carefully, I moved around the desk and placed a hand on his shoulder. He turned to me, patting his leg. I sat across his lap, my hands going to his neck as I pressed myself close. One of his arms draped over my middle, the other hand going to my hair and gently pulling, his fingers nimbly breaking apart the tangles.

"I'm impressed that you managed to make it here," he murmured, offering a gentle smile. "You're making beautiful progress."

"...I'm becoming like you?"

Dana reached to his desk, holding me securely as he opened the top drawer, pulling out a square that opened up to a mirror.

"Take a look."

One hand still around his neck, I took the mirror and turned it to my face.

I had not seen my own reflection in months. For so long, I had been sure that my entire body was covered in open sores and weeping red wounds. Staring at my reflection in the mirror, I was shocked to see that it was me, a face I recognized. But there was so much *more* to me. Even with the tangled, dirty hair and the eyebrows that had been left to their own devices, I felt exceptionally beautiful. My skin was smoother. The pores that I had started complaining about when I was thirteen were smaller, making my face look flawless. The color differences that were around my cheeks and forehead had cleared completely, leaving my complexion smooth and even, like I was wearing porcelain foundation. My lips were a darker tint and seemed fuller than I remembered. After my eyes had traveled over the planes and slopes of my face, my gaze settled on my eyes.

No longer were my eyes a dark hazel. They were brighter, like copper with a golden tint around the edge. They were larger, surrounded by thick, dark eyelashes, captivating and strong.

"You see?" Dana said. "You're coming along beautifully."

"I'm..."

"Nothing has changed," he said, plucking the mirror out of my hand. "When I saw you for the first time, this was how I saw you. This is what was inside of you, scratching and clawing, needing to get out." He took my hand and played with the digits.

"But...I'm beautiful now."

"You were beautiful before," he corrected. "But you were taught not to see it. Society put up a barrier for you that separated you from who society wanted you to be. I just tore it down, and you are finally reaching your potential."

He turned his eyes on me, pride and tenderness in the expression.

"You're emerging from your cocoon."

"I'm still afraid," I whispered.

"That will disappear," he assured, pushing my head back to his chest, cradling it to his neck as I breathed in his metallic scent. "Just like for me. Suddenly, everything will fall into place. I promise."

* *** *

I wanted to believe that everything would fall into place like Dana said, but I wanted to know when. Impatiently, I paced my cell. Dana ordered my testing to be pushed to the next day, which allowed me ample time to contemplate what he said, as well as the reflection I had seen in the mirror.

I was changing, and I was terrified. But it was not the same fear I had felt before. The fear I remembered from before was strong, fighting against the inevitable as I tried to push back against Dana. Now, I was terrified not because of the erratic behavior and frightening power Dana displayed, but because I was worried I would not be the same as him. If I didn't have him as an example, as a teacher…what would I become?

Dana was already the leader of the Commission of the People. He was the one everyone turned to, worshiped, even. Who would I be when I was at his side? Surely I would never measure up.

Would he even let me out in public? Would he let me see the outside world again? Would he let me control anything in the same way he did?

I had no choice but to learn some things on my own.

During my next test, I tried something on Corbett.

I looked him in the eye and studied his gaze as he locked eyes with me. He flinched away, unsure what to do in response. I continued to stare, trying to figure out if I could make him do what I wanted.

He was watching my vitals as another injection made its way into my system. I did not feel pain, just a strange pressure moving through my veins as my blood was displaced by the serum, which allowed me to keep eye contact with the scientist.

Corbett swallowed hard. I watched the knot in his throat bob.

He reached out and placed a hand on my arm.

"Are you alright?" he asked.

I nodded, turning away.

He had obeyed.

Next time I was with the B-Group, I tried to pull at the restraints, but Randy saw what I was doing and ordered me to stop. I did.

When I was in my cell for the next long period of time, watching the food come and go, I decided to be daring.

As the food cart came in my direction, I turned my head and looked at the three young men out of the corner of my eye. I watched them look around the cells, being sure they had given food to all of us. One of them saw me and stopped.

Capturing his attention, I moved forward, extending my body as I crawled to the glass, blinking slowly and parting my lips. I pressed a hand to the glass, pulling myself to a kneeling position. I now had the attention of everyone delivering meals. They were watching me very closely, interested and slightly frightened, like curious puppies.

I reached for my collar with the other hand and pulled at it, exposing my collarbone and straining the top button of the red uniform.

The cart moved and I found all three of them standing above me on the other side of the glass, intrigued.

I bit my lower lip and pulled more, feeling the button give way and exposing the top of my breast. Their pupils dilated. Two of them had their mouths open. Those two must have never been with a woman— maybe once or twice as awkward teenagers feeling around foreign territory nervously. The third one had been with a partner before, which was obvious from his steady stare. I wasn't teasing him. It was a prelude to something he had already experienced.

I pulled the shirt closed and turned, sitting with my back to the glass, telling them they could go.

Those simple, unsatisfying tasks were the only tests I could do in my prison.

My spirit was dying. The excitement from learning my new body and testing new limits was fading. Everything was familiar again.

None of my tests hurt, and after learning everything there was to know about the scientists in charge of me, there was nothing I could do to test them further. I had managed to break Randy into having sex with me, which had been a meaningless test because he did not have much to work with, but it proved that I was becoming as seductive as Dana.

But there was no fun in it.

I went about my testing with a crying spirit. I was longing to break free, to move within my full capacity, to be around people I did not know, to test my abilities, to learn from the man who had already mastered the techniques...

I needed something to do.

Before I knew it, the T-Team had returned and were taking me back for the fifteenth boring test since I had come so close to death.

I was back on the table again.

I didn't even bother to pull my restraints. What would it matter if I was free anyway? I was stuck, once again, waiting for the needles, waiting for the general routine...wondering why the hell the T-Team had walked out of the room and left me there.

"Here we are again, Little Lily," that cold voice whispered. I shivered, my eyes rolling back in my head as I felt myself go limp on the table from the feeling the voice brought. I gave in. The voice was so perfect...so smooth it was clear that he was not human.

"Why aren't you fighting anymore?" Dana whispered. I could not answer. Didn't he already know? I was bored and tired of playing boring games. I wanted something that would actually test me. Besides, the restraints had been changed four tests ago when it was discovered that I could break them. "Little Lily...why don't you struggle?"

It wouldn't yield any results. It was always the same. I struggled...the needle slipped under my skin...that annoying, peppy music played...There was a time when the table used to bring fear. But since it had been so long since I felt pain from tests, I knew the only thing to be afraid of was another minute passed without fully flexing my abilities.

"Why can't you fight?" Dana's voice was suddenly against my left ear, hearing my thoughts. The shiver ran through my body and I knew it was not from the cold air against my naked skin. My body was revving, trying to rise to the challenge, though there was still some part of me afraid of my capabilities...of what I still had to learn about being who I had become...

"I...I...can't..." There were so many meanings behind the two words. Dana understood all of them.

"Try..." he breathed so low that it was almost inaudible. I shivered at the power of his voice. A command...he gave me a command to fight...to struggle...he liked it when I struggled...

Come to think of it...I kind of liked it, too.

"Try," he commanded again. Something still stopped me, something that told me the command was to fight him as well...

There could only be one of us...

"Little Lily, don't you see?" he asked, backing away. "I already have you trained." I heard his feet walk around me. "Make sure that a child who has very little strength cannot get away, and when they get stronger, they don't realize that the same thing that held them when they were children would give way if they put forth the slightest effort."

I was not in the mood to hear one of his obscure lectures about the lessons of life and how humans were. I was no longer human, not after being on this table. Everything that had been human about me had been systematically sliced away...

...but he was right...I *had* become stronger.

"Try, Little Lily," Dana whispered, standing at my feet.

I opened my eyes and turned my head to look at him. He was standing in his suit, staring down at me with his powerful eyes, not blinking, expecting me to fight. While his eyes were locked on mine I could not look away. When he turned his head, my eyes followed his gaze and I saw a knife on the rolling table next to me.

I turned to look at him again, not sure what the knife was for. He smiled when he saw my confused expression.

"Try to fight, Little Lily."

I looked at the knife once again. If I could grab it...if I could break the fabric restraints...if I could move fast enough...

I moved my hands, testing the familiar feeling of chafing against my already-raw skin. I cringed and my hands went limp again.

"Come on, Little Lily," he chuckled. "I know you can do better than that." I closed my eyes and took a few deep breaths, trying to temper the intense feeling of excitement that ruptured my stomach. He moved away from my feet and walked to the table with the knife. My eyes opened when I heard him move.

Good, he's getting closer...

"Are you going to forget?" he whispered. "Have you already forgotten the game we played? The way we danced so perfectly together before you came here? You were alive then, Little Lily. I know you felt the thrill...the power...the pleasure of being so secretly powerful...You enjoyed the game just as much as I did, I can assure you."

I tried to block out the words, but they penetrated my barriers, hummed through my skull, and sparked my already whirring system...

"You want to feel alive again, don't you?" he said, a dangerous and pleased smile creeping over his face. "You want to regain the control I took from you. That's what this is all about."

I pulled harder on the restraints I had been putting pressure on since he walked to my side. My muscles trembled, but not from strain, it was from only using part of my strength. He was right. He could see into my deepest desire, seeing that I was suffocating in my current cage.

"I know exactly how you operate," Dana whispered, getting closer, his eyes locked with mine as I tried to discreetly break the restraints. "You and I are exactly the same. We live for the fight, live for the struggle, and we feel most alive when we are hunting...when we're both predators with our goal in sight..." He leaned even closer. "And because we're so similar, I knew exactly what to do to you to make you stronger, to remove those barriers that limit your ability to enjoy the hunt. All you have to do is keep fighting."

I pulled harder...something was about to give way.

"Try, Little Lily."

The metal rings snapped on my restraints and as soon as the pressure was released, I let out a shriek, launching off the table and grabbing the knife, clumsily swiping at his throat as he backed away.

I missed his neck.

I swiped again, screaming, blinded by the adrenaline. I felt flesh give way under the blade and the imbalance of the feeling caused me to halt and stare at where the knife had made contact.

I saw the red bleed into the pristine white fabric of the shirt, which had been sliced at Dana's chest. The gash in his chest was long, but not deep, and his shirt and vest had been cut, showing the blood dripping from the long wound. The leader of the Commission of the People did not stop to study the injury. He grabbed the knife from my hand and flung it away, grabbing my wrists and pushing me to the ground, settling over my hips. I continued to fight, even getting one of my arms free to hit the cut at his chest, struggling out of instinct and habit.

He caught my wrist again, pinning them above my head, breathing hard, his eyes alight with playful fire, a crooked smile on his face.

"Very good, Little Lily."

I stared into his eyes, feeling the adrenaline coursing through me. I was breathing as hard as he was. My skin was tingling, my hair standing on end.

It felt amazing.

Dana released my hands. I remained where I was, staring at him, my blood pumping furiously through my veins, caught in an alternate state of mind. It felt good. I *did* have power.

Dana pressed his hand to the shallow wound in his chest, studying the blood on his palm. He shuddered and lowered his hand to my face, turning it over and pressing the bloodied fingers to my lips.

The touch was electric.

My eyes slid shut and I sucked in a quick breath, feeling the spark run through my entire body as the fire spread to my fingers and toes before spiraling back like a hurricane to hit my core, where the fire pooled and worked its way through me once again, empowering me.

The blood was warm on my mouth, and while I never thought of blood as being soft, it felt like the softest silk on my skin.

His fingers smeared the blood over my mouth as I drank in the intense feeling inside me, moaning.

I could take it no longer.

I moved my hand to his chest, touching the damp fabric of his blood-soaked shirt. He drew in a sharp breath and rolled his hips against mine at the touch. The feeling of the blood trickling through my fingers, running down my arm, leaving a trail of stained skin behind, teasing me, tantalizing every inch of skin as it rolled closer, was too intense.

My breath was heavy, but for entirely different reasons.

Dana's gaze locked with mine as I moved my hand away from his chest and brought my fingers to my neck, painting my skin with the red ink, wanting to feel the soft warmth over my entire being.

His eyes locked on my hand as my fingers moved down my neck, over my collarbone…trailing down my sternum and finally coming to rest over my breast. I groaned at the contact and I saw his eyes grow darker.

I was in power, now.

I groaned once more as the feeling that had been encompassing every fiber of my being once again spiraled out of control. I watched his eyes as my hand continued its journey down my belly, my skin seeking the touch as it drew closer to my hips. I felt the goose bumps rise as the warm blood marked my skin. Finally, I reached the point where his hips covered mine, and my hand lifted along the front of his pants, teasing him through the seam.

He leaned closer.

"That's my girl…"

His tongue darted out to enter my mouth as I met him full force, my hand still working him. When his warm blood dripped onto my chest from above, my arousal soared to new heights. I shivered, becoming pliant against the floor, even as every muscle in my body tensed.

Seeing my reaction, he pressed his chest to mine as he kissed me, rubbing the blood over my sensitized skin.

I moaned loudly into his mouth.

He backed away and repositioned himself, releasing his erection and burying himself inside me as I shuddered and groaned loudly. I had never felt such intense pleasure in my life. My hands went back to his chest, fisting the wet fabric, feeling the blood trickle once again down my arm and cloud my head in intoxication.

Dana pounded into me mercilessly but all that did was build the pleasure deeper within. It grabbed every part of my being, held it tight, kept it close, waiting for just the right moment…

I wasn't sure who was making all the sounds echoing around us in the empty lab. There was only intensity and gluttony. The hunger in my body refused to be satisfied, even with the incredible pleasure that left my nerves singing. I wanted more. I *needed* more.

I pulled him closer, wanting to feel his blood over my skin again. When he was close enough, I wrapped my arms around his shoulders and bucked my hips, using one of my legs to hook his calves and roll him so I was straddling him.

He did not stop me, his hands settling at my hips as his mouth went to my shoulder, biting, the pain of the wound only adding to my arousal.

I rubbed myself along his bloodied chest as I rode him hard, groaning, my vision white. My eyes rolled around in their sockets, useless as I shut off all sensation other than touch.

I sat straight, my hands moving to my chest, rubbing the soft blood over my skin as if I was covering myself in a blanket, feeling the pleasure spark to an even higher level.

I saw him smiling, his expression calm apart from the intense fire in his unnatural golden eyes. I groaned once again and his smile turned into a chuckle. I grinned, continuing to grind on him as I brought one hand to my mouth and fingered my already bloodied lips, feeling the power radiate through me.

He sat up and his arms wrapped around my waist, pulling me closer, countering my movements. I pressed my hand to his mouth. He nipped at my fingers, licking the blood as if he were a cat. As I smeared the blood over him, he groaned and pushed himself deeper into me, his eyes sliding shut as I felt myself reach the precipice. I pushed my fingers into his mouth and he moved his tongue over them, thrusting into me deeper and deeper.

I felt it…I was at the edge.

My vision went white and my body lit on fire, coursing with something that I had never felt before. Every muscle within me was bound tight, tense with pleasure, and soon, it was going to be too much. I welcomed the feeling.

My back arched and I felt myself slip over the edge. My eyes rolled back into my head and everything went black.

I knew then.

I could fight.

I was still powerful.

I could play the game on his level.

I was a predator…

He was a predator…

And we were each other's prey.

I was alive again.

* *** *

The game started again.

For several days, I was unable to enjoy the hunt. I was left to rot in my cell. No tests were done, nothing changed, Dana did not come to see me.

For someone who said he knew how I operated, he seemed to ignore how I hated to be caged.

I was pacing, concocting ways to regain that feeling from our time in the lab, like an addict chasing a high. I did not sleep. I could not eat. Every time the food came I would stare at the tray, seeing the dead slab of animal and the bastardized vegetables that I had been receiving for the past three meals. Dirt seemed more appetizing.

The emptiness in my belly was not hunger. I needed to hunt. I needed to play.

When I was retrieved for another round of testing, my body perked up immediately, recognizing who was coming into the cell. The T-Team leader crouched in front of me to bind my wrists. I watched him approach, scrutinizing his face.

I remembered his slightly crooked nose that always led me to look at his narrow eyes set into the wrinkled face. I had always hated the way he looked. I wanted to slice at the corners of those narrow eyes and make them wider, see how large his eyes could really be...fix the angle of his nose...slice away at the wrinkles until they were channels of blood...I had so many plans for my T-Team.

I was hauled to my feet and led out of the ward. I studied the leader, trying to decide how best to change his face as he walked beside me.

I had found my prey. My toy.

He had no idea what I was thinking of doing to him—that was the most exciting part.

It was a short walk to the lab and I obediently got onto the table, my eyes sliding to glance at the narrow-eyed leader. His eyes were green...they were a pretty color...it was too bad I couldn't see more of them around the wrinkled skin of a smoker.

The fabric restraints irritated my skin as I was fastened to the table. I growled, annoyed.

I closed my eyes and drew in a deep breath. When my lungs were filled with the stale, chemical-tasting air, the stretch of my muscles caused my body to ignite. The power surged through me. I was ready...

"We're running a B4.1," one of them explained as the others busied themselves with the vials. I used to count their steps. I used to note the number of vials. Counting...numbers...solid facts...they didn't matter anymore. All that was left was feeling...touch...sound...stimulus that caused my body to react and my brain to fire different signals. Immediate gratification...

Latex was on my arm as a hand touched me...It was not the feeling I wanted.

The needle pricked my skin and the cool serum pumped through my arm as my unusually steady heartbeat pushed the blood through my veins.

I turned to the narrow-eyed man. The movement caught his attention. I smiled at him and parted my chapped lips. He was watching...he was interested...

I moaned and my eyelids fluttered.

Watch me...

He blinked once…twice…surprised…*excited*.

I moaned again and tightened the muscles in my abdomen and thighs.

"This is not a recorded reaction," one of them said.

The narrow-eyed man was watching me with those pretty green eyes. I could feel the trail of his gaze as it traveled down my body. He was pretending to study my reaction to the test. He was really watching me because he felt a fire within his own veins. He was reacting to my arousal.

Good boy…

I groaned again and bucked my hips.

"What should we do?"

I took careful account of where everyone was in the lab as I gasped and turned my head. I didn't need to see them, I could *feel* them. I could feel my prey watching me, wanting to get closer…wanting to reach out and touch…

"I don't know…" the one on the left side of my head muttered.

I opened my eyes slowly, tantalizing my prey, urging him to come closer…

He swallowed hard. I watched his throat contract.

"Check her vitals," another ordered. My eyes were locked on his pretty green eyes hidden by skin and too many wrinkles. I wanted to see more. I felt my power reach out and wrap around him, pulling him even closer.

He stepped forward. I saw the muscles in his hand tremble as he extended his fingers toward me. He reached for my neck. The hand was cautious as it approached.

He knew he was the target. He knew I was controlling him. He knew that he was in danger. I could see all his thoughts playing behind the narrow eyes.

But he still could not resist.

How could he? I was pulling his strings.

His fingers brushed the base of my neck, searching out a pulse.

I pounced.

Breaking the restraints, I grabbed his wrist. I heard their shouts, their surprise, but I was intently focused. The others could do nothing to me. They were not part of the hunt.

I pulled him closer, throwing the leader down on the table and wrapping the chains of the restraints around his wrists—they were such delicate wrists for a burly, older man. I pulled them taught, seeing the skin break and the bone strain as he released a pained cry. I rolled off the table, still attached by my left ankle. He was half-splayed, his wrist fastened across the dirty metal so that his face was pressed to the head rest.

I cackled, unfastening my leg.

At this point, the other scientists buzzed forward like irritating flies, attempting to restrain me, but they were powerless and pathetic. I kicked two of them away with little difficulty, watching one of them crash into a rolling cart, spilling beakers and cutting himself on the broken glass and scalpels.

I turned to the other distractions.

Two more flies to worry about, and they were buzzing about my prey, trying to unwrap the chain that dug deep into his skin.

I lunged, teeth bared, biting deeply into one of those fleshy arms, feeling the fabric and skin break beneath my teeth. He reeled backwards and I did not let up, pulling away fabric and loose skin as he retreated. The coppery taste on my tongue fueled me...reminded me of soft, soft blood...how much I wanted to feel it over my skin, between my teeth, on my tongue, down my throat...

I moaned at the acute sensation in my abdomen and straddled my face-down subject's back, grabbing the last fly's face, bringing him close to me, looking into his wide, terrified eyes. His eyes were brown but there was no life in them...he was not interesting.

"This one is mine," I growled, pressing our noses together and looking deep into his eyes. "Don't you dare take him from me." I pushed him away, feeling his neck jerk sharply as his body followed the force of the shove.

A hand tried to grab my knee and my attention went to my prey. He was trying to grab at me to remove me. He was adorable, thinking he could fight.

"Oh, no worries...we have plenty of time, pup," I cooed. I rubbed my hips across his back before scooting down to sit over his flabby, untoned buttocks. "I plan to enjoy this *slowly*."

I slid off, standing behind him, my pelvis pressed to his trembling thighs.

"Do you like it this way?" I asked, pressing closer, grabbing his hips and rutting against him. I felt his tremor. It was surprise, not pleasure...it was fear, not excitement...it was exactly what I wanted. "Or do you only like to do this to girls who can't fight back?"

I looked at the flies, still buzzing angrily nearby.

One of them had obtained new restraints and was starting toward me. I saw the nervous flick of his eyes, the way the muscles around his mouth quivered. He told me that the other one was starting to walk toward me from behind. They were trying to trick me, distract me...

I smiled when I saw him take another step.

I heard the whistle of air behind me and ducked, grabbing one of the fallen scalpels, smiling at the crumpled scientist clutching his wounded neck from where he had fallen on a beaker. I didn't know where the fourth fly was, but I was unconcerned. He was no longer in the room.

When I ducked, one scientist hit the other in the face with the chain intended for me. As the other fell, I placed my hand over his crotch, my fingers squeezing enough to make contact as he halted, surprised. I watched as his eyes slowly fell to me and I smiled, flexing my fingers around him.

Every cell on my hand was a different sensor, able to feel only what was in that area. I felt the heel of my hand close to a warmer part of his body…a throbbing, pulsing vein…

I pinpointed the location as if I could see the pliant tube of blood, lifting my scalpel and sliding it along the inside of his thigh, over the artery, severing it as the blood struck my face, chest, and arm. I gasped, a wave consuming me as I was tossed about in a violent storm of sensation that I sought no shelter from.

He screamed. He crumpled. His life was leaking out of him. I watched the process, fascinated, even as he tried to clamp his hands around the wound. Shivering fingers tried to undo his belt. He wanted to make a tourniquet.

I ignored him. It mattered little to me if he lived or died. It was inconsequential. I had someone who needed my attention more.

I glanced at the scientist with the bleeding neck, satisfied that he was no longer going to interfere.

The scientist who had been hit by the chain had a broken jaw. It was a funny face and I had to laugh.

It was time to get to the business at hand.

I crouched and sliced at that thick cord of tendons on the back of my prey's ankles, watching the blood leak into the frayed fabric of his damaged socks. I could just imagine the blood leaking into his shoes, squishing with that delicious sound every time he moved. His feet were now useless, just limp fish on the ends of sticks. His hand that had been trying to work the chain out of his skin and away from his bone suddenly fell limp and I could taste his scream on my tongue as it echoed in the room.

I grabbed his ankle, feeling the severed flesh give way under my fingers as I lifted his leg. He was dead weight, too limp from pain to offer assistance as I maneuvered him clumsily onto the table. I laughed when he continued to scream, tears streaming down his face, following the crevices and wrinkles, as if obeying some sort of traffic law on his face. His skin glistened from the tears in the dim light. It strengthened my desire to see his eyes, like a stone when wet. I was sure those eyes were even more beautiful drenched in tears.

Once he was on his back, I pulled his legs to the two restraints I had freed myself of and strapped him in, the rigid leather wrapped in sweat-stiffened fabric digging into the deep wounds in his ankles.

"You're not going anywhere, pup."

"P-Please..."

"P-Please what?" I imitated with a giggle. "Straighten out," I ordered. His arm, still trapped in the chain, was causing his torso to bend in an awkward angle. When I saw that he could not straighten, I groaned, annoyed.

I stomped over and roughly twisted the chain, his wrist breaking under my strength, allowing me to position him the way I wanted. He screamed and cried, a sound I was starting to believe I could sing to. I giggled and skipped to the other side, wrapping the chain around his other thin wrist.

"There we go...now, you won't disobey me," I said, taking the bloodied scalpel and pressing it to his cheek, spinning it on its tip, watching the blood well around the blade and drip down his face. His eyes opened, turning in an attempt to focus on the scalpel.

I was right. The glistening in his eyes made the color even more outstanding. The green was so beautiful that I was filled with a sense of calm. I wanted more...I wanted to be engulfed by that feeling. I needed to see more.

I pulled my scalpel down his face, leaving a small, red canyon in his skin before dragging it down one of those two tendons in his neck to the fabric covering his chest.

"Are you frightened?" I whispered.

His lip was quivering and his eyes were focused on me, tears running down his face. The skin was getting red around his eyes and nose...but that blood was on the other side of that thin membrane. I wanted to see it *outside*.

"Answer me, are you frightened?" My scalpel never left his chest, sometimes snagging in the fabric of his coat or sweater, scraping over the cheap plastic of his name tag, bumping over the pens in his coat pocket, causing his skin to prickle in response to the placement of the blade.

He hesitated, and then shook his head.

I slid toward his face, angry.

"Don't fucking lie to me."

He nodded quickly, closing those eyes tight. I watched him shake, his tears falling from under clenched folds of skin that could have been considered eyelids when he was younger. I straightened, my scalpel continuing to dance over his chest.

"How frightened are you?" I asked, watching the silver metal beneath the blood glint in the dim light. "Scared? Terrified? Petrified? ...*stupefied*? Or just plain stupid?"

I climbed onto the table and straddled his waist, causing his eyes to fly open again.

That's it, my little puppy...Look at me.

I lifted the scalpel to my mouth and pressed it to my lower lip, my gaze never leaving his. I saw his eyes dart between my eyes and the bloodied scalpel against my lip. I straightened, pressing one hand on his soft belly, arching my back and thrusting my breasts forward to catch his attention as I dropped the scalpel to rest against my bare sternum.

"Are you excited?" I whispered, my body shaking with excitement, with lust, with overall need, hunger, and heat.

His eyes were frightened. They were confused. The emotion playing in them was more fascinating than any of the great theater productions in the history of humanity.

I laughed, throwing my head back as I dropped the scalpel to my belly and my navel. I shivered, my eyes sliding shut at the sensation.

"Do you want to fuck me?" I asked. "Do you want to be inside me? Do you want to feel me writhing on you?" I circled my hips over his and moved the scalpel up to my right breast, running the side of the blade over my nipple and feeling electricity shoot through my nerves.

He shook his head.

"No? But you had no problems raping me, or any other girl that you strapped onto the table," I said. "You wanted that power...that high...and you didn't care about violating anyone else for it, did you? You could ignore the screams, the pleading, because in the end, you were the one who would walk away with the benefits, right?"

I swiveled my hips on his pelvis harshly. I did not feel any blood rushing beneath me. His heart was beating fast out of fear, not pushing blood to engorge his genitals.

"What? Can't get it up now?" I challenged. "Not that there was much there to begin with..."

He began pleading pathetically.

"Ple-please...p-p-please...I'm so-so-sorry..."

"You're sorry?" I stopped grinding, dropped the scalpel to his belly, and leaned over his face, taking his chin in my hands, focusing him, my nails digging into his skin. "It's too late now, isn't it? You allowed the corruption to consume you, to defile you just as you defiled those girls. Just as you bastardized all the humans that you found in front of you on this very table." I turned my head to the side. "Do you know what happens when you do things like that? People get upset...people snap...you create monsters that are stronger than anything you ever thought possible..." I laughed. "What do you have to say about that, old man?"

He did not say anything. He stared, those eyes shining with frightened tears.

"Ah..." I crooned. "I love those eyes...so colorful...so expressive...so wasted on garbage like you." I sat up and bucked my hips again. "You're lucky I'm in such a giving mood. I'll let you fuck me before I cut your eyes out of your head."

His expression became mortified. Now his eyes were larger than normal, showing off their brilliant color. It tested my patience. Maybe I wouldn't be able to hold out through fucking him before I needed those green orbs in my hands.

He shook his head.

"No? You don't want to fuck?" I sighed and shrugged. "Fine." I leaned forward. "Then why don't we skip to the good part?"

I moved the blade to the side of his face, staring at the corner of his left eye, the eye I wanted to start with. He started shaking his head violently back and forth, desperate to avoid the blade, his eyes clenched tightly shut, muttering 'no, no, no' over and over and over again. What an annoying puppy...

"Stop moving," I warned. I didn't want to damage my pearl. I just had to get around the shell, and that shell was moving too much for me to successfully extract my prize.

"Stop!" a voice caught my attention. I glanced over my shoulder. There was the fourth fly, standing next to Dana, who was looking over the situation calmly. I felt myself shiver in anticipation at seeing him there. The scientist started forward before Dana spoke to him.

"You stay put," he ordered.

The man stopped and turned to the leader of the Commission incredulously before obeying. I sat straight, watching as Dana took slow, measured steps toward me, his gaze scanning my work.

He stepped to the side of the table and looked over the man head to toe before his golden eyes settled on his face.

"Good evening, Greg," he said with a cold grin. He looked at me. "Come here, Little Lily."

I hesitated. I didn't want to lose my prey. I was worried he would tell me I couldn't have him. I wanted him. I would take those eyes anyway, no matter what Dana said.

I climbed off, though, and sat on the edge of the table, my legs swinging over the side. Dana stepped up to me, wedging his hips between my thighs and looming over me, smiling darkly. I grinned. I was proud of my catch and knew he was pleased at the sight. I had caught my first real prey and he was proud.

His hands rested on my hips and before I realized it, he lifted me, flipped me over and planted my feet on the ground, grabbing my hip with one hand and pulling me against his pelvis, causing me to moan loudly. His other hand grabbed my wrist and jerked my arm behind my back, forcing me upright as his mouth settled next to my ear.

I didn't struggle. I moaned. I wanted him to bend me over and fuck me right there. I was hungry for sensation.

"Are you causing trouble?" he sang against my ear. I shivered and pushed my hips back against his trousers. He laughed and bit my ear. "You've been a naughty girl, Little Lily." He moved away from my ear, wrapping his arms around my torso, holding me tight.

"This is a very sloppy job," he scolded. I growled. *I* was not disappointed.

"Oh, Little Lily, you're like a puppy that has just figured out she has teeth," he said with a disapproving tone. "You know they're there but you have no idea how to really use them." He leaned back to my ear. "Do you see him? Lying there...helpless...at your mercy...but not immobile."

I was confused. He wasn't able to get off the table...

"You frightened him but you need to petrify him...make it so he cannot disobey you..." He smacked my thigh. "Get back up there."

My heart leapt at the realization that I could keep my prey.

I clambered back on the table, excited.

"Good girl." Dana handed me the scalpel and we both turned to my victim.

"Sir?" he whispered, his voice choked, his gaze locked on his boss.

"What?" Dana asked. I giggled and squirmed. The little pup was so entertaining. He thought we cared what he wanted to say.

"Look him in the eyes," Dana told me.

I turned and caught his terrified gaze.

"Hold it..." Dana whispered. "Pull him into you...feel your power around him, keep him close...don't let him go..."

I watched those eyes minutely twitch as I held his gaze, seeing the muscles straining not to blink.

"Remember...you are in control...you have his life in your hands...make sure he knows that...make sure he feels nothing other than how helpless he is."

I smiled at my prey and placed a hand against his cheek, stroking the loose skin with my thumb. He could not escape. Even the eventual blink of his eyes could not break my control.

"Very good."

I moved the scalpel to my prey's face, toward the corner of the left eye—the starting point for my game—and pressed the blade to the very point where his top eyelid met the bottom. He did not move, his eyes locked with mine. He barely flinched at the touch of the scalpel.

I pressed harder. He did not move.

He could not scream as I stared at him. Dana instructed me in cutting around the eye, slowly moving the flaps of skin as they were peeled away to reveal the incredible large orbs of white, painted with that circle of green flares that moved as if the eye itself was breathing.

"So pretty..."

"Do you want them?" Dana asked. "Take them."

I looked around for something to gently remove my prize, not wanting to harm my delicate pearls. Dana grabbed a spoon-like instrument, handing it to me. I set to pushing through the swollen, irritated flesh around the eye, rolling it carefully out of the socket and unraveling the nerves that connected the eye to the skull. My prey was shivering. He was in shock. It was nice to finally work in quiet.

I moved to the other eye and, with the same delicate hand, I removed it.

Then, I took the scalpel and carefully cut at the nerves until the two eyes were loose in my hands.

"They are pretty," Dana agreed, retrieving a metallic bowl and holding it out to me. I smiled at my little treasures as I placed them in the bowl. I then glanced at Dana, beaming with pride. He set the bowl aside before also turning to my prey. He wasn't nearly as interesting anymore—just a sack of skin, blood, and bones.

"Well...he won't be able to work with a scalpel anymore...he's useless now." Dana grabbed the scalpel and sliced at the artery in the pup's neck. I leaned down to watch the blood pump out, bobbing my head with the beat of gushes. I watched it form a pool on the metal table as the man shivered under me.

Fingers came to the blood and dipped in, coming away coated in burgundy. I looked at Dana as he took the blood and ran it over the skin of his fingers. He locked gazes with me, alight with fire.

"S-sir?" a voice said distantly.

I groaned and quickly turned, angry. Why was he here, that little maggot?

"How...how could you..." the fourth fly whispered. I scrambled off the table, pushing him backward, angry.

"Little Lily," Dana called, grabbing one of the fallen chains on the ground. I glanced at the other three scientists I had dealt with earlier, suddenly recalling their presence. The one with the severed femoral artery was dead. The one with the bleeding neck was either dead or unconscious, I didn't care which. The one with the broken jaw was shivering, unable to do anything with that funny-looking face of his.

"It would appear that we have another subject to test on," Dana laughed, swinging the chain. The scientist I had pushed was looking between us, frightened, trying to crawl backwards on his hands along the cold floor.

"W-What?"

"I can't have you telling the others what happened in here, so we're going to deal with you in a way that allows you to live and is beneficial for the Commission," Dana explained. I giggled.

"It's your turn on the table," I sang, winking.

He tried to stumble to his feet, but Dana was after him immediately. I loved watching Dana move. He was so powerful.

He wrapped the chain around the scientist's neck twice and twisted it, pulling him roughly back as the scientist choked.

"You can't get away from this," Dana jeered. He turned the man over and wrapped the chain around his mouth, forcing the metal between his lips and teeth, and then began to drag him to the other three scientists.

"Can't we play with him?" I whined.

"No," Dana said, shaking his head and jerking on the chain, fastening it to the metal frame of the table next to the fly with the funny face.

"Why not?"

"Because you need to be punished," Dana said sternly.

"What did I do?"

"You were sloppy. You should have done this better. I've lost five scientists. You could have played with just one."

"The others were trying to stop me," I defended as Dana straightened, looking annoyed but amused. My smile widened. "I was bored. You didn't see me..."

"It's not my job to entertain you."

"So I entertained myself."

"You need to learn better control."

"I had control!"

"No, you had power, there is a difference." He turned to face me fully as I approached. "Power is the means to knock someone down, to take their life, to hurt and abuse them. Control is the ability to make someone do all of that to themselves without so much as laying a hand on them or saying a word. Control comes from an unspoken threat. You only have as much power as people give you. So you make them believe that you have all that power and more...*that* is control."

His voice was stern, powerful, commanding, and it drew me closer. I was pressed against him by the time he finished speaking. I was so proud of myself and my hunt that I wanted a reward. I wanted to feel the way I had before, and I knew he could give it to me.

I reached for his belt and he grinned, catching my wrist.

"No."

"Why not?" I asked, rubbing myself against him.

"Because I am going to punish you. You need to learn."

"Punish me while you're fucking me..." I murmured, trying to free my wrist. He laughed and backed away. He was playing hard to get. I had to hunt him, now. I knew I could win. I knew he wanted to fuck just as much as me.

"No," he said. "If you wanna fuck so badly, find something to fuck yourself with."

I looked around the lab. There were scalpels, pens, rubber tubing, test tubes...

"Nothing's as big as you," I said, once again reaching toward him. He stepped away and I followed. He was chuckling, as was I. "I'm not asking you."

"Oh? You're not?"

"No."

I pushed him to the ground, using my leg to kick his out from under him. He fell heavily, but I knew he was willing.

"You want me to find something to fuck myself with, well..." I reached back and cupped his groin, "I choose this."

"No."

"What? You want me to fuck you instead?" I giggled. "That would be fun. Get something to shove inside of you...I bet you would love it."

"You have a long way to go before you can do that," he said. He grabbed my wrist and rolled me over, pinning my hips under his. I moaned loudly and wrapped my legs around him, canting my pelvis, wanting him inside me so desperately I was sure I would die if I was left empty much longer.

"What am I going to do with you?"

"I can't wait to find out," I said.

"Be careful about surrendering to me, Little Lily," he warned with a smile that made my whole body jolt violently. I licked my lips.

"Why? Are you going to force yourself onto me and make me take my punishment?" I taunted. He wagged a finger in front of my face.

"It doesn't work like that anymore," he breathed. "I'm sure you noticed that your body doesn't react to pain the same way."

His finger moved down my sternum, down my belly and over my pubic bone, finally pushing inside me. I let out a choked groan. His finger was joined by another, both of them crooking to stroke the front wall. I shuddered, smiling at him and looking him in the eye, trying to bend him to my will and get him to fuck me, hard and fast.

Dana's finger pushed deeper and I let out a thrilled cry, finally feeling something I had been craving.

"The only effective punishment now," he whispered, crooking his finger three times before violently pulling them out and standing swiftly, "is denying you."

With a frustrated moan, I got to my feet, staring at him defiantly.

He grinned knowingly. "You're not going to let this go, are you?" I shook my head.

He extracted his phone from his pocket and pressed the screen a few times, lifting the phone to his ear.

"We're going to need discreet cleanup in Lab Two," he said shortly, hanging up and smiling at me as he replaced the phone. "Get dressed, Little Lily."

"No," I snapped, crossing my arms, thrusting my breasts forward. I knew I caught his attention with the way his eyes dipped to look at my chest. He sighed and rolled his eyes.

"I don't remember being this stubborn..."

"It was a long time ago," I reminded him. "Maybe in your old age you can't remember what it's like to be teased and then left hanging."

"Have you forgotten, Little Lily, all the times you've teased me in the last year and half?"

"Then you should understand how upset I am right now."

"Trust me, sex won't cure that," he said. "At least for now. All it will do is fuel your fire and then you won't let me go for a few weeks, I'm sure."

"Ooh..." I said, blinking slowly and stalking forward, being sure to put as much movement into my hips as possible. "That could be fun."

"Not when I have a country to run." Dana shook his head, though he allowed my hands to wander over his hard chest. "Get dressed."

"No."

"Staying naked will not make me fuck you."

"Maybe not, but I'm sure the people coming in here to clean wouldn't refuse." I raised my eyebrows, rolling onto my toes and wrapping my arms around Dana's neck. "I've been practicing..."

"Yes, I saw." I cocked my head to the side and his grin widened. "There are cameras everywhere, Little Lily. I was impressed, truly. Randy is not easy to seduce at all."

"Why are you being so cruel to me?" I whined, my hand tangling in the hair at the base of Dana's neck.

"Are you forgetting already?" he asked, glancing at the scientists littering the lab. "I'm punishing you because you were greedy. You took the power and used it over them, but rather than going after the one you wanted, you went after him with the others as *my* collateral damage."

"They were dicks," I told him shortly.

"I know," Dana said. "But that's why they were so good at doing all the nasty tests the others couldn't stomach. Now I have to assign that to another team."

"I'll help you," I assured, pecking him on the lips. He looked me over with a knowing gaze, shaking his head as I groaned and rolled my eyes, lowering from my toes, my hands resting on his shoulders. "How is it that you can resist me?"

"Because I have more control over this than you do," he said, placing a finger on my chin and lifting my head. "But don't worry, I'll teach you."

A warmth spread through my belly at the words.

He kissed my forehead just at the time the door opened and another face I had not seen in what felt like years entered, three men with him.

"What the hell happened in here?" Sean gasped, his eyes wide in horror at the scene he saw. My whole body went on alert when I saw the head of security. There was something about him that was incredible, so stable and yet so electric and powerful. It was like staring in amazement at a mighty tree that dominated all the others in the forest.

I let out a squeal and ran to him, but Dana caught my wrist, halting my advance.

"Ah, ah, ah," he scolded. "No."

"Why?"

"M-Miss Sandover?" Sean blinked, shocked to see me standing naked among my carnage. I pulled against Dana's grip.

"See? He knows who I am! Let me go!" I whimpered.

"No, no, Little Lily, Sean is mine."

"That's not fair!"

"It has taken me years to get Sean to this point and I will not have your newbie antics breaking all my hard work," Dana snapped, though he was chuckling, pulling me back and wrapping his arms around my shoulders to hold me still, even as I looked over Sean hungrily. I could not even place what it was about the head of security that was so intoxicating. I felt like I needed to hover around him and draw off his strength and simplicity.

"Dana, what—"

"I told you she was going to become like me," he said. "Here she is…*almost* complete."

I glared at him.

"Well, you still have three little tests and some training," Dana answered my silent huff.

I huffed.

"Sean, give her your jacket."

Without hesitating, the head of security shrugged off his jacket, handing it to me. I was tempted to leap out and grab onto him, climb around him like ivy, but from Dana's increasingly strong grip on my shoulders, I could tell he was warning me against it.

I took the jacket and wrapped it around my shoulders. It was big enough to reach half-way down my thighs, so it covered me substantially.

"Dana…do I even want to know what happened in here?"

"Go look at the footage if you're curious." Dana pointed to the scientist chained to the table. "Take him to the holding cells," he said. "And run his blood. The other three need to be disposed of, and this one…" Dana reached down, having released me to place his hand on the head of the fly with the funny face. "I don't actually know what we can do for him…" He turned his head, hearing the man cry out in garbled pain. "Call Stacy. Let her see him. She can make the decision."

"If he can be fixed?"

Dana shrugged. "Put him in the holding cells as well. And run his blood work. I want everyone on file."

"Yes, sir."

"Excellent." Dana motioned for me to follow. "Alright, you, come with me."

I skipped after him, throwing glances at the others in the room as I moved. I was looking forward to playing with all the people Dana had in the Commission. There were so many people I could learn about, and I fully intended on using them as practice for my own new abilities.

Realizing we were walking to the security office, I turned to Dana. "You're not taking me back to my cell?"

"No," he said. "You're bored as hell back there. I think it would end up costing me even more money. I think it's time you became my assistant."

"Your assistant?"

"If anyone asks, that's what you are."

"What am I really?"

"My protégé," he said.

Both of us passed through the security checkpoint without being stopped and we walked down the hallway leading to the door that would lead to the offices of the Commission. But we continued walking, passing his office.

I followed, briefly studying the walls. I was surprised by how much colors played a factor in how I felt. The darker walls of the offices immediately soothed me from the bright white colors in the back of the Commission. The change was immediate. I was thrilled to be out of the back.

"Excited?" Dana teased, opening the door into the empty meeting room.

I skipped and twirled into the meeting room, spinning around once before running to the podium and standing in front of the room, looking among the empty tables and chairs. Dana stepped up beside me.

"What do you think?"

"When's the next meeting?" I turned to him with a grin.

"Three days," he said. "But you will need a little time before you can stand in front of the Commission."

I pouted, sticking my lip out as he laughed.

"Trust me, it won't take long."

He took my hand and led me through the other door, the door I only had been through twice, though I could not precisely recall what happened during those times or what was beyond the door.

There were more doors marked with numbers. I blinked at the silver plates of engraved numbers as Dana led me down the long hallway, turning right at the first junction. He took me to the end of that hallway and then opened the first unmarked door on the left.

Dana slid his card over the lock on the door and it clicked open, the lights turning on as we walked in. I saw a large, suite-like room, similar to the one that I had been in when I first came to the Commission, but that one was larger and grander.

There was a large bed with a simple black frame on the far wall, covered in a silvery gray bedspread and adorned with pillows. Next to the bed were two black nightstands. One had an empty glass on it used for hard liquor. The other was covered in files and papers with the contents sticking out at mismatched angles.

"Do you even sleep?" I asked once the door had closed behind us.

"No. Sometimes I like to pretend, though, when I'm bored and there's nothing or no one to do."

I nodded to the glass.

"Have a guest last night?"

"Yes, I did."

"A man?" I said knowingly, judging by the glass.

"Yes," Dana repeated. "Speaking of, give me that jacket so I can give it back to him," he said, reaching his hand out for the coat. I blinked at him, pretending to be shocked as I realized the identity of his guest.

"Mr. Christenson? You've been mixing work and pleasure?"

"That's the only way to live, my dear." He took the jacket as I slid it from my shoulders.

He put it over the back of the chair that was tucked under the desk, which was large and littered with papers and a closed laptop. The whole surface was a complete mess. I was able to see law books, as well as a few anatomy books, and files on the experiments with a blood work readout on top of everything.

I glanced around the room, my eyes filled with wonder. The pictures on the walls were grand, impressive works of art, including two Dalis. I skipped to one of them, one that I recognized immediately.

"This looks like the original."

"They all are," he affirmed. "The Picasso over there is the original. And the two Van Goghs..." He motioned to the pictures.

I studied the amazing colors and shapes of the pictures. It felt like being in a palace.

"Expensive tastes."

"This is only part of my collection."

"But, I'm surprised. No 'Starry Night?'"

"I'm not one for the general favorite." He spanked me. "Enough with those. Through there is the bathroom. Take a shower and we'll get you cleaned up because...you desperately need it."

"Fuck you," I teased, walking into the bathroom, putting a swing to my hips.

The bathroom was heavy with grays and concrete, silver faucets and a large round, modern bathtub that stood out against the simple colors. The shower was huge, with several different faucets that went in many different directions.

Extremely excited, I danced to the shower and looked at the controls, turning it on easily and adjusting the temperature before stepping in and allowing myself to be engulfed by the heat of the water and the pressure of the spouts.

The feeling was heavenly. I closed my eyes, allowing the water to run over my skin, feeling each droplet roll down my body in a horribly tantalizing manner.

Finally, I managed to pull my arms up and run my hands over my head, pushing the water through my hair. The feeling of the droplets over my skin was too much. The ache of being denied earlier returned with a vengeance.

I ran my hands over my breasts, rubbing the water over me and feeling the sparks that radiated as my palms passed over my nipples.

The door opened and another figure joined me. I smiled, looking over his naked body appreciatively as he came up behind me, leaning his head to my neck, licking a line from the base of my nape to the back of my ear. I shivered and collapsed against him.

"How do you even get through a shower?" I breathed, feeling need tug at my belly.

He nipped at my ear lobe. "Practice."

His hand grabbed my hair, pushing me forward so my hands rested on the glass wall in front of me, bending me over as his other hand grabbed my hip.

I turned over my shoulder, breathless.

"What happened to punishment?"

"Punishment's over."

* *** *

I have become Dana's personal doll.

He shaved me in the shower and washed my hair, even though both actions led to a rough romp in the hot spray. It was an incredible roll of amazing feelings. It was also fascinating, watching him shave my legs, under my arms, even gently around my genitals.

"No one's complained," I remind him with high eyebrows.

"You're in a different weight class now," he said, placing a kiss on the inside of my thigh.

"What is that supposed to mean?" I narrow my eyes playfully. He shook the razor in the water to clean it. "Are you saying that the scientists in the back are not as shallow as the members of the Commission?"

"No, they have lower standards," Dana laughed. "Speaking of which, you do not submit to them now that you're with me, understand?"

"Possessive?" I laugh, setting my leg down as Dana stood, switching the water off.

"No. But now that you're not an experiment, you have to act like you're in charge of them."

"Am I?" I challenge, easily catching the towel as it's thrown at me. He smiled, grabbing the other towel and placing it around his shoulders.

"Of course. I'm training you to lead beside me."

"Take over for you one day?" I test, cocking an eyebrow. He shrugged, walking into the bedroom as I study his back appreciatively.

"If you ever manage to get rid of me, I suppose," he said, shrugging off the mild threat. I follow him, pulling the towel over my head and trying to dry my hair as much as possible. It's difficult not to watch him as he moves, and I find myself unconsciously licking my lips.

"Here," he said, walking to his closet and pulling out a robe, tossing it on the bed before pulling out a suit from the closet, setting it next to the robe. "Wear this until I get back."

"Back?"

There is a knock at the door that causes me to whirl around.

"Yes?" Dana called, not startled.

The door opened and young, beautiful woman walked into the room, holding a tray in front of her. The tray had a covered plate and another domed silver setting with a glass of wine in the corner.

"Just set it over there, Lydia," Dana instructed, toweling his hair dry, jerking his head to the round table under the Van Gogh painting. The young woman passes me with her head dropped in embarrassment. I watch her small, round butt move in the pencil-skirt and my lips purse. I try to decide if I like the shape or not.

"Will that be all, Mr. Christenson?" Lydia whispered, setting the tray down.

"Yes, Lydia, thank you," Dana said, walking to the mirror on the closet door, moving his fingers through his hair. I watch her leave. I see her hurry out, her little butt moving quickly.

I chuckle and shake my head, putting the towel around my neck and reaching for the robe.

"She's cute."

"She's standard," Dana said, moving away from the mirror and grabbing his shirt from the hanger, pulling it over his shoulders.

"She's got a nice ass," I continue, pulling the robe around me as Dana began to button up his pristine white shirt. I am having trouble not watching his every move, even the small, precise movement of his fingers.

"It looks better with clothes on," he said, glancing at me with a cocky smile.

I snort. "Have you had everyone?"

"More or less. There are some I simply do not care for, so I continue to tease them." He jerked his head to the table. "That's for you."

I step to the table, tying the oversized robe as I walk. I remove the bigger cover from the tray and my nose twitches at the smell. There is a large slab of roasted, dead meat on the plate, along with potatoes and bread. I cringe away from the food and set the cover back down.

"No," Dana said, walking to me as he fastened his trousers. He removes the cover as I groan. "You need to eat."

"*You* don't eat," I point out.

"Little Lily, take the robe off and look at yourself in the mirror."

Eager to get away from the disgusting food, I prance to the full-length mirror, dropping the robe, shivering at the feeling of it passing over my skin. I look at my body—the first time I have seen my full form after my transformation. My hair, now washed and clean, curls around my smooth face, drawing attention to my bright, golden eyes. My lips have not changed color since the last time I looked in the mirror in Dana's office. My neck is thin, draping into my shoulders. I can see the entirety of my collarbone for the first time in my life, and my ribs are visible along my sides. My belly is thin, sloped, tucked between my hips, which are also thinner and leaner.

"What?" I ask.

"You look terrible."

"What the fuck are you talking about?"

"You need to gain at least seven kilos," he declared, walking behind me and straightening his tie behind my reflection.

"I think I look good," I say softly, running a hand down my side and resting it on my hip.

"Believe me, you'll look much better when you have curves to work with again," he said, smacking my hip as he walked away to pick up the vest. I sigh, reaching up to cup my breasts. They have gotten much smaller...it would be nice to have those again.

"Why are you changing suits?" I ask, stooping to pick up the robe, pulling it over me again, trying to avoid the food on the table.

"Because that one," he pointed to the one hanging over the back of the chair over Sean's jacket, "is worth four thousand dollars," he said. "And this one is only worth one thousand." He smoothed the front of the vest and reached for the jacket. "I don't want to ruin the four thousand dollar suit."

"Why?" I chuckle, walking to him and placing my arms around his waist, snuggling close. "What are you planning on doing?"

Dana pulled away, pointing at the table.

"You will get to do plenty soon enough," he said. "I have a few appointments. You need to have that finished by the time I get back."

"Is it even possible for me to eat?" I whisper, casting a wary eye at the unappetizing meal.

"It is possible, but not advised. Your metabolism is running at a completely different level now. You should only need to eat for about a week, and you'll have gained the weight back."

"Girls like to be skinny," I whine.

"You're not a girl, you're a woman. A woman needs to have something to her to be a woman." Dana traced a finger along my jaw. "Trust me. I'm a man, I know. I will be back in three hours." He began walking away, glancing at the watch he had just fastened around his wrist. "Don't try to throw it away, either. I will know."

I grab the towel around my neck and snap it at his backside, though he did not react, laughing as he walked out of the room.

"Don't leave, either."

I sigh, staring around the room before cautiously stepping to the table and glaring at the covered food with disgust.

For twenty minutes, I wander the room, opening the large closet and walking in, studying the suits and shoes on one side as well as the watches, cufflinks and ties at the far end. Next to those, I find ornate, beautiful necklaces with matching earrings, gold and silver bracelets, and rings laid out in perfect display. Running my fingers along them quietly, I question why they are there.

"Well, Dana, I didn't know you were into drag," I say with a giggle. I walk up the other side of the large closet and find an array of women's clothing, from stiletto heels to dresses and backless shirts. I look among the beautiful colors and chic styles, running my hands over the soft fabric. Finding one particularly soft black dress, I pull it out of the line of the others. It is a thin, smooth fabric, wrapped in a draping style.

Realizing it is far too small for Dana, I realize that it's for me.

It is my house-warming present.

I crouch and look among the beautiful shoes, finding a pair of strappy stilettos that immediately catch my eye.

Pulling them out, I move into the bedroom, placing the dress on the bed and the shoes at my feet. I skip back into the closet, opening the drawers under the jewelry and finding a selection of incredibly beautiful lace bras and panties. I pull out a red set with black trim. I shed the robe, putting the lingerie on and moving to look at myself in the mirror.

I am stunning. The red against my pale skin causes a shock to my eyes and makes me feel warm and excited, despite the fact that my breasts did not fill the cups of the bra.

Ignoring that insignificant detail, I put the dress on, slipping it over my skin and trying to control the immediate sparks that ran through my body at the feeling of the fabric. Once I settle the straps over my shoulders, I slide my feet into the shoes.

Before my newfound balance, stilettos were terrifying. I used to feel impossibly perched when I wore them. Now I am able to adjust my center so easily, as though I had been walking in stilettos my entire life.

Standing in the mirror, I hardly recognize myself. The dress is a little large, but as I gain weight, I know it will hug my hips and breasts beautifully. I am suddenly excited to eat again. I can spend time looking through the makeup and jewelry Dana has put there for me afterward, and maybe even style my hair to see how beautiful I can make myself.

I pull the dress off and set it on the bed, but as I walk past the mirror to grab the robe and towel I had abandoned, I decide against taking off the lingerie, feeling far too sexy to consider departing with the bra and panties.

I pull the robe over my ensemble, leaving the shoes on as well, and walk to the table to attempt eating.

It is much harder than I expect and I find myself spending two hours angrily jabbing the food with my fork and forcing it into my mouth. I force it down, growing angrier with each bite.

But I finish everything, even the cold soup. I could not taste the food so none of it brought any pleasure, and it sat like boulders in my stomach.

For fifteen minutes after finishing the meal, I brush my teeth furiously, trying to get rid of the horrid taste and desperate to take my mind off the disgusting deed.

Satisfied that I have cleaned my mouth completely, I walk back into the room and look around at the paintings and files on the desk. There are a lot of notes on Eina that I read, learning about his sister, and how they had yet to see one another following her transformation.

Rehan's testing is going to be finished today.

I feel myself start a little in surprise when I read the memo.

It's exciting.

But my investigation into the current happenings with the Machine of Neutralization is interrupted by Dana returning.

He smiled when he saw me holding the notes.

"I see you have done some exploring."

The smile spreads across my face, cat-like and slow, as I set the papers down and spread my legs in the chair, knowing that my position allowed him to see the bra and panties.

"You have incredible taste, Mr. Christenson," I purr.

"I know," he said. "Now," he walked around the back of the chair, pulling his four thousand dollar suit away and moving to the bed, where the hangers were sitting from his other suit, "what did you find?"

"Rehan's going to be finished today," I tell him directly.

"She is," he said, methodically hanging up his suit.

"I want to see her."

"Tomorrow."

"Why not today?" I pout.

"Because she's sleeping," he said, still looking at his suit. "Final diagnostics will be run tomorrow."

I huff but say nothing in protest.

"So," Dana started, walking into the closet and putting the suit away, "I see you found everything I bought for you."

"I did."

"And that was the one that caught your attention first?" he asked, coming out of the closet and pointing at the dress on the bed. I nod.

He walked into the bathroom, rummaging through some drawers and cabinets.

"I ate everything," I declare triumphantly, looking at the empty tray at the other table.

"Excellent," he said, closing a drawer and walking out of the bathroom with a small bag and a larger bag. I blink at the two items, curious. "We're going to have a little bit of fun," he said, setting the things down on the table and pushing the tray out of the way before removing his jacket and flinging it onto the bed easily. He unbuttoned the cuffs of his shirt and rolled his sleeves back.

"There are some things that you need to understand," he said, sitting in the other chair, grabbing the leg of my chair, pulling me closer. I let out a squeak before lifting my leg, setting my ankle on his shoulder.

"Yes?" I whisper, canting my hips with a grin.

He grabbed my ankle, pulling it off his shoulder and looking at my foot in the stiletto. I find myself biting my lip as I watch him stare at the curve of my instep.

"Those look very good on you," he said. I place it back on the ground as he releases my ankle. "Little Lily, ease of access is not the image you want. Your goal is not to fuck everyone."

"It's not?"

"No. You want control. Remember what we talked about in the lab?" He grabbed the smaller bag, opening the zipper. "You make them come to you. With sleazy men, it's easy to get them to bend to your will if you just show them a little cleavage and a flash of leg."

"Is that how you get the boys?" I tease.

"No, I must work much harder to get the men to come to me, just as you will have to put in some effort to getting the women to come to you. Most people today," he continued, pulling out a pair of tweezers and leaning forward, putting one hand on my face and setting to work on taming my eyebrows, "have been taught to believe that they should never be attracted to the same sex. That it's wrong and punishable by imprisonment in the Commission. Your task is getting them to desire you so much that they fall into your trap and surrender to you, even though they are in the Commission itself."

"But you've already had everyone," I point out. "They think that it's okay to have sex with the Commission leaders."

"Oh, they never think it's okay," Dana corrected with a smile. "That's the beauty of it."

"I want to know how to read people the way you do," I whisper. "How do you do it? How do you find everyone's weakness?"

"It's far simpler than you think. Humans are very simple creatures, and when they're uncomfortable, it shows so clearly that it's impossible not to exploit it."

"But you would have to learn when they're uncomfortable," I press.

"Also not difficult." He removed his hands from my face and looked between my eyebrows. "Do you remember how I used to get you uncomfortable?"

I shake my head.

"It starts with the eyes," he said, running his fingers over my brow bone. I lean into his touch. "See if they look you in the eyes, if they look away shyly, if they stare at you in fascination…and as soon as you have that feeling from them," he returned to his work, "push it until they back away completely."

"But I'll frighten them away."

"Fear is your greatest ally," he told me. "It's how we're going to get what we want."

"And what do we want? In the grand scheme of things?"

I see Dana's smile as he continues working.

"I think *we* want to be challenged." He pulled away from my face again. "We're hunters, Little Lily. It's in our nature. Our bright colors and elegant speech are the tools we use to attract our prey. But we always leave them wanting more."

I sigh, waiting for him to finish with my eyebrows. I know the real thing I have to work on is not wanting more myself.

He sat back and put the tweezers down, smoothing over my eyebrows with his thumbs.

"Don't worry, you'll learn control." He opened the larger case, showing me the various types of makeup. "Let experiment, shall we?"

He tells me that appearance is our most powerful asset. He explained that it did not matter what we were thinking, we always had to keep a mask of power. Even if we are thrown off by what the people do—and he assures me that there will be times I will be surprised—we need to keep up our appearance.

Apparently, Dana put a lot of care into his general appearance, but it did not take him much effort to look as stunningly handsome as he did. Similarly, it does not take me much to match him. A little accent to the eyes, a little accent to the lips, and that's all it takes.

Dana trims my nails for me, but tells me never to paint them, saying it's unnecessary. And then he brushes through my hair as though I am his doll, moving it around my face in a certain fashion before motioning me to try on the dress.

Excited, I pull the garment on, making a show of it for Dana, which I see he appreciates.

Then, I saunter to the mirror to look myself over.

I look unreal.

I look like a fashion model right out of a magazine—admittedly without much cleavage. My hair is perfect and my smooth skin acts as its own foundation for the little makeup I don. The dress, still a little loose, is beautifully made and the quality is apparent.

Dana walked up behind me and put his hands on my shoulders, looking at the two of us with a smile.

"Perfect."

We are perfect.

* *** *

Eating is my least favorite part of the day. Dana forces the three meals down my throat and threatens that if I do not eat, he won't let me see Rehan.

I don't know how I managed the horrible practice of mastication before. I make this an inappropriate joke for Dana. He rolled his eyes, but still laughed.

Walking down the halls of the Commission at Dana's side, my heels clicking on the floor and my hips hugged by the skirt, showing just a little bit of cleavage accented by a large pendant, my hair falling in a naturally perfect way and the makeup empowering me, I feel like the most powerful creature alive.

Particularly as I use my own card to open the doors leading into the back of the Commission.

"You've settled well," Dana noted, removing his hand from his jacket where he was reaching for his clearance card.

I place the corner of the card between my teeth as I turn away from him and breeze past the security desk. I can feel eyes fall on me from the guards and I stop myself from smiling at being able to attract their attention.

The experiments look confused as I walk past them. I glance into each cell, seeing fascinating creatures I was sure I had never seen before. Everything appears different from the previous day. I smile and feel a tightening in my abdomen as I think about the incredible fun of yesterday.

I look down at my extremely expensive Rolex and smile, realizing I now knew that it was, indeed, yesterday that I claimed my prize of the two green eyes that Dana had placed in a jar to preserve.

Dana and I walk side by side as we move to Lab One. I can't stop the smile on my face as we walk in and everyone jumps, surprised.

"Mr. Christenson," one of the scientists gasped. His eyes fall on me. "Is...is that—"

"This is my assistant," Dana said. "You may address her as Miss Sandover."

I hide my pout that I don't get to change my name like Dana did.

"Yes, sir," the scientist murmured. "Miss Sandover." He bows his head and motions me closer.

I step up to the table and look over the beautiful creature strapped there. It feels like looking at a doll perfectly preserved in a box, still tied to the position of packaging. She looks like Eina, her light hazel eyes half-closed from the drugs, and her long, sandy hair falling to the side of the table. Her breasts are full and perky, despite her thin frame. From the smoothness of her skin, I can tell that she barely has that downy, light hair that generally covers the human body. Her legs and arms are smooth, even her pubic area is devoid of hair.

"What do you think?" Dana asked, coming to my side and wrapping an arm around my waist.

"She's stunning..." I whisper.

"Sir, all final tests have cleared," the scientist said with a nod. "Her charts match her brother's exactly."

"Excellent."

I turn to them.

"She and her brother are infused with lion DNA?"

"Yes, miss."

"What is the progress on other animals?"

"W-well…we're still running test on those in the holding—"

"Surely many of the prisoners already have shown the same genetic anomaly displayed in Rehan and Eina," I interrupt. "Yes?"

"…yes, miss."

"Then why have you not tested other animal DNA?" I press.

"We have been focused on Rehan, and we will be artificially inseminating her—"

"I am fully aware of what you will be doing. I read the file." I stop him again. I feel how proud Dana is next to me. "But as soon as the fetus begins to grow, there is very little you need to do, and we must be sure that you are kept busy."

"Yes, o-of course."

"Kyle, is it?" I ask, discreetly moving my eyes to the plastic tag on his jacket.

"Yes, miss."

"You're the head scientist on the Machine of Neutralization project, and yet you seem extremely disinterested in its development."

"I do not think it is wise to rush ahead," he said, lowering his eyes. He was feeling emasculated. While Dana did not seem concerned with it, I wanted to test how quickly I could change his mood.

"Well," I say, shifting my weight and tilting my abdomen, softening my outline, "of course, I trust your judgment on the speed of the program, but I do hope to expand our range. After all, this is the most profound project of the Enterprise Labs. I want to make sure that you reach your full potential with it."

He was taken aback but not in a bad way. I could see his eyes widen and heard his heart skip a beat. I slowly blink, smiling gently.

Dana's thumb, still at my hip, is lightly stroking my back—he's applauding my work.

"Thank you, Miss Sandover," Kyle mumbled.

"Do you think that you could let me know when you have another subject ready to go forward with new DNA?" I ask. "I would love to be part of the process."

"I will, Miss Sandover." Kyle bowed his head.

He had relaxed in many ways, but was still tense, curious about who I was and how much power I had over him.

"Miss Sandover," another scientist with the name of Michael addressed me. I turn to him slowly, keeping my expression soft once I see that all seven of the scientists in the room are focused on me. "Later tonight, we are going to fertilize some of Rehan's eggs. In a few days, we should know if any will develop. If-if Mr. Christenson agrees, perhaps you could be the one to choose the first embryo we will implant."

"Oh." I pretend to be flattered. As if I *wouldn't* be a part of it. "I suppose, if Mr. Christenson agrees..." I turn to the leader of the Commission, who has a slight smile on his face, but the greater smile shows in his eyes, like a proud parent.

"I think that would be wise," Dana said. "After all, women have an intuition that men do not."

I turn back to Rehan, who is looking at me with her tired, brilliant eyes. As with Dana, I feel a certain clash of our respective powers. I vaguely recall Eina's amazing ability to see right through me, to see wounds that I thought were present. Perhaps Rehan could see the person I had let go of...the person I used to be.

Her power is great. I can feel it in the way it makes my body shiver with anticipation and excitement.

"She's exceptional," I murmur, turning to the scientists. "Well done, gentlemen."

"Thank you, Miss Sandover," they mumbled back, their heads bowed.

"Go ahead and take her back to her cell," Dana ordered, taking control of the situation. "Let her rest until we pick the embryos to implant. The most important thing now is to keep her healthy and not cause undue stress."

"Absolutely, Mr. Christenson," Kyle agreed.

"Keep her out of the Dome and, as usual, keep her away from Eina. We will reunite them after we understand the fertility of these creations. And, as Little Lily is eager to see, we can start to observe social interactions as we expand the project."

"Very good, sir."

"Wonderful job, gentlemen. You can expect a bonus in your next checks."

"Thank you very much, sir," they said quickly, their eyes lighting up from the mention of bonuses. I realize that I must ask Dana about the living situation for those who work in the Commission of the People. There is still so much I need to learn.

"We will leave you to her," Dana said. He leaned over to Rehan and ran a hand over her head before leading me out of the lab with a gentle hand on my lower back. When we are away from the labs, walking through Ward Six, I turn to him.

"How do you have the money to pay them?"

"Central pays them," Dana said. "And we own Central."

"Ooh, that's nice to know," I say. "And why do they need money if we provide their food and lodgings? I could have sworn I heard some of the scientists talk about having families…"

"Some do," Dana confirmed. "Just as the members of the Commission of the People are allowed to go out and interact in society—within restrictions of the NDA—so can the scientists. The guards are the ones who are always permanent residents."

"Let me guess," I say with a dark smile, "most of the scientists eventually end up living down here anyway."

"Of course." Dana returned the smile. "It's hard to do what the scientists do, and sometimes they simply cannot interact with their family anymore. Husbands and wives must keep it secret what they do. Secrecy like that can destroy a relationship."

"Are there any secrets in *our* relationship?"

"A few."

"Such as?"

"I assure you, Little Lily, within a month or so, there will be no secrets," Dana whispered, his fingers tightening around my waist.

"Well that will be boring," I realize.

"That's why we'll just have to continue to try and undermine each other," he teased.

"I was not undermining you," I protest lightly. "I was establishing my own power among the scientists. I would never think to compete with you."

"That will change."

We walk through the door leading into the Termination Cells and I startle at a familiar face approaching us, his black uniform contrasting sharply with the white walls.

"Frank," Dana greeted. I smile as I approach, remembering the ambitious young guard who was seriously lacking in natural assets from a few months previous. Or was it years? Maybe it was only last week…

Hell if I remember.

"Mr. Christenson," he said, his eyes going wide when he saw me follow the leader of the Commission. "Sir…is…isn't that…"

"Oh, Frank, how rude," Dana chortled, turning to me and reaching his hand out. I place my hand in his and am pulled to the conversation. "You have already been intimately acquainted with Little Lily."

"W-well...yes, sir, I-I guess I have," he said, looking me over. I turn shyly away, giving him an alluring smile. I need the practice, after all. "Sir...I...I—"

"Oh, don't be so flustered," Dana said, patting him on the shoulder before straightening his collar and tie. "If you had done anything I didn't expect you to, trust me, you would have found yourself on the table next to her." He straightened the lapel of the suit and patted Frank's cheek. "You did your part."

Dana breezed past him. I turn back to the guard and smile, carefully moving my hips in perfect time as I walk to him. Wrapping one hand around the back of his neck, I lean up, rising slightly on my toes to whisper in his ear, feeling the shiver wrack his body from my breath.

"You certainly did..." I whisper.

My finger expertly hooks in his belt and I smile against his face. "Thanks."

I pull away and walk to Dana, who is waiting for me.

"Very well done," he complimented. I smile at him and roll my wrist in front of my chest to show him my prize as the last door closes behind us, bringing us into the main offices of the Commission of the People.

"Want one?" I ask, shaking the almost-full carton of cigarettes.

"Why not?" Dana shrugged, opening his office door and ushering me inside. I tuck the carton into my cleavage and turn to him, stepping backward to lean against the front of his desk. He closed the door behind him and walked to stand in front of me.

"Are you not going to have one?"

"I will," I say, grabbing his tie and pulling him to me. "I've always wanted to try smoking a cigarette after being fucked."

"I think that can be arranged," he whispered. His lips crash on mine, hungry, biting and nipping, his arm extending behind me and sweeping everything off the desk easily. His hands are on my hips, hard, strong, lifting me onto the smooth surface of the desk. I hook my leg over his hip, pulling him closer, one of my hands hiking up my skirt and flashing the top band of my thigh-high stockings. He smiled and bit his lip before looking up at me with a hungry fire.

"I like those..."

* *** *

Three days of mundane tasks and I am starting to understand why Dana used to go so stir crazy in the Commission. I have been following Dana around for three days, force fed meals and bored out of my mind as he forces me to help him file things away and learn the way he handles the Commission.

It's a "watch and learn" experience.

I am completely bored.

He does nothing but read the things that the Central office drops off for him, which is currently about the manhunt for the strange angel creature and the remaining survivors of the Central Angels.

It's boring.

All survivors are in the holding cells and Chris is already in the back. I saw him on the random walk-around Dana and I did the other day.

I entertain myself by teasing Sean and the others who come into the office. Some recognize me, others don't, but all of them hardly interact with me until I get bored and introduce myself. Then, I do what Dana told me to do. I find their weaknesses, study the way they look at me, allowing my instincts to take over when reading their body language and deciding how to act further.

I had managed to fluster most of the men easily, but the women were far more difficult. I had not expected to struggle getting a woman to react. After three failed attempts with Sarah, one of the scheduling aids, I finally got a reaction out of her while Dana was on the phone. Touch was a last resort. After my fingers brushed her chest when I reached for her necklace to compliment it, her body shivered and she looked at me with a slightly confused, frightened, and interested expression.

I return from brushing my teeth furiously after my lunch that third boring day to find Danielle Markus in the office with Dana. It is the first time I have seen her in a very long time. She looked different. She was pretty and strong and it was obvious that she was a driven woman, but her face was showing its age, and there was a tension in her shoulders that got much worse when she saw me.

"Mrs. Markus," I greet with a smile, closing the door behind me and approaching her, bypassing the handshake to hug her. She is frightened, and I know exactly why.

"L-Lily?"

"It's so good to see you again," I say amiably. "How have you been?"

"Um...well...I-I've been well," she said nervously. "Um, I wonder if you could excuse us." Her smile was forced.

"There is no need to be so awkward, Mrs. Markus," I say, brushing past her and walking to Dana's side, sitting on the desk and crossing my legs as Dana drifted the back of his fingers over the exposed side of my thigh, his attention still focused on Mrs. Markus, just like mine. "There are no secrets between the two of us."

"Dana...you didn't tell me that you..."

"Had a new assistant?" Dana completed. "Little Lily is more than an assistant, she is my partner in the Commission. Which reminds me, prepare on the agenda her introduction—or reintroduction, I suppose—to the Commission meeting this Saturday."

I glance at him briefly before turning my eyes back to the flustered main advisor for the Commission of the People.

"S-sir?"

"You heard me."

"Dana, she is a known criminal. Her parents are out there, as well as the parents of the children she conned into her revolution. Did you forget that I lost Clark because of her?!" she snapped.

"You didn't lose him. He's in the back, I saw his file." I roll my eyes.

"You bitch," Mrs. Markus snarled.

"Ladies, ladies," Dana said, stopping the words coming out of my mouth. "As much as I would love to see this come to scratching and hair-pulling, the Persian rug is brand new and I do not wish to stain it with blood." I smile at the indignant expression on Mrs. Markus' face. I am going to have a lot of fun playing with her...

"Danielle, be a darling, and work it into the schedule," Dana said.

"Fine," she bit. "Also, the car will be ready for you at eight-thirty this evening," she said, acid dripping from her tone.

"Wonderful. Thank you, Danielle," Dana complimented, honey coating each word, which noticeably calmed her. She still looked upset, but her shoulders relaxed of their own accord. "You may go."

She left as Dana and I turned to one another.

"Whenever you two actually have it out, make sure I'm in the room," Dana said, leaning down and kissing my knee before standing and walking to his table on the other side of the office, sifting through the papers there.

"What's going on at eight-thirty?" I ask, swiveling on the desk to look at him.

He turned to look over his shoulder.

"It's a surprise."

As had happened at random intervals the previous days, my attempts to get any information out of him end in a hurried, flustered, hungry fuck in his office that we both relish immensely, even though neither of us really desire the romp.

At eight-thirty, we walk through a secret passage in the back of Dana's office that leads into the area of the car elevators.

"That's sneaky."

Sean was waiting for us near the closest open elevator door, the car idling inside.

"Dana, Miss Sandover." He greeted, motioning to the car. I wink at Sean as I pass. I have been begging Dana to let me have a few hours alone with the head of security, but Dana is adamant that I am to keep my hands off his Sean until I prove that I am able to control myself properly, a statement that makes me pout every time.

As Dana had said, denying me is the only way to effectively punish me.

Sean drove us silently to our destination, followed by two security cars and a large entourage of vans that I had never seen before. Once I get bored of waiting to reach wherever the hell we are going, I lean down in the back seat to suck Dana off, a random whim I decide to follow to tantalize Sean.

Dana did not stop me, but released a quiet chuckle to let me know that he understood my purpose for the intimacy.

Sean was silent, but the few times I cast my gaze to the rearview mirror, I see him staring.

When I sit straight again, we are close to the airport.

We drive through two large gates opened for us by uniformed members of the American military, and drive onto the airstrip of the darkened airport, continuing to the cargo terminals.

Glancing at my watch, I realize it is only nine at night, and it seems strange that everything is so dark around the airport.

"We close the airport every now and then when we're expecting a shipment," Dana answered the question he sensed within me.

"A shipment?"

There was a tap on the window and Dana rolled it down, allowing both of us to look at the man outside.

"The plane was delayed on its departure. It will be here in thirty minutes, sir."

"Very well, we will wait," Dana said, rolling the window back up and unbuckling his seatbelt. I wait for an explanation. "It's a surprise for you...a gift, actually."

"You bought me something?"

"I bought you a lot of somethings," he said with a sly grin. He turned his body to me and rested a hand on my thigh, which makes me shiver, still turned on from my oral service to Dana earlier. "You were so kind to me, I figure I should repay you," he said, his strong fingers moving my legs apart.

I turn my body and open my legs for him as he lowers himself closer to the seat.

"Can you two not do that right now, please?"

"Oh, Sean, that's just cruel," Dana teased, his breath ghosting over my thigh. I am doing my best to put on a show for the head of security, eager to get him hot and bothered so he would seek me out—without Dana's approval. There was something about his energy, his *being*, that made him irresistible. "You allowed Little Lily to service me, and now you expect her to sit here unsatisfied?"

"I feel like I'm the slab of meat being fought over by two lions," Sean grumbled. "Don't think I don't know the games you play, Dana. You both were looking at me while that was going on."

"You should have been watching the road," I say.

"And you are our slab of meat…" Dana said. "Don't pretend you don't enjoy it." His head moved down to me again, trapping my clit in heat and moisture. It was a good thing I didn't wear panties that day.

"I don't enjoy it, Dana—will you stop!"

"Stop being so stiff," I groan. "Oh…I guess that is the problem."

Sean rolled his eyes. "It was bad enough when there was only *one* of you."

"Come back here and join us," I tease. Dana pinched my thigh, but I ignore it and moan louder for Sean. "Come on…I've already sucked him off, he won't be able to get it up any time soon. I need someone to come back here and fuck me."

"Hey, you sassy bitch," Dana said, biting the inside of my thigh. "I can get it up just fine."

"Prove it."

"I hate both of you," Sean huffed, getting out of the car and slamming the door behind him. I turn to Dana and we both start laughing.

"It's fun to work him up," Dana said.

"Think he's hard?"

"Probably not. He was probably getting hard and that's why he left."

"Why can't I play with him?" I whine.

"You can, just not yet."

I sigh, looking at him with raised eyebrows.

"Can you really get it up again so soon?" I ask, skeptical.

He grabs my ankle and pulls it to his groin, allowing the top of my foot to press into his erection.

"I'm impressed..."

It's a fast fuck in the limo that does not even muss up our hair, though I do have to adjust my clothes when I get out of the car.

I am excited for my presents, though I have no idea what they are. Knowing I need to work on my patience, I do not ask Dana, waiting to see for myself.

The cargo plane moves closer and stops, the engines slowly winding down as I wait patiently with Dana.

Five minutes later, the steps are rolled out to the plane and seven people, two women and five men, disembark to greet us.

"Mr. Christenson," a woman greeted with a thick French accent. She's not particularly pretty, but her face looks younger than her age with the way her hair is pulled back tightly.

"Madame Duchamp," Dana greeted with a flawless accent, taking her hand before kissing her on each cheek. "This is little Lily Sandover, my partner in the Commission."

"Miss Sandover," she said, reaching her hand out. I also lean forward and kiss her on both cheeks, smelling her faint perfume.

"We just need your signature," she said, grabbing the clipboard from the man behind her and extending it with a pen to Dana. I watch as he looks over the papers, tapping the pen on the board.

"Madame Duchamp, you and I have shared a wonderful relationship, of course, but I don't always trust what they put on these slips..." he said.

"Of course," she said knowingly, motioning for us to follow her. Dana nods to me and we both walk across the tarmac to the plane, ascending the metal steps as my stomach jumps excitedly. I can hardly wait to see my presents.

I step into the plane, following Dana as we move into the back. The two men who followed us pulled out flashlights and shined them into the space of the cargo. My heart leaps in excitement and I turn to Dana with wide eyes as he smiles at me.

"What do you think?"

I grab the flashlight from the man next to me, turning it to the cargo, shining it on each unique face, looking at the ones with darker skin, the ones with narrow eyes, the ones with similar faces to ours...all of them flinching away from the light and shivering in fear.

"What is this?" I ask in wonder.

"Our pharmaceutical programs always need subjects. It's one of the biggest businesses in America," Dana explained, stepping to my side with another flashlight and casting it around the men and women confined within the plane. "A few decades ago, we had quite an assortment of subjects. After all, we don't just test for Americans, but for those all over the globe, and to know how each medicine or technique works on each person, we need variety."

"Slaves?"

"Criminals," he corrected, walking up the second of six rows of at least eighty people, crammed into the space, chained together in their sitting positions. "Some countries are desperate for money, and they round up the homeless and prostitutes and sell them at auction."

"You bought them at auction?" I giggle. "Big spender."

"Like I said, we make a lot of money off them," Dana said. "Besides, since they outlawed animal testing, the techniques have become a lot more precise, since test subjects are so expensive now."

"And these are for me?"

"I'm letting you handle them, yes," Dana said. "You will handle their paperwork, assign them to various areas of the holding cells— which you now understand—and make sure you look over all their blood work for our little side project."

I wrap my arms around his neck, pulling him close in the dark cargo hold, kissing him in front of everyone, thanking him for my presents.

*   ***   *

Two days later was the Commission meeting.

I am so busy with my new pets that I hardly notice the time go by. However, as the pets are all assigned to their pens and put on a schedule for testing their blood, I am left without their entertainment. There had been a total of four hundred, seventy-nine new pets, and I was anxious to get their blood work back so I could assign some to the Machine of Neutralization project.

Dana even allowed me to work out the price of each pet based on their sex, age, and ethnicity. It was one of the most fascinating undertakings I had ever had and it taught me much about what I had never known about our endeavors in the Commission of the People.

Then, I am reminded of the Commission meeting, and suddenly, that is all I can think about.

Dana changed into an expensive suit. I pick a sexy set of lingerie to wear under my skirt and blazer to feel more empowered.

I am not nervous as I walk with Dana to the meeting room, arriving at exactly eleven, when the guards closed the doors loudly. Mrs. Markus walked up to the podium, going through the ceremony of opening the meeting while I look around the room in fascination at the amount of familiar faces, and the amount of shocked stares I am receiving.

The room looks very different from this angle. It looks much bigger, much more like a theater. It brings out the artist in me.

"Now, we will start the meeting with our leader, Mr. Dana Christenson, and his news pertaining to the leadership of the Commission of the People," Danielle said, turning to us.

We walk forward, my stride long and confident, trying to thrust my now-fuller bosom into the cleavage of my shirt as I feel my hair bounce around my face. I am the most powerful, sexiest being in the world, and not only did I expect them to be enthralled at seeing me, I could *feel* their rapture.

"Ladies and gentlemen," Dana greeted, standing next to the podium with me at his side. I look around the room, spotting parents of children I had once known, and catching sight of Sean standing guard in the back corner. There are two particularly shocked faces that make me smile and one more face that I am surprised to see in the audience.

"As you can see, and as I can tell from your surprised faces, I have someone very special here with me tonight. Many of you already know her…in fact, I'm sure all of you do. This is my assistant, Miss Lily Sandover and, as of today, I have made her partner in the leadership of the Commission of the People."

There was stunned silence followed by one man clearing his throat and standing up.

"Mr. Christenson, this is the former leader of the terrorist group you sought to annihilate…" he whispered.

"Yes. What better way to rehabilitate her?" Dana said strongly. "I assure you, I have fully educated her, and she is now one hundred percent in agreement with the Commission's actions, and is also an active member in the Machine of Neutralization project."

"You cannot expect us to accept this," one woman snapped. "After what she did…after what she did to our *children*."

"Ah, technically, what *you* did to your children," Dana corrected. "No one thought to go after their children? To lead them back down the correct path? You basically gave them to me when you agreed we were going after the Central Angels. What you, as parents, did was far less noble that what Little Lily did."

I raise my voice to address them.

"People of the Commission, you know that I was part of the Central Angels, and I'm sure you feel extremely uncomfortable with me being before you today. But I can assure you, I have seen the error of my ways, and I have changed in ways you could never imagine. Rather than attack Mr. Christenson about bringing me on board, you should be celebrating him. He has proven that the Commission is powerful enough to withstand even a direct attack because, in the end, people will always come around. He taught me that the true power of the Commission, of Central, of America, was the peace the Commission of the People has been able to maintain." I turn to Dana and smile, raising my hands. "Let's applaud Dana Christenson for all he has done for this nation."

I start clapping alone, but the applause follows shortly after as Dana turns to me.

"Too much..." he whispered with a smile.

I participate in the meeting as I never have before. I listen from the side as the different presenters talk about the coverage of the false manhunt for Chris, and the plan of finally releasing Eina only for the purposes of taking down Chris and proving we have the power to remove the terror.

International relations were discussed and plans were laid out for the week. The three hour meeting passed with amazing progress, and I was able to pay attention to the information while still staring around the room at the faces that were trying to ignore me.

However, when the meeting was over, those people could not escape me.

I move like water among them, conversing with parents who had only heard of me as the one who corrupted their children and destroyed their families, possibly even their reputation. After some flirting, the fathers are practically licking the palm of my hand and the mothers are shifting uncomfortably in their seats.

Of course, that's not the technique to use on my own parents.

"Lily..." my father whispered when he saw me approach.

"Dad." I nod to him. I turn to the woman at his side. "Mom."

"Lily," my mother murmured. "We...we thought you were dead."

"Your daughter is dead," I say with a smile. "That must make it much easier to handle."

"Lily...please, understand..."

"I'm not upset, Mother," I say brightly. "How could I be? Do you see how powerful I am now? I'm just like Dana. You should be happy."

"Are you happy, Lily?"

"Dad, really?" I bark a laugh. "I have never been happier. And you don't have to worry about me being rebellious against the Commission now. I really understand its role and how important it is in keeping the peace of the world."

"Well, Tommy, Karen," Dana said, stepping up behind me. I feel him approaching long before and am not startled when he puts a hand on my waist. "What do you think?"

"I…I don't know what to say, Dana," my father said. "It's such a shock. I would have preferred if you had told us that she was in your care."

"We assumed that she was…" my mother whispered, looking frantically between us. It was obvious she was frightened. I have a sense of excitement at the feeling and find my smile growing.

"I was not sure how you would react," Dana said. "To be honest, you were so quick to turn her over to me, I wasn't sure if you even wanted to know what happened to her."

"Is this going to be uncomfortable?" I ask, trying to sound concerned. "I mean, after all, we're going to be working together. I would not want anything from the past to hurt that relationship."

They are both surprised to hear me talk in such a manner. It really is comical how they cannot seem to get their thoughts together enough to talk to me.

"It will be difficult, of course," my mother murmured.

"But manageable?" I say.

They looked between Dana and me, but then slowly nodded. Not like we gave them any other choice. Of course they would have to learn how to work with us. There was no way for them to get out.

"Excellent."

"Now that that's settled, Little Lily, if I may speak to you," Dana said, motioning for me to follow him. I smile at my parents once more before stepping away.

"See?" he said, putting his arm over my shoulder and hugging me. "Let your instincts take over and you can play everyone in the room perfectly."

"I never realized people were this easy."

"Extremely simple creatures," he agreed, looking around as we cleared the area with the tables and made our way back into the cold stare of Mrs. Markus. I ignore her.

"You don't want to do anything to them?" Dana asked, turning to face me as I glance back at my parents, knowing exactly what he meant.

"No," I say. "I think it will be enough that they have to confront me every week."

"I love the way your mind works."

"It works just like yours, I'm sure," I tease, winking.

"Why do you think I love it so much?"

I gently run my hand along the lapel of his suit. "I think I have been a very good girl, lately..."

"I would have to agree."

"And, as a reward, I think it would only be fair if you let me play a little," I whisper, blinking at him slowly. He sighs and looks hesitant as I press myself close to him.

"Come on, let me try..." I pout. Dana gently ran his fingers over my cheek.

"You think you're ready for the big leagues?" he challenges me. I nod.

Looking thoughtful, he glanced around the socializing room.

"Fine, you think you're ready?" He turns me around and leans close to my ear. "Pick a target."

I scan the room of potential prey, singling out the few that catch my interest. Finally, I see the one I want in the crowd. She was nervous, constantly casting an eye around, knowing that a predator was near.

"That one," I tell him, nodding to my victim.

Dana smiled and his hand skimmed down my waist as he nipped at my ear.

"Very good choice," he complimented. "You have six hours," he tells me, smacking my backside and making me feel twice as empowered.

I take a deep breath, finding the center I need, and then I walk to my target. As I am walking, Sean approaches me, nervous.

"Lily, what are you doing?" he asked, his tone tight with concern. I pat him on the lapel, winking at him.

"We'll play later," I promise, continuing toward my target. I admit, I am impressed with Sean's ability to see my entire demeanor change with the object of my game in sight. It makes me want him more. But not tonight.

My hips are moving smoothly as I stride to the group, gently weaving through the others and finally approaching my target's back.

I tap her shoulder.

The way she stiffens before she turns around tells me that she understands exactly who is behind her. She turned anyway.

"Lily..." she whispered, her eyes wide.

"Becca," I greet. "I'm surprised to see you here. Dana didn't tell me that you had joined the Commission."

"Well...y-you know, with my inside knowledge...he kinda had to let me in."

"Without your parents?" I ask, looking around her at the group staring at me.

"...yes," Becca admitted. "But he's thinking of bringing them in, since my mother is having an affair with your father as it is."

She tried to make the comment sharp, but all it did was make me shiver, thrilled at the twist of fate.

"Is that so?" I giggle. "Good for them. Must be thrilling."

"You're not upset?"

"Why should I be?" I chuckle. "Are you?"

"Of course," she snapped. Her face softened and her eyes became fearful. "How long have you been down here? How much do you know?"

"I've only been out of the back for two weeks or so," I answer. "I'm still learning everything. I would love to catch up with you. I have been wondering what you're up to." I glance at the rest of the group, silently telling them to leave. They obeyed, bidding quick goodbyes to Becca. I motion for her to sit at the nearby unoccupied table, taking a seat myself. She remained where she stood until I was seated completely. I chuckle when she does not join me.

"It's alright."

Hesitantly, she lowered herself to her seat, crossing her legs and pulling her skirt over her knees. I proudly let my hemline rest at my upper thigh. I look over Becca's nervous frame, taking in her state of mind and seeing what I can exploit. Admittedly, I cannot remember much about our last meeting other than that we were in an alleyway. I need to relearn her to play my game with her.

Six hours is more than enough time.

"How soon after our last meeting did you get pulled into the Commission?" I ask bluntly. She blinked, leaning back in her seat, surprised at how simply I had asked the question. I smile, warming my expression. "There is no need to be concerned. I bear no grudge against you."

"You don't? Even after..."

I lean forward and place my hand over hers on her knee. She jumps, surprised at the sudden contact and I change the look in my eyes, adjusting my entire body to show sincerity and undeniable warmth.

"It's in the past...and regardless of everything, we're going to be working together here in the Commission. I want to make sure that we can be friends."

"But...you've changed so much..." she murmured, her eyes flicking back and forth between my hand and my eyes.

"So have you," I purr, but gently, being sure not to come on too strong until I had her relaxed. "To think, someone of your particular tastes in the mouth of the lion."

She lowered her head. I squeeze her hand and she glances back up at me.

"It's alright," I whisper. "This is probably the safest place. And after everything you did for the Commission, I'm sure that you're safe."

"Really?" she asked, her eyes hopeful.

"I'm sure of it," I say. "If you were going to be captured, it would have happened already. Besides, I'm sure Dana likes you."

"...he's kinda frightening," she chuckled brokenly, her body relaxing. My hand is still on hers, being sure to establish physical contact early. I laugh and nod.

"He can be intense."

"I thought you hated him," she whispered, leaning closer. I look around, pretending that the watching Dana does not know what I'm trying to accomplish, before also leaning forward.

"I didn't understand him before. He's still intense, of course, but I understand a little better now."

She is skeptical, I can tell. But she is more relaxed, which makes it easier for me to talk to her.

"No one at school knows you're a Commish Kid?"

"There are no more Commish Kids," she muttered. "And I don't want anyone to know."

I nod. She leaned close again.

"What happened to everyone?"

"The Commish Kids?" I ask. "Well, ten of those in the rebellion were killed. Three surrendered before the final capture and, as far as I know, are with the other survivors in the holding cells."

"What's going to happen to them?"

"I don't know," I tell her, looking at the ground. "It just depends..."

"On what?"

"A lot of factors."

"Lily, there's a lot I want to say to you," she said. There was the first crack in her barriers. I squeeze her hand, trying to provide some comfort so she would relax further. She opens her mouth again, but stops when I move. I look around the empty room, noticing that even Dana had left with Sean. There are a few guards around because we are there, but I realize quickly this is the best moment to exploit the weakness in her armor.

"Actually," I say, nodding to the guards in the quiet room. "Maybe we should go somewhere a little more...private?"

She looked around as well and nodded.

"Good idea...where can we go? Do you have an office now or something?" she tried to laugh, though I can feel her nerves getting high again.

"No, I share an office with Dana. But I have my own room." That's a lie. I plan to move to a specific room. I move confidently, my hand no longer on hers, as I lead her into the back. I tell the guards that she is a close friend and I can see them smile knowingly. Surely, with Dana, they came to understand the way we play. One insisted that he follow, just in case there was any trouble, as was ordered by Dana.

Becca follows close as I lead her down the numbered rooms to the third door without a number, which was one of the four rooms that belonged to Dana. The third room is one I remember well as the room in which my transformation began.

I slide my card over the lock and hold the door open for her. Becca stepped inside worriedly, looking around the simple room as if waiting for something to jump out and attack. I turn to the guard, who positions himself next to the door, pretending he does not know what is about to happen, even though I can see the knowing glint in his eyes.

I close the door and turn to Becca. She is standing still in the middle of the room, wringing her hands nervously behind her back, which I know from the tensing muscles in her arms.

Knowing I have to calm her down before I can do anything else, I motion for her to sit on the bed, walking to the chair by the desk and wheeling it out to sit near her, but not right across from her, giving her some physical space.

She slowly lowered herself to sit on the bed. I am disappointed that the chains that were once attached to the headboard are no longer there. They would have been very useful...

I'll have to improvise.

"Lily...you said that there is no grudge between us," Becca started, rubbing her hands together in her lap, avoiding eye contact. I sit in the chair, looking at her, being sure to keep my arms uncrossed to avoid appearing defensive. "Are you sure you can forget that?"

"It's not forgotten," I lie, "but it's understandable why you did what you did...and truthfully, it was for the best in the long run." I only have a small inkling of what I'm talking about.

"You really believe that? After Josh?"

Who?

"Yes," I say. "It was hard at the time, but...you know, sometimes things happen that we just can't understand until we reach the other end of the tunnel."

"I feel so guilty," she murmured. "I got so scared...I was terrified that you were actually killing people, and that it was Mykail who was attacking Central...but then I got here and I learned that you had been right."

I listen to her, vague memories of distant times bubbling to the surface. They are unclear, out of sequence, and it is difficult to determine what ones were from a dream and what had once been my reality.

"I spent months agonizing over what I had done."

I tilt my head to the side, my eyes remaining soft. There was a tremor in her voice. She was close to tears. I see the situation play out in my head before it even happens.

What a fun game.

"And then I see you...like this..."

"What do you mean?" I ask, sounding genuinely curious, even though I know I am reading from a script to get what I want from her.

"Well...you're just...not Lily anymore."

"What are you talking about?" I chuckle lightly, shaking my head. "Of course I'm Lily."

"No...you're someone else," she said, her voice trembling as she fought the tears. I wait on each passing beat, knowing she is going to break soon. "You've been changed by Dana...and...it's all my fault."

There it was.

She bowed her head, the tears gathering in her eyes as she hiccupped, trying to control herself. I make my move, sitting next to her on the bed, wrapping my arm around her shoulders and pulling her close. She leaned her head on my shoulder and sniffed, reaching to her face, becoming intelligible as she mumbled into her hand.

"I shouldn't have been so weak...b-because of me...people are dead...changed...h-how could..."

I rub my hand over her arm, reestablishing touch after our departure from the meeting hall. I remain silent, letting her cry and babble against me, offering comfort and drawing her close slowly, putting pressure on her shoulder that brings her closer to me.

She cries for seven minutes, releasing tension in her body that had been there for months, and her entire being weakens in exhaustion. I pull her closer and closer, until she has one hand on my leg, my own hand covering hers while the other strokes her shoulder. I am no longer pulling. I am merely trailing my fingers over her skin, gently pushing the edge of her sleeve upward.

Becca started to lift her head every now and then to wipe the tears away, which was a sign she was calming.

I watch her as she finally lifts her head to look at me, our faces close. I hold back every part of me that wants to leap forward and attack her right then. I had to make her come to me…

I look down at her parted lips before looking at her eyes. She is watching me through red, puffy eyes and I am forced to look at her lips again to avoid reacting to the pathetic expression on her face.

I lean closer, our breaths mingling in mid-air, and I wait…

Within moments, she closed the gap between us, kissing me once before pulling her lips away, shaking.

"I'm sorry…" she breathed.

"Don't be," I say, my fingers once again trailing over her shoulder.

"I've been so confused ever since entering the Commission," she whispered. My fingers are gentle, barely touching enough to be registered on her skin. "…it's like…I-I can't think straight."

"I know," I murmur, my fingers closing around her shoulder and gently insisting she move closer again. "I went through the same thing."

This time, I kiss her once…twice…feeling her soft lips on mine. There is a part of me, a hungry part, that wants to force her down and take her, but there is a bigger part of me that is enjoying the tantalizing dance. I am delaying my own gratification.

Her breath shuddered out of her. I am close to winning. As expected, I feel a small amount of resistance start to bubble within her. She breaks the kiss and looks at me with a shy, frightened smile.

"I'm sorry… I…I shouldn't…"

"Stop apologizing," I say, lifting my hand with hers in my grasp and gently running my thumb over the side of her hand. "I am actually very happy that you're here with me…"

"You…you are?"

"I am…" I nod, finally working our hands properly so we can lace our fingers together. Her hand is shaking, but the adrenaline is causing her body to go hot, which makes me realize I am winning. I feel my power over her.

I tilt my head, knowing that she needed to close the distance this time.

As scripted, she did.

Her other hand came to my neck, pulling me closer as her lips worked against mine. Surprisingly, she was inexperienced, clumsy and rushed. Enjoying the slow dance too much and not caught up in the moment like her, I move my hand to her neck as well, softly moving my thumb over her skin, urging her to calm down and take things slow. My lips move slower, trying to calm her frantic body.

Funny...I had wanted her to surrender to me, and now I wanted her to slow down.

I guess it makes sense, making her want me, leaving her wanting more...

Taking a small chance as she starts to slow, I push gently, guiding her to lay back on the bed, moving as slowly as I can so I don't startle her. She continues to kiss me, her hand wrapped around the back of my neck as I settle over her.

While I had no experience kissing women, I did not think there was anything different about the way her lips moved. The motions were a little more hesitant, but the actions felt no different from a man.

Until I lower my body to rest on hers, allowing our chests to touch and causing a surprisingly tactile sensation, so intense that she broke the kiss and gasped, her eyes tightening.

I kiss her cheek, moving down to her neck, intent on keeping her intoxicated while I explore the differences between sex with men and sex with women. This is practice for the future. Maybe I could even succeed with the red-head Veronica, who Dana had failed to seduce.

"Lily, wait..."

I hesitate, rising to look at her as she licked her red lips and tried to catch her breath.

"I-I don't think this is a good idea..."

Deciding against words, I sit back on her hips and begin pulling the blazer over my shoulders, tossing it to the side. Her eyes are watching me intensely. I instantly understand Dana's sense of power. I reach down, grabbing her hands and raising them to my chest, placing her hands at the button for my blue blouse.

She hesitated, and then worked the first button open.

I raise off her hips when I feel her attempt to move, allowing her to sit up and continue her work as I place my hands on her shoulders, keeping our lips apart while she took control of unbuttoning my shirt.

Of course, I was in control of the situation completely. I was pulling her strings, feeding off her fear, confusion, and need for companionship.

She pulled the tails of my shirt out of the waistband of my skirt and slid the fabric from my shoulders. I shiver from the smooth feeling of her hands and the fabric moving down my arms as her eyes scraped over my blue bra with black lace, pressing her face between my breasts for a brief kiss. I take control, pushing her insistently back to the bed.

She blinked, surprised, but not opposed.

My hands move from her shoulders, over her breasts, gently squeezing them and opening my mouth to swallow the moan that bubbled out of her. My right hand moves to the side of her dress, immediately locating the zipper I had spotted earlier, allowing my finger to trail along the skin as the side of the dress was opened.

Becca shivered. The fear was back. There was apprehension in her features. Needing her to remain calm for only a little while longer, I kiss her, deftly moving my hands to pull the shoulder strap over her head, breaking our kiss for only an instant.

When I pull away, my hands are at either side of her body, sliding the dress down, over her bust, down the smooth curve of her waist, and over her full hips. I lick my lips as I stare at her rounded hips.

Quickly sliding the fabric off her and allowing it to drop to the floor, I move back to her mouth, sliding my chest along her skin, letting her feel the contours of the bra's lace, smiling to myself as I think of how quickly our encounter was going to change without her knowledge.

I occupy her mind with another kiss, pushing my tongue into her mouth and tasting the spearmint toothpaste she had used a few hours before, probably just before the Commission meeting. She does have a slight chemical taste from lip gloss, but I choose to ignore it, focused intently on grabbing her hair with one hand while the other uses two fingers to stroke up the side of her thigh, over the lace of her panties and up her side to her breast, which I palm through her simple bra.

I can tell that her brain has shut down. She is completely in my domain now, but she has only just surrendered. I need to keep her there and get all her barriers down so that she won't fight me.

I press my breasts to hers, rubbing them over her as she moans into my mouth. I can taste the adrenaline and pleasure coursing through her.

It would appear that she is a virgin.

Or at least a virgin to being with a woman. Surprising and yet not surprising, considering her tastes.

I try to recall all the places Dana has found on me that make my hair stand on end and my blood sing in bliss, pressing the pads of my fingers into the side of her breast as I gently squeeze. She has very nice breasts, now that I'm actually playing with them. They're soft, warm and cause those cute little sounds in the back of her throat that empower me further.

I reach around her back with one hand, hooking under her, unclasping the bra, pulling away from her mouth to remove the undergarment. She is self-conscious and looks away from me as I toss the bra to the side, somewhere far away.

Both of my hands cup her breasts, moving them in circles, squeezing tenderly. She moaned, her eyes sliding shut and she bit her lip, trying to stop the sounds from escaping her. I smile at how easily she has succumbed, how much she is enjoying my ministrations. I turn my nails to her skin, pushing them down her breasts, scraping over her nipples, which makes her back arch high off the bed. Her nipples are far more sensitive than mine, which makes me want to explore them, fascinated with the reactions.

With one hand on the right breast, I pull the left breast up, squeezing it to form a peak before closing my mouth around the nipple. One of Becca's hands flies down to her side, gripping the bed spread, while her other hand moves to my hair, running her fingers through the strands and holding me to her chest.

I roll the small nub in my mouth, sucking before pushing my tongue back around the sensitive center. She is so responsive, so incredibly aroused, that when I shift to the right breast, my leg falling between hers and pressing against the junction of her legs, her reaction is nearly violent.

She releases a choked cry and her back arches off the bed, forcing my head upward. I break away from her breast, smiling as she tries to catch her breath.

Her hips are rocking, rubbing her panties along the edge of my skirt, desperate for friction. I let her writhe, allowing her to lose herself while I reach for the thin belt on the skirt.

I extract her hand from my hair as she grinds against my thigh, kissing her palm to soothe her before looping the thin belt around her wrist, grabbing her other hand bringing them both above her head, wrapping them together. When I pull the two ends tight, she gasps and her eyes snap open, her hips still moving in wonton circles, possessed.

There's a stronger fear now. She knows she's vulnerable, and now that her hands are tied above her head, she's in more danger if I change the nature of our encounter.

We stare at one another for several long moments. Her movements begin to slow. I know she can feel the change in my energy.

Wanting to throw her more off-balance, I return to my treatment of her breasts, prompting her to start moving against me again. She knows she should run—I can tell with the way her muscles quiver. Her brain and her instincts were telling her to leave, knowing things were about to get dangerous, but her body was begging to stay for the attention it had never known.

I move to her sternum, kissing and lapping at the spot between her breasts before sliding my tongue down the center of her abdomen, moving my arms to rest behind her bent legs, hooking around her thighs as I drop to kneel next to the bed, pulling her hips a little and settling my face between her thighs.

I stare at the wet spot on her panties and smile, thrilled at the reaction I was able to draw from her. She tenses again, looking down at me, frightened at what I would do next.

I lean forward and gently kiss her panties, pressing my tongue to the already-wet fabric and ripping a startled shout out of her as her head falls back onto the bed, thrashing back and forth.

I hook my fingers in the waistband and pull the last scrap of fabric from her, dropping it to the floor.

She moves her arms down in an attempt to cover herself, but I grab her wrists, slithering back up her body and pinning them above her head. She's frightened again. I'm dominating her and she is not sure she can trust me. I shake my head slowly, before reaching back with my other hand and pulling my tight skirt up to rest on my hips, exposing the matching panties and thigh-high stockings I am wearing. I have really come to love stockings.

Pushing my hips forward, I come into contact with her and she gasps, her hands desperate to grab at anything. I have to push them back down to the bed. I rub myself against her. I am turned on myself, but I am not the same type of slave to my passions as I was before, where I would lose my mind and reasoning when aroused. Now, I was always aroused, and just had to find the right way to sate myself.

I smiled, watching her writhe and shake as I thrust against her, rubbing our sensitive bodies together in a slow, agonizing rhythm.

A few more thrusts later and my pet lets out a frustrated sob.

"Do you want more?"

She cannot say anything, her eyes tightly closed, but she lets out a whimper in answer.

"Feel everything," I whisper, pushing a little harder against her.

She gasped and choked back a moan.

I stop moving and her eyes flutter open. I smile, reaching to finger the wet lips, parting them. She looks at me nervously, her expression curious and unwilling to stop, but frightened to continue.

I push my middle finger into the tight warmth. She gasps and cringes a little, confused by the pressure.

"So tight..." I breathe. I crook the finger forward, searching for a particular spot...

She wails in confusion.

There it is.

I crook my finger over and over again, feeling the sensation building in her. Her body is producing so much lubricant that it's easy for my finger to move. I pull it out only long enough to insert another finger. She gasps again and her body moves awkwardly, unsure how to react.

"You're dripping wet..." I say, watching my fingers move in and out of her. She moans again, though she looks uncomfortable. "Do you want more?"

She shakes her head quickly, knowing that pain would come if I inserted a third finger. I look at the tight cavity my fingers are exploring and sigh. "You're going to have to know at some point..."

I add another finger, forcing it in, meeting resistance from her body. She lets out a cry and her face contorts in pain.

"It only really hurts the first time," I tell her. "Well...that's not entirely true. But you're so wet down here, you'd be ready to take a man..."

Her eyes fly open and that is my cue.

I remove my fingers and stand, grabbing my clothes. For those few stunned moments that Becca remains on the bed confused, I stride to the door and open it. As soon as it was open, she scrambled, trying to untie the knot I had purposely made lower than her fingers could reach.

"Quincy?" I ask sweetly, turning to the guard who jumped to attention outside the door. "Can you do something for me?"

He glances at me and then peers into the room.

"She's all yours," I say, stepping aside and letting him in the room. "I prepared her for you. She said she doesn't like men, so I figured I would give her a helping hand in getting ready."

"Lily, what the fuck?!" Becca wailed, clambering off the bed and attempting to find a way out as she tried to untangle her hands.

"It's Miss Sandover to you," I correct coldly, watching Quincy advance. "Trust me, you'll feel better once you get it over with."

I close the door behind me after hearing a scream. I walk down the hall, swinging the blouse and blazer over my shoulder, walking to the first room and tossing my blouse on the bed. I cannot hear anything from the other room, which makes me intensely curious about what is going on in the room I just left.

I fix my hair, combing through the messy parts with my fingers before swinging the blazer over my shoulders and closing the three buttons, leaving a little peek of the blue lingerie underneath.

I pass through the halls toward my destination, finally turning and knocking on a door.

"Come in."

I open the door and smile at the man who is sitting, startled, at the desk.

"Miss Sandover…"

"Sean," I greet. "Don't worry, I'm not here for you. Actually, I am hoping that you can take Miss Davis home. She'll be ready in about five minutes in my old room."

"Your old—" He stopped, his eyes going wide. "Lily, what did you do?"

"You worry too much," I say with a wink. "You'll know soon enough."

I walk out of the office, moving across the hall to another door, not even bothering to knock before swinging the door open. Dana is sitting at his desk, expecting me, tapping his finger on the arm of his chair.

"I must applaud you, Little Lily." He grinned wickedly. "That was superbly executed."

"I learned from the best," I say, walking to him as I unbutton the blazer, flashing the bra to him.

"Is that her punishment?" he asked. I lean against the side of his desk.

"Yes. I don't remember what happened. I just know that I was furious with her about something at some point in time. It's not important anymore. But she knows what she did…and she's going to think that's what that was about, and she will turn that over and over in her head…"

"Bravo," Dana said proudly.

"Now, I want a reward."

"Come and get it."

I did. I crawled into his lap and enjoyed the rough play we had taken part in so many times. There was nothing like enjoying one another as equals, feeling the clashing power in both of us. Even as I tried to choke him, he did not flinch away, responding by biting my neck hard enough to draw blood, and thus heightening our pleasure.

When I finish refastening the final snap over my stockings, Dana is motioning for me to follow him.

"I have another reward for you for playing Miss Davis so perfectly," he said, crooking his finger in a similar motion to earlier.

I giggle and hop off the desk, buttoning my blazer again.

"You certainly are spoiling me," I say, following him out of the office and toward the back of the Commission. "Did Bryant Morris give you all kinds of goodies when you became Dana?"

"I guess," he said, using his card to open the door leading into the security office. "I guess I took my rewards, really." He flashed the broken pocket watch to me as we passed the guards, who bowed their heads to us. "I mean, I did take the entire Commission when I cut his head off."

"Big or little head?" I joke, already knowing the answer.

"First one and then the other," he said with a devilish smirk. I lick my lips and then bite my lower lip, imagining the blood that must have poured from the decapitated body.

"Died from a stroke, huh?" I leer.

"Decapitation was a little too nasty to report to the press and the delicate ears of the people of America," Dana said. "That's why no one said anything about what I did to Thomas Ankell, either."

"Figures."

We walk to the back of the wards, coming across the large room connecting the major hallways of the back. I am confused when we pass the lab, but I figure we were going to see one of the Machines of Neutralization, so I say nothing, excited for my surprise.

We turn into the west side of Ward Ten—the side I have never been in.

"We're going to see Rehan?" I smile, skipping next to Dana and latching onto his arm like a child.

"No. I have a new pet for you, since the others are locked away in their kennels. You can do whatever you want with this one."

"You gave me an experiment?" I laugh. "Again?"

"I would have given you the old one, but Mykail died before we got him back to the Commission," Dana said. "We probably wouldn't have been able to save him anyway."

"Too bad, he would have been fun to play with," I pout, though I can't really remember who Mykail was.

"Here we are," Dana announced, turning around the corner of the more complicated half of Ward Ten and motioning to the figure in the back corner of the cell. My whole body perks up and excitement runs through me at an alarming pace.

"*Really*?!"

"He's all yours."

I grab Dana's card, running it over the lock, entering the cell and approaching the shocked experiment in the corner.

"L-Lily?" Clark choked, terrified.

"Clark."

He stands and starts toward me, but stops immediately, retreating.

"No..." he whispered. "What *happened* to you?"

1247

"What do you mean what happened to me?" I chuckle. "What about you? You're all bruised and bloodied."

"I've been fighting back, what about *you*?" he snapped.

"Ooh." I shiver, excited by the sharp tone of his voice. I feel Dana walking into the cell behind me. "I fought as long as I could, but then I realized I was fighting for the wrong side. Isn't that a bitch?"

His eyes go wide and he shakes his head, looking hurriedly back and forth between me and Dana.

"No…you gave into him? After everything? After all that Griffin and Tori died for…after Josh and Mark…you gave in to him?!" His voice is tight with tears as he looks between the two of us. "And you became like *him*?"

"I don't know who you're talking about, but you need to let go of the past," I tell him with a shake of my head. "I did. And it helped me immensely."

"You motherfucker…" Clark growled, tears falling down his cheeks as he turned to Dana. "You destroyed her."

"I think it's an improvement, personally." Dana shrugged.

"What the hell do you want?" Clark barked. "You want to show me what happened to you? Well, I've seen it. You can get the fuck out now."

"Was I this much fun before?" I gasp, turning to Dana.

"That and more," he laughed. "I wanted to play with him a little, but it turns out that my time with him before still has him obedient to me…so, I give him to you. He is your pet and toy until you tire of him. But you will have to figure out something to do with him, eventually."

"What the fuck?!" Clark gasped.

"You belong to me, now," I tell him, walking forward as he backs away, pressing himself into the corner. When I get close enough to touch him, he tries to shove me backward, but I grab his arms and pin them to the side of his head, leaning close and looking at his dirty and swollen face with a dark smile. "And I am going to have so much fun with you…"

* *** *

Rehan is pregnant—at least for now. It was worrisome when we were not sure if her incredible immune system was going to reject the embryo, but it took and, two weeks later, the embryo is beginning to grow in her uterus.

This means seeing Eina to discuss how he felt about his offspring. Dana accompanies me and we both move excitedly toward the cell,

1248

where Eina is bound with The Teeth and sedated just enough to still be coherent for our chat.

"Eina," Dana calls as we close the door behind us. The first Machine of Neutralization lifts his head slowly, blinking at us with forced exhaustion. "Kyle tells me that you have been trying to destroy his equipment when getting your checkups."

"How could you?" Eina hisses.

"How could I what?"

"Rehan..." He lowers his head and breathes heavily.

"When I was in the Dome with him, he was able to see things that weren't there...he seemed to be able to read my mind." I look over Eina. If possible, he is even more beautiful now than when I last saw him. His skin is flawless and perfect, and despite his poor nutrition, his body is in amazing shape. Kyle tells me about his incredible health, and I look over his charts all the time, excited to see how resilient he is. He heals from injuries within hours, his hearing is so acute he can hear through the soundproof walls, and his speed is unparalleled.

"Well, considering everything else he is able to do, I would not be surprised," Dana laughs. He takes two steps and Eina growls. I resist the urge to growl back and protect Dana. I know that we are not really in danger, but I am very protective.

"Is that the case?" Dana presses. "Can you see into people's minds? How do you know what's happening with Rehan?"

"I...I can feel her..." he whispers, his gaze dropping as he tries to fight the drug-induced exhaustion. "And I feel the other life inside her."

"You can feel her?" I repeat. I know the feeling. I can tell when Dana is nearby, but the two Machines of Neutralization are separated across the Commission from one another. "What does that mean?"

"I can't explain it..."

"Come, now, Eina," I say, walking closer, ignoring his growl and crouching to look him in the eyes. "Remember? We were able to talk in the Dome..."

"You're different now." He shakes his head. "You're just like him."

"I know," I agree. "And I'm proud to be like him." I lean closer. "But you told me about a lot of things in there. You told me about the angel, about the rebellion...about a dragon..."

"A dragon?" one of the guards echoes, skeptic.

"Go with it," Dana says behind me. "He's been on about a red dragon ever since his testing was finished."

"He's *real*..." Eina growls, glaring at the both of us.

"You know that the same way you know about Rehan being pregnant, right?" I continue, trying to stay on subject and away from the strange fantasies of his mind. He turns those beautiful hazel eyes on me and then nods. "You feel it?"

"Yes."

"Do you want to kill the child?" I ask bluntly. His eyes widen, surprised. Dana is quiet and apprehensive behind me. "Eina? If the infant is born as a Machine of Neutralization, would you want to kill it?"

He is torn, his eyes moving back and forth rapidly along the floor as he thinks about my question. I allow him time to consider. I do not entirely understand how he can still have such intense human morals. I have no particular feelings toward the offspring of the two Machines of Neutralization. There is a lot that can go wrong. They are brother and sister, and the inbreeding is a problem we might be facing until we can find another strand of animal DNA that works with the genetic anomaly in some of our current prisoners. If the child is born with defects, there will be no choice but to put it down, so getting attached is pointless.

"Why...why are you asking me this?" Eina asks, his head swaying as he tries to think around the drugs.

"Here's the thing, Eina," Dana states, crouching next to me. "We've had two successes, and we're working toward making more, but to create a sustainable force, we need to be able to breed you and the others. But infants need care, and they need to be raised to understand themselves and their bodies. The offspring of the Machines of Neutralization stand a great chance of needing the care of older Machines of Neutralization, like yourself, in order to learn how to live."

Eina started chuckling, shaking his head.

"How...how the hell...am I supposed to teach him anything...when I don't know what I can do myself?" he asks, looking at us with an exasperated expression.

I glance at Dana, who returns the look. We share our silent conversation before Dana sighs and turns back to the experiment.

"What can we do to facilitate you learning your abilities?" he asks. "We do not know how to set up an environment for you. I will admit, you are the guinea pig. We don't know what to do for you, so everything is going to be trial and error."

"I want to go outside..." he pleads, looking at us with sad eyes. "I want to feel the sun on my face, the wind...I want to be out in the open air."

"Do you think that will help you learn more about your abilities?" I ask, raising an eyebrow. "Or is that just something you want?"

"I don't know," he practically sobs. "I just feel like I'm suffocating down here...I need the sun."

Dana sighs.

"That is not going to be easy."

"You're letting me out soon anyway," Eina growls. "You want me to kill Chris."

"I do."

"If I do that for you...will you find a way to let me be outside? I know I will be able to learn more about myself up there."

"As if you have a choice to kill Chris," I bark a laugh.

"I will turn against you if you double-cross me," he snarls, the growl coming from deep in his throat. "I may not know what I am capable of, but I know I can overpower the both of you..."

"I know you're not foolish enough to threaten us, Eina," Dana warns. "We put you together, and we can take you apart."

"You won't, you *need* me."

"Do we?"

"Why else would you be here now?" He leans close. "I want to go outside...I want to have room to run at top speed. I have no means to test my limits down here and it's killing me."

"If we provide a facility for you to be outside and to hone your skills, will you care for your offspring and raise it to know its abilities?"

Eina looks between the two of us, his eyes trying to focus. He finally sighs.

"It's my child, isn't it?" he whispers. "Of course I will. I want him to know himself better than I know myself."

"Very well, Eina," Dana says with a grin that mirrors my own. "We will see what we can come up with. It might take a while, and you will have to deal with Chris before we can deliver our portion of the agreement. But we will be sure to let you in on our plans when we have them."

Dana places a hand on my back and leads me out of the cell.

"This is a hiccup," he grumbles.

"How? We can build him a facility. It would be more beneficial to put our money toward him so that he can train others."

"But the funds are not divided that way. The sponsors of the Machine of Neutralization project are expecting numbers first," Dana explains. "This is the new nuclear arms race. People saw Mykail and Chris and the international community quickly moved to make something stronger. Now that we have it, we need to market it, but we can't do that if we don't have the supply to match the demand. And we sure as hell can't risk the information leaking."

"Kyle is working on some more DNA today," I say. "He told me that by the end of the week, he should have something for us on other possible animals we could use for the same strength profile."

"It might not be the same." Dana shakes his head, leaning against the wall next to the door leading out of the eastern portion of Ward Ten. I lean next to him, watching his face. "This project has incredible potential. But we need to cover our asses as well and be sure we don't get fucked over."

I sigh and thoughtfully stare at the ground. It's true. The Machine of Neutralization is an untested weapon. There is no way of knowing Eina and Rehan's capabilities. Having come late into the game, I still do not know who is sponsoring the project and for what reasons. That is what Thursday's meeting is for. There is still a lot I need to learn, but I am just as interested in the project as Dana, and I want to ensure its success.

"Maybe we can pitch something to the sponsors," I suggest. "Who are the big spenders?"

"The Greater United Kingdom at the moment. Germany is also heavily invested." Dana sighs and runs a hand through his hair. "And that woman will be at the meeting, as well."

"Veronica Harris?"

"Yes, who apparently has no birth certificate, no known contacts, and should not even exist according to records. I have checked databases across the globe, and instead of finding answers, I have discovered I am not the only one searching for her."

"Are you going to let her invest?" I raise my eyebrows. He looks at me with a shrug.

"I think if she buys into this idea of building a facility for the Machine of Neutralization, absolutely. If she wants to fund, the least I can do is milk her of her money."

I chuckle. There is a large part of me that is thrilled at seeing Miss Harris again. I feel myself already starting to plan what to do when I see her again.

"We release Eina tomorrow," Dana says. "It's going to be a tough sell to the public."

"I have been thinking," I say slowly. "Don't let Eina kill him immediately. Let him get away, let Chris make a few scenes over the next few weeks, and that will swing the people in favor very quickly."

"Be a dear and call General Matthews and General Perkin," he says, tenderly tucking some hair behind my ear. "Tell them that I want to speak with them and tell them they will have cameras following them."

I see the plan immediately. Release Eina, be sure that we are in close proximity in case he gets any ideas, but then let him work with the military and have the military superficially sponsor the Machine of Neutralization as a weapons acquisition against the threat of Chris.

"Come on, we have a lot to get done in the next few hours if we want to plan Chris' next few moves," he says, standing straight and turning to leave.

"Dana," I call. He turns back. "There is one other problem with introducing this to the public."

"Which is?"

"Well, if we start breeding them, then we're going to create a new class of people in America...particularly if we build Eina a facility. That is going to start us spiraling on the path of discrimination again, and people might see that as us taking a step backward."

"We will simply make sure the people know that these things are not human. They are weapons to be used, and that is all." Dana grins. "Come on."

"I want to see the puppy," I say, walking toward the door to the western section of Ward Ten. Dana chuckles behind me and I throw a devilish smile at him.

"Fine, enjoy him," he agrees. "But be sure you come back soon. We have a lot of work to do."

"Will do, sir," I tease with a wink before opening the door and walking past the guard.

Forgetting everything we discussed for the moment, I skip toward the far end of Ward Ten, rounding the corner and studying my little puppy, who is crying in the corner. I feel my lip extend in a pout, though I am not sure what I expected from him.

I slide my card over the lock and open the door, grabbing his attention. When he sees me he stands, his eyes wide, warily watching me approach as fear and anger passes down his spine.

I smile, slowing my step, not wanting to startle him.

"What do you want?" he snaps. He doesn't want me any closer. I stop and smile, looking over his swollen eyes and red face. He looks very different without the glasses I always remember him wearing.

"Has your eyesight gotten better?" I ask, tilting my head to the side.

"What?"

"You're not wearing your glasses."

"There's not much point back here, is there?" he bit.

"I guess not."

"What do you want, Lily?"

"I want to play," I say, deciding there was no need for formalities in this setting.

He tenses. I can feel his muscles flex. His heartbeat begins to pound against his ribs. I chuckle and shake my head.

"No need to worry," I say. "I won't touch you."

"Lily, please, listen to me, there has to be something left of you in there..."

"There is," I agree. "But it's not the part you want...or maybe it *is* the part you want. Who knows? You have a devious side in you than your simple appearance hides, if memory serves."

"If memory serves," he sneers. "You remember me, but you don't remember the others? You don't even remember Mark?"

"No." I shake my head. "He's dead, right?"

Clark's tears began to flow again.

"How could you?" He swallows hard. He is in a very high emotional state, and I know it will be easy to shake him up. Clark is still clinging to the idea that I am the bastardized character I was a few months ago...that, somewhere, the false person still lingered. Forcing him to realize I had shed the façade is going to be fun, and could lead somewhere fascinating in our play.

"Clark, really, I'm much better now that I've let go of everyone. You should be happy for me that I finally have some semblance of peace."

"*Peace*?! You've completely lost your mind!" Clark darts forward and grabs my shoulders. I feel how desperate he is. I am the one he's clinging to in order to believe there is still a reason to fight. I am his four-eleven forty-one. As long as he did not see me, I was the image he could hold to against the testing and torture. My new reality is too much for him.

I had him set up on a simple testing schedule for the last two weeks. Basic tests that might make him a little stronger, but really were just to give him experience on the table until I can find something brilliant to do with him.

I decide to glance over his blood work again and see if he shares the same anomalies as Dana and myself.

And then I immediately decide against it.

Dana is my prey. Once I understand everything about the Commission, I fully plan to do to him what he did to Bryant Morris, and I know that he is anticipating it. It's part of the fun. Having someone else be another player in our game is unacceptable.

"Lily...please," Clark pleads. "How can you not remember everything we fought for? Everyone fought for you so that you wouldn't become like this. You were willing to die before submitting to Dana."

"I did die," I say. "That's what I'm trying to tell you. The Lily you knew is dead. This is what is left of her, grown stronger and more resilient than ever."

"I refuse to believe it. You are so much stronger than this, I know you are."

"You think what we were doing before was proof of strength?" I bark a laugh. "It was an exercise in futility. You still won't fight against Dana, even now, when you have absolutely nothing to lose, because you know he's superior, and you know that you will never be able to defeat him."

"Not without help."

"You tried that already," I remind him shortly. "Honestly, there is nothing you can do. You are one person, without a rebellion behind you, and you are stuck in this cell, crying in a corner because you feel nostalgic for the days when you were led to believe you had some power to change things." I shake my head. "That's not the way the world works, duckling."

He lets out an exasperated laugh, forcing the air out of his lungs as he backs up to the wall and slowly slides down to sit.

"You really have lost it…" he whispers, shaking his head. I smile and step forward, lowering myself to my knees and sitting back on my heels, looking him over. "I can't believe it was so easy for you to forget everything…"

"*Easy?*" I bark. "Like hell it was easy. I had every part of me sliced away and turned inside out…every moment I was on the table, I was begging for death. I'm sure you haven't had that happen, yet."

He does not answer, but he does not need to. I already know.

"But I learned so much about myself in that time," I say, leaning closer. "I learned about fear, about pain…I learned about how to survive and how to become powerful enough to rise out of nothing and become something great."

"You used to believe that it was for the betterment of the country that we fight against Dana."

"Argh, Clark, enough about what I *used* to believe," I groan. "That's not me anymore. That part of your past is gone, and you need to let it go."

"I can't."

"And why not?"

"Because I refuse to lose sight of those who gave everything up to ensure that we would have some sort of chance against Dana. I won't throw away Mark and Josh and the others like you did. You say that we were weak for fighting Dana and the Commission, but you were the weak one because you couldn't hold on to the people who really mattered."

"Clark, no one really *matters*. They didn't matter, you don't matter, hell, even I don't really matter. We're small blips in the universe, waiting for our time to be put out."

"Well, congratulations," Clark growls. "We're getting close. With the fucking Machine of Neutralization, you've created an arms race that probably won't end in a cold war or a standoff."

"No?" I challenge. "Where do you see it going?"

"These are not weapons controlled by people," he whispers. "These are living creatures with their own free will and the ability to destroy things with a flick of their wrist."

"Well, that hasn't actually been tested yet," I admit, bobbing my head from side to side contemplatively. "We have to build a facility that is strong enough to hold Eina and allow him to really see how far he can go."

"Lily! You are going to destroy the planet with him!"

"Not just him," I croon, putting a finger to my lips. "But with his sister, and his offspring."

"...offspring?"

"We have to see if Rehan can even deliver the child, but yes."

"You are *sick*."

"Oh, puppy," I playfully whine, running my hand over his hair, even though he flinches from it. "So are you. You have all these little holes that are festering in your heart. When all those people you loved died, they tore a part of you open, and you keep letting it get infected." I take his face in my hands. "Do you know how to take care of a wound like that? You cut out the infection, and sew it back up."

"...what happened?" he whispers, his eyes sliding to avoid my gaze and resting on the scars on the inside of my wrists.

"Transformation is a bitch," I laugh, dropping my hands and shaking my head. "Did you ever consider how much strength it takes for a butterfly to rip through its cocoon? I had to do a lot of ripping to become this beautiful."

"You're not beautiful anymore, Lily," Clark chokes. "You're a hideous creature with no love or compassion. You have become the thing that you opposed."

"Well, there is the old adage, those who oppose the government become the government. While it's not entirely applicable to this case, it does ring true to some degree." I lean forward and bite my lower lip before saying the next part. "And try telling Becca I'm not beautiful. She didn't resist when I had my hands on her…"

Clark reaches forward and shoves me. I straighten from the force, but I am not knocked off-balance. I never am anymore. I always know exactly how people are going to move.

"You bitch!" he snaps. "You're just saying that to get a reaction!"

"If that was true, it certainly worked," I giggle. "But let me assure you, I had Becca. Well, for a while. Then the guard had her. She's a little trooper, that one. She's still coming to the meetings and interacting with me on a civil level, though she won't let me touch her again."

"Wait…" Clark choked. "You…you *raped* her?"

"No, no," I say. "She was mostly willing for me. The guard is the one who raped her, I guess." My eyes widen as I straighten. "Have you been raped, yet? And I mean full penetration. It seems to be the initiation ceremony around here."

He cringes and turns his head away.

"Still a virgin, huh?" I smile. "This brings out the artist in me…"

"Fuck you, Lily."

"Don't tell me that if I spread my legs for you, you wouldn't take advantage of the opportunity."

"I *wouldn't*."

"You know nothing about yourself, yet." I shake my head, reaching out and playing with his tangled and matted hair. "Still a puppy…you'll get there, little one."

His head moves and I let him retaliate. Just like a puppy, he has to learn where the line is. His teeth find the flesh of my hand and he bites. There is no pain—there's never pain anymore—so I stare at him, waiting for him to continue. He has not broken the skin, expecting me to move away.

"Well?" I challenge.

He glares, but I see the gears of his mind trying to figure out the best way to act.

"Oh, come on, are you going to even try?" I jeer. "Put some muscle in it. *Bite.* Bite as hard as you can," I urge, my voice quiet, traveling on wavelengths that resonate in the lower part of his skull. "Come on, bite me. You're angry, prove it! Bite harder!"

He becomes distressed and the tears rise to his eyes, but he cannot disengage his teeth from my skin—my words won't let him. I smile and lean even closer.

"You want to prove your strength, then *bite* me."

He sobs and my other hand goes to his hair, pulling a section of it sharply.

"You want to teach me a lesson? You think that you're stronger than me? Then why aren't you taking the opportunity?"

He sobs again and I sigh, bored. I pull his hair harder and his mouth opens to squeak in pain.

"See? This is where it's obvious our natures are different," I tell him shortly, wiping my hand off on his red shirt. "You know that I'm more powerful, that I'm the master and you are my puppy. I have the power to hurt you, even when you have my hand in your mouth and you're about to take off my thumb. I own you completely."

I push his head away and stand.

"My nature is to become powerful enough to do something," I laugh. "Who's the weak one here?"

I leave him to cry, hearing the sobs rise inside him as my heels echo around the cell.

* *** *

I cannot deny I am excited to sit in the plush chair in the large meeting room, even though my father is acting awkward next to me and my mother refused to come because I would be there. Nothing can break my mood.

Every time I walk into the daylight, I feel a sense of life pump through me at a velocity that causes me to stop and catch my breath. There is so much energy among people that it is impossible for me not to take notice

It is my third time out of the Commission during the day, but it is my first time in the temporary building that was erected after the destruction of Central Hall. The meeting was supposed to be yesterday, but a sudden—of course, unexpected—attack from the angel of the Central Angel terrorist group was spotted again. The military, working closely with the new soldier from the Commission, codename Leo, made a big show of pulling Chris to the ground and fighting him, though Eina let him go for one more attack before killing him.

Now, the meeting is taking place on Friday as cleanup occurs on the streets below.

Dana turns to me.

"Ready?"

I nod, ignoring the glare from Mrs. Markus and the uncomfortable shifting of my father beside me.

It is going to be an amazing day.

Sean opens the door and I smile. Someday, I'll have him. I'm sure. Dana says I can only have one pet at a time, and since I have been having fun with Clark, I cannot play with Sean. But I know my time is coming.

"The convoys just arrived," Sean announces, walking to stand next to Dana.

"Excellent."

A few minutes later, we are greeting Leader Simon as he joins us. There is a little scarring on his face from the fire that had torn down Central Hall, but it is only noticeable when he turns to the right, which is why I chose to be on his left side, so as not to be distracted.

Leader Simon takes his seat at the head of the table and adjusts his jacket.

"Miss Sandover."

"Leader," I greet warmly. My voice does not have the honey quality of Dana's, but I am able to make it sound like silk so it wraps around the person I direct it towards, bringing them closer. I am still learning the art of changing my voice.

It is another fifteen minutes that we're waiting until the other leaders file in. Everyone stands and walks to one another, shaking hands and kissing cheeks for formalities. Translators are working with us, all signing non-disclosure agreements to be sure that nothing leaves the confines of the room.

We have leaders from twelve major countries, most of them with a translator or one advisor. Several of the leaders are able to speak English, which I know from Dana, so we understand that the translator is often a shield to protect them from answering quickly, or sometimes is another advisor that they are trying to sneak past us.

We allow it because we know the potential translators have for altering the course of meetings. Sometimes, Dana tells me, that's when the meetings get really fun.

Before the General of State from Spain shows up, a lone woman walks into the room, her auburn hair framing her face and her skirt hugging her round hips perfectly, her bosom barely accented under the blouse. Her bright hazel eyes scan the room as she closes the door.

She draws a lot of attention.

"Miss Harris," many of those within call to her, moving to say hello to the representative from the often-silent and secret World Convention—I had not even known about them until becoming part-leader of the Commission of the People. I am staring at her through new eyes. She is so powerful, so mysterious, and so alluring that I want to get inside her and figure out what makes her tick. There is something otherworldly about her that I noticed our first meeting, but now the feeling is magnified. She's not only fighting against Dana's energy, but is also commanding the space in the room full of politicians, both male and female, that are scurrying to her.

The realization hits me like a freight train.

She is the most powerful person in the room.

"Miss Harris," Dana greets as she approaches, extending his hand to take hers, kissing the back of it.

"Mr. Christenson," she greets, her voice sending shivers down my spine. She turns to me and offers her hand. "Miss Sandover."

"It's a pleasure to see you again."

"You as well," she says, her hand leaving mine. "I can tell you've changed since we've last spoken. I greatly look forward to hearing what you have to say in this meeting."

Veronica is pulled away by Leader Simon, allowing me to turn to Dana.

"We really found *nothing* on her?" I hiss, raising my eyebrow.

"Nothing."

"I can't decide if I like her or want to kill her."

"I'm saving my judgment for after the meeting," Dana whispers. "If she has the money we need, then I'm willing to work with her."

Finally, the representative from Spain and his translator come into the room and the final greetings and formalities are made before everyone takes their space at the large table, seated in front of their country's name. A few assistants from the Commission begin passing out the folders to each leader in the room with the respected translation, leaving one for a registered advisor.

"Ladies and gentlemen, welcome," Leader Simon starts, looking around the table. "Even though I know you have all met them in the past, I would like to recognize that Dana Christenson and his advisor, Danielle Markus, are the ones bringing forth this project. Seated next to Mr. Christenson is the new co-chair of the Commission of the People, Lily Sandover, and her advisor, Thomas Sandover. Also on the project, we have Dr. Kyle Patton, who will be answering all your medical questions regarding the project."

"Well, we are all aware of what the project entails, Greg," Daniel from the Great United Kingdom says. "After all, it would have been against World Convention codes to conduct such experiments without the knowledge of the international community."

"Some of us are not immediately leaping in to fund such a project," Catherine from France snarls. "Not all of our countries are willing to pay for such research."

"We know that there was controversy at the late date that the project was shown to you," Mrs. Markus says. "However, we were unsure if the project was going to be successful, and did not wish for you to throw your money at something that was not proven to be efficient or usable."

The leader from the Korean Peninsula begins speaking to his translator.

"We agree that the experiments of the Commission of the People have been beneficial to all of our countries. Are you not concerned that this weapon will spark war, rather than rid the world of it?"

"We have no such illusions of being able to cure the world of war," Dana says. "There are still many countries scraping with one another, fighting for some form of control. When the nuclear disarmament happened, the world was sure that there were nuclear weapons still active, and that led to many attacks out of fear and sparked wars all over the world. We understand that this is going to cause a new arms race, which is why we bring this proposal to you now."

"Are you saying that you have full understanding of what this creature can do?" Veronica calls from her spot.

I hesitate, as does Dana.

"No," I admit. "We do not know what this weapon is capable of. There is still more research that needs to be done."

"And what steps are being taken in the direction of that research?" she asks.

"That is outlined in the proposal," I say.

"What are the current statistics on production time of each of these weapons?" the translator for the Prime Minister of China asks.

"At the moment, we're looking at four months for complete alteration," Kyle explains. "However, this is only possible with subjects who have a particular genetic anomaly."

"And that's when you infuse...lion DNA?" the Prime Minister of the Japanese Archipelago asks, looking at his folder and flipping through some pages. "I have never seen this weapon but this sounds like the work of science fiction."

"What this weapon is capable of appears to be beyond anything we have ever known before," Kyle admits. "There is a tremendous amount about him that we do not know. He can heal at remarkable speeds, there has even been evidence to suggest he can read minds."

That earns a laugh around the table.

"Come now, be serious," the woman from France laughs.

"We are being serious," I say.

"A creature with such capabilities is indeed unrealistic," the advisor from Pakistan said with a shake of his head. "There must be a logical explanation."

"Perhaps there is," I nod. "But more research must be done if we are to know the full potential of this weapon."

"If you are able to use lion DNA, is there any other animal that you can use as a substitute. It says here that there are no physical animal traits on the subjects...would it matter the DNA used?" the woman from Russia asks through her translator.

"It seems to have an effect, yes," Kyle admits. "Preliminary tests have occurred to find other animals and other strands of DNA that we can use. However, no subject has been tested with the new formulas yet."

"Are funds limited?" Daniel asks.

"Slightly, yes," Kyle says. "Creating the formulas for the subjects is expensive as it is, but holding and caring for the subject as the transformation occurs is the most costly to the Commission of the People. These are powerful weapons, and they do not understand control, which causes a lot of damage."

"Is there any way to combat those effects?" Daniel continues.

"We have only been successful with two subjects at the moment, a male and a female of the same family, and we are trying to breed offspring to see the results."

"You want to create a breeding species of these creatures?" Veronica asks. "I thought that you made your subjects sterile when you start their testing."

"Normally, yes, we do," Dana affirms.

"The male is sterile," I add. "The female was created for the purpose of trial breeding. Tubal ligation was not performed. We used artificial insemination."

"And the progress?" Hashita from Japan asks, curious.

"So far the embryo is progressing healthily, albeit rapidly," Kyle tells them.

"If she managed to produce a healthy offspring, you're telling us that breeding these weapons will be quick?" Duncan of the Australian Regime asks, his eyebrows high.

"At the moment, it does look that way," Kyle says. "But there will be other complications faced with breeding. Space, nutrition, care, and education...we still do not know what these weapons will produce when breeding."

"As you stated, this could become the next nuclear weapon," Francesca from the Republic of Brazil starts, calling our attention to her. "And here in the proposal, it states that you are willing to trade."

"In a manner of speaking, yes," my father says, jumping in on his specialty for the proposal. "It is unfair that we ask the rest of the world not to notice the weapon we have created and not realize the potential for another super-weapon. Therefore, we agree that the countries of the world should be allowed to purchase these weapons as all other weapons are purchased over the globe."

That causes murmuring to spread through the room as I glance around at those who are part of the Commission. We share the knowing glance.

"You are suggesting that we pay you for these weapons and throw money at you?" Klaus sneers.

"No, no," Leader Simon says quickly. "Not at all. As it says, we are willing to trade. We do not want this to be secret. We want the people of the world to know that these are weapons we created and that every country has them. As stated in section five of the proposal, we are willing to remain at an equal or lower number of the country with the most of these weapons. We will only breed or sell as needed for other countries."

"This will be an intense economic haul," Veronica says. I notice that she has not opened the proposal once. "The Commission has already stated that it does not know what these creatures need for care, or what sort of medical treatment they will need in the future from any complications. The trade of this weapon would mean that facilities would have to be built for them, and they would have to be strictly regulated. Numbers would have to be closely monitored to be sure that everyone is keeping up with only their registered number of allowed weapons."

"That could be regulated through customs," Daniel says.

"Which seriously lacks in authority," she counters simply. "There is a branch of the World Convention that can be redirected to handling the regulation of numbers, but it will be an economic boom of constant buying from the Commission of the People to a bust when they can breed within their own facilities. This could be devastating to the economies of countries. And if you plan to tell the people about it, there is no guarantee that they will agree with the expenditure."

"Thanks to the winged creature from the Central Angels, the entire world is in fear with their eyes on America," the man from India explains. "There have been calls for stronger weapons and assurances against such creatures attacking. The people already understand that this is an arms race. The people want what keeps them safe. Perhaps you forget the horrors the entire planet faced seven decades ago."

"I have not forgotten, but there is great potential for this to throw the planet back in that horrible state."

"You are right, Miss Harris," I agree. "Perhaps it is still too early to discuss trade and economics when we know so little about these weapons and their capabilities. Perhaps our attention could be focused more on the discovery of their abilities."

"What do you mean?" Daniel furrows his eyebrows.

"Our male has agreed to be our subject of observation. What we would need, though, would be an outdoor facility, a large camp or enclosure that would allow us to further test him. That will also allow us room to grow the numbers of these weapons as we discover new DNA to use."

"The funding calls for *quantity*, Miss Sandover," Klaus says coldly.

"I understand that," I reply. "However, we could be losing a lot of money if we mass-produce these weapons without knowing everything we can. These are living weapons, and we must be sure that we understand them completely before we release them to other countries."

"You have done so with other experiments," the Korean translator relays from her leader.

"We understood those experiments and what they were capable of," Dana interjects. "There were no surprises with their abilities, because it was what we designed. With this project, there is no telling the full extent of what he can do. So far, he has been one surprise after another. I agree that it would be foolish to go ahead with sale and trade when we do not understand them, including their needs and upkeep, as well as breeding restrictions."

"But you are asking for fourteen billion more dollars to construct such a facility!" Daniel gasps, flipping through the papers in the folder and seeing the schematics we had designed for a possible facility, though I know we're going to change them. "We've already given you nearly eighty million to develop these weapons!"

"We understand that—"

"Fine."

The soft voice causes everyone to turn, cutting my father off, mouth open in shock.

Veronica looks around the table.

"I said fine," she repeats. "I'll fund the facility."

"Miss Harris," Leader Simon says slowly, being the first to recover from the shock. I glance at Dana, both of us trying to read the bizarre situation. "This is fourteen *billion* dollars…and you know when constructing anything you always need to double the price."

"I will fund what it takes to build the facility," she says. "I have all the funds you need."

"The World Convention won't—"

"I am personal sponsor," Veronica cuts me off, turning her bright eyes to me. "If you are going to mass-produce these creatures, I'll be damned if you're going to do so without understanding them. As long as I have an active role in the development of the project, I will fund the facility and what it takes to run it."

No one can speak for several long moments. I turn to Dana and he leans to me, allowing me to whisper in his ear.

"I thought she was against the project."

"I did as well."

We straighten and Dana turns to her with a smile.

"We would appreciate your generosity, Miss Harris. Provided, of course, that everyone else agrees."

Diplomats turned to their advisors and Leader Simon turned to Dana, asking him with their eyes if he thought it was a good idea to involve someone from the World Convention. I stare at Veronica, who is also looking at me. We share an intense stare as I try to figure her out, though I am unsuccessful. A part of me is concerned about the sudden support and her willingness to throw so much money into the project, but I figure that by working side by side with her, I would have more of an opportunity to get to know her.

After the deliberation, Leader Simon looks over the other leaders.

"All in favor of allowing Veronica Harris to privately fund the construction of a research facility?"

Every country except for Korea raises their hand.

"Majority rules."

"Miss Harris, we would like for you to come to the Commission as soon as possible and discuss the facility," I tell her, never once breaking eye contact.

"I would be happy to, Miss Sandover."

"What are you calling this project?" the man from India asks.

"We're calling it the D.E.M.O.N.," Dana answers with a grin.

* *** *

My high from the meeting is not broken when we return to the Commission, even after the guard comes up to me and tells me that my puppy has been badly hurt in the back. I'm a little annoyed by the news, but my mood does not change.

Rather than join Dana for a celebratory shower and fuck, I have to go and deal with the puppy.

By the time I reach his cell, Clark is bandaged and crouching in the corner, crying. The guard walks up next to me as I look into the cell.

"What happened?"

"He fucking lost it," the guard sighs. "He was suddenly screaming and bashing his head against the walls. He started smashing his face into the wall over there, which is why his face looks like that."

"Fine, I will talk with him," I groan, rolling my eyes and reaching for my card. I can think of so many other things I would rather be doing right now...

"Miss Sandover, do you think that's a good idea?" the guard says. I turn and blink in surprise, shocked he would think of telling me what was really none of his business.

"Excuse me?"

"I-I just mean...he's upset, and you have a tendency to make it worse."

"Be careful what you say, Jeremy," I warn. "You're lucky I'm in a good mood. I won't throw you into the holding cells today."

His eyes widen and he backs away.

"Yes, Miss Sandover, please forgive me, that was out of line."

"Yes, it was," I agree, opening the lock and stepping inside the cell, motioning the young guard away and quickly forgetting about him as I look over the face of my puppy. One of his eyes is bandaged and the other is nearly swollen shut. There are dark spots forming all over his face and his neck is in a brace, his hands covered in mittens that are locked to him to keep him from scratching at himself.

"Clark..."

"Stay the hell away from me," he practically gurgles.

"You look like something from beyond the grave," I say. "I guess I really have broken you."

"*Broken* me?" he hisses. "You're a fucking psychopath! How could you become this?!"

"Oh, you're so dramatic," I groan, rolling my eyes. "Really? You just bashed your face against a wall and you're talking about *me*?" I straighten. "Oh, wait, I've heard about this...is this a ploy for my attention?"

"The hell it is!"

"Am I not spending enough time with you? I thought we had fun last time. I know I left you hanging, but things came up. If you want, we can start again right now and maybe I'll let you finish this time, if you're a good boy…"

"Fuck you! Stay the fuck away from me!"

"Oh…maybe we should wait until your face heals," I agree. "But I'll try to be better. Things have been so crazy lately, I know I've been ignoring you."

"I didn't do this for your attention!"

"No?"

"No! I was trying to kill myself, you fucking psycho!"

I continue to stare at him, surprised at how easily he broke. It was far too easy. I guess Dana did a lot of the work for me long ago. It was finally time to decide what to make out of Clark. He was not going to be any more fun in his current state.

"You were trying to kill yourself? For heaven's sake, why?" I laugh.

"Anything is better than being here with you," he growls, putting up a cute display of defiance, even though his face diminishes any spark of ferocity he might have had.

"I made you do this?"

"Yes! You're a monster!" he screams. I love the fear in his voice. The way it echoes off the walls and reverberates in my core makes me shiver. A smile creeps over my lips. I must make it a priority to be there when he starts his testing so I can hear his screaming.

"Apparently, I'm not the only one," I sing, looking over his battered face. I do not understand how he can bash his own face in like that just because he is trying to get away from me. I know I did a lot to get away from Dana at first, but bashing one's face takes an immense amount of self-discipline.

Then again, I guess he couldn't really use his teeth after I had proven how weak his bite truly was.

He starts crying, curling forward on the floor, shaking and sobbing. I feel the muscles in his body relaxing, but in exhaustion and defeat. His final barrier has fallen and he has crumbled at my feet, ready for me to mold back into a beautiful, powerful form.

He's in the perfect position.

"Aw…you broke him," a voice says at the door of the cell. I turn to Dana and my heart beats quickly at the sight of him. Dana smiles, walking to stand next to me. "I heard what happened. I was wondering why you weren't with me."

"Well, he is mine. I figured I needed to come see what kind of trouble he's gotten into," I groan.

"How bad is it?" Dana asks curiously.

I lift my foot and toe Clark over, exposing his mangled and swollen face. Dana cringes.

"That's a new one. I've never seen anyone do something like that before."

"He's totally broken."

"I can see that."

"He won't be too much fun as he is."

"Then we need to decide what is to become of him. Do you know what you want to do?" Dana asks, his arm going around my waist as we both look at the subject on the ground, crying and screaming in an agony that was not physical.

I look at Clark and smile, glancing over his face, watching how it contorts in agony...

"I think I have some ideas for what to do with him."

Epilogue

Veronica sighed as she felt the elevator slow. She could feel the approaching disaster in her bones and she was desperate to find a way to minimize the damage. There was no way to avoid it completely, but perhaps she could curb some of the larger repercussions.

However, considering how much everyone supported Dana and his associate Lily, there was no way Veronica would have enough leverage in her current position to change much.

Sixteen months and twenty-one billion dollars later, the facility was finally ready for the transfer of the first D.E.M.O.N. prototypes. It would also be the first time that Veronica would see the twelve individuals in the same space. Dana would not let her observe them in the Dome when they socialized with each other. As much as they could, both Lily and Dana limited the amount of contact Veronica had with their prized experiments.

She walked out of the elevator and to the door leading into the offices of the Commission of the People. Sean greeted her, almost colliding with her.

"Oh, Miss Harris," he said, holding the door open for her. "I'm so sorry. I guess I'm a little late."

"No, not at all," she assured with a gentle smile. "Actually, I'm a few minutes early." She liked Sean, and despised the way the crazy twins pawed and scraped over him. But she understood that there was no way out for Sean. If he did not obey, he would become subject to further torture.

She also liked him because he was similar to her, wanting to keep the damage as minimal as possible.

"Getting excited?" Sean smiled knowingly.

"I'm curious," she corrected gently. "Tell me, where are Dana and Lily?"

"They're overseeing the loading process. They asked me to come and get you. Do you wish to ride with them? Or would you rather have a separate car?" Sean asked, leading her through the now-familiar door that led to the security checkpoint into the back of the Commission.

"Oh, there is no need to waste more resources on me," Veronica said, stepping forward and flashing her own card to the security desk, even though they knew very well who she was and had been letting her through without a fuss for over a year. "I will ride with them."

"...are you sure?" Sean asked. "There's a lot of excitement over what's going on, so they're going to be...well..."

"Thank you for your concern, Sean," Veronica said with a small smile. "But I can handle myself."

"I've noticed that…" Sean agreed, opening another door for her and leading her through the lab to walk into the holding cells and to the car garages. "You need to teach me your ways."

"I wish I could," Veronica said. "But if I told you how I managed to stay strong against Dana and Lily, you would never believe me."

She brushed past the confused head of security and walked through the aisles of the holding cells, looking at the faces behind the glass. She was able to see each and every face as she passed. There were a few who deserved to be imprisoned, but she also noticed that several of them should never have been locked up. It tore at her heart to see such horrid circumstances for those people, but there was an etiquette to what she was doing, and she knew she had to act very carefully in order to save as many people as possible.

Sean opened the door to the car elevators, where voices immediately greeted their ears.

"Remember, if you try to run, these will detonate and blow your head clean off. So, just sit like a good girl, and wait for us to bring you to where you'll be living," one of the guards told one of the D.E.M.O.N.s. Veronica sighed heavily and started forward.

"Do you think it's safe to move them?" Sean asked. "Their strength tests have been frightening."

"I'm afraid that nothing is really safe with them," Veronica said. "They are too powerful to be contained by human means. Thankfully, they still retained their humanity and react to fear and intimidation all the same. It's the only thing keeping them in line."

"But…what if that changes?"

"Hope that you're gone before that happens," Veronica told Sean sadly.

"You really think they're going to fight back?"

"I am certain of it."

"Ah, Miss Harris," Dana called, seeing her round the corner to the second row of car elevators. "Excellent, you're right on time."

"Mr. Christenson," she greeted, allowing him to kiss her hand. "Miss Sandover."

"Miss Harris," Lily returned the greeting, her bright golden eyes unwavering on the older woman. Veronica did not feel uncomfortable with the leaders of the Commission of the People. She knew she was more powerful than they were, and that allowed her to brush off their intimidation tactics, but that did not make her any more at ease.

"We've loaded everyone up," Lily declared. "Even the little ones. We're about to go."

"Wonderful." Veronica forced a smile. "Do you mind if we share a car?"

"Mind? Of course not." Lily grinned, brightening up immediately at the thought of having Miss Harris cornered. Over a year of working with the mysterious woman and she had yet to learn anything about her. She thought that she would be able to learn Veronica's background and family ties, but Veronica gave nothing.

It was as if she had appeared out of nowhere.

Dana was not as pleased with riding in the car with Veronica. He had been just as eager as Lily when he first began to dance around Veronica Harris. However, he had used every trick that had ever worked for him and nothing swayed the woman. It was also not uncommon that he would look at Veronica and find himself legitimately afraid of her.

He had not been afraid in so long that the feeling frightened him just as much as she did.

Dana was now very wary of Miss Veronica Harris. The younger Lily was bolder and not as fearful as the older and calmer Dana.

The three of them got into the limo and Sean slid into the driver's seat, pressing some buttons in the car to bring the car to the surface streets.

"How was France, Miss Harris?" Lily asked, striking up conversation.

"Beautiful," Veronica said, noticing how Lily moved to her section of seating in the limo while Dana had remained afar.

Veronica had also noticed the change in Dana. He was the older animal, no longer curious about things that could hurt him. He knew that when something felt as dangerous as Veronica, it was best to stay away. He had tried to warn Lily before, but she could not be swayed.

"What were you doing in France?" Dana asked.

"I had a meeting with the president," Veronica explained. "I told her I was coming to finally transfer the D.E.M.O.N.s to their facility and she said she's very excited to see the progress we've made."

"Is she upset about the time it took?"

"Not at all," Veronica answered Dana's question. "A year is not so long, really. Everyone has been convinced that it is a good idea to test them before we continue mass-production."

"I apologize for the scheduling," Dana chuckled, his eyes flicking to Lily, who was slowly inching closer to Veronica with every turn of the car. "You must be exhausted, flying in from France and then coming directly here."

Veronica laughed lightly.

"Like you, Mr. Christenson, and most other politicians, I do not sleep." She smiled. "Thank you for your concern, but I am not tired."

"You never sleep?" Lily asked skeptically.

Veronica just smiled mysteriously.

"I notice that you don't travel with security guards," Sean pointed out from the front seat, breaking the awkward silence. "Is that wise?"

"I am not well-known enough to be a target," Veronica said, brushing away the question.

"We used to have a spectacular experiment security unit, but the surviving ones are all in other countries," Dana said. "Otherwise I would have insisted you purchase some for your own protection."

"Oh, you are too kind," Veronica forced herself to say. "But I assure you, my safety is not something to be concerned about."

"Well, it would be a shame to have something happen to such a beautiful woman," Lily said. "And especially so young. You don't look a day over thirty."

"Thank you, Miss Sandover," Veronica said politely, even as Lily began running her fingers up and down Veronica's arm, gently moving the fabric of the blouse, trying to be as discreet as possible. To the older woman, it felt like Lily was shaving the skin off her arm. She chose to ignore it, settling herself easily.

"If you don't mind me asking, Miss Harris, how old are you?" Lily pressed. Veronica was silent for a moment, her eyes blinking slowly as she decided how to answer.

"I'm much older than I look."

"I would assume, considering that you have the personal funds to throw into this project. You must have had time to amass your wealth."

"I come from old money," Veronica said. "Very old money..."

The car was silent for four turns leading to the freeway. Finally, Dana spoke, first calling Lily to come back to his side, which she obeyed.

"You must have heard the news about the Altereye Team." Dana tried to strike up conversation.

"I did."

"They will be doing some exploration before starting their seven-year journey back," Dana explained. "Imagine, finding a planet like earth, with similar atmosphere composition, water, even animals."

"It's not so difficult to believe," Veronica said. "The universe is a large place. Presuming to be alone in something so vast is self-centered, wouldn't you agree?"

"No humans have been found, yet," Lily challenged.

"Yet," Veronica repeated. "And animals prove evolution, which means that, eventually, a highly-intelligent life form would come into existence."

"You believe in aliens and extraterrestrial life forms?" Dana teased.

"I believe in a lot of things that would sound strange to you," Veronica admitted. "Aliens are not one of them."

"But you believe in other intelligent life," Lily pointed out.

"I believe in evolution into a bipedal, 'intelligent' life form evolving with opposable thumbs across the universe," Veronica said.

"But nothing besides humans?"

"In evolution, no."

"Why not?"

"Because humans stop their own processes," Veronica explained. "They make everything evolve around them. Their further evolution comes from the things they create." She fixed the two with a hard stare. "Like the D.E.M.O.N."

"Well, one could argue that the D.E.M.O.N. is just a higher evolution of a human," Lily chuckled.

"It's the bastardization of nature," Veronica said strongly. "When they split the atom all those years ago, they never knew what would come of it. Now, you've split the basis of humans, and power is going to erupt from that."

"I thought you were in favor of the project." Dana raised his eyebrows.

"My feelings are far more complicated than simply stating I am for or against this project," Veronica said. "You could never understand."

The car pulled up to the tall gates of the first ever D.E.M.O.N. site, clearing through the gates as the twenty-three cars made their way in, driving up the long road over the flat terrain, passing by large, open fields and slowly coming upon the five-story laboratory facility, where Kyle and his team had been setting up the previous month, duplicating the files needed for the D.E.M.O.N. project and starting work on more DNA tests to move away from the first three animals that had been perfected.

As Sean was pulling into the parking lot, the other vans carrying the D.E.M.O.N.s drove to the other side of the laboratory, where small homes were lined up, all one story and minimal in appearance, but separated, to allow for a sense of privacy.

There was nothing over the top of the enormous grounds, and the walls were about ten meters high. Veronica knew that the demons could easily leave the grounds, but she was confident that they would not. She wanted them to have their space, the open air, and a chance for the sun to shine down on them but, for now, she wanted them contained behind the walls.

This would be the first time the D.E.M.O.N.s had seen the sun since they were captured by the Commission of the People.

Walking with Dana, Lily, and Sean, Veronica moved around the side of the lab, not bothering to check the structure as the other three did, since she had been at the project site only a week previous.

She was more curious about watching the D.E.M.O.N.s unload from the cars.

The first two vans opened, allowing seven individuals out. In the first van, a man and a woman, obviously related, were standing close to the car, allowing the guards to take the cuffs off their necks. On the male's hip, a young boy was held securely, though his eyes were wide in wonder and he was squirming in his father's arms.

"Papa! I want—"

"Hold still..." his father whispered, holding the young D.E.M.O.N. still as the guards removed the neck cuff. The female was looking around, her eyes wide, filling with happy tears as she stepped away from the car, free of her cuff, holding the silent infant in her arms, who was also looking around, though he did not experience the same wonderment as the older ones.

From the second van, a young man with pale skin and nearly-black hair cringed away from the sun when he first got out, but soon was closing his eyes and standing in the sun's rays, relishing in the feeling of being outside once again. He turned and laughed as the four D.E.M.O.N.s of the other car, free from their restraints, started running toward the rows of houses, falling in the green grass out front. The young boy laughed and leapt on his father as they playfully wrestled.

"It's hard to believe that he's only a year old," Dana said, stepping to Veronica's side as they watched the family play in the grass. "Six month gestation, and then to mature to speech and motor skills so quickly...it's remarkable."

"Indeed," Veronica agreed. "But, like you said, we don't know anything about these creatures. It's important to let them grow as they can and observe quietly for a while, to see if they will continue on their own."

"Well, for Eina, we'll have to interfere," Lily chuckled. "He can't get Rehan pregnant on his own."

"They had a natural conception, correct?" Veronica asked, nodding to the pale young man and the young woman at his side, who was holding onto an infant as well.

"Yes, they did," Dana confirmed. "Clark! Nancy! Come over here and thank Miss Harris."

The two turned to Veronica and she sighed sadly, watching how frightened the two were as they approached. She knew that it took time for people to get angry enough to cause drastic change, but the D.E.M.O.N.s were so terrified after everything they had endured in the Commission that they were obedient and frightened of everything. Veronica wanted to tell them that they were more powerful than Dana and Lily, that they could fight back and win, but she refrained.

It would be a few generations before one of the D.E.M.O.N.s became angry enough to fight back and smart enough to organize the others to rebel. Veronica had to be patient.

Clark and Nancy approached Veronica and bowed their heads to her, whispering quiet and worried thanks.

"What do you call yourselves?" Veronica asked.

They both looked at her, confused.

"Your real names."

They looked at one another, confused and unsure what the woman meant or if they should answer.

"It's okay, you can tell me."

"We probably should not promote the use of those silly names they make up for one another," Lily said behind Veronica.

Veronica turned to Clark, "Jyara, right?"

The young man blinked, nodding slowly.

"What about you?" Veronica asked, turning to the female.

"Lyrra," she murmured.

"Beautiful." Veronica smiled. "And who is this beautiful little girl?"

"Nau," Lyrra said, turning her body to bring the infant closer to Veronica. The older woman gently ran her hand over the infant's hair.

"What a beautiful name," she murmured.

The young D.E.M.O.N. reached out for Veronica, clenching her little fingers repeatedly, trying to reach for the redhead.

"May I?"

Lyrra carefully transferred the baby to Veronica's arms. Veronica held onto the young girl, turning to see the last four adult D.E.M.O.N.s released from their vans and running to explore the facility.

She turned to Lyrra and handed the baby back to her mother.
"You look like a natural," Dana teased.
"I've had experience with children," Veronica said.
"None of your own?"
"No," Veronica said. "I don't want any of my own." She nodded to Lyrra and Jyara. "Please, go find a home that you like and be comfortable there."

"Thank you so much." Jyara bowed his head again and took Lyrra's hand, both of them walking to the houses.

"You're not afraid of them?" Dana asked Veronica.

"No," she said. She turned and sighed, studying the families darting to the different houses, disappearing inside before coming out to greet each other, playing and laughing as if they were in a stereotypical suburban neighborhood.

"I am thrilled to study what they are capable of..." Lily shivered. She walked to Dana and wrapped her arms around his waist, snuggling close. "Look at our babies..."

"You did good, Mama." Dana said, running his fingers over the back of Lily's neck.

"You, too, Papa," she giggled. The two shared a passionate kiss that had Sean feeling awkward while Veronica paid it no mind.

She took a deep breath and looked around the facility slowly, her eyes settling on the small area where the D.E.M.O.N.s were playing.

It was for the best. She knew it was. She saw the way things would progress from here, the way the public would change as fickly as they always had, and the D.E.M.O.N.s would become the most feared creatures known on earth...and possibly many other places as well. She had to get as many people that were worthy of surviving off the planet as soon as possible. She had to fund projects to move people because, as the D.E.M.O.N.s would grow more numerous, there was a greater chance that the one who would rally them together would be born.

"I am going to speak with Eina," Veronica said, walking toward the first D.E.M.O.N. family, who were letting the young boy pick the house they would explore.

"Hyreyna?" she called.

The first D.E.M.O.N.'s back stiffened and he turned, shocked by the use of his proper name. He saw the woman standing behind him and blinked at her, unsure what to say. "We've never actually met, but my name is Veronica Harris. I'm the one who built this facility for you."

"...thank you," Hyreyna breathed. "You don't know what this means to me...to us..."

"I can guess," Veronica said with a gentle smile.

"Do I know you from somewhere?" Hyreyna asked, tilting his head as he looked over the woman.

"It is entirely possible," Veronica said. She looked at Rehan and the two children with her. "I would like to speak with you, if that's alright."

"Of course…" Hyreyna turned to Rehan and nodded once. The female D.E.M.O.N. ushered the excited boy into the house he had picked. Veronica and Eina watched the family disappear, also nodding to another D.E.M.O.N. who was wandering in awe, running and laughing as he played in the sun.

Veronica looked over her shoulder at Dana.

"I don't have much time, but allow me to ask you something."

"Yes?"

"A favor, actually," Veronica said. "I won't be around often to help you, so I need you to push yourself as hard as you can. Find every limit you have, find how to use your powers, hone them, and then teach the others what you discover."

"Powers? What are you—"

"The scientists aren't able to comprehend what you're capable of, so make sure that you know fully and use it to your advantage," Veronica continued in a hushed whisper, cutting off the D.E.M.O.N. "Hyreyna, one day, a day that you *will* see, someone in your bloodline will rise up and they will rally the D.E.M.O.N.s against the humans. D.E.M.O.N.s will destroy the humans, so you have to be sure that you know the powers you have and how to control them. Then teach that control to the others. If you have any D.E.M.O.N.s that are out of control, the whole program will be shut down, and you'll all be killed."

"You…you want us to destroy everything?" Hyreyna hissed, his eyes wide.

"It seems to be the only way to reset everything properly," Veronica said.

Hyreyna's eyes widened further and his mouth opened slowly.

"It can't be…you…you're…"

There were three long seconds that hung in silence as the two stared at one another.

Slowly, Hyreyna lifted his right hand, holding his palm out to Veronica, who stared at it before pressing her hand to his.

He gasped and backed away, staring at her, half in fear and half in fascination.

"It's you…it's really you…I knew you were real."

END

More Works by K.J. Amidon

Inside
(Written as Kyra Anderson)
Inside – Pt. 1
Inside – Pt. 2
Inside – Pt. 3
Inside – Alternate Part 3
Inside the Commission

The Coalition Trilogy
(Written as Kyra Anderson)
Forged Under Fire
The Rising Tide
With Banners Raised

The Significant
(Written as Kyra Anderson)

The Significant Expanded Story
(Written as Kyra Anderson)
The Degenerates
The Deserted

The Faith
(Written as Kyra Anderson)
The Faith
The Sacred

The Dimension Guardian Series:
The Realm of Beasts – The Guardian Tournament
The Realm of Darkness – Blind Ambitions
The Realm of Humans – Fate
The Realm of Light – Imbalance
The Realm of Demons – Scars in Time
The Realm of Exile – Continuum

The Roadside Paradise Series:
Into Oblivion
Wander the Lost
Until Dawn Breaks
Hiding from Sight
For Fools
Challenge Gods

www.ingramcontent.com/pod-product-compliance
Lightning Source LLC
Chambersburg PA
CBHW030548020726
47494CB00005B/1532